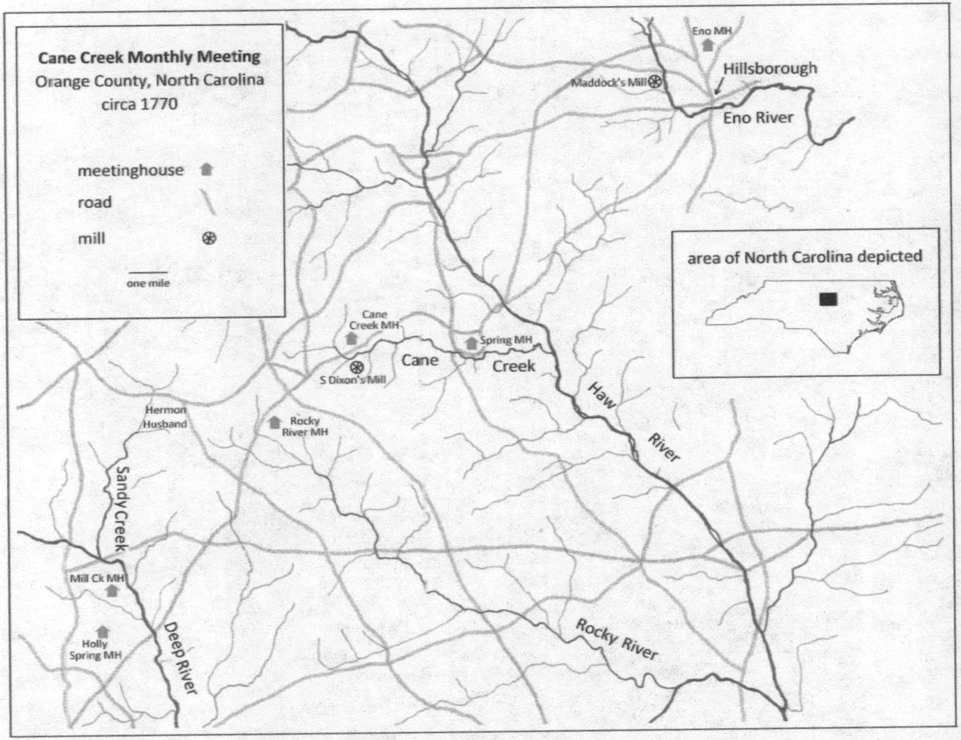
Cane Creek Monthly Meeting
Orange County, North Carolina
circa 1770
meetinghouse
road
mill
one mile
Eno MH
Hillsborough
Maddock's Mill
Eno River
area of North Carolina depicted
Cane Creek MH
Spring MH
Cane
Creek
S Dixon's Mill
Haw
River
Hermon Husband
Rocky River MH
Sandy Creek
Mill Ck MH
Holly Spring MH
Deep River
Rocky River

I0660985

The Frontier Chrysalis

The Story of Charity Wright Cook

Barbara Schell Luetke

BARCLAY PRESS

Newberg, OR 97132

The Frontier Chrysalis
The Story of Charity Wright Cook

©2025 by Barbara Schell Luetke

Barclay Press, Inc.
Newberg, Oregon
www.barclaypress.com

Printed in the United States of America

Interior design by Mareesa Fawver Moss
Cover design by Eric Muhr
Cover art by John Corcoran

ISBN 978-1-59498-176-0

To my children, sons-in-law, and granchildren; may you
be inspired by my writing to stand up for peace and
social justice: the families of Breeze Elizabeth Richardson
(Kelsey, Gus, and Iggy); Hannah Luetke-Stahlman
(Rick, Tripp, and Madison); Mary Pat and Tim
McAlevy, Marcy and Robert Byrd.

Contents

Family Tree of Rachel Wright and Charity Cook

Rachel Wright formerly Wells

Born March 27, 1720, in Prince George's County, Province of Maryland

Daughter of Joseph Wells I and Rachel (unknown) Wells

Sister of Joseph Wells II [half], Margaret Wells [half], and others

Wife of John Wright—married 1736 in Prince George's County, Province of Maryland

Mother of William Wright, Mary (Wright) Brooks, Joseph Wright, Margaret Wright, Charity (Wright) Cook, Rachel (Wright) Coate, John C Wright, Sarah Wright, Hannah Wright, James Wright, Susannah (Wright) Hollingsworth, Elizabeth (Wright) McCool, Nathan Wright,

Thomas Wright, Keziah (Wright) Hanks, and Isaac Joel Wright

Died December 23, 1771, in Bush River, Newberry County, Province of South Carolina

Charity Cook formerly Wright

Born November 13, 1742, in Prince George's County, Maryland

Daughter of John Wright and Rachel (Wells) Wright

Sister of William Wright, Mary (Wright) Brooks, Joseph Wright, Margaret Wright, Rachel (Wright) Coate, John C. Wright, Sarah Wright, Hannah Wright, James Wright, Susannah (Wright) Hollingsworth, Elizabeth (Wright) McCool, Nathan Wright, Thomas Wright, Keziah (Wright) Hanks, and Isaac Joel Wright

Wife of Isaac Cook—married 1762 in Newberry County, South Carolina

Mother of Joseph Cook, Sarah Ann (Cook) Hollingsworth, Rachel (Cook) Lewis, Thomas Cook, Mary (Cook) Brady, Charity (Cook) Brock, Ruth (Cook) Furnas, Marion Wright Cook, Isaac Cook, Susannah (Cook) Lewis, and Keturah (Cook) Madden

Died November 13, 1822, in Caesar's Creek Monthly Meeting, Clinton County, Ohio, United States

A Short Glossary of Quaker Terms

Birthright member—a Friend recorded at birth on the membership rolls of a meeting because the parents or grandparents are Quaker and intend to (or did) raise the child in the manner of Friends. Members who are not birthright Friends are referred to as "convinced Friends." An attender is someone who comes regularly to meeting for worship but has not sought membership.

Clearness committee—a group of Friends appointed by the meeting, a committee of the meeting, or suggested by the focus person to help any member (or members) achieve confidence of divine guidance in their life about a certain decision or course of action. The members help the focus person (or couple) discover whether there is clarity (clearness) to move forward with a matter, wait, or take other action. This may entail worshiping together, listening deeply to the questions and concerns brought by the individual, questioning the individual in a careful, gentle, and open-ended manner, reflecting back on what has been heard, and trying to find clarity.

Clerk—a member of the meeting who has been approved in a business meeting to administer a Friends' committee, monthly meeting, or other body and be sensitive to the guidance of the Spirit in the conduct of the business of that body. This may include preparing for the business meeting; coordinating with those who will be presenting at the meeting; facilitating a spiritually grounded and worshipful process during the meeting; starting and ending the meeting; ensuring worship throughout the meeting; recognizing those who wish to speak; discouraging dialogue between members on a topic; interrupting people who burden the meeting by repeating what has already been said, speaking for too long, or who use a tone and language that is hurtful to others; inviting minority views; keeping the meeting focused on the matter at hand; periodically summarizing what has been discussed; and so forth to eventually discern if the group comes to a sense of the meeting on an issue. Initially, the clerk also recorded the minutes of decisions made. These days, there is a recording clerk for this purpose, but the clerk is responsible to see that the minutes are accurate.

Elder—a member of the meeting who supports and encourages those who give ministry in the flowering of Spirit-led ministry (and discourage behavior and speech which inhibits messages). This leadership (called eldering) can include logistical support, honest feedback, prayer, and helping with spiritual discernment. Historically, elders were appointed to foster the life of the meeting and individuals in the meeting. Today, elders are not appointed but sometimes are informally asked to serve the meetings or an individual.

George Fox (July 1624–January 13, 1691) was an English religious dissenter who is credited with founding the Religious Society of Friends (commonly called Quakers or Friends). He traveled throughout Great Britain, preaching, performing hundreds of healings, and was persecuted by the disapproving authorities. In 1669, he married Margaret Fell, a wealthy widow and a leading Friend. In the years 1671 to 1673, he traveled to the British colonies in the Caribbean and to the American colonies, strengthening and organizing the existing Quaker communities, especially in Maryland and Rhode Island. He spent his final decade working in London to organize the expanding Quaker movement. Those who worked with Fox to spread the Quaker way to the most populated areas of Great Britain in the years of the faith have been called the Valiant Sixty or First Friends.

Inner Light—a term that represents the direct, unmediated experience of the Divine. Similar terms used in Quaker writings include Christ Within, Holy Spirit, Inward Light, Light, Light of Christ, Spirit of Truth, Seed, Guide, Inward Teacher, and that of God in every person.

Leading—a sense of being called by God (or Spirit, etc.) to undertake a specific course of action that often arises from a concern. A Friend may submit a leading to the meeting or to a clearness committee for testing by corporate wisdom.

Recorded minister—a member of a meeting who has been recorded in the minutes as having a special gift of service to the meeting or the community (e.g., vocal ministry). Such recognition is accompanied by the meeting's commitment to provide oversight to the ministry (often in the form of a clearness committee) and perhaps other forms of support as well. Itinerant or public Friends are those who traveled to preach, reinforcing religious ties among the sect and across geographic areas. They flourished in the eighteenth and nineteenth century to form a great transatlantic bond. Today, some meetings record ministers.

Meetinghouse—a building where meeting for worship is held. Typically, Friends meetinghouses are plain in appearance and do not utilize steeples, altars, pulpits, or religious icons. Quakers do not believe that meeting for worship has to occur in any special place, and early Friends often met for worship outdoors or in local public buildings.

However, as the Religious Society of Friends grew, special meetinghouses were needed. Some Quakers also refer to their place of worship as a church.

Meetinghouses built in a traditional style usually have a large room for worship (which traditionally had a side for men and a side for women, sometimes with a divider that was used to separate men's and women's business meetings). The seating was originally long, hard wooden benches. Seating arrangements vary and may include pews or chairs arranged in a circle. Some meetinghouses have a facing bench where weighty Friends and those traveling in the ministry would have sat. There may be an elders bench, too, as well as a gallery for extra seating. Early meetinghouses had high windows so that worshipers couldn't be distracted by what was outside. Meetinghouses built in a more modern design will usually consist of a large meeting room, smaller rooms for committees, children's classes, a kitchen, and bathrooms. They may have windows that provide a view into the meetinghouse garden or woods. In the novel, I chose to spell the word as a compound and to capitalize it only if it refers to a particular place.

Monthly meeting—a congregation of Friends who meet regularly for worship and to conduct corporate (typically monthly) business. A monthly meeting is usually part of a regional gathering of members, traditionally, on four occasions each year. This is called the quarterly meeting. In the Greensboro, North Carolina, area, where this story takes place, Western Quarterly Meeting is referred to as Quarterly Meeting or Western Quarter. The yearly meeting consists of monthly meetings from a geographically extended area and whose members are invited to gather in an annual session to worship and conduct business together. This term is also used to denote the total membership of the constituent monthly meetings of a designated area. At the time of this story, there were separate men's and women's meetings for business.

Moved to speak—led by the Spirit to speak, especially in meeting for worship.

Plain dress—the witness of early Friends to the testimonies of equality and simplicity was to dress simply, in undecorated garments.

Plain speech—the witness of early Friends to the testimonies of equality and integrity by speaking plainly to all, regardless of social status. This involved the use of the singular "thee, thy, thou, thine" for all people, instead of observing the custom of using the plural "you" for a person of higher status.

Not everyone who consulted on this novel agreed with how I used "thou/thee" language. Two Quaker historians suggested that Charity and others in colonial Quaker communities would have used "thou" and "thee" (etc.); however, they disagreed as to which of these would

16

be used for the subject case and which for the object case, and since this is a work of historical fiction, I chose to use only "thou," "thee," and "thy" (with "thou" as the subject case, etc.) when the speaker is addressing a single person (and "you" when addressing two or more people) to give the reader a flavor of the usage. Today, Friends continue the practice of plain speech by using full given names and no titles when referring to themselves or addressing others. Most Quakers no longer use plain speech.

Quaker—originally a derogatory term for Friends, coined because their excitement in the Spirit when led to speak was sometimes expressed in a shaking or quaking motion. Today, this term is simply an alternative designation for a member of the Religious Society of Friends and is more widely recognized by the general public than "Friend."

Testimony—speech or action that derives from and demonstrates deeply held beliefs. Most Friends would list the testimonies of the sect as equality, simplicity, community, integrity, and unity. At the time of this story, these intentions were not so specifically named.

Travel certificate/papers/minute—the endorsement a meeting gives to one of its members who is traveling in ministry or under the weight of a concern. It is usually a letter carried by the traveler that has been approved by the meeting and signed by the meeting clerk.

Weighty Friend—an informal term for a Friend who is respected for spiritual depth, experience, or wisdom.

Note on Bias-Free Language

The text of this book generally follows the guidance found in the chapter titled "Bias-Free Language Guidelines" in the *Publication Manual of the American Psychological Association*, Seventh Edition. For this reason, racial and ethnic groups are designated by proper nouns and are capitalized: Black, White, Native American, and Indigenous.

The Journey*

Mary Oliver

One day you finally knew what you had to do
Though the wind pried with its stiff fingers
At the very foundations. . .
The road full of fallen branches and stones.
But little by little as you left their voices behind,
The stars began to burn through the sheets of clouds,
And there was a new voice
Which you slowly recognized as your own,
That kept you company
As you strode deeper and deeper. . .
Determined to save the only life you could save.

*from *No Voyage and Other Poems*, 1963

PART 1

PART I

Chapter 1

Rachel Wright sat on a hard bench on the women's side of the meeting room, her heart beating so strongly that she could feel the palpitations vibrate in her chest. Normally, as a recorded minister, she'd have been sitting at the front of the room, elevated and separated from the others, but five months pregnant and showing, she'd thought it best to sit among the rest of the women and as close as she could to her daughter, Charity. Shifting now on the backless bench, Rachel rearranged her skirts and crossed and uncrossed her unadorned black shoes. Charity, her nearly fifteen-year-old daughter, stood just in front of her, within reach, but turned toward the front of the room so that Rachel couldn't see her young face to assess how she was faring.

Thou are loved. Thou are held. Rachel chanted internally as she fixed on the cascade of chestnut curls that fell down Charity's stiffened back. She shifted her gaze to the bow of her daughter's apron, neatly tied at her backside, and scrutinized her gray, homespun dress. The girl could have been mistaken for either of her two older sisters or for Rachel herself for that matter. Like a handful of nails, the Wright women were all slender and tough, the lot of them with thick, long hair that they left uncut, although the older ones pulled theirs into buns as did their mother.

You are my friends if you do whatsoever I command thee. The Bible verse came into Rachel's consciousness. Jesus had said that to his disciples. It was why those of the Quaker sect called each other Friends. Today, of all days, Rachel needed to trust that the women of Cane Creek would be loyal friends to Charity and wrap her in their favor.

Rachel had been worried about Charity for days. Why just yesterday, when taking a respite from cooking to step into the cool of the winter air, she'd noticed again how reserved her daughter was behaving. Charity was with her Negro sister, Danise, doing the laundry, an almost daily task that couldn't wait for warmer spring weather. The rhythm of their work had mesmerized Rachel, the girls' brown and pale hands alternating to first scrub a tan bodice, a newish blouse, and finally, the best of their skirts. It seemed to Rachel that the two had switched personalities. Usually it was Charity who was a bit bossy and Danise delicately subtle; Charity who was carefree and quick for teasing, Danise cautious and slow to reveal how she was feeling. But when Danise had given a splash from the large, oblong wash tub, Charity had ignored her. When Danise had picked up a twig for an affable poke, Charity had only twisted away, a visible frown on her otherwise comely face.

Seeing Charity's odd behavior, Rachel had stepped forward, hands on her hips, intending to remind her daughter that she was a child of God and "held in the Light," as Quakers were fond of saying, to assure Charity that whatever happened at the upcoming women's business meeting, it would be the right thing. They would bear it. But she'd stopped herself and reconsidered. Wasn't *she* the one who needed to trust her faith? Best not to give Charity cause to think that her own mother was fretting about the outcome of the specially called session. And hadn't it been decided that Danise would be allowed to attend? That alone held promise and would bring comfort to them all.

The scratch of Mary Jackson's goose quill pen brought Rachel back to the square little meetinghouse with its undecorated walls, few windows, and plank floors. The simple room had been adequate when it was built some twenty years ago, with benches arranged to separate the men from the women. In the last years, with the increase of families migrating south from Pennsylvania and Maryland to the Carolinas, the women sat like shingles on a roof, tight against each other in their allotted space.

Peering over her shoulder to the last row of benches that were designated for Negroes, Rachel gave a smile of assurance to Danise, her adopted daughter. She didn't know the details of what

Charity had told Danise, but she figured that, as close as the two were, she knew the most about what had happened on the awful night in question. Rachel had only found out the morning after the ravishing. She'd bent to pick up Charity's soiled dress off her bedroom floor, seen how it was torn—and the blood stains—and sought out an explanation. Charity hadn't been able or willing to tell her mother much, only that Jehu Stuart had attacked her, that she'd gotten away and run home. Of course, Rachel had immediately taken her in her arms, but they'd only talked again of the incident when Charity had been called to the women's meeting. Rachel counseled her to tell as much as she could because Mary Jackson, clerk, would never allow a Negro to speak during the session, to allow Danise to share what she knew of the details of the assault. Charity would be on her own to convince the women of Cane Creek that she had no part in what had happened.

Rachel turned back to face the front of the meeting room, screwing one hand inside the other and jiggling the foot that was crossed over her leg. She hoped Charity would control herself and behave as was expected—with respect, obedience, and modesty. And she as well. She said a quick, silent prayer that she would maintain restraint and be able to manage her bold and brassy ways. Like the others at the meeting, Rachel would need to wait to be called on by the clerk and keep her voice polite. For although she was a recorded minister and overseer of the meeting, she had to remind herself not to succumb to pride or be self-righteous, to not try to use her position to sway anyone away from what they felt in their own heart. Today of all days, it was important that she conduct herself as an esteemed and cherished Friend, a long-time member in good standing of the Cane Creek Monthly Meeting, and the mother of properly raised, pious children.

Rachel shifted her gaze to Mary Jackson, who was middle-aged and graying a bit, her form cut in half by a table that had been moved to provide her a writing surface so that she could take minutes, notes of whatever decision was made. As Rachel reined in her scowl, she thought back to how joyous the two of them had been eight years ago when they'd traveled to the Cedar Creek Meeting near Richmond, Virginia. Mary had been the one to suggest they ride astride as the men did, laughing deliriously with the freedom of it. She certainly hadn't been so serious and full of herself then. She'd respected Rachel on that trip, eagerly taken her advice, and seen how she was admired by those they visited.

Now Mary sat behind the clerking table with what seemed to Rachel to be a look of importance, busy with arranging the gavel, ink well, paper, and pen so they were positioned to her liking. She wondered if, as clerk, Mary would be able to control the other women in attendance if things got out of hand. Many of them were opinionated and didn't hesitate to express their thoughts, no matter the expected behavior.

But why should things get unruly, Rachel tried to console herself. *Most of these women have known Charity since she was a little girl. Please,* she begged internally as she glanced around the room, *take pity on her, hear her out, find her innocent of any wrongdoing.*

When Mary finally lifted her head from what Rachel supposed was her recording of the reason for the meeting, Rachel tried to catch her eye. *Look at me,* she silently commanded. She wanted some sort of signal that all was well, that all would ultimately end favorably. Instead, Mary pressed a finger against her lower lip and overlooked Rachel's strained smile to survey the last of those who were coming through the women's door of the meetinghouse. Disappointed, Rachel turned to the tender expression of her mother, Margaret Wells, sitting beside her, and to her oldest daughters, Mary and young Margaret. The older woman found her daughter's hand, caught her eyes, and tipped her head slightly to indicate that Abigail Pike had seated herself at the end of their same bench.

Rachel gave a nod of understanding. She knew well the importance of the esteemed minister's choice in sitting beside Charity's allies. As a recorded minister, Abigail Pike could have chosen to sit on the facing bench as well. She'd held a position of honor and leadership among the Cane Creek Friends for over a decade—since she'd stood before the first of them and announced to the families in attendance that "if Rachel Wright will go with me, we'll attend the Western Quarter at Little River and ask permission for this gathering to be officially designated as Cane Creek Meeting."

"Oh, wipe that worry off thy face," Abigail had laughed at the rise of that past meeting when Rachel, mother of seven children by then, had come to her wide-eyed. "Have we not husbands to mind home and farm while we're gone? No one will starve or be put to bed past their usual bedtime."

"I'm not opposed to the idea of it," Rachel's husband, John, had told her when the couple had talked of the trip later that day. "If thou are truly led by God, as I am confident thou have established, then thou *must* go."

Rachel and Abigail had ridden the rough two hundred miles to the far eastern part of the colony. They'd traveled for six days through dense wilderness and miserable weather, the rain trailing off their wide-brimmed hats and their damp skirts holding them on their horses like heavy feed sacks. They'd eaten their meager meals around struggling fires and slept on the hard ground with their backs up against each other for warmth, only to return as heroes with cracked lips and chapped hands to give their report: it was official. Cane Creek was now recognized as a monthly meeting in its own right. Soon after, Abigail and Rachel had organized a Cane Creek women's meeting to take up the business that the men thought was beneath them—assisting their poorest neighbors, overseeing those who wished to marry, and counseling women members. They reported the most serious offenses to the men, then to the quarterly meeting, and sometimes to the yearly meeting.

Rachel looked over to the men's side of the room, the men meeting for the same purpose as the women. She couldn't quite see her husband, John, but it was easy enough to imagine him, sitting as he usually did beside Richard Henderson and waiting for the men's session to start. He'd be ramrod straight, his feet planted firmly on the floor, as was his form when he worshiped. A smile escaped Rachel. Her John could sit like a fox for hours, not shifting his weight, not turning his head, not twisting his hands. Still, today was a different day. In her mind's eye, Rachel saw John Wright's forehead lined with worry and a callused hand fiddling with his graying beard. *It will be alright. The right thing will happen*, Rachel wanted to whisper to the good man. John trusted his decisions to God, but she knew he expected the other men to treat his daughter fairly and acknowledge that she had been raised with the expected Quaker values. After all, almost all of these neighbors knew John and Rachel as founding members of the meeting, as overseers, and Rachel as a minister. The Wrights were held with great respect in the Cane Creek community.

And is Hermon Husband there in the Men's Meeting? Rachel stiffened with worry. She hadn't seen her old foe outside, and as the men entered the meetinghouse through a different door, she was unsure whether he sat among the others, dressed as they were in a collarless coat, plain shirt, gray breeches, and buckle-less shoes. It would be fortunate, indeed, if Herman was back in Maryland with his parents, as he often was, or out speculating on land. Still, she could easily imagine the contrary man, a hand fussing through his tousled hair as he sat with an air of confidence. No doubt, there would be a smug expression on his beardless face. *Hermon Husband*, Rachel worried. He was no friend to women and certainly no friend to the *Wright* women. If he were in attendance, he would certainly have an opinion against Charity.

If only this matter could have been settled privately, Rachel fretted, *without the likes of Hermon Husband and his followers*. But, no, Jehu Stuart had gone around the Cane Creek settlement bragging unabashedly about his conquests over several young women. He'd single-handedly tried to destroy Charity's good name.

Suddenly, a loud squawk sounded from the Men's Meeting. *Do not sound thy trumpets and proclaim him innocent*, thought Rachel, her eyes still on the men's side of the room. In the Bible, the Hebrew king of Israel was depicted as cunning and bloodthirsty, known for his acts of violence. King Jehu had been responsible for Queen Jezebel's murder. *And Jehu Stuart is just as guilty, responsible for all that is happening to Charity. Her only crime was to go with him that night. Ours for allowing it.*

"Why not reward those who have left the energy to let loose a bit?" That's what John had said on the Sixth Day in question. "The young people deserve a night of fun." And it hadn't seemed unreasonable to Rachel that a group of them could enjoy an evening walk together, get away from their large families, and have a bit of privacy. She and John had allowed it of William, Mary, Joseph, and Margaret when they'd become young adults, and there'd never been any trouble. Rachel tried to relax her hands in her lap. *If only Danise had gone with her. . .*

"Friends, Friends," Mary Jackson tapped a flat hand on the clerking table, calling the meeting to order. She pushed on the edge of it to stand, the pen knife for her quill clattering to the floor. "Thank you for thy attendance today, this good day, this unpromised day that the Lord has given us," she began, ignoring the dropped knife and already seeming uncomfortable in leading the session. "May God be our guide in the serious matter before us as we take up our business this First Month in the year 1761." She glanced around the women's side of the room. "A moment of silence, then."

Sitting in their places, looking like rows of dark sunflowers, the women bowed their heads for their practice of internal worship. There was some rustling and a little coughing, and then quiet descended on those gathered. This was their belief, that in the corporate time together, the Holy Spirit, ever present, would come into each warmed heart and assist them in their challenges. But no sooner had Rachel sought out the beauty of the private quiet, searching for God's peace, than a vision of Jehu Stuart loomed up in her mind's eye.

Good girl? Good girl? the imagined Jehu taunted her. His face was scruffy, his eyes menacing.

Rachel squeezed her lids shut further and raised her clasped hands to her mouth. *A very good girl!* Rachel retorted mentally. Charity, an extrovert, loved to laugh. She might be too energetic around the supper table, too teasing in her way with her siblings, too quick to finish her chores, but outside the safety of the family, she was a model of modesty. She'd not put a bow in her hair when she went with Jehu, not worn a shortened skirt or applied beet juice to her lips. Heaven's no! And Rachel couldn't imagine Charity saying a word to make the young man think she was anything but an innocent Quaker girl, raised in the manner of the Religious Society of Friends.

Thou are the guilty one. Thou are the guilty one, Rachel repeated, the vision of Jehu Stuart never disappearing until she blinked open her eyes to vanish him. She turned to one of the windows, finding a soft shaft of the winter day coming through it. *Light. Light,* she prayed, watching the dust motes dancing in the smoothing light. She stretched her spine, closed her eyes again, and moved her conscience down into the shadows of her mind.

Light. It was a holy word to Friends, the single breath of it capturing the mysterious presence of God. Rachel internally chanted the synonyms that helped her to deepen into the silence. *Holy Spirit, Inward Light, Christ in Thee, that of God in everyone.* The naming drained her anger. *Guide those on both halves of the meetinghouse, Rachel prayed, to remember that they've known us all these years. That we are good people. That Charity is a pious girl.*

Mary Jackson cleared her throat to end the time of inward prayer. "Thank you, Friends." She allowed a lengthy pause, and in it, Rachel opened her eyes and watched Mary unfolding her hands and slowly rising from the table. "As you know, the matter of Charity Wright and her alleged carnal misconduct with Jehu Stuart has come to our attention." Mary Jackson glanced toward the other half of the room. "The young man is now before the Men's Meeting as Charity is with us."

Sara Reyerson stood to speak. There was no agenda. Those who were moved to speak rose and were recognized by the clerk.

"Sara Reyerson," acknowledged Mary Jackson.

"Before anything is said against him, I want to say that Jehu Stuart is from a good family. He works for us on occasion. Puts in a full day."

And is a predator through and through, Rachel mentally added, her shoulders tensing. She'd seen Jehu Stuart at work. Oh, yes. Him offering an arm to this or that young woman after meeting for worship on First Day. Had she not seen him try to steal a kiss from a young maiden when he'd thought no one was watching?

"The way I've heard him tell it," Sara Reyerson was saying, "Jehu's been trapped by girls the likes of this one." She pointed at Charity. "They won't leave him alone. 'Tis them that come after *him,* encouraging him in his advances—"

Mary Jackson interrupted with a question as a point of order. "And thou have witnessed this, this

34

way that women . . . that they badger Jehu Stuart for inappropriate attention?"

"Well, no. Not directly," Sara Reyerson admitted. She knew well, as they all did, that Friends were to share only what they themselves had seen or heard. They were not to spread gossip.

"Thou are aware that, as Friends, we are to speak from our own experiences?" Mary Jackson asked.

"I am," Sara Reyerson mumbled. She sank down.

Rachel's mother, Charity's Grammy Margaret, stood and was acknowledged. "Charity comes from a good family, too, and you all know it well. She's been raised with the Bible, dressing and acting as modestly as any of us."

Marcy Byrd interrupted Margaret. "Charity might have flirted improperly with the young man," she called out, not bothering to stand or wait for the clerk's acknowledgement. "Egged him on, no?" She cocked her head and held it like a confused chicken, scanning those around her for affirmation.

"Are the other young women among us?" asked Sarah Beals, wife of Thomas Beals, the two of them having walked years ago with the Wrights from Maryland to North Carolina. Sarah stood to ask her question but didn't wait for Mary to call on her. "Are they here, the ones rumored to have been molested as well?"

The questions hung in the air for a moment, but no one identified themselves as also being one of Jehu's victims. Sarah sat down.

"Charity is equally at fault for what happened, is she not?" asked a woman behind Rachel, her voice high-pitched. "What did she do to dissuade the young man?"

The dam broke, remarks drowning appropriate conduct as women offered up their thoughts and talked over each other. Mary Jackson let it go on, not doing anything to create space between the comments and accusations.

Tears of worry pricked in Rachel's eyes. She expected the women of the meeting, the ones she'd organized and counseled, to support Charity, to be understanding of what had happened to her daughter. *Not this. Not women defending Jehu against Charity.* Rachel felt the damp under her arms. *Calm,* she prayed. *Trust the Spirit.*

The comments continued. Some pointed out Charity's small stature against the strong lad, while others defended her respectable character. But others supposed that Charity had somehow provoked Jehu and could have done more to stop the assault.

"She had to know what was going to happen if she went with a lad with such a reputation," suggested Mary Hiatt, her voice loud enough that it stood out to Rachel. She was a woman of good standing in the women's meeting, but Rachel had long thought Mary Hiatt was jealous for the admiration Rachel and Abigail enjoyed among the Cane Creek women's meeting.

"Were they drinking to excess?" asked Rebekah Marshall, a good friend of Mary Hiatt's.

Rachel clenched her teeth together so forcefully that she felt the pressure of it in her upper jaw. Fury colored her face, and she pressed her fingertips into the oak of the bench on either side of her to keep herself from screaming out her rage.

"Ah, Charity Wright—" Marcy Byrd, puffed up like a mad hen, began. She was on her feet, her eyes narrow, her lips thin. "Thou sit here meek and mild before us today, but I know thee to be so sure of thyself and so carefree in thy youth, the result of thy mother's tutorage, yes?"

Rachel turned from Marcy Byrd to the dumb-founded Mary Jackson, willing her to do her job as clerk by calling out the inappropriate remarks.

Mary caught her eye and slowly raised a hand to signal the women to order, but then she let it drift back down again and remained silent.

Marcy seemed to take Mary's inaction as permission to continue her rant. "I wonder what hindered thee from crying out, crying out in *protest* when this *rape* was happening. For thou did not, did thou? Perhaps thou found thyself *enjoying* Jehu Stuart, a willing *partner* in his attentions!"

Rachel saw Charity stiffen. Then she turned back over her shoulder to her mother and grand-mother, Margaret. Wide-eyed, she was once again a baby-faced child with smooth cheeks and ripe lips. Conflict shown in her eyes. Was she to wait for Mary Jackson to ask for her side of things or respond to Marcy's inferences?

Rachel reached a hand to her daughter, hoping with all her heart that her facial expression conveyed all the love she held for the girl. As she found Charity's tearful eyes, she lost her composure and glared at Mary Jackson. "Might thou . . . please . . . *clerk* . . . this meeting?" Rachel demanded, each word measured.

"See how she behaves? Ha!" Marcy Byrd bellowed. Rachel stared at her, thinking the woman was taunting her so that she would lose herself to inappropriate conduct. "Thy Charity is no different than thee!" She sat down with a thump of arrogance and began to straighten her skirts as if she were royalty.

Mary Jackson pounded lightly on the table. "Friends, Friends!" she called to the women at large. "Might we hear Charity Wright's side of it?"

Charity turned forward, stood, rolling back her shoulders, and tilting up her chin. "I am falsely accused," she began, her right hand on her heart.

Rachel could hear an unexpected confidence in Charity's tone of voice. She watched her daughter turn slowly from the clerk to the women seated on the benches around her.

"I am falsely accused," Charity repeated. "I know Jehu Stuart, yes, and I've talked with him on several occasions when my parents or siblings or other adults were present," she clarified. "But I never led him on. The night of the . . ." She couldn't find the words and started again. "The time he, he . . . surprised me . . ." she stammered, beginning to drain of the resolve she'd had at the start. "Back when it happened . . .

It was Sixth Night, and we'd all labored through the week as is expected of us. Jehu came to our cabin, arriving after we'd eaten. He politely introduced himself to my parents."

Charity drew a sharp breath. "A couple of others met up with us as we walked, just talking as we do and . . . and we came to an abandoned cabin on Simon Dixon's property. It wasn't planned . . . us being there. We, we just arrived there, at that unlocked place." Charity swallowed loudly. "So we all went in . . . and Jehu Stuart and I . . . we, we became alone . . . in a separate room." Charity brought her hands to her face and held them hard against her cheeks. "I, I am so angry with myself . . . for my foolishness in trusting him, for separating from the others, and I apologize to all of you for it." Charity gave a quick jerk to where her mother and grandmother sat.

Rachel saw the sweep of her daughter's eyes as they glanced down the row of her allies, taking strength from them. "It, it worried me that we were alone together," Charity continued, her eyes fixed on Rachel's. "At first, Jehu and I were just talking . . . same as we had on the walk . . . but then he looked oddly at me and moved closer. I thought maybe he was going to try to kiss me, and I backed up a bit."

Charity turned to Marcy Byrd. "Sister Byrd, thou are wrong. I didn't act impetuously. I did not encourage Jehu Stuart. I put my hands up in protest when he came too close." Charity turned toward the rest of the women to demonstrate. "He grabbed my arm . . . hard." She held it out as if the marks were there and visible despite her long sleeves. "He seemed agitated and mad at me for not understanding what I did not. He clenched his arms around me, locking mine tight at my sides. And then he . . . he smashed his lips hard on mine." Charity's voice quivered. "I knew then . . . I truly felt the trouble I was in, and I tried to move toward the door to the room where the others were . . . but he held me fast, and I couldn't get away from him."

Rachel felt like she was suffocating in the small, stuffy room. Every woman had stilled, all of them at full attention for the telling. She hoped the men who were meeting across the way, only a narrow aisle between the two groups, couldn't overhear what Charity was saying. *Oh, God, be with her,* Rachel clasped her hands and pressed them hard against her lips.

"He came at me," Charity went on, "and I didn't realize at all what he was wanting." Her voice began to quaver. "The next thing I knew he had his fingers on my—" she searched for a word she could use in public, "—my bosoms . . . squeezing clumsily and grunting like a, like a pig. I should have called out then, the others were just in the next room, but I didn't. I didn't want them to hear what Jehu was doing to me . . . and then, then he was on me so heavy, like an anvil . . . and I, I couldn't get away. I told him 'No.' I did. 'No, no, no.'"

Charity stared down at her shoes, her hair falling forward so that Rachel saw the white of her innocent neck. "He didn't listen to me. He, he pulled at my, my

. . . drawers—" came the meek voice. "It was so . . . so quick . . . and I didn't cry out because there was such pain . . . red hot pain."

Charity stood back and straightened. She inhaled and exhaled loudly. "Danise and I have talked of what it'd be like to fulfill the, the wifely duties of our wedding nights, but, but when Jehu ripped into me—" She caught herself and went silent.

Rachel tilted her head back as if it were hinged and searched for God in the rafters. She knew the rest. Charity had gotten out of the cabin. She'd run home, limping with the hurt and bleeding. She'd stopped at the privy washstand to clean herself. Once in her bed chamber, she'd ripped off her dress and thrown it down, seeking Danise, who was asleep in their bed. She'd woken her sister, snuggled her pale face up beside Danise's, wanting only to know that it was over and she was safe.

"Clerk," Abigail Pike demanded, rising. "Has she not told enough? 'Tis like she's being ravished all over again!"

When Mary Jackson didn't react, Abigail remained standing, and then the whole row of Charity's relatives slowly came to their feet in silent support of her. Rachel didn't have to look to the back to know that Danise was standing as well. Still, more women than she would have guessed remained on the benches, either uncertain of what they thought of Charity's story or not believing it.

"Abigail Pike?" Mary Jackson finally squeaked.

"There is clearly no unity here," Abigail noted firmly. "Might we give this matter the seasoning it deserves? A month until we are to meet again to think on how we want to proceed?"

Mary nodded her approval of the delay. It was right order that a decision on the matter be allowed to simmer. "Silence, then?" she asked, calling for the period of worship that traditionally ended their meetings. "We are adjourned, Friends," Mary announced a short time later.

There were no handshakes or hugs as there often were at the end of First Day worship. Mary Jackson picked up her bonnet and, without looking at Charity or Rachel behind her, moved from behind the table and made her way to the women's door. Dismissed, the others gathered their winter cloaks and began to exit as well.

Rachel reached her arms to pull Charity to her.

"Oh, Mama—" the girl whimpered softly as she came briefly into the embrace and then wrenched back out of it. Tears dripped down her face like scars. She drew in a ragged breath, but then, her shoulders slumped like melted wax; she went to Danise.

The last one to leave the room, Rachel wrapped her cloak about her and rested a hand on her pregnant belly, the one life she could protect. She met John and the others outside. Charity was already in his arms. "'T will be alright, dear heart," Rachel tried to comfort Charity. The words seemed hollow, even to her.

"There was division in the Men's Meeting, too," Richard Henderson informed her. Rachel heard hope in his voice. "Jehu has been bragging about his numerous conquests, but there's no way to know if the 'acts' were consensual."

John eyed Rachel over Charity's head. "The issue has been carried over."

Trust, Rachel prayed. *Trust in God.* It was the touchstone of their faith.

Chapter 2

Rachel looked ahead to the sway of Abigail's skirts, she and John Pike walking ahead of her and John on the path just behind Danise, Charity, and the oldest Wright children. She was glad they'd walked to meeting and not ridden horses; the winter daylight coming soft through the trees and the birds singing despite the cold season helped to calm her nerves.

What does it mean: Abigail asking for a delay? Rachel worried, ringing her plainly gloved hands. *Does she not believe Charity? Does she think the poor girl could have done something to stop Jehu?* The possibilities for disapproval galloped through her mind. It hurt her to think the Wright family didn't have Abigail's wholehearted support. *Will the Cane Creek women shun her now? Think her conduct sinful?* Rachel sucked in her worry, John turning to her at the noise of it.

"Does thou think the Pikes feel Charity wasn't raised up proper?" she fussed. "That I'm not a moral mother, us allowing our daughter to go off with Jehu in the first place?" It seemed symbolic to Rachel, Abigail's turning away from her on this day of what amounted to Quaker court.

"John said nothing to indicate any of that during the Men's Meeting," John Wright answered, referring to their older neighbor. The two of them watched the older couple take the fork in the lane that led to the Pike farm, their own just beyond it. "I'd hate to lose their friendship," John Wright added carefully. "You and Abigail have logged a good many miles together. She knows thee, Rachel. She knows our children."

Not sure what to say, Rachel repeated what she'd already been told. "The men were divided as were the women today?"

"They were, yes."

"And many believed Charity had done all she could to stop Jehu?" Rachel surmised hopefully.

"Some did, yes."

"And Hermon Husband wasn't there?"

"He was not."

"But does thou think some of those who are close to him would have confused Charity's situation with Hermon Husband's dislike for me? With the way he complains that I have forwardness in my manner and that I work too zealously to establish women's meetings?"

"'Tis possible," John admitted, taking her hand, "but might thou let it rest for a time? 'Tis our faith to trust in God, is it not?" He glanced over to his wife.

"Thou are a recognized, respected minister, Rachel, thy good work sanctioned by the meeting."

Rachel gave up a brittle smile, grateful to have her husband's unwavering loyalty. She willed herself to accept his counsel, drifting back as they walked along to when he'd chosen her. John had been a shoemaker then, living with his parents in the Hopewell Meeting community in Virginia. She'd been new to Quaker meeting, surprised not to see a minister leading the service or that no one read from a prepared text during the hour. Those in attendance sat in a holy silence unless one of them was moved to speak and deliver a message. Soon after Rachel had begun a regular practice of attending, John had approached her at the rise of the worship. She'd let the quickening of her heart be God's nudge that she should accept his interest.

As was true of many Friends, John's Quaker family had come originally from England and then to Massachusetts, New Jersey, and Pennsylvania. His parents, James and Mary Wright, had been pioneers in the settling of the Hopewell Meeting when it had formed in 1735, James already serving as a prominent minister and well known in the Philadelphia Yearly Meeting. John's Aunt Martha had been recorded as a minister when she'd been only twenty years old, recognized for the depth of her faith and not because of any formal education. And another aunt, Hannah, was also appreciated for her ability to preach.

Rachel knew little of her own relatives. Her father's father, Thomas Wells of Prince George's County, Maryland, had been a boisterous and opinionated man, an enslaver. He was prone to fights with men of his own kind, with countless charges of assault against him. Rachel quivered now at the thought of her lineage, glad she was no longer in contact with the uncles who had inherited her father's tobacco plantation. Quakers worked to find that of God in each person, but for the most part, those in the Hopewell Meeting shunned the owning of another human being.

Her own father, Joseph Wells, was cut from the same cloth as his father. In Rachel's childhood, he'd been a womanizer and a drunk, the cause of much gossip. When she'd been old enough to read, she sought out the records at the All Hallow's Protestant Episcopal Church where she'd been told her birth was recorded. She'd found the name of a woman, "Rachel," with no last name listed beside her own birthdate, 27 March 1720. Her birth mother had died in childbirth, and she'd been named for the sacrifice.

Soon after, Rachel's father married Margaret Swanson, a good woman whose relatives had also come to Pennsylvania from England. A soft smile crept up Rachel's face as she remembered her many childhood days aside Margaret Wells, the only mother she'd ever known. She had memories of the forty-acre farm along the Monocacy River in Maryland where they'd moved after her half-brother, Joseph Jr., was born. They'd called the place Boiling Springs Farm, and Joseph Wells Sr. had worked the acreage himself. When Joseph Jr. was old enough, he'd been apprenticed to a furniture maker and showed great aptitude for the craft.

For Rachel, there was no such option, no apprenticeship or schooling outside what was required around their home. In her boredom, she discovered the Friends, two groups of them, in the Hopewell Meeting and with Fairfax Friends who were a hundred miles away. She busied herself learning the Quaker way of things—Rachel practiced not saying things that seemed vain and arrogant or to act in any manner that separated people. She dropped the use of titles and ranks.

On the rough meetinghouse benches, sometimes in one meeting and sometimes in the other, Rachel became familiar with the silence, feeling relief in the great quiet. It was usually the image of a planted seed that she took—still used—to take her down into the murky depth of the imagined soil and assist her in the meditation. With her whole being, her complete self, she came to accept that she was a beloved child of God, that the Holy Spirit would take all her worries and awkwardness from her and speak with her directly as a guide if she would but sit calmly and listen. She knew no Bible verses or songs to repeat as she sought growth and opportunity. Instead, she would conjure up images—a flame she was to tend, yeasted dough she was to knead, radiating light through clouds, a butterfly emerging from its dull, brown case transformed and perfect. She would allow the impressions to spread through her, drift within, and open like meaningful blossoms. With humiliation, she would carefully and honestly examine whatever came into her heart, accepting her weaknesses, taking responsibility for her ways, and praying that a door of private understanding would open, that she'd grow from the seed, be warmed by the sun, take wing like the butterfly. Her desire to heed the Holy Spirit, coupled with an enveloping desire to improve herself, resulted in a hopeful joy. She hadn't tried to explain to her father or Margaret.

Out of the discussions Rachel had with John's sisters, Hannah and Martha, around that time, she came to understand that the Wrights didn't care about her having been born out of wedlock, that her grandfather had owned slaves, or that her father had once been a drunk and a womanizer. Instead, the women were against war and dishonesty and worked to uphold a simple, God-focused life. They had a great love for their fellow "peculiar people," their communities that were "separate from the world," as non-Friends described them.

The Kingdom of Heaven did gather us and catch us all, as in a net. . . . And from that day forward, our hearts were knit unto the Lord and one unto another in true and fervent love," Hannah Wright had recited over tea early on in their meetings. It was a famous quote from one of the Valiant Sixty, the first Friends who traveled and preached in the seventeenth century to spread Quakerism. To Hannah and Martha, and all

50

the Wrights really, it seemed the flawed fragments of Rachel's background had been what had brought her to the Friends. They saw great potential in her gifts of intellect and engaging energy.

Cautiously at first, Rachel shared her joy of corporate Friends worship with Hannah and Martha. She told them of her lack of church attendance as a child, that she had never memorized Bible verses, and only knew of other religions that had been mentioned in social conversations. Hannah and Martha shared some of Quaker history, of how the first Friends, as they liked to call them, the seventeenth-century Friends, had been severely punished by the Church of England, the only acceptable faith at the time. Many of the followers of the founder, George Fox, had come to the colonies seeking religious freedom. From that point on, Rachel would imagine John's ancestors sitting with her and the Wrights as they worshiped on First Day, solid in their testimonies, their vows of equality, simplicity, and community.

Abigail Pike had been the first woman Rachel had ever witnessed give a message in meeting. Sitting in Fairfax Meeting, she'd heard the rustle of women's skirts and then the confident feminine voice. She'd popped open her eyes to see everyone, eyes closed, taking in the ministry as if it wasn't at all unusual. But it was. Rachel knew enough about the society outside the meetinghouse walls to know that women ministers were an oddity. She came to learn that Friends valued women as spiritual equals, recognized them for their gifts of speaking, and encouraged them to travel to share their faith with others.

Abigail explained that she was a birthright Quaker, born to parents who were Friends. She'd grown up in a monthly meeting where women discerned messages and women's meetings for business had been long established. Literate when her protege was not, Abigail told Rachel that the separate women's and men's business meetings had been George Fox's idea. The founder of their sect had observed how the women were hesitant to speak their minds in front of their husbands and other male relatives, and he'd listened to the women when they'd told him that they felt nearer to the Spirit when they were separated from the men. The logical solution had been to form women's meetings, first in England, then throughout New England, and then in Pennsylvania and Maryland.

Eventually, Rachel had requested official membership in Hopewell Monthly Meeting, appreciating how her opinions were valued and warmed by the friendship of Abigail Pike and the Wright women. No one seemed to think that her sex, her youth, or her lack of literacy prevented her from being of service to the sect.

In 1736, when she'd been sixteen years old, Rachel married John, who was twenty. Her own parents were members of the meeting by then. There was no clergy and no one gave her away. Quakers were so influential in the Pennsylvania colony, and non-officiated marriages, or self-united marriages, as some called them, were considered legal. James and Mary Wright saw to it that John and Rachel's marriage certificate was of the finest paper and so large that it covered a good part of a table. It was signed first by the newlyweds, then by John's parents, and then by the rest of those who had witnessed the wedding pledges. Rachel's brother, Joseph Jr., had framed the certificate, and they had hung it above their bed.

Just a few years after their marriage, Rachel and John were made meeting overseers, although they were both still in their twenties. William Dewsbury, a young Friend himself, had created the position of overseer in 1653, proposing that each meeting appoint one or two of those who had most grown in the power and the life of discerning of truth and that they take responsibility for the spiritual welfare of the meeting. With Abigail Pike as her mentor, Rachel took the work extremely seriously, wanting all of those in the Quaker community to learn, as she had, how to become closer to God.

#

Back in those early days in Virginia, Rachel had been on the comfortable side of Abigail's sharp tongue and indisputable wit as the older woman clerked the women's meeting sessions. Rachel had seen how skillfully Abigail conducted the business and wrote the minutes of accomplishments. Rachel saw through Abigail's stern ways to her soft heart as she eldered those who seemed "uppity" or inexperienced. When Rachel first gave ministry herself, it was Abigail who found her afterward with compliments that made Rachel feel faint. Not much later, after she'd preached several more times, Rachel's gift was officially recognized by the meeting, and she was recorded as a minister, the distinction documented in the meeting minutes. After that, Abigail and Rachel, allies in the work of organizing women and giving them their voice, began to ride to each cabin along the Opequon River to set up women's meeting for business in the small meetings of the vast Hopewell Meeting jurisdiction.

Rachel loved the freedom of the travel, even though one or two men usually rode along, too. She and Abigail made the visits in all seasons, often seeing more Cherokees than settlers and sleeping beside each other on the hard, cold ground, their faces to the stars. Rachel was the one to rise early, like some nocturnal animal, and start the fire for their coffee. The air was often so cold that the haze of her breath blocked her vision as she listened to wolves on a nearby ridge singing the sun up. Then, as Abigail and the men rose, ate, and readied, Rachel would pace around like a colt kicking in a barn stall, more than ready to leap into the day.

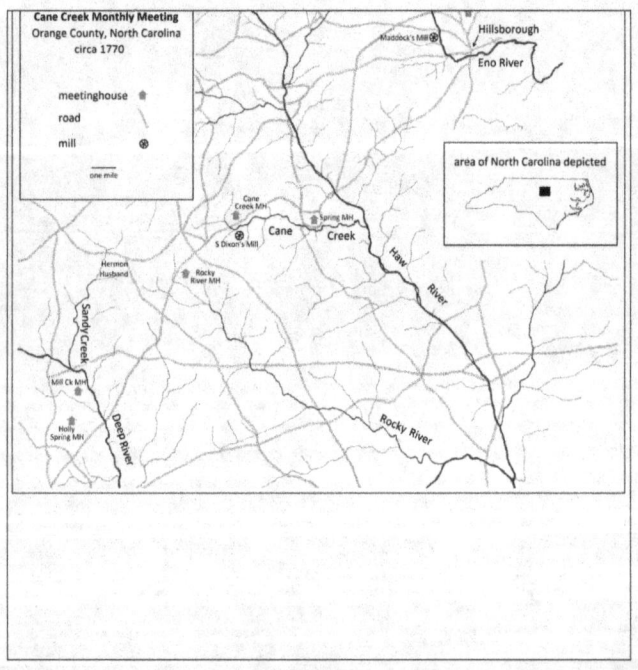

Map originally published on page xx in *Cane Creek, Mother of Meetings*, by Bobbie T. Teague (Snow Camp, NC, Greensboro, NC: Cane Creek Monthly Meeting of Friends; North Carolina Friends Historical Society: North Carolina Yearly Meeting of Friends, 1995) and used with permission of the publisher.

Chapter 3

It was from Simon Dixon, a member of the Hopewell Meeting in Virginia, that John and Rachel learned the history of Henry and Hannah Phelps, the first Friends in the Carolinas. Simon was organizing Friends to move to North Carolina and a new Quaker settlement.

As Simon told the story, Henry had a reputation in the Massachusetts colony for being a troublemaker. He avoided the Sunday services of the Anglican Church, refused to tithe to what was the colonial version of the Church of England, and didn't abide by the colonial laws. In 1658, Henry and his brother, Nicholas, were the first to hold meetings for worship in the manner of Friends in their home. They were arrested for doing so and fined heavily. Others in the meeting suffered, too. Members had their ears cropped off and were publicly stripped and whipped and then immobilized in the stocks. Eventually, the

Phelps house and property were confiscated for the offenses of their brothers.

When Nicholas died in 1665, Henry married his widow, Hannah Basket. The couple set off south for Albemarle Sound, a large estuary on the northeast Carolina coast in the Outer Banks region. They had settled in the swampy eastern Perquimans region that had been named for King Charles I. In the spring of 1672, an esteemed Irish Friend, William Edmundson, who was one of the Valiant Sixty, came first to Barbados and then to the Carolinas. He traveled further inland through the "pathless backcountry" in search of other Friends until lost, cold, and abandoned by the men who were supposed to be guiding him, he miraculously came to the Phelps homestead. Refreshed by a nap but still dirty and disheveled from over a year of travel, William Edmundson sent out word that he wished to invite anyone interested in hearing him speak to the Phelps home. People came by boat, horseback, and on foot to the cabin. The family and their neighbors were pleased for the diversion and hoped for news of England. William greeted them and then entered into worship, letting the Holy Spirit inform his words.

Had the Spirit led the seventeenth century preacher to find Henry and Hannah on the wild inland narrows of the Perquimans River? Rachel wondered. He'd written of it in his diary:

"Having not seen a Friend for seven years before, Henry and Hannah Phelps wept for joy to see me. It was a First Day morning when I got there, and I was weary and faint and my clothes all wet. They left me to alert others in the area that there would be a meeting for worship later in the day. At the appointed hour, many people came, but they had little or no religion, for they sat down in the meeting, smoking their pipes, their dogs panting loudly in a corner. Still, the Lord's testimony arose in the authority of his power, and their hearts were reached with it, several of them tender enough to be convinced. After that meeting for worship, they requested more, a thirst unquenched."

William stayed for several more days with the Phelps to meet with the families and preach. When he left, the settlers continued to hold worship in the manner of Friends that he had shared with them, without priest, prayer book, or song.

In the November of that same year, 1672, George Fox, heartened by reports of William Edmundson's reception, also visited the Albemarle. He stayed first with the governor of the Carolina colony and then visited the Phelps and the other settlers. He stayed eighteen days, strengthening the seeds that William had planted. Thus, Simon Dixon noted, not having seen other Quakers in years, the first to worship with Henry and Hannah Phelps in North Carolina were two of the most famous!

#

When Simon Dixon spoke to John and Rachel about migrating to North Carolina, already a distinct colony from South Carolina, he'd already purchased acreage from Earl Granville's colonial agents. The Earl, originally awarded a land grant by King Charles II, knew that the hills and valleys between Virginia and the Carolinas that had been stolen from the Natives. He'd instructed his agents to sell plots and send the profits back to him in England. Simon bought his land, located in the north-central part of North Carolina, from an agent in what he thought was a fair agreement. It included an eastward meandering creek that eventually merged with the Haw River and then the Wilmington River. He'd cleared a small plot for corn, built a simple cabin, and returned to persuade others in the large Hopewell Meeting to move south with him.

"Where the river cane grows so high that it's obvious the soil is richly fertile," Simon told the Wrights. "There'll be no Anglican Church and no tavern." John joined the group that Simon organized of men from New Jersey, Pennsylvania, Maryland, and Virginia to go see it for themselves; to partake in Simon's dream of a Quaker settlement, cheap land, and a longer growing season than in the north. Once en route, some of the men—Simon, John Wright, John Pike, Thomas Beals, Richard Henderson— spent their evenings sitting around their campfire talking of the tenets of their faith and farming. There'd be no plantations, no enslaved people. The family farms would grow grains and keep livestock and resist the growing authority of the king's East Coast colonial agents.

Upon arrival, the men had each chosen acres for their own. It was hotter in North Carolina than John had expected, but large sections of the land had already been cleared by the Cherokee so that the men had been able to help each other seed a field each. Together they'd built a one-room cabin for each family and covered the dirt of the floor with a smooth coat of pulverized quartz, found nearby in abundance. The homes had stone mudcat chimneys at one end, the mortar made from the same clay concoction as what the men had slapped between the cabin logs. Then they returned to their wives, fully set on the move.

John told Rachel he'd picked a section of farm that butted up to a gentle spring at the back end of the land so that it'd be easy enough for Mary and Margaret, their oldest girls, to come with their buckets and fetch water from it. The plots of their closest friends were in a row, fanned out from the river like a grand sundial, John Pike and Simon Dixon beside the Wrights. Thomas Beals and Richard Henderson were close by. A parcel of acreage in the middle of the land had been set aside for the meetinghouse and grounds. With his oldest children around him, John named all the trees he'd seen, tapping each of them on the head in succession as he listed them: shortleaf pine, oak, cedar, persimmon, cherry, walnut, and so on. "All kinds of birds sing the day long, and flowers tumble like laughter off the bushes," he grinned. He looked over at twelve-year-old William, his oldest. "We'll need to see about thy long rifle, son. It's a hunter's bonanza, crowded with buffalo, deer, and black bear. Eden."

"And Natives?" Rachel interrupted, biting her lip. It was why they weren't moving to western Pennsylvania. Natives had been attacking those who tried to take their land to settle there. The horrible stories had been floating back to those in the East for years.

"Didn't see many," John shrugged. "They live north of Cane Creek in the forested mountains." He'd only had one encounter—a band of deer hunters, their skin the color of copper. One of them had looked to be part Negro and knew some English. When the group of them had approached John in his worship, the man had served as go-between so that John could convey that he was a peaceful man, no threat. He kept his voice soft, saying, "Friend, friend," and kept a smile on his face while slowly picking up his hat and pointing to the wide brim. They'd seemed to understand, to recognize that he shunned conflict and used his gun only for hunting. "For whatever reason, they rode on," John told Rachel.

The caravan of travelers left Hopewell, Virginia, in the spring of 1749, their wagons and farm animals stretched out like a string of ants on the Great Wagon Road. John led a horse hitched to a wagon and walked with their oldest boys, William and Joseph, and little Mary, who basked in his attention as he taught them the names of trees, wildflowers, and birds.

Rachel guided a lineback dun that held two-year-old Rachel in one basket and one-year-old Johnny in another. She stayed close beside six-year-old Margaret, who rode on the family's oldest and most reliable mare, and instructed her to hold tight to four-year-old Charity.

Their group of five or six families was so large that, some days, they only progressed about ten miles or so as they moved down the barely visible trading trail. The Great Wagon Road was anything but a road, and sometimes, they lost the way of it altogether as it wound through dense forests, across rushing streams, over savannas, and up foothills and mountains. The trail was littered with wheel hubs and broken spikes, horseshoes, and empty barrels from those who had preceded them.

It wasn't long before every one of the pioneers considered the trip both dull and arduous. Their feet ached relentlessly, almost all of them with an incessant bloom of blisters. Still, there was excitement, too. One day, they saw a band of Natives watching them from a ridge. Rachel clenched her pregnant belly and stared as wide-eyed as the children at the bare chests and arms, the riders sitting ramrod straight, barefoot, and without saddles on their brown Mustangs. John said they were only out to hunt, but Rachel had pulled the dun horse tight to her and instructed Mary to grab the reins of the mare and guide it behind the wagon for what little protection it provided. John and some other men rode out to meet the bronzed-colored men, and were able to convince them that their group meant no harm. The Natives let them pass, unharmed, and later that evening, John reminded the children that there was "that of God" in everyone. He was sure he'd seen the evidence in the Native hunters.

The evenings as the group traveled were for nourishment and socialization. After the cooking was done and the men had attended to the animals, it was easy enough to ignore the worsening stink of the boys' jackets, flax-wool shirts and pants, and filthy socks, the girls in their stained cotton dresses, and to gather around the circle. Rachel, four months pregnant and sick at times with all the riding, barely got seven little faces washed, matted hair combed out, and the diapers changed on Johnny and little Rachel before the youngest children fell asleep. Then John and twelve-year-old William would set to repairing boots and shoes for the nine of them—and anyone else in need.

The travelers ate bear bacon, dried fruit, and lots of deer and fish—and on lean days, they filled their hungry children with bread and biscuits from the flour they'd brought along. They drank mulled cider and fresh water from the streams they encountered, filling their jugs whenever they had the chance. After an entire month of travel, the group arrived in North Carolina, exhausted but relieved. At the little cabin John had built the year before, the Wrights got the youngest ones down from the horses, while William, Mary, and young Joseph jumped about like grasshoppers. Rachel laughed at her babies, mimicking their siblings without any understanding of what was being celebrated. Then William and young Joseph helped their father herd the rake-thin horses and cow, their ribs protruding, into the waiting pen that John had loosely constructed the previous year. Rachel put seven-year-old Margaret in charge of four-year-old Charity, two-year-old Rachel, and baby Johnny, confining them to the cabin so the wagon could be unloaded. Before she'd done much of anything else, the Negro, Majer, came riding into the yard. He was owned by Joel Brooks, who was fond of Charity's sister, Mary, and had been apprenticed to Joseph Jr. back in Maryland. "Can you come to the plot set aside for the meetinghouse?" Majer asked. "Simon Dixon has called a meeting for worship."

The Wrights found the other travelers sitting in the field among the wildflowers, some on fallen logs, in a loose circle. To shade them from the sun, the men wore wide-brimmed hats made from beavers, and the women had "sugar scoop" bonnets, the brims large and stiff and the backs flat. The men had brought their guns and dogs as protection against wild animals and now made teepees of the guns. The group sat as divided by sex as was possible. Rachel had a time of it, getting her little ones to stop their running about and settle down beside her and John, but even before Simon welcomed everyone, baby Johnny had fallen asleep in the soft, red fescue grass.

Twenty-one-year-old Simon stood near his young wife at one edge of them all, shoulders back, legs planted wide. His shaggy head was bowed, the locks swinging forward, and his hands were clasped against his chest as if their safe arrival amazed him, too. Rachel watched him for a few moments, the sun shining on him as if it were holy Light. She bowed her head in gratitude that Simon, and all of them, had been wrapped in God's favor on the journey, no one falling terribly ill, drowning as they crossed a rushing stream or breaking a leg falling from a horse. They'd trusted this young man with their lives, and he had not disappointed them. Here was the result, all that they had dreamed of, this island of a community of only Friends, where they could predict the honesty and integrity of their neighbors in any given situation, work large plots of rich farmland, and live in peace.

In the following weeks, sawdust sweetened the air. Everyone was improving their cabins, adding rooms or working on the interiors. John Pike and John Wright helped each other construct sleeping lofts on the caramel-colored walls of the back rooms. They laid more substantial roofs and improved the chimneys they'd made hurriedly the year before. By that first fall, the men and John Wright's oldest son, William, had laid floorboards throughout both their homes. Rachel's brother, Joseph Jr. had married in Virginia and returned with his wife to live nearby. He and Majer, both skilled craftsmen, brought over a table, chairs, a long bench, and several, three-legged stools. The two had made a beautiful cradle especially for baby Rachel. And before he left, Joseph Jr. had shown William his technique for driving pegs into the walls for jackets and helped Rachel to suspend John's rifle on antler hooks above the door.

By the time the new baby, Sarah, was born in December 1749, Joseph Jr. had a sawmill up and running, and the Cane Creek women had assembled their looms. John and his boys had started on the rails for fencing around the farm and found arrowheads in the dirt. They'd built a box in the river to keep their milk, butter, and cheese from spoiling, and nine-year-old Joseph had come back from the work full of pride as to how he'd chosen the stone that weighed down the lid. It would keep the beavers and foxes from stealing their food. Meanwhile, Rachel had enlisted ten-year-old Mary to collect chicken fluff, bird feathers, and grass to fill the large mattress encasements she'd sewn on the trail. The family had dug pine saplings from the nearby forest and planted one for each member of the family, letting some of the children tend to the watering. "For our coffins when they're needed," John told his brood.

Chapter 4

Four years old when she had moved with her family to Cane Creek, Charity was six when the impressive minister, Catherine Payton, visited the Wright farmstead. The weighty Friend and her companion, redheaded Mary Peisley, arrived at Cane Creek, quivering like dry leaves, Mary with a barking cough. Rachel and Abigail had taken the two in like precious pieces of silver, infatuated by their presence, honored to have the renowned women in their homes.

Over cups of peppermint and honey tea, Catherine and Mary told their story. They'd met in Ireland two decades back, when they were both in their twenties, the Holy Spirit alive in their conscience and not letting them alone. They were released by their meetings to travel and preach, and although blessed in their work, they'd found it as much of a burden as a privilege. They missed their families, but they'd seen great sites and were sure they were responsible for the convincement of a great number of people.

"Mary is my second self, my 'yoke-mate,'" Catherine Payton had grinned. "The two of us called to visit all around Great Britain before enduring six weeks of horrible storms and nauseating seasickness to come here to the colonies. I saw hell on that voyage," Catherine said plainly. "The leaky, cramped living quarters, the malnutrition, the poor hygiene, and the considerable weeping and vomiting."

"At least we weren't accused of witchcraft and thrown overboard, as some Friends have been," Mary reminded her, her Irish brogue a delight. She moved a hand and rested it on one of Catherine's. They'd been in Pennsylvania, the revered Quaker colony founded by William Penn in 1682, and according to Catherine's journal, had visited almost two hundred families. They'd attended six meetings a week while in Philadelphia and visited anyone who was ill or distraught. Then they'd come south to Charleston.

"My goodness, what a hectic and dirty city, that Charleston," Mary Peisley sighed. "A disappointment to us, these colonies being so young."

"'Tis where the remarkable Mary Fisher is buried," Catherine cut in. She'd put her hands to her lips and glanced skyward, as if to say a quick prayer. She realized that no one knew about Mary Fisher. "She was one of the first itinerant Friends, one of the Valiant Sixty—about thirty years old when she was convinced by George Fox. She was the first of us women to be stripped and whipped in public for preaching." Catherine straightened up. "When Mary Fisher was arrested for it, she sang and praised God all the way to jail. And later, still a young woman, she went all the way to the Ottoman Empire to visit and expound our faith to the Sultan Mehmed IV."

Catherine searched around the table to see their reactions. "And then," she went on, "a couple of years later, Mary sailed to Boston where, even before she got off the boat, her pamphlets were burned, and she was accused of being a witch." Catherine shook her head. "And if that wasn't enough suffering, a 'woman' jailer, who turned out to be a man in disguise, insisted on *checking* her for signs of the craft." Catherine made a face to indicate to the older ones at the table that more had been done. "She was locked in a cell for six weeks with no way to earn food or water."

"And did she die?" young Margaret wanted to know.

"No, no," Catherine replied, turning kindly to the child. "But many of the first Friends did die for the horrible things that were done to them. Mary was helped, just as your family is aiding us now. At one point, a man stopped to listen to her preaching through her cell window. The words that God gave her convinced him that he had that of God within and didn't need clergy to have a direct relationship with the Holy Spirit. He brought Mary supplies until the authorities forced her back to England. Later, when she was older, she married and came to live in Charleston."

Rachel sat, chin resting in her hands, and watched Catherine through what she called "a telling." She saw how her manner held the interest of all ages of those bunched around the table, conveying the history and sacrifice of Friends and the importance of the current work of the women.

"Tell us about thy travels in Britain," fourteen-year-old William bravely asked Catherine.

It was what Rachel wanted to hear, too. "Thou've managed a women's meeting at the yearly meeting level, have thou?"

"No, no. Not at all," Catherine shook her head and rubbed a knot on the slab table. "There's still no official women's meeting at London Yearly Meeting. We gather and write epistles, but we've been specifically *told* by the male elders to take our *concerns* to the men." She twisted her mouth a bit with her disdain.

"Though we are," Mary frowned, "and this is an exact quote, 'to be careful not to speak too much or take up time that male Friends could be using to speak.'"

"We've read thy letters," Abigail informed her, "and we are in much agreement that women's meetings should be set up at all levels—monthly, quarterly, and yearly." She leaned forward to share a confidence. "Rachel and I are led to do the work in these parts, too, but we—we haven't begun as yet."

"If it is a leading," Catherine said sternly, "if thou are being asked by the God of Love to act, then thou must make a way of it." Her tone increased with the importance of her words. "Love is Holy and persistently at work all around us. We must only have eyes to see it, a heart to feel it—and be faithful to its call for action." She emphasized the word. "Don't be tempted by the thoughts in your head that tell you otherwise, that make you doubt yourself, that tell you something can't be done." She looked around at them all. "It is evil that tries to make you think you are not to go, that you are not strong enough, not smart enough, not worthy enough to do the work that the Spirit has called you to do. Because," she wagged her finger at them, "it's not so. The truth is that Love is at work in us and in those we influence. It is winning and growing—and will triumph."

Catherine turned directly to Rachel. "Thou have things to say now, don't thou, Rachel? Don't thou suppose God wants thee to say them?"

After Catherine and Mary had left Cane Creek, Rachel and Abigail went before the women's meeting to request that they, too, be allowed to travel to outlying meetings in the Western Quarter. When permission was granted, the two women set about visiting all the women in the Cane Creek jurisdiction, no matter that, in some areas, the Indigenous people were almost constantly at war with the settlers for taking their land and that the British and French were at odds with each other in the colonies. They shared news of the women in the other meetings, how they were progressing in establishing their own business meetings.

The work wasn't easy. Once Abigail and Rachel pitched their tent in a fierce, unexpected wind-storm, only to wake to ankle-deep snow, frozen drinking water, and damp firewood. Another time, they were offered a room that was partially exposed to the weather. It rained all night, soaking them both, but they rode on, bent against the wind and coughing continuously.

It was after Rachel began to travel as an itinerant minister that another traveling Friend, John Woolman, visited the meeting. He was a short, slender man, not fifty years old; the humble preacher came to them on foot. He wore undyed homespun, his shirt and breeches the natural color of wool, a contrast to the dark, indigo-dyed jackets of the Cane Creek men. When he entered the meetinghouse, he took note of Majer and his wife, Anarcha, the community midwife, who were sitting on the back bench, the one designated for Negroes, and he went over to them and shook their hands. Then he walked to the front of the room, respectfully removed his floppy, drab hat, and scrunched it in his hands.

Perhaps he's but a ghost, thought Rachel. *Come to shame us for our treatment of the Negroes among us.* She watched as John Woolman fixed his gaze on his buckleless boots and waited patiently for the room to quiet. Then, well-seasoned in the manner of Friends, he lifted his head, gently pressing a dark curl back from his eye, and closed his eyes. Rachel knew what he was praying, that God would give him the words needed to reach them, to make comprehendible the message he was called to deliver.

May the Holy Spirit guide thee, Rachel prayed, too. She recognized the divine moment, saw it in the way John's chin quivered as he began to address them.

"I know, I know, you don't have enslaved people here in Cane Creek," the preacher began, looking over their heads to the couple sitting against the back wall. "You don't call them that. You say servant or apprentice or midwife." He looked first to the men's benches and then to the women's, his voice quiet, but unyielding. "I know. I know. You have only kept and cared for the few who were in your families in Pennsylvania, Maryland, and Virginia. Probably most of them the offspring of those bought by your parents or grandparents and given to you somewhere along the way. You've made sure they have food and clothing. You've taught them to read."

Well, yes, thought Rachel. She didn't dare turn her head to the back.

"You are good to them, yes, but Friends, they are kept, they are not free. They can't eat or wear anything of diet or apparel that is produced by their labor, no matter your kindness. They have no say over their lives." He rested his gaze on Majer and Anarcha, and let the room go quiet.

'Tis a complex situation that deserved sorting, Rachel thought. But she had to admit that she'd never talked with Majer or Anarcha about their thoughts on the matter, if they were happy with their lives in Cane Creek. She vowed to do so, and in that same moment, she put a hand to her heart and pledged she'd talk to any enslaved people directly that she saw in her

travels, taking up the issue of slavery with Quakers when she made her round of visits in the jurisdiction.

Rachel stared at John Woolman as he stood stoically. *Thou are led to take up this difficult issue, moved by the strength of an inner conviction.* She had felt it, too, that feeling that impels a person to do as they are divinely directed, no matter the struggle. John Woolman had left his wife and daughter behind to travel through Virginia, Maryland, and the Carolinas with his leading. Rachel knew the pain of it. She had left her John and their children for weeks at a time, riding the rutted, rough old Cherokee trails that John Woolman walked, the both of them knowing the beauty and perils of the unspoiled paradise, of the rich soil and rushing rivers—of the challenge of the Friends who held enslaved workers.

"Do you know of Friend Benjamin Lay?" John Woolman was asking, bringing an end to the uncomfortable quiet. He didn't expect anyone to interrupt him to answer. "Quite a remarkable man," he mused aloud. "A dwarf who was appalled—appalled at Friends' institution of slavery when he came from Britain and saw how Negroes were treated in Barbados and Philadelphia. He's been preaching against slavery for years. Twenty years ago, he came to Philadelphia Yearly Meeting dressed as a soldier to deliver a diatribe against slavery. He has tried all sorts of ways to get our attention," John went on, "standing outside of meeting in winter with no coat and his feet in the snow to show how the enslaved are made to work in such conditions. He temporarily kidnapped the child of enslavers to show them how Africans felt when their relatives were sold away from them. He was disowned, of course, but Benjamin befriended the powerful Benjamin Franklin, who printed his book *All Slave Keepers That Keep the Innocent in Bondage*. I advise you to read it if you haven't as of yet."

John walked to the back of the meetinghouse and returned to the front. He looked right and left at all the congregation. "My White brethren, your actions here and in the Carolinas go against the Golden Rule. 'Tis not right that you sit Negroes on the back bench there," he pointed, "their hearts and souls hungry. It is not right that Negroes in the colonies are whipped, chained, and sold off—separated from those they love as if they had no feelings, no heartache." The preacher put his hand up again in protest. "I know, I know. Not by you, you are saying, but perhaps by your relatives and certainly by others in the Religious Society of Friends. And why is this?" John let a poignant silence fill the room. "The only Christian way to treat the enslaved is to set them free."

Chapter 5

A month or so after John Woolman had left them, close to Charity's eighth birthday, the Wrights met Danise and her little sister, Chelsea. They came bouncing into the yard with Charlie Mayer, a big, burly frontiersman, and his wife, Peggy, who lived in Old Fort, about thirty miles west of Cane Creek. With them were their help, an aging Negro couple, and the two little girls.

"I brought you Dan-eee-sssss and Chellll-seeee! A birthday present!" Charlie Mayer called out as he pulled the horses to a halt and spied Margaret and Charity in the Wright's front yard. He lifted first one and then the other girl down from the creaking wagon, his cheeks ruddy from the whipping fall wind. Danise was taller, the two of them dressed in simple shifts, frayed at the bottom, boys cast-off trousers underneath to protect their stick-thin legs, but no stockings or shoes. Both their little faces shone bright with the anticipation of playing with the Wright children.

Charity was in awe of the tiny, tight, chocolate curls that crowned Danise and Chelsea's heads. She'd never played with Negroes, hardly ever talked with Majer or Anarcha.

Danise, with her high cheekbones, thin nose, and buoyant grin, didn't hesitate to thrust her hand toward Charity. The gesture was a Quaker custom that implied equality. "I'm Danise. Eight already."

"Are they your grandchildren?" Rachel asked the aged Negro couple.

"In a manner of speaking," Ol' Toby answered.

Why are Ol' Toby and his wife raising these little girls? Rachel wondered. She thought it imprudent to ask.

Danise motioned for her little sister, Chelsea, to come closer to her. "This is Chelsea," she announced, moving a hand in an odd manner on her cheek. "She doesn't hear."

"We think Chelsea's about six," Peggy Mayer added.

"Are there bear here?" Danise asked then, jerking a thumb toward the forest that surrounded one edge of the Wright farm. She repeated the question in sign, bending her hands as if they were claws and holding them up in front of her chest. Bear. She raised her eyebrows to indicate that she was asking a question. *"Any bear here?"*

"No, honey," Rachel assured her. "Not that thou need worry about." She awkwardly copied the "bear" sign and shook her head. *"No Bear."*

With that, Margaret, Danise, Charity, and Chelsea giggled a bit in their newness of each other and then bounded off like fawns, Margaret in the lead as they raced toward the creek. Rachel watched them kick up the brown and gold leaves that covered the ground as they ran. When they returned, they were all holding hands. They danced around the Wright family and their guests and then joined them for Charity's birthday picnic.

As they ate, Rachel watched Danise and Chelsea talk in their manual way of it. Back and forth in one-handed and two-handed gestures, palm in, palm out, Danise dutifully filled the void of what Chelsea was missing of the other's comments. If Chelsea signed something, only unintelligible sounds came from her mouth, so Danise told them what she was meaning. It seemed that the girls had gestures for each food—meat pie, fried potatoes, and ginger cake—and expertly threw the signs at each other as they ate.

"Good cake," Chelsea smiled when it was dessert time. The flour had come from the Dixon Mill, built only recently by Simon and his sons. It was some of the first the Dixon family had begun selling outside the needs of their own family.

"Can thou show me thy names in that?" Rachel asked Danise, rolling her hands loosely in front of her blouse. She, Margaret, and Charity all copied the name signs that Danise showed them. She was a natural teacher, holding up the handshapes for them to imitate, stopping at the placement until they each had their hand there and slowly moving the gesture so they could duplicate it. *"Danise"* was two taps on the heart with an open hand. *"Chelsea"* was signified by a hand that curved up one of her cheeks to extend her toothy smile.

"And ours? How will thou make *our* names on your hands?" Rachel asked.

Danise pressed her long, thin fingers to her cheek to think. She started with Charity, considering her long wavy hair. "What about this for thee?" she suggested, making eye contact with Charity. She gently waved an open hand, moving it from her head to her chin. "Because of her lovely long hair."

Charity beamed. "And for Margaret?" she blushed.

Margaret was ordinary in her features. Her clothes were almost identical to Charity's—a gray smock and long sleeves with no cuffs, a white apron, stockings, and hard shoes. Nothing that stood out for a sign name. "Perhaps an *M* at the heart?" Danise suggested.

"An *M* at the heart?" Rachel repeated. She stood and went over to where Danise was sitting by Charity and Margaret to get a closer look at the three bent fingers the delightful girl held in her right hand.

"There is a way to make the *ABCs* on your hands," explained Danise to them all. "Here, we'll show you." She sat back stiffly, ready to teach. "We aren't allowed to read, but a woman taught me these letters for our hands."

For the rest of their time together, the Wrights were freer in how they gestured, trying to incorporate signs they copied from Danise into what they were saying. There was both shyness and laughter as they tried out the new way of talking.

When it was time for the Mayers to leave, Charlie Mayer gave each of the Wright girls a whirl, scratching their cheeks with his wiry beard, and shook hands with John and the boys. Peggy, the strings of her white cap dangling down her cheeks, pulled each child into her side for a soft hug.

It was only a year or so later when the Mayers were attacked and murdered outside Old Fort by an angry Native war party. The North Carolina Colonial Assembly had been harassing Friends to muster with the local militia as pioneers of other faiths were doing. Friends were told that they could line up with a good axe, spade, shovel, or hoe in place of the regular musket if they didn't want to face heavy fines. Most refused.

Rachel was sure that Charlie Mayer hadn't gotten involved in the "French and Indian War," as it was called, and she imagined him and Peggy trying to talk reason with their attackers on the day of their deaths. She didn't want to hear the details of it when the elderly Negro, Toby, made the trip to tell them, Danise and Chelsea sitting quietly beside him on the driver's bench.

"We can't a-keep them," explained the gray-haired Toby. John and Rachel helped the hunched man down from the wagon, while Danise and Chelsea jumped down on their own. "Don't know how me and the wife will manage now to feed the two of us, our masters dead and gone, and you've got the many children here for playmates." He wobbled with grief.

John nodded his approval of the plan and glanced over to Rachel. She indicated her acceptance of it as well. There were plenty of other families in Cane Creek who had taken in abandoned children for all kinds of reasons, none of them Negroes though.

Toby turned to Danise, a crack in his voice. "Be good and a helper. Say thy prayers." He hugged her and then handed her a lovely quilt and the floppy handles of a small canvas grip. He kissed Chelsea's head, hugging her tightly. Then he accepted John at his elbow to drag himself slowly back up on the buckboard.

Later, Rachel wondered if it had been God in her heart when she'd seen the girls, down-faced and sorrowful, wiping tears from their puffy cheeks. It wasn't the time to ask how Toby had come to raise them or to question why he hadn't given them any ownership papers.

It was over the next weeks that Rachel came to fully realize what it meant to have a Deaf child, to fetch and tap Chelsea every time she wanted her, and to learn a sufficient number of signs so that her new daughter could understand her requests. When it came to any real conversation, though, Rachel had to rely on Danise. The two of them worried that Chelsea's deafness might put her in more danger than the rest of them. There were wild animals and Natives sharing the forest nearest the cabin, and they were not keen on the settlers. Their hunting diminished by the farming efforts of the settlers, they sometimes wandered up to the cabin, asking for food. While it was true that the Natives mostly let the settlers of Cane Creek alone, there had been attacks in the region of late so fierce that even the bold and independent Rachel was forced to pay attention when she went visiting.

"The Natives are ravishing British forts," Majer warned her. Majer traveled for Rachel's brother and his furniture company and took head of the goings on. "Fort Dobbs isn't far from us." The log fortress on the western frontier had been named for the governor. Its soldiers, traders, and colonial officials were attempting to provide protection from French-allied Natives, but recently, the Shawnee, Delaware, and Cherokee, as well as the French, had been escalating their raids on isolated settlers and any fur traders they found on the trails. They ruined crops, burned farm buildings, and murdered families. In retaliation, the governors of Virginia and the Carolinas had banded their troops together in a joint campaign, trying to completely crush the Native way of life. They were responsible for sending thousands of men, women, and children into the hills to starve.

How will I protect the girls from such things? Rachel wondered. There were no other Deaf people that she knew to ask for advice. She worshiped on it for weeks before the idea came to her to visit with Thomas and Sarah Beals. They now lived in New Garden and were good friends. John and Rachel had been witnesses at their marriage, and they had all come together on the caravan from Hopewell, Virginia, to Cane Creek. Rachel hadn't seen the Beals much in these last years, but she always looked forward to catching up at the quarterly meetings. She knew that Thomas was very involved with both Natives and Negroes. He'd told of his work at the quarterly sessions, of how he held many satisfactory meetings with the Mingo and Delaware, as well as of how he and his wife had labored with a Friend who'd owned and abused Negroes—split up families and raped the enslaved women as if it were nothing. Rachel didn't know the outcome, but she'd been told that Thomas also met with another man at the Pasquotank Monthly Meeting in the Eastern Quarterly Meeting, where slavery was prevalent. After meeting with the Beals and other Quakers, the Friend agreed to stop buying and selling Negroes, understanding that those in the New Garden community would continue to meet with him, worship with him, and seek justice. Yes, Rachel decided. It was worth the day's ride to New Garden to seek the sound advice of the Beals as to how to keep Chelsea and the other children safe. She was anxious to discuss what to say should a slave trader or colonial government man come asking to see papers for the girls, ownership certificates that she and John didn't have.

As it turned out, Thomas didn't think the Natives would bother the Cane Creek community. They understood that Friends upheld a peace testimony and wouldn't fight them. He also felt that, since Friends didn't use the colonial courts, the lack of proper paperwork for Danise and Chelsea shouldn't be a worry. "Trust God," he'd advised. "It is right that you have taken them in as your daughters. Cane Creek Meeting will vouch for you should it become necessary." The embarrassing part of the visit had been when Sarah Beals had asked about Danise and Chelsea's parents, about how they'd come to live with the Mayers.

"I don't know," Rachel had admitted. Upon her return, she gathered her family in the front room and asked Danise to tell her these things.

"One minute," Danise signed, holding up her index finger. She went to the bed she shared with Charity, pulled the quilt Toby had left with her from it, and returned to the waiting family. Kneeling beside Rachel, she patted the spot on her other side. *"Come. Sit,"* she signed to Chelsea.

"Ah, thy story quilt," Rachel smiled.

Pointing to Chelsea, Danise signed, *"She wants to know about us before—before we came here."* She turned back to Rachel. "I only know the bit that Mister Mayer told me," she said, glancing around the room to the others as she arranged the quilt over her and Chelsea's laps. *"This,"* she fingered one of the neatly appliqued squares, *"tells our Mother's story."* This quilt tells our Mama's story," Danise repeated.

"It starts with this one. This is Africa—*Africa*." She indicated a dark green shape. "Here's the ship that brought Bibi, my Grandma, from the coast there to the coast here—to the Orton Plantation far east of here." She drew a finger from one continent to the other, shifting her gaze to John Wright and her Wright siblings. "Our Bibi was brought to the Carolinas some fifty years ago." She pointed to some little round circles of fabric below the blue of the colonies. *"Island,"* she signed to Chelsea. *"Far, far away."*

Chelsea nodded. She put her chin on her fist, waiting for more.

"Master Mayer thought this is Barbados," Danise explained, "but I'm not sure who in my family came from there. The enslaved people were working the sugar cane and starving, so men, plantation owners on the Carolina coast, started growing rice to ship there to feed them." Danise looked to Chelsea. *"Slave slave work work,"* she signed, repeating and exaggerating the movements, her facial expression reflecting the pain of the enslaved workers. "With sugar . . . and hungry, *hungry*," Danise moved the handshape down her chest and mouthed the word with a pitiful expression.

"Because rice can't grow in this Barbados place?" Charity asked innocently. "Because why didn't the enslavers in Barbados grow rice for the people themselves?"

"Because they were—are *greedy*," John butted in. Rachel thought that perhaps he thought Danise was too young to explain. "They wanted only sugar on their plantations," John continued. He glanced over to Danise who gave a nod of approval for him to say what he wanted. "Sugar was the money crop. Then and now, the plantation owners in Barbados want only to grow what brings the most profit, the most money in their pockets."

"And where do Friends stand in all this?" asked eleven-year-old Margaret.

"British merchants, some of them Quaker, are the main force behind the slave trade and the ones bringing the Negroes from Africa," clarified John, his attention on William, Mary, Joseph, Margaret, and Charity, all of them old enough to comprehend the severity of it.

"Because we take them from their beds, Papa?" worried Margaret.

"Well, not us, but some Friends and others, yes. Fathers and mothers and children." He looked at three-year-old Hannah playing with Rachel's skirts.

"Friends who own the ships and pay the sailors to kidnap the Negroes and bring them from Africa," interrupted William, now sixteen and a voracious reader. William turned to his father for permission to continue. "Majer got a copy of the *Gazette*, that new newspaper. He told me that more and more people are captured each year—eight hundred brought here in the early 1700s, six thousand midcentury, and now more than forty-one thousand."

"The numbers seem right," John agreed, frowning. "Friends, Quakers, both here and in Britain, are caught up in these money-making opportunities." He leaned back, his hands on his head. "Why, if we were to go to Barbados right now, we'd see as many enslaved workers as there are trees in the woods." He looked around the circle of children.

Charity was slack-jawed. She only knew four Negroes in all of Cane Creek—Danise, Chelsea, Majer, and Anarcha.

"Been like that for a hundred years," popped William, pleased to be respected for what he knew of it and the exact numbers he'd recalled. "When George Fox preached in Barbados, on his way here to the colonies, he found at least six Friends who owned more than a hundred enslaved people." He shook his head, "A hundred!"

"Friends who *own* other people?" whispered Mary, turning to her oldest brother. Surely that wasn't right. Like her sisters and most of the other girls in Cane Creek, her world was very small. She'd never been out of the Cane Creek settlement.

"Well," her father admitted, sucking his lips as he thought about how much to explain, "it's not much discussed in this community, but the plantations in Barbados and here on the coast can't grow their tobacco and sugar without the Negroes. They couldn't make money without the cheap labor. It's hard work, and they need a lot of help. Once enslaver owns another man, that man can be forced," he looked with uncertainty to Rachel, "forced to have babies,

90

increasing the number of slaves he owns, increasing his wealth."

"When George Fox sailed to Barbados, he could have stopped it then, no?" William asked, addressing his father. "At least among the Quakers. For in our tutoring we've read that he stayed months on the plantation of his relatives there, and of course, they were Friends—*enslaving Friends*. George Fox saw the treatment firsthand, but didn't condemn it."

"'Tis true," agreed John, catching William's eye. "George Fox only reassured the governor that he wouldn't encourage the enslaved people to rebel and preached for the owners to be 'mild and gentle' in their dealings with them."

"To be *better* enslavers but enslavers, nonetheless?" snorted young Joseph.

"'Tis why we struggle with it now," suggested Rachel. She knew there were at least a hundred people owned by those in the yearly meeting, most belonging to Friends on the coast. "It's no better in the Carolinas."

"And now we share, as do all Friends, in the complicity of it." John glanced over to Mary, Margaret, and Charity. "The Negro people, the enslaved people, are *property*, like cattle or our corn crop. They can be bought and sold, used to ensure repayment of money that is borrowed from the colonial bank, and passed to relatives when their first owners die. Out on the coasts of the Carolinas and Georgia, the enslaved people work in the fields, but other places, they are the ones who build the roads and levees, the ones that clear the canals and rivers. If thou were to go to Charleston or the big cities in the north, thou'd see the enormous buildings they've constructed with their talent. And even so, they have no rights."

"Then, if they've done so much," asked Mary innocently, "why aren't they allowed to be members of our meetings?" It was a hard, honest question.

Rachel looked at John. In Cane Creek, Danise, Chelsea, Majer, and Anarcha came to meeting on First and Fourth Days as did the rest of the Wright family, but they typically weren't allowed at business meetings.

"We're working on that," John finally answered. "As a whole faith." He glanced at Danise, providing the only excuse he had. "At yearly meeting, Friends come from the communities all over the region. It's those on the coasts, the plantation enslavers, shipowners, and merchants who thrive off the slavery, and as members of our yearly meeting, argue against it." He sat back with a creak of his high-backed chair, done. "Cane Creek abides by habits of all the other meetings," he added weakly, looking down to the hands that rested in his lap.

Rachel patted Danise's shoulder. "'Twas about thy family I was wanting us all to hear," she redirected, realizing that John and William had taken her intention way off course. "Might thou tell us more of thy family, please, Danise?"

Danise found a square of the quilt that told the next part of the saga. "Master Mayer said that on the Orton Plantation there were about two hundred and fifty Negroes doing the back-breaking rice work, clearing the trees from the swamps, and building the flood dams." She stopped to paraphrase what she said in sign for Chelsea. "Our Bibi was one of them," she went on. "Living with a Necoe man, a Native, who maybe was our Grandpa, because look—"

Danise found a square with a man, a woman, and a child between them. "That's our mama. These two," she pointed to the couple with the child, "are our grandparents. She pointed at them. *"grandparents,"* she repeated, hesitating, and then continuing. "Maybe, I'm not sure. They were found dead on their pallets one morning; others think they died from malaria."

Danise took a deep, shaky breath and then moved the quilt so they could see the next part. "Their children—well, one of them was our mama—were sent to people in Wilmington after their parents died. I don't know why." She laid a finger on the next shape. "That's on the coast, too. See these stick figures? Those are the enslaved people who were already there. Our mama grew up in the big house, sleeping on the kitchen planks. Lots of scrubbing, emptying of chamber pots, toting water. She was never branded, though."

Rachel pulled her braid to the front of her bodice and cleared her throat, an indication for Danise to curtail the telling a bit for the sake of the youngest children.

"Branding," asked Margaret anyway. "Like the cattle?"

Danise nodded glumly but went on. "I don't know our Mama's proper name. This is her here." She fiddled with an edge of the quilt. "I think she and Papa loved each other." She dug a charm from her pocket and displayed it. "You all know I carry this, my good luck charm. I'd like to believe that our first papa made it."

"And thou don't know his name either?" asked Rachel.

"Not first, not last," Danise confirmed. She gave no reason for it.

Rachel began to gnaw on the edge of a fingernail. *Even young Margaret knows our full names and those of our relatives.* Rachel's own birth mother had died when she'd been born, but she knew the first and last names of generations of folks on her father's side. London Yearly Meeting had them all recorded— births, deaths, and travel certificates from the 1730s forward. *But not of enslaved workers, she realized. Not unless they're listed in the property rolls and then only by sex and age.*

And Rachel knew more than just the names of those in the Wells family. She knew that her grandfather, Joseph Wells, had been a farmer and enslaver. She knew that her father and brother had learned cabinetry techniques in the North and were now, along with Majer, renowned furniture makers. She knew which of her women relatives made the best pie, canned the sweetest pickles, and were the most accomplished quilters.

Danise fingered the three little hammered, intertwining rings. "Our mama said our papa was a blacksmith. She called these rings of love and belonging. *Love, Belonging,*" she signed. "He was maybe a Seneca man, is what Ol' Toby thought, for there's always been a lot of mixing among us on the coast." She rotated an arm as she handed the rings to Chelsea, who was bored with the story that was unavailable to her unless Danise stopped to interpret. "Majer thinks it's so from our features and that we have no hair on our arms." Danise held up an arm, but didn't bother to push back her long sleeve.

"Our mama was sold off as a breeder to someone on the outskirts of Wilmington." Danise's voice quivered with the remembering, and Rachel leaned over to rub her back. "It was Christmastime," the girl whispered, turning to Rachel, "and when I woke up, she, Mama was gone. Just gone . . . it's hard to talk of it." She looked around the group of them, all the faces as sad as her own.

"And how did thou come to live with the Mayers then?" Mary asked after there'd been a long, solemn pause.

"When my mama was sold off, Chelsea and I came to live with them. I don't know who sent us or why, but whoever it was made sure I had my mama's quilt. The Mayers were members of South River Monthly Meeting and saw to it that we were allowed into Friends worship. We sat by ourselves with the others of our kind under the stairs, not on a bench."

Chapter 6

Life on the Wright farm was tense during the Second and Third Months of 1761, as the Wrights waited to hear whether Charity's disownment would be upheld. Friends were known for their laboring, their seasoning, their needing of consensus, but when no decision was made at the first meetings of the year, Rachel had found it difficult to trust God that things would turn out as she prayed. One evening, the children asleep in the back rooms, she worked to quiet her worries over the situation. Sitting by the spring fire, she sought the relief of worship, but unable to settle, suddenly rose from her hardbacked chair to right the little stick horses that her seven-year-old son, James, had galloped across the hearth. Then, she busied herself, puffing at the soot to move it back closer to the ambers. Next, she reached for nine-year-old Chelsea's heap of knitting to put it back into the bag that lay beside it. Finally, she plopped restlessly back down in her chair.

Things change so slowly, Rachel lamented, thinking first of the process of Charity's appeal but then about how there was still such inequality between White Friends and the enslaved families who faithfully attended meetings for worship. Back a few years, Philadelphia had arranged a mostly segregated meeting for worship for Negroes to be held on the Fourth Day afternoon, following each quarterly meeting.

"We must be about supporting our children," Rachel whispered to the embers, "all our children. We must work harder to keep them in the fold of Friends, not offending them with our actions, no matter how well-intended." She found a candle, lit it from the hearth, and banked the coals with ash so they'd be available for breakfast the next morning. Moving into the short hallway to the room where Margaret, Danise, Charity, and Chelsea slept, Rachel carefully opened the jib door and peeked inside. She found exactly what she'd expected. Charity and Danise were snuggled side by side in one bed and Margaret and Chelsea balled up in the other. The four had shared the room since the first night Danise and Chelsea had come to live with them.

Rachel went to each of the girls now, tucking their quilts and giving each a kiss. She hesitated over Charity, the aroma of lavender from her hair rising up from the sleeping form. Only four months back, this brave daughter of hers had stood unaccompanied before the facing bench of the women's meeting.

Rachel had smelled the lavender then, too. *My precious girl, thou of great things.* It was difficult to await the final decisions of the Cane Creek men and women's business meetings as to whether Charity was guilty of any misconduct, any "disorderly walking."

Rachel touched Charity's smooth cheek. There was something, something undefined as yet, budding in the fifteen-year-old. Catherine Payton had seen it years ago. She'd prophesied that Charity would travel, too, and share in the itinerant preaching and visiting that she and her companion, Mary Peisley, and Abigail and Rachel had been led to do. For Charity stood out among her sisters, coming to Rachel about the time her monthlies had started with a solemn, personal commitment to the Spirit. She'd told her mother with the seriousness of an adult that she'd not shrink from the life of convincement, choosing Quakerism for herself and not simply because she was a birthright Friend. After that, she sat with Danise and Chelsea on the back bench.

#

Finally, in late March 1761, Jeremiah Piggott, clerk of the Men's Meeting, rode out to the Wrights. *This is not a good sign,* Rachel fussed as she watched Jeremiah and John talk, Jeremiah still astride his mount. She knew the handsome man well. He'd come to the cabin on occasion to discuss the work of the women's meeting, and once, he and Mary Jackson had ridden along on one of her visitation trips.

As it turned out, Jeremiah had come to ask John to step aside and not attend the upcoming Fourth Month discussion of Charity's disownment. When John agreed, Rachel, pregnant and not feeling well, decided she and her oldest daughters would stay away from the women's meeting as well. If they were absent, Rachel reasoned, perhaps the membership would realize how hurtful the whole circumstance was for them.

Now, a day or so after the business meetings, Jeremiah was returning with Mary Jackson, the women's meeting clerk, trailing a ways behind him. Most of the family was out in the yard, but when Charity saw the two of them come trotting up, she went quickly to stand behind her mother.

Without so much as even a howdy or fanfare of any sort, Mary Jackson maneuvered her mare alongside where Rachel and Charity stood. She pulled out a paper from her skirt pocket.

"April 4, 1761," she read, loud enough for them all to hear. "The women's meeting, after repeated extended labor, disowns Charity Wright for having carnal knowledge of Jehu Stuart." Disownment meant Charity could attend worship on First Day but not participate in the women's business meetings. It meant that everyone in Cane Creek and the jurisdiction would know of the decision, the news spreading like prairie fire.

"Oh—" Charity whimpered. She cupped her eyes with her hands.

"Thou are no longer able to attend women's meetings," affirmed Mary, her face stiff.

"Mary Hiatt and Rebekah Marshall have been made overseers for the meeting," Mary Jackson further announced from her lofty perch atop her mare. She stared at Rachel. "As thou have been so, so improper these past months."

"Promoted for their part in this," Rachel fumed with furious eyes. She could feel the heat of humiliation and anger moving into her cheeks. "'Tis not right," she seethed, throwing up her hands. "How can it be that they believe our girl enticed that man or didn't do what she could to stop him? How can they not think I would do all I could to proclaim her innocence?" She made her way to Jeremiah, leaving Charity shocked still where she stood. She didn't even try to contain her anger. "Disownment certainly has its time and place when couples choose to be married by a justice of the peace or decide to wed outside our faith, or take up arms to fight. 'Tis not for when a girl is ravished!" she pleaded, hands atop her sunbonnet in disbelief. "Is this what we are coming to?" There was a desperate edge in her voice. "That a person can be read out of meeting for not yelling loud enough when she's being violated?"

"And the men?" John challenged in his own quiet way. He walked slowly over to Jeremiah's horse and took hold of the reins.

"They concur, yes, and have disowned Jehu Stuart as well."

Rachel wanted to stomp around and scream, tears pushing at the back of her eyes as she watched the rumps of Jeremiah and Mary's horses as the pair left the yard.

Oh, if Catherine Payton would only come riding to them now! She'd stand strong with her arguments on Charity's behalf. She made her way back to Charity. *And remind me that God has a plan, unknown to us, and that the right thing will happen.*

"I'll not change my telling," Charity sobbed. She stomped a defiant boot, but her cheeks had gone chalk pale. "I'll not say I encouraged Jehu Stuart when I did not." She wiped at her tears. They all knew the process. A committee would be out to the cabin and ask her to acknowledge her fault. They'd expect Charity to ask for forgiveness for what they'd concluded she'd done.

"We'll move," Rachel announced suddenly. She grabbed at her daughter's hand and held her brown eyes. "Thy father and I have talked of the possibility."

"Where?" asked a startled Charity. She meekly searched Rachel's tired face with both surprise and gratitude.

"Bush River," Rachel and John said in unison.

"Near Newberry, South Carolina," Rachel clarified, sounding more confident about the decision than she felt.

"It's a newer settlement right on the border of the South Carolina colony. Cherokee country," added John, one hand gesturing vaguely as if creating the location of a map out of thin air. "Friends came to it as they did here, from Virginia and Pennsylvania to escape religious persecution and because the land is cheap. They've built their cabins on both sides of the sluggish little river there."

"We'll make an appeal to quarterly meeting that thou not be disowned," Rachel assured Charity, "and we'll hold the others in the Light who Jehu molested, hoping they'll step forward. But we will also apply for certificates of transfer so Cane Creek is aware that if they insist on this disownment, they will lose us all."

It was another two months of waiting before a quarterly meeting committee responded to Charity's appeal. The whole time of it, the sixteen-year-old was like a jumpy deer trapped in a cabin corner. She had bouts of anger and times of unnatural quiet, going off to the oak grove with Danise more often than their chores allowed. Rachel didn't know what to say to her daughter, and as far as she knew, Charity didn't talk to anyone but Danise about her feelings over the matter. None of her girlfriends came to visit, and the other girls Jehu had bragged he'd molested never broke their silence. Even Abigail Pike and Margaret Wells seemed to visit less often.

Somehow, thought Rachel, *there is a gift to the disownment, a way it will assist Charity in her life, if only I could see it.*

Finally in June, Charity was called to New Garden to appear before a panel of fourteen men from Centre, Deep River, and New Garden Meetings to discuss her appeal. The Wright women were directed not to speak unless called upon and to sit apart from

John Wright, Joseph Jr., William, and young Joseph who'd accompanied them to the special session.

Rachel looked at the wall of the committee members as she waited for things to start. Their relatives were German Lutherans and Reformed settlers, as well as Scots-Irish Presbyterians, who had come initially to the northern colonies before migrating south as her family had on the same Great Wagon Road. They'd built their cabins in the open, grassy spaces that had once been Cheraw's farmland, just as she and John had done in Cane Creek. The similarities gave Rachel an odd comfort. *Aren't all Friends family? Won't these men see the wisdom of keeping Charity in the fold?*

Rachel glanced across to where the men sat and found Thomas Beals, Sarah's husband, sitting just behind John. The Beals were pious and peaceful. They'd offered their cabin to about twenty Friends for meeting for worship when there was no meeting-house. Since those first days, Friends had migrated like bees to the New Garden settlement so that now it was a good-sized meeting. The Beals were considered weighty Friends, elders. Thomas had been so reasonable when Rachel had gone to see him a few years back to seek his counsel with regard to Danise and Chelsea. Sarah had come all the way from New Garden to support Charity at the very first sessions regarding the rape. Surely they would want the girl's continued membership in the sect and sway others to her defense.

Oh no. Rachel's gaze flitted from Thomas Beals to Hermon Husband. He was sitting like an eagle on a post, watching from a few rows back for his opportunity to strike. Rachel averted her eyes, supposing Hermon would be gloating about the Cane Creek disownment, a victory in his years of battle with her.

Abigail had told Rachel of Hermon Husband's background, that he wasn't a birthright Friend, not born into a Quaker family, but rather was the son of wealthy enslavers who were members of the Anglican Church. As the story went, he'd been "deeply touched" in a moment of truth at one of the Great Awakening revivals of 1740, when he was sixteen years old. He'd laid in a fetal position on the ground, making infantile sounds as he was birthed into the Protestant faith.

"No, no 'tis not so strange," Abigail told an amazed Rachel. "First Friends did much the same, rolling on the ground, and speaking in tongues and incantations. They honored the seed, feminizing faith as a new creation, a promise fulfilled. 'Tis not the devil when we see such behavior now," Abigail had assured Rachel, "but only that we have matured from the sudden dazzling and transforming experience of the seventeenth century to a slower and subtler path to God."

Hermon had found Friends as a young man and had been taken under the wing of businessmen in the Deer Creek Monthly Meeting north of Baltimore. He'd gotten involved in land speculation in the North Carolina frontier. Earnest in his understanding of the history and proper way of things in the sect, the young Hermon was soon made an overseer. By 1750, he'd written about his religious odyssey in a published pamphlet. Abigail had secured a copy. According to the tract, Hermon had been to both Barbados and North Carolina and was familiar with the slave economy in both places. A few years later, he'd come through the backcountry of North Carolina as an agent for a land company and decided the paradise of Cane Creek was where he wanted to settle. He bought property near Simon Dixon's mill, began to raise wheat, and set up a public gristmill. He worked as a surveyor and sold land, returning frequently to Maryland to see his parents but attending Cane Creek Meeting often enough that he eventually asked for membership.

Almost as soon as Hermon was an official member of the meeting, he started complaining. He claimed that he'd taken the motions of membership very seriously, implying that others did not. He was alive with the fire of his great awakening, concerned that Friends had fallen away from the faith as it was originally preached in the seventeenth century by George Fox and the Valiant Sixty. "Thousands of those who bear the name of Quakers know nothing of the saving power of God," he proclaimed, "and have set up forms, complex ways of decision-making under which they shelter." Recently, during meeting for "waiting worship," as he called it, Hermon had shouted out, "Where is our spontaneity, our immediate inspiration? Must we anticipate the decisions about our actions from those who travel from the monthly to the quarterly to the yearly meeting and back again to inform us as to what we are about?" He'd gathered a following, people who believed him to be more than a land speculator and farmer, more than a spiritual pilgrim like themselves. Those who were at odds with the decision-making process among Friends, of the time it took to reach consensus and have it recorded, fell into line behind the leadership of Hermon Husband.

Rachel and Hermon had a lengthy and complicated relationship. They were about the same age, although Rachel could give countless examples of how Hermon had shown his disrespect for her work in the meeting. Still, she tried to consider his arguments, worried as he traveled among those in the region who were lapsed in their attendance at meeting for worship and who were known to be loose in their habits—dancing and card playing, vanity in their garments, and greedy in their obtainment of wares. And, of course, it was true that elders, ministers, queries, and books of Quaker discipline hadn't existed in the seventeenth century, as Hermon often complained. But that was where the two parted ways. Rachel didn't think the absence of the tools among first Friends invalidated their use now. She disagreed that the recognized ministers and overseers were "select Quakers," as Hermon called them, and were held in higher regard than others in the congregation.

"And where is the evidence of women's meetings in the good book?" Hermon Husband often nagged when Rachel and Abigail were reporting on their leadings. He admitted that he found their work appalling. "Thou want only for a reprieve from thy duties as wives and mothers. Stay home where thou belong," he would repeatedly chastise Rachel.

How many children must we have? Rachel wondered. Pregnant again, she rubbed the bulge that obscured any indication that she had a waist. *How stable and loving must our homes be before the likes of Hermon Husband will grant us women the use of our talent?*

Hermon didn't like strong and assertive women. When he talked to them at the rise of worship, it was always the young ones who twittered nervously with his attention and were meek in their replies to his questions. Recently, he'd married a young, comely, and soft-spoken woman, who was never heard to contradict his opinion.

But there was more. Abigail Pike believed she'd found the root of his disdain for Rachel in one of his tracts. He'd written that, once, while hurrying home to pray, a woman was walking in his direction on the same road. He blamed his instant lust for her on Satan and admitted that he'd wanted to embrace her as she'd passed by. He'd felt "ashamed" and disclosed that, though his pace had been quick, the woman caused him to "slack his stride to enjoy her flesh and the devil." As Abigail and Rachel pondered the particular phrasing of his words, they saw that he took no responsibility for his desires, that his perspective was that this innocent woman and perhaps all women "ensnared" him.

It was his second pamphlet, "The Second Part of the Naked Truth," that had mortified Rachel. Hermon had actually *named* her, writing that, whenever she was in the company of "younger men" when she traveled, she stayed with them all hours of the night, drinking alcohol to excess. In the tract and with his rumors, Hermon claimed that Rachel, mother of a gaggle of children and happily married to John, went to bed "in mixed company" on many of these nights, that she had lain beside Jeremiah Piggott—clerk of the Men's Meeting, for heaven's sake—and who Hermon described as a "young man," although in truth, he was about their same age. Hermon charged that, as they camped, Rachel had come into Jeremiah's bedroll, complaining of the cold, and opened her blouse to him.

The truth of it was that Jeremiah had asked to go on the visit with Rachel and that Mary Jackson had gone, too. They wanted, Jeremiah had explained, to better understand what was involved with the visits the itinerant ministers made to the women in the out-lying meetings. "And men usually do accompany you women, for protection should you two come across Natives or wild animals," he argued. *Ha*, Rachel had thought at the time of his suggesting to tag along. *I can shoot a gun as well as Jeremiah Piggott, take out a pheasant on the wing if need be, and am certainly the better cook and conversationalist when it comes to engaging strangers.*

It was curious to Rachel that Mary Jackson, who had lost control of the initial women's meeting about

Charity's rape, hadn't challenged Hermon over what he'd written in the pamphlet. Or Jeremiah Piggott, clerk of the Men's Meeting, either, for that matter. Yes, she'd been with Rachel and Jeremiah in 1753 when the three of them had ridden to Cedar Creek Meeting, the visit approved by the meeting. Both Mary and Jeremiah knew firsthand how she'd behaved and that the allegations Hermon made against her were both false and of malicious design. Perhaps Mary and Jeremiah had their sights on positions of prestige in the meeting and didn't want trouble from the influential man. *God has a plan, unknown to us,* Rachel reminded herself. *And Hermon has a growing group of supporters of his ways. Best to let it lay.*

Now, Rachel wondered what had motivated Hermon to make the hard ride from Cane Creek to New Garden for the quarterly meeting committee meeting that would consider Charity's disownment appeal. *Is it that he sees me in Charity's personality, capable of trapping him in sin, as perhaps he thinks she tempted Jehu Stuart,* Rachel fretted. *He wants her halted before the meeting recognizes her full potential for a ministry of her own.* Rachel picked at her top skirt. *Hermon Husband wants a negative mark on any future work Charity might do, not wanting any more of the Wright women riding the wilderness to encourage women to have confidence in their public speaking and in their ability to debate men.*

Rachel went on with her mental torment, wondering if Hermon had even read the "Book of Discipline," sent down by London Friends to the Philadelphia Yearly Meeting. Copies were stacked at the back of the meetinghouse, filled with queries, the questions after each section of the book that had been written by a thoughtful committee. Hermon, of course, complained that neither the process nor the questions were in the Bible, but Rachel and others thought the query discussions were exceedingly important. Their faith practice did not include the recitation of a creed; the queries assisted each of them in taking personal responsibility for their spiritual development and their behavior in their daily life.

Still, there was no denying that, in the tracts Hermon had authored and with his charismatic personality, the man was influencing others. Prominent Quakers in North Carolina, like Joseph Maddock and Jonathan Sell at Eno Meeting, had become his close allies, embracing his judgmental "moralism." They'd begun to crack down on the Eno Quakers who were distant from humble living and not attempting to embrace the testimonies of peace, integrity, plainness, and equality. Likewise, Quakers at Mill Creek Meeting on the Deep River had become passionate moralist supporters as well, agreeing with Hermon that the likes of Rachel Wright riled up their women folk and insisted it was permissible for them to express their opinions in public. There was no denying that there were irreparable consequences from the rumors Hermon Husband had spread.

Have I not fallen out of favor with the women of Cane Creek? Rachel worried, her head in her hands. Suddenly, she was unsure of herself and physically sick with worry for Charity. She needed air. Rachel

held her swollen belly, wobbled to her feet, and loudly
made her way out of the committee meeting before
Hermon Husband or any of the other men had their
say.

Chapter 7

The news was not good, but if she was honest, Rachel had expected it. She couldn't think of a time when a quarterly committee had overturned the decision of a monthly meeting. In addition, John reported that Hermon Husband and his cronies had stood in the way of Charity's appeal, seeming to convince the majority of the others in attendance that she could have stopped Jehu Stuart's "advances" had she wanted.

"Is it that we simply move?" asked Rachel, the Wrights and their allies circled outside the New Garden meetinghouse. "Take our chances with being accepted by Bush River Friends?"

"'Tis a frontier community," John nodded, not at all objecting to relocating, "not at all as organized as here. A chance to start anew, yes?" He reached an arm to Charity and pulled her into his embrace.

Not long after, one of the committee members from New Garden came with a letter of apology that the quarterly committee had written. They didn't want Charity disowned. All she needed to do was sign the letter, and she could retain all the rights and privileges of membership in Cane Creek Meeting:

WHEREAS despite my having had a sound Quaker education, I have not given careful mind to the leadings and directions of the Spirit of Truth, that unerring Guide, which would have preserved me. Instead, I did give way to youthful pleasure and my own inclination and kept inappropriate company with Jehu Stuart, a young man of my Cane Creek Meeting who wickedly offered unclean and abusive usage to me, and I did not resist. Being overcome and defiled by him, I have much suffered the truth. To clear my name and to let the world know of my transgressions and great wickedness, I fully admit that I did not resist to the utmost of my power and ability but gave way to behavior that I hereby freely and heartily condemn. I desire to be continued in membership with Friends, hoping that, through divine aid and assistance, my future conduct may be attended with such care and circumspection that it will not be rendered by me again on any occasion.

Charity, of course, refused to sign.

"Thy brothers and sisters are already packing," Rachel told her daughter, "for us to move and assist the fledgling Bush River Meeting." She kept her voice calm and steady, not letting her own doubts and anxiety invade. She had once been a valued member of Cane Creek Meeting, recognized as a preacher in her own right, her abilities treasured by their community. It was lost to her now, partly due to her behavior in standing with Charity and partly because of the influence of Hermon Husband.

John sent William, now twenty-three years old and married, to Bush River to find a proper cabin for them, one nearby as well for his own family. The travel certificates had been requested.

On a sunny afternoon, Charity went to visit the meetinghouse one last time before returning thoughtfully to the cabin. Danise, Chelsea, and Margaret were there, sorting and folding, taking Rachel's lead in deciding which things would go and which would be shared with another family. As Rachel wrapped objects passed down from relatives, she thought about the family names they'd given their children. It came to her that she'd never heard of the last name of Majer and his wife, Anarcha. Rachel cocked her head to one side. *And what of Danise and Chelsea? What do they consider theirs?* Rachel bit on her lip. She turned to young Margaret. "Fetch Pa for me, yes? And as many of the others as thou can find."

Rachel swiveled to Danise and Chelsea, the Deaf girl never far from her older sister. "I was thinking about thee, thee and Chelsea, just now," she addressed Danise, her voice wobbling. She caught Chelsea's attention. *"Think,"* she signed, pointing to her temple and then to herself. Chelsea stopped her packing of sawdust in the barrels of preserved vegetables and herbs and watched Rachel.

"You two," Rachel pointed at them. "I was thinking about the two of you." She circled her index finger by her forehead, *"wonder,"* and pointed to them. "I was wondering if you two—" She moved her hands, bent like claws, in a horizontal circle at her waist and made a quizzical face. *"Family?"* She kept her eyes on Chelsea. *"Family with us, yes?"*

Both Danise and Chelsea nodded in unison. They were confused about where Rachel was going with this, and their faces showed it.

"You girls have been shuffled from place to place with no say in the matter," Rachel continued, speaking and signing. "And now, we are moving you again." It was not quite what she wanted to say. "You are young women, and we haven't even asked your opinion." She made eye contact with each of them.

"We want to go with you," Danise assured her, signing and speaking as they all did now when Chelsea was in the mix. "We've thought ourselves thy children for eight years now and a part of this community." She looked a little worried. "And we might not be considered free outside it. We aren't manumitted." It was a brave admission.

The rest of the family had come into the room and circled around Rachel, Charity, Danise, and Chelsea. Rachel gazed around the circle of them, wondering if they understood the term. It had been used in a letter from Philadelphia Yearly Meeting,

116

read recently at the rise of meeting for worship. The members of Cane Creek "who hold slaves . . . use them as fellow creatures and do not make too rigorous a demand of all their labor—to manumit them when their owners die." It was also requested that Friends "not go patrolling to keep Negroes in subjection" and advised that "the life of religion is almost lost where enslaved people are very numerous; and it is an impossible practice, being contrary to the spirit of Christianity." Not assured that the youngest children understood, Rachel gave a definition. "Manumitted means freeing Negroes, especially after their owner dies."

"Not sure how we'd do that," said John. He kept his eyes on Rachel. "What's being discussed here?"

"I was asking Danise and Chelsea about moving with us, how they feel about it," Rachel explained to them all.

"I just assumed it," John admitted. "Did you not want to go?" he asked Danise, confused. He waited for her to catch Chelsea up with her interpreting. "You two are daughters to us. And you know we have no papers. Besides," he rubbed at his chin, "manumission is prohibited by law unless a person has done 'meritorious service'—and that applies to adults. You'd need to be eighteen. Both of you."

"And how would we make a living if we were freed and not with you?" Danise asked, still puzzled by the intent of the conversation. She had no trade outside of housework and gardening, and all the rural women knew how to do those jobs.

Rachel put an arm around Danise's shoulder, loose enough so she could continue to sign. "Of course, we want you to go. The two of you are family, but there's a sorrow heavy in my heart," she said softly. "It's a deep hurt that you two are in such an odd place with us. You are our daughters, but you don't have our name, our last name, a name that belongs to you."

"We do not," Danise replied. *"No family name, you and I,"* she signed directly to Chelsea.

"And the names of folks, well, they tell a story—they give a history," Rachel went on. What you've told us of thy birth parents and know of your time with Charlie and Peggy Mayer and of the years that you two have lived here with us." Rachel swallowed. "And I was wondering if the two of you might like to be officially adopted as our children, taking the Wright name as your own. And when we get to Bush River, to sit with us in meeting, or if that's not allowed, well then, we'll sit with you." Rachel looked at John for his agreement.

John had already gotten hold of the family Bible and was turning to the last pages where such things were recorded. "We could write thou name and Chelsea's here with ours?" he offered Danise. "Danise Wright. Chelsea Wright. Right after baby Thomas."

Danise and Chelsea nodded. Young Margaret went to fetch ink and pen and handed the supplies to her father. Then, John wrote the names carefully, as was his duty, while everyone watched.

PART 2

Chapter 8

Two years after the Wrights moved to Bush River, Charity felt the call to speak out of the cherished silence during meeting for worship. The idea that she was suddenly to share a message shocked her. What would the members think? It was well-known that technically, because she'd been disowned, she was allowed to attend worship but not give ministry.

The decision is documented for all eternity, thought Charity, *available for my siblings, children, and future grandchildren—and for any Friend to know of my disgrace. But I am nudged to speak.* The fear of judgment crawled over her. Would someone halt her in her obedience to the higher authority? She put a hand to her hammering heart, trembling with the idea of it.

God, Light, Spirit would not let her be. Charity's indecision swirled in her head like a jig. Exasperated, she opened her eyes and surveyed the room. It was filled with her new neighbors, those who had welcomed the Wrights when they'd come with their wagons of goods, their livestock, and their many children. The family had moved into a two-story cabin of oak logs, weathered gray. The previous family had planted flowers all about the perimeter of the large, rectangular cabin, with porches on the front and back. Inside were four bedrooms and a sleeping loft, a kitchen area, and a family room. Not far from the back door was a sturdy, two-seater privy, and sufficiently far from that, a drooping clothes-line between two slanted poles. A huge garden occupied most of the expansive front yard. There was a large barn, storage shed, and corn crib, as well as extensive fields for farming and grazing. A creek ran through the far end of the land as it had at the Cane Creek home, moving so slowly that the water often reflected the pale blue of the sky like a mirror. Birds and bees loved the place, as did snakes and mice.

The Wrights hadn't met any other Negroes, but the first day that they came to meeting for worship, Danise and Chelsea were shown to the back bench by an elder. As pledged, the Wrights had taken their place with them as a family, all of them lined up like mourning doves on a branch, men on one end of the row and women on the other, with the youngest children in the middle.

Charity gazed down the string of Wrights and wondered if their defiance in sitting together was where the message lay? Was she to speak on it, explain their position? Charity dug in her brain to find the kernel of what it could be that she was being asked to share.

Might I have direction? Charity whispered internally. She held her chin toward the ceiling, her confidence as thin as an egg shell. Soberly, she willed herself into the quiet and sat for a while longer. *What will be lost*, she wondered, *if I don't deliver whatever it is that is nagging at me?* Finally, she drifted up from where she'd been sitting and stood. When she felt a tug on her skirts, she looked to see Danise offering her the tiny chain of rings. *Thou are loved.* She returned her sister's smile and took them. Then she slowly edged her way forward past the rows of benches and to the front of the meeting, her eyes caught on the partition that usually divided the large room. It was pulled back so that the men and women were worshiping as one; the assembly of about two hundred people was intimidating. It seemed to Charity that, although she only saw closed eyes, people were listening to the scrape of her hard shoes on the wooden floor planks and knew someone was moving to the front of the room to give ministry.

I don't want to disappoint these good people, Charity worried. Bush River Friends had welcomed the Wrights so warmly into the cocoon of their community, a safe haven from the pain they'd left in Cane Creek. The memory of other women preaching fluttered through her mind and gave her strength. When she reached those on the facing bench, she turned from them to face the larger group. "Is it not one of our testimonies," she began, a definite stutter impeding her first words, "a vow, a course of conduct, to assert and promote equality of all persons; that there is an equal measure of divine in us all? That in the eyes of the Spirit we are all God's children? And are we not to bear witness to this belief in every aspect of our everyday lives? To be committed to action arising out of our experience?" A rhythm emerged in her delivery—as if she were someone else speaking. As she went on, the sentences broke into distinct phrases with accents for emphasis. Charity listened to her message as she gave it, her speech not at all its usual pitch but alternating from low to high and back again.

"Praise God. Praise God that we are to find—find soon—very soon, a way through the laws and the desires, a way that opens to the end of the buying and selling of those who are enslaved, for they are God's people," Charity continued, gaining confidence. The message pleased her. It was spontaneous, compelling, and the truth. When she'd finished, she returned to her seat, sat down, and tried to settle into the quiet. Some of what she thought she'd said bubbled up in her again. She'd mentioned Catherine Payton, the first outspoken and daring preacher she'd known, as well as the seventeenth-century preachers, Margaret Fell, the mother of their sect, and the young, bold Mary Fisher, one of the first ministers. Charity was sure she had quoted Philippians chapter four, verse eight: "Whatever things are true, whatever things are honest, whatever things are just, whatever things are pure, whatever things are lovely, whatever things are of good report, if there be any virtue and if there be any praise, think on these things." She couldn't remember the rest of her ministry.

At the rise of meeting, several of the women, none of them well-known to her, came forward. Her first thought was that they were going to chastise her for preaching, but they complimented her instead.

"Thy message touched my heart," one began, taking her elbow. "Thou are so young to be so gifted."

Charity felt the warmth of validation gallop through her veins. She was pleased, delighted in a way she hadn't expected, that she'd served God well. She let the warmth of the acceptance and worth wash over her.

"Was very brave of thee," offered another as Charity tried to remain stone-faced. The elder invited Charity to the women's meeting, to come with her mother, the esteemed Rachel Wells Wright, who they knew from quarterly and yearly meetings.

"We're not so formal here," another woman coaxed, "not so organized, for heaven's sake, as to turn away the Wright women."

In trying to meet the kind eyes and remember some of the names of those who introduced themselves, Charity saw beyond the gaggle of those around her to a comely young man who was standing behind the group. He seemed to be patiently waiting his turn to talk with her. *Do I know him from Cane Creek? From quarterly meeting?* Then a more likely possibility dawned on her. *Had he been at Grandfather Well's wedding?*

The lad saw that she noticed him and held her gaze. His eyes twinkled, and he gave her a broad grin.

"Does thee remember me—Isaac Cook?" the young man asked, coming to her when the women had left her. She went slowly to collect her hat and shawl and ready for home.

Tall, Charity mused as he stood beside her, more than a head taller than she was. They shook hands. *Of course, it was the wedding*, Charity decided, considering Isaac's face more carefully. His mother, Mary, had married Charity's grandfather, Joseph Wells.

"Might I walk thee home?"

"Thou might," Charity replied, her voice quivering with uncertainty. He looked safe enough, dressed nicely for meeting in a dark and collarless shirt with suspenders that held up his First Day breeches. She looked into his blue eyes with their fringe of long lash. *But Jehu was Quaker, too,* she thought. Her heart raced. It had been two years since the pain of the rape and the shock of the disownment. She was unsure if it was wise to walk unaccompanied with a young man, to trust again that nothing bad would happen. Charity glanced at Danise, who was just tying up her bonnet, for confirmation. Her sister beamed at her. *She seems to approve*, thought Charity as she watched Danise take Chelsea's hand and turn away from her to exit the women's door of the meetinghouse.

"We're related through thy grandfather Wells, are we not?" Isaac asked, the two of them following Danise and Chelsea at a distance.

Charity could tell he was searching for small talk. She relaxed a bit, taking in the cloudless day, and how the light seemed to come not only from the sun but was reflected off the chartreuse leaves as well. It had been so long since she had a normal conversation with a boy—a boy that was not a brother or uncle. She always had her guard up, avoiding deep conversation and didn't attempt much small talk—to complain about the stubborn milk cow, how endless it was to sweep the cabin, or how limited her progress in altering one of Margaret's dresses. Always the effect of the rape was with her, enveloping her like a raincloud. "Related? I wouldn't say *related*," Charity replied, managing a half-smile. She was relieved that she and Isaac were far enough behind Danise that she couldn't overhear but nervous enough to be glad her sisters were in sight. "Thou were at thy mother's wedding in Cane Creek, then?"

"Yes, yes, of course," Isaac stuttered. "'Twas my mother's third time, but of course, we children were all there." He swallowed so loudly that Charity could hear him. "I live here now—in Bush River, not far from your farm. I'm a farmer, too, like my parents and all those before them."

"Thou'll leave nothing for me to weasel out of thee," Charity teased, Isaac's fumbling helped her to relax. "And who *did* come before thee?" she asked kindly.

"My grandparents were married in Cheshire, England." Isaac feigned an English accent. "They came to Pennsylvania some thirty years after William Penn established the colony."

"Oh? They were part of the Philadelphia Yearly Meeting, then?" Charity replied, ignoring the accent. "'Tis the grandest of the colonial meetings and influences us here." She caught herself. It was a useless thing to say. Of course, all southern Friends were aware of the sway of the mother meeting.

"Well, not exactly," Isaac answered, with no hint of disapproval for Charity's comment. He was walking beside her but not too close. "My father and mother married in Warrington, which is near Philadelphia but has its only monthly meeting." His conversation came more easily now. "They were prominent members there, urging Friends to take no part in the conflicts with the British or French."

"We come from Pennsylvania, too," said Charity, "though I was born in Maryland and only four years old when my family came to Cane Creek."

"From a large family, I hear—"

"Ah, yes." Charity's lips turned slightly up at the corners. "Thou've already investigated the thirteen of us then, have thee?" She felt gay, light—safe. After her disownment, she'd been moody, often crying for no clear reason. Now, Charity blushed with optimism, wanting the sun to be a sign of hope. She was eighteen years old, clearly at the age for courting, but for months now, she'd battled the itch of dread that she was "spoiled."

"I'm the fifth of eight, but my oldest siblings are married," continued Isaac. He was looking ahead on the path.

"My two oldest are married, too, and stayed in Cane Creek, Charity replied, "and my mama's due to have a baby again soon. But the rest of us are here."

"I believe I know the fellow who courts thy sister, Susannah. Doesn't like my suspenders and thinks them an 'unnecessary innovation,' a savoring of pride. He's given them a yank once or twice, he has."

"Big Isaac?" Charity smiled. "He has a rough exterior but an excellent heart. He probably took to thee because thou has the same name." They continued their small talk, Charity listening to the chirping calls of the birdsong. Isaac's hand brushed her skirt. She distanced herself a bit and brushed absentmindedly where Isaac's hand had touched. *Isaac is not Jehu*, she tried to remind herself.

"Thy delivery today reminded me of Catherine Payton," Isaac complimented.

"Oh, have thou met her? She stayed with us when I was eight years old," Charity offered. "Her leading, 'of living in the cross,' greatly impressed my mama." She stared at Isaac's arm, pale and marbled as the tiny pebbles in the creek sand, and swinging slightly as he walked along. She hadn't considered a lad since the rape, all the muddled feelings still festering. On the days when she was brave enough, she replayed the details of her evening with Jehu in her mind, her grief nuanced. She was not the innocent youth she had been before the ravishing. Instead she was anxious and unsure of herself, in need of public praise, but doubting the sincerity of it. She turned to Isaac now to share a treasured memory. "Catherine Payton saw great promise in me and predicted that, one day, I would serve as an itinerant minister, too."

"And now, led by the Spirit, that time has come."

Charity considered Isaac's profile, wanting to believe it was true. "I'm not so sure," she admitted. "I felt pushed out of my comfort this morning, called to surrender to the Inward Guide and deliver this message." Immediately, Charity felt the blush of her immodesty. She quickly changed the subject. "And thy thoughts then about enslaved people?"

Isaac steepled his fingers in front of his chest. "Seems Friends are of three bents: those who want to keep the ones they own, always taking the time to comment that they were inherited and not purchased; those who won't take part in the discussions; and," he tapped his fingertips thoughtfully, "those who believe that enslavement is contrary to our witness to equality but don't actually act."

"Slavery has created a cycle of evil, has it not?" asked Charity with great seriousness. "It rips at self-worth and devalues people. It'd be helpful if Catherine Payton or, better yet, John Woolman were here among us now to speak out against the immoral practice so that all the enslaved people could be set free."

"True, true, true," agreed Isaac, caught by her intensity. "Perhaps it is the work we are to do."

Charity stopped their walking. "And what is thy stand on it?" she asked Isaac directly. "For I have two Negro sisters, Danise and Chelsea." She pointed to where her sisters were, so far ahead on the path they were almost invisible. Charity wished she'd have introduced them to him before they'd all left meeting.

"I know of them. The younger one can't hear?" asked Isaac before he was suddenly distracted. He put a hand on Charity's back and one to his lips, signaling her to quiet. His stare went over her head and then to the bush in front of them. "I think there's a Native out there." He gripped her shoulders to stop her from turning around. "No, don't, don't look back."

Charity felt the flush of her cheeks, her heart pounding. For the moment that he held her, she examined Isaac's sapphire eyes and the freckles that ran over the bridge of his nose. He had the sparse beginnings of a mustache and barely a beard. She could hear his breathing.

I should not be considering him so, Charity warned herself. She wiggled away, fighting to trust that the hands that held her fast were not a harbinger of another mistake made in trusting a lad. Then, in her mind's eye, Jehu loomed up in front of her, the one that Isaac thought was in the bush. Her forehead knotted in confusion as the ghost of Jehu stepped in front of them, his shirt untucked and wrinkled, his breeches heavily stained.

I demand thee defend thy chattel, Charity imagined Jehu challenging Isaac, the issues of slavery mixing with his assault on her. *Her market value has dropped now that I've had her. And surely thou know she's accused of lustful ways and disowned for it,* the apparition taunted, unkempt hair hanging down over the dark, hollow eyes.

Isaac sensed a threat. He encircled Charity in his arm again and surveyed all directions.

Charity could smell the aroma of soap and tobacco. *Of course, Isaac knows of my rape? Of the blame? Of my disownment!* She felt her face color with the shame of it. "Are not Colonel Grant's three thousand troops," she found herself saying, "right there in the woods, ready to run off the Cherokee from their homes?" she escaped him a second time and pointed.

Isaac checked back over his shoulder and looked passed her. "I keep thinking I hear something." He directed his gaze at her. "The Natives have a right to be angry. Not a year ago, the military destroyed fifteen thousand acres of Cherokee homes and crops."

Charity gave him a weak smile, the two of them mutually deciding to continue their walking. "Not that a good Quaker lad would engage in a fight," she tried to tease.

"Oh, I've learned the lessons of my faith," Isaac assured her. "I know that Margaret Fell made our position clear to King Charles II and was made to learn the famous quote by heart as part of my schooling." He stood straighter and cleared his throat. "We do utterly deny all bloody principles and practices, all outward wars and strife, and fighting with visible weapons."

As Isaac recited, Charity imagined him standing tall and unabashed as he turned to face Jehu. *But no*, she thought, *Isaac, steeped in the way of Friends, would never fight Jehu or any other man.* Her virtue would go undefended. She stopped abruptly and stared down at the red dirt.

"For any end or under any pretense whatsoever," Isaac was saying, "and this is our testimony to the whole world."

She's yours then, Charity imagined Jehu Stuart huffing. *Spoiled as a rotten egg, and everyone knows it.* She saw him move off like a wild rooster, songbirds scattering above him as he bobbed from side to side back into the woods. The high, familiar calls brought Charity back to Isaac.

"That the Spirit of Christ, who leads us into all truth," Isaac finished, "will never move us to fight and war against any man, neither for the kingdom of Christ, nor for the kingdoms of this world." He looked over to Charity, stopped on the path. "Charity? Charity, are thou okay?" Isaac bent his head to her.

"I am but property, *chattel*," Charity mumbled. She was close to tears. "Considered inferior goods no matter what my abilities and not someone for thee to walk with." Her deepest worries tumbled out. "Neither the meeting nor the courts are ever going to punish Jehu, because ravishing isn't deemed a crime; women are considered property, just as the enslaved workers."

"Charity, no." Isaac faced her, his look earnest. "Thou are yours, yours alone, Charity. And valued

here. No one at Bush River considers the disownment. And isn't it still under consideration with
yearly meeting?" He reached to her to cautiously put
a finger near her lips. "And don't let any member
persuade thee otherwise."

Over his shoulder, Charity saw an undulating
butterfly darting on the path and then flying off as if
it had better things to do. She took in a deep breath,
letting her chest slowly fill, and worked to believe
Isaac's kind words, to open her heart to him.

"Why, thou were just magnificent this morning.
As bright as a star," the lad said firmly.

Chapter 9

"Did thou know that Clerk Coffin knows sign, formal sign?" Danise asked Charity as the two stood ankle-deep in the large creek after which Bush River Meeting had been named. "He's teaching some to Chelsea and me, ones we need but hadn't invented as yet." She began to scrub a large, heavy skillet that had been set on the rocks to soak.

"Tristram Coffin?" asked Charity. "How do thou know that?"

"Majer. He took us to see him. Tristram Coffin's mama is 'Great Mary,'" replied Danise. She lifted her eyebrows and held them in the habitual way she had developed from signing with Chelsea. "Have thou heard of her?"

Charity shook her head. She wasn't surprised. Danise soaked in information like a wash rag, seeking out long discussions with Majer, whose quest for information seemed insatiable and who was able to travel safely from one Quaker community to another.

"Here, will you set this in the sun to dry?" Danise asked, handing the heavy skillet over to Charity. "When Friends first came to the colonies," she began, an arm waved to coax Charity to leave the work and join her on the bank, "they didn't go to Martha's Vineyard where the people were mostly Baptists and Presbyterians. They settled instead on Nantucket or 'Sandy Island,' the land of the Wampanoag people—until smallpox all but wiped them out." Danise let out a noisy breath. "The Coffins were among the first settlers there. One day, they were visited by Thomas Chalkley, a Quaker missionary merchant from Philadelphia, who read the Advices and Queries to them and showed them how the entries could guide behavior."

Charity leaned back against the rough tree trunk.

"Tristram's mama was Mary Coffin Starbuck. She was raised as a Friend, and she and her husband were weighty among the Nantucket Friends. They hosted the first meetings in their home, where Mary gave powerful ministry. It's said that people wept at her words."

"Did she travel? An itinerant minister?"

"No. She was needed there with her extensive business interests and civil affairs, far exceeding her father in her judgment and clarity of understanding issues. Well, that's what Tristram said, but she was his mother, of course, though he hasn't seen her for years. He told me that the Nantucket women were responsible for any dealings when their husbands were out whaling, and they oversaw their families, large as any here. His mama could read and write proficiently." Danise raised an eyebrow again; the abilities were remarkable for most of the women in Cane Creek. "People called her 'the Great Mary' because she had an elegant way of expressing herself and was a model to the Nantucket women in her piety."

"But how does this lead to Clerk Tristram signing?" asked Charity, her head tilted to the side.

"Oh!" startled Danise, the purpose of her storytelling lost in her tangent about Mary Coffin Starbuck. "'Tis that the tiny group living in Chilmark on Martha's Vineyard had their roots in gray whaling. Same as those who lived nearby on Nantucket. They communicated on the boat in sign, exaggerated motions but a complete, manual language, nonetheless. It'd come to the islands by way of Jonathan Lambert, who'd come to Chilmark from England in the mid-seventeenth century. He and his children were Deaf with generations of relatives who, likewise, couldn't hear and signed. They don't value speech and formed deep friendships with other Deaf people. They used Kentish Sign Language—from Kent, England—and mixed it with the gestures used by the Wampanoag people. The hearing whalers started to pick it up, signing to each other when they were out on the high seas—the distance between the boats and the slap of the waves making it difficult to hear each other." Danise looked up to the clouds. "These days, the whole island of them can sign as naturally as they speak, and in every conversation, even the hearing people, one to the other." She turned to Charity with a wishful expression.

"Now wouldn't that be nice," Charity agreed. "Deafness, Friends, small worlds within larger ones," she considered. She smiled at her sister. *"Love thee,"* she signed, crossing her fists over her breasts. *"Love thee."*

"Ah, yes, *love*," Danise signed back and giggled. "It's in the air, don't thou think?"

#

In the summer of 1762, Charity and Isaac composed a letter of intent to wed. When it was finished, Isaac delivered it to Phoebe Coffin, clerk of the Bush River women's meeting. This was right order, the couple wanting their engagement to be under the care of a clearness committee who would talk with them and make sure their marriage was the right course of action. Arrangements were made, and on a sunny afternoon, three older members of the Bush River Care Committee met with Isaac and Charity to assess their sincerity to marry.

Charity had already decided that the meeting would be a challenge. She'd been blamed for not doing enough to ward off Jehu Stuart, had refused to apologize for the charges against her. Subsequently, she'd been disowned and barred from ministry and meeting for business in Cane Creek. In Bush River

Meeting, although her status was no secret, she had given divine messages and attended the women's meetings—and more than once—but Charity felt that the whole situation needed a good airing. She still had nightmares of Jehu Stewart, of him groaning as he lay on top of her, his head turned upward so that, in the dim light, she only saw the pale skin at the stretch of his throat. A thousand times she'd gone over her part in the rape, the feelings of shame and sadness rising up in her, shining like old tin scraps just below the surface in a river. *What was I to have done?* Had it been her dress? What she'd said to him? The way she'd walked? Charity couldn't think of a way she'd been misleading, but hadn't the majority of those in her beloved Cane Creek Meeting—and they'd finally heard—decided differently?

Am I really in good standing? the insecure young woman wondered. *Do they all agree that I've behaved as led by the Spirit?*

The constant, internal struggle gripped Charity, and she worked to stop the gnawing shame that was always close at hand. She willed herself into the holy darkness that she loved, and when she could not, she imagined herself instead into the pitch black of her bedroom. Danise beside her, her breath soft on Charity's shoulder. She offered the smile that came to her then to Gunnel Clark, Alice Friedman, Teriann Pollock, and Celia Matson when she greeted them at the door.

Sure enough, Isaac and Charity had hardly seated their guests and served tea, and the huddle of them sat in worship for a bit, when Alice, head cocked and leaning toward Charity, asked about the ravishing. "I'm wondering if the affair with Jehu Stuart continues to any degree."

"Continues?" asked Charity incredulously. *Affair?* she repeated internally. *It was never that.* "Absolutely not," she answered curtly. "I was an innocent girl." She clasped her hands and worked to keep the bitterness out of her replies. "I have sat long hours thinking through that evening and how I was with him, and I can't see anything that would give him the impression that he could tackle me to the floor and, and . . ." She closed her eyes for a moment. "I didn't expect to be read out of Cane Creek Meeting, and I'm hopeful you will allow Isaac and me to marry without disowning *him* for doing so."

"Marriage is a spiritual union," agreed Celia, looking eager to move on. After all, Charity had given brilliant ministry multiple times in meeting, and the women's meeting felt fortunate to have her and her mother involved in the business they took up. "And thou are of deep faith," she added, reaching a hand to each of Isaac and Charity. "The two of you are well-suited to be 'yoke-mates,' as first Friends said of marriage."

"Do thou stand ready in it," Terriann asked, "prepared to assist each other in what the Spirit requires and allow God's will to take precedence over the duties of hearth and home?"

"We do," Isaac nodded. "Yes."

"And you are waiting until you are married for any 'involvement' with each other?" asked Gunnel.

"We are," said Isaac, his eyes on the floor and a flush crawling up his cheeks.

Celia went on, keen to keep asking questions as was the due of the clearness committee. "Will thou create a companion marriage, essential for a godly household so that thy children can experience the inward Light?" she asked in a crisp, business-like tone.

"And as partners, seen by the children as examples, clearly witness thy submission as instruments of the Spirit?" interrupted Terriann over Celia.

Charity and Isaac nodded. Yes.

Alice cleared her throat, giving some space to the session. "We ask that, in private, the two of you discuss thy anticipations of each other and how those might change over time."

"We will," Charity assured her.

"And have already," Isaac clarified. "Our own parents and grandparents have been models of the support we intend to give each other," he added, checking with Charity for her agreement.

"We've seen our mothers manage their flocks," Charity amended Isaac's reply. "Our children will be raised up to be of the faith and to be helpful members of our family and community. They'll live our testimonies as solemn vows. We have a good communication between us," Charity blushed, nervously fussing with the bun she now wore. "When the Spirit brings change, children, we will discuss the consequences."

Isaac sat back, sounding sure of himself. "We wish to have a large family," he confirmed, the farmers in Bush River well aware that an ample number of children were needed both to help work the land and carry on the faith. "And they'll be better educated than we were. We are pledged to that."

"Isaac's been teaching me to better read and write," Charity eagerly explained. "And Danise and Chelsea, too."

Alice cleared her throat. "Have ye considered the possibility that one of you may receive a leading that takes you away from Bush River, puts you in harm's way, or causes financial strain?" she asked, seeming not to want to discuss Negroes and literacy.

"If God wills it, we must heed, no?" replied Isaac. "There have been itinerant ministers in both our families."

"And we've experienced thy gifts," Celia nodded to Charity. "It must be thy priority to labor in the work of the Spirit." She made eye contact with Isaac. "The meeting is here to support thee and thy family should Charity have drawings to travel."

"We expect nothing that is asked of us will affect our love as a couple," confirmed Isaac, "as a family, as a community. Our marriage will be sacred, as will our work in and outside our cabin."

Charity wanted to take Isaac's hand but thought it too bold for the committee members. "And it will last our lifetimes."

#

On the day Isaac Cook and Charity Wright were married, during the Fourth Night meeting, the perfumed smell of the dogwoods and azaleas drifted into the meetinghouse on the warm breeze. There was no officiant; no one gave away the bride. Isaac and Charity sat with their eyes closed and at an acceptable distance apart on opposite ends of a bench that had been moved to the aisle between the men's and women's sides. Charity wore a white, flat-brimmed hat of beaver that Isaac had given her to mark the day, a plain brown dress, and her mother's nicest shawl. Isaac's face was shaven clean and his hair combed back. He wore a shirt and pair of pants of undyed cotton that had been sewn lovingly by his mother.

Charity tingled all over. She basked in her sister Mary's sweet words as they had walked up to the meetinghouse, and her Mama's parting hug as they'd entered the building. Warm with joy, she let the thoughts float off, opened to God, as she had done a thousand times in her life, and made herself available to the Spirit.

All seats in the room were filled, some two hundred people there to witness the union of the young couple. Family and friends sat on the benches closest to Isaac and Charity, no one protesting when Danise and Chelsea sat beside Rachel and their female siblings at the front. The special occasion began with a good, long period of silence, and then, various relatives and friends took turns standing to confirm their witness of the love between Charity and Isaac and to give their support for the union. When Isaac felt moved to stand, he went to Charity and gently touched her shoulder. Her eyes twinkled open, her smile so wide that her cheeks dimpled, and she rose to meet the handsome face.

"In the presence of God and before these our family and friends," Isaac proclaimed, "I take thee Charity Wells Wright to be my wife, promising with divine assistance to be unto thee a loving and faithful husband so long as we both shall live."

Charity was silent for a few moments. She glanced around to her family and then into Isaac's kind, twinkling eyes and knew she could love this man forever. "'In the Lord,'" she began, quoting the Bible, "'woman is not independent of man, nor man of woman; for as woman was made from man, so man is now born of woman. And all things are from God.' First Corinthians chapter 11, verses 11 and 12." She paused and then spoke the traditional words the witnesses expected to hear, "In the presence of God and these our friends, I take thee, Isaac Cornell Cook, to be my husband, promising with divine assistance to be unto thee a loving and faithful wife so long as we both shall live."

Isaac and Charity went to the marriage certificate laid out on the nearby table with a quill and a bottle of ink beside it. They each signed their names and sat down again. Tristram Coffin rose and came to read the words that were familiar among Friends:

"On this day, Six Month 10, 1762, in a solemn manner, Isaac Cook did openly declare his taking of Charity Wright to be his wife, promising through divine assistance to be unto her a loving and faithful husband until death should separate them." He cleared his throat for the next part, added by the young couple and not ever appearing on a certificate as far as anyone knew. "And Charity Wright openly declares the taking of Isaac Cook to be her husband, promising through divine assistance to be unto him a loving and faithful wife until death should separate them."

"Come." Tristram cracked a faint smile. "Come each of you here and sign the certificate as witness to this marriage."

Isaac and Charity didn't kiss in public, but later that night, when they were alone in Isaac's cabin, the groom held his wife's chin and bent down to softly caress her lips with his own. In the gesture, Charity found all that she cherished. She was sure she would be a good wife to this deserving man and a loving mother to their children. As Isaac turned her to untie the laces at her back, she prayed he'd say nothing related to the rape but would only move slowly, carefully, helping her to relax in her love for him and in her trust that, when he came into her, it wasn't going to feel at all as it had the first time.

Chapter 10

Thirty-year-old Charity stood in the Cook's yard and watched her parents, siblings, and John Pike, their old friend from Cane Creek, as they dismounted and tied their horses. Her oldest boy, nine-year-old Joseph, watched, too, as he held his six-year-old sister Sarah's hand and tried to prevent her from running to the group of family and friends who'd come calling. Little Thomas was asleep in Charity's arms, and little Rachel clung shyly to her skirts.

As the visitors moved toward the cabin, Charity's eyes were on her mother. Rachel was the last in the line and moved with difficulty. "Thou should come by wagon, Mama," Charity called to her, Rachel not at all looking like her once vibrant self. She was pale and haggard, multiple strands of her graying hair escaping from her bun.

When Danise and Chelsea reached her, Charity handed little Thomas to Danise. "Mama does look good," she whispered and then turned to the others. "Needing a respite from that long list of chores, are you?" Charity greeted them. "Come on, children," Charity counseled the oldest of her little flock as Rachel reached them, "give Grammy a kiss." She embraced Rachel herself and whispered, "Really, Mama, it's 1775. Everyone uses a wagon these days. Do you need to keep riding?"

Charity signaled Chelsea to manage her youngest siblings, ten-year-old Keziah and eight-year-old Isaac, who had come along and were playing an impromptu game of tag with some of their Cook playmates, too close to the adults. "Come, Mama. Sit down. Let Chelsea watch the children."

Rachel waved a hand to Charity as if bothered by a bee. "I'm fine. I'm fine. Did thou hear of Jehu Stuart?" she asked, redirecting the focus from her to anything else, and she'd always relished having the latest news to share. "The minutes from the most recent Cane Creek Men's Meeting state that he's condemned his former conduct against thee and the others." She coughed. "No longer disowned."

Tears started in Charity's eyes, her good mood seeped away. She hadn't thought about Jehu in a long while, but now she felt as if he'd punched her in the gut. "No longer disowned?" she echoed. "After all the women he bragged to have molested? Us left with our ravaged bodies and souls." Feelings about the awful time came flooding back into her. In a flash, she saw Jehu as the lad he'd been when she herself was only just coming of age, his weight on her as he painfully pinned her to the planks, the cool evening air on her naked thighs. Then the ripping, searing shock of the rape.

"He's a member of New Garden Friends," Rachel went on, unaware of Charity's turmoil. "Married now and with some little ones."

Charity closed her eyes. It was the core belief of her faith that there was that of God in Jehu. If she couldn't accept it of him, she'd live a hollow lie of Quakerism. Anger rose up in her as she saw his ghost in her thinking. *Thou'll not take my faith. No, no.* But could she forgive the lad she remembered? Could she forgive those in Cane Creek who had blamed her, then turned her out? Charity wasn't sure.

It was her father who noticed Charity's frozen stance, and odd expression on her face. He pulled her into him. "Thou are loved, Charity," he whispered, with heartfelt sincerity. "Thou are a child of God and *nothing, nothing* is going to ever change that."

Charity wiggled out of her father's embrace, embarrassed that the others were watching them. "Come sit, everyone," she offered, letting the company distract her.

"Have you been notified of these taxes?" John Pike huffed, ignoring John Wright's comment. He waved taxation paperwork like a fan. "Them going higher and higher?" His legs creaked as he folded into one of the wooden chairs that were arranged in a circle by the cabin door.

Spirit heal me. Keep my attention on my family, my mother, prayed Charity. She sank onto a stump that had been brought from the woodpile.

"Hello, good Friends," called Isaac, loping from the barn toward the Cook cabin. Majer was with him, the two of them taking a break from the repair of some tools when they heard the welcome commotion of visitors out in the yard. The men, covered with dirt, reached the circle of friends. "Good to see thee, Mother," Isaac greeted Rachel, bending to her sunken frame. He shook hands with John Wright and Danise.

"I overheard thee talking of debt," Majer addressed John Pike. "Anarcha and I certainly haven't escaped it." The Negroes had recently been freed by Charity's sister, Mary, as directed in the will of her husband, Joel Brooks. Still, it had taken the authority of Charity's brother, Joseph Jr., now a well-respected businessman and the executor of the estate, to see the request through the colonial court system.

Majer and Isaac took the available chairs on either side of John Pike. "There've been so many Scots-Irish immigrants migrating to the Carolinas in the last years. Someone has to pay for the bettering of the roads around here and the sheriff and such." John Pike opened his coat like a wing and checked for his pipe.

"And they're responsible for our higher taxes?" Isaac challenged.

"Oh, there are so many parts to it," sighed John Pike, turning to him. "I didn't mean that, not entirely.

150

It's just that the new families migrate down here from the north and take land to farm from the Natives or those White people who are otherwise illegally settled on it. The government has allowed it all these years because their farms form a buffer between the Cherokee and the incomers, but now it appears that money is needed to support a militia because the Natives are on the warpath to defend themselves. Settlers can't safely farm, and they've got no crops to harvest to use for barter. Some of them have begun stealing from others in order to feed their families." He took a breath. "And now the lot of farmers have joined in with any other troublemakers who can't pay the county taxes." John waved his tax assessment again. "Everyone gets upset when those yokels in New Bern or Hillsborough come up with ideas for raising money like that fool Stamp Act—they're taxing newspapers, almanacs, pamphlets, legal documents, dice, and playing cards." He took a deep, exasperated gasp of air.

"And thou have need of dice and playing cards?" Isaac asked sarcastically.

"I just might," replied Majer, taking over the tax lament. "For then, here comes the sheriff, riding these difficult roads, he does, with no taverns along the way to soothe a sour mood. Him greedy for the fines that pay his salary, collecting what is owed and taking his cut.

"And not properly recording that the farmers have paid," John Pike jumped back in to complain.

151

John Wright rubbed at his chin. "Thou seem to know a lot about it, Majer."

"I do," Majer nodded confidently. "My wood-working takes me around to plenty of good folks who owe their hard-earned money to the county government. Some have taken their complaints to the local courts but report that the ordeal of it 'tis a nightmare, the lawyers as corrupt as the sheriff. They use their know-how to an unjust advantage against them who are unfamiliar with how the system works."

"Or find that their paper money's no good," added John Pike, "and the way we barter to cover costs unacceptable to those in their wigs and three-cornered hats."

"Lots of squabbles taken up in the regional courts, are there?" asked John Wright, his brow furrowed.

"By Friends?" Rachel asked over him. She sat slumped over, caved into herself.

"No, no. Now Rachel Wells Wright," coddled John Pike, "thou know we have our own ways of airing our disputes. Haven't you two and Abigail and I all served as members of pastoral care teams at one time or another. No, no. No courts for Quakers." He leaned toward Rachel and met her gaze. "But it seems that thy ol' friend, Hermon Husband, has little care for our ways now that he's finally disowned for spreading his discontent of Friends far and wide." John Pike sat back, patting at a couple of pockets for his tobacco. "He's a loud, willing voice among those who disagree about taxes."

Disowned? Charity thought back on it. Hermon Husband had been read out of meeting for crabbing to anyone who would listen about the failure of Quaker ways. He'd taken his appeal of disownment to the Western Quarterly in August, just after baby Sarah was born. Charity looked over at Danise, playing finger games with four-year-old Sarah, and recollected John Pike telling them of the ruckus a group of Wright supporters had made at the Western Quarterly, stomping and hollering so loudly when Hermon Husband was trying to address the men that he couldn't be heard. He'd marched out of the meeting with his supporters—Joseph Maddock and Jonathan Sell from Eno Meeting, as well as a large contingent of men from Mill Creek and Rocky River. The sordid man's influence, his ability to manipulate, should have been a warning to them, then. "And the people are looking to him as their leader?" Charity asked of John Pike and Majer.

"'Tis what I hear, yes," John Pike confirmed. "That he's done with Friends; he and his followers not coming any longer to meeting for worship. Haven't been for a long while." John looked down at the dirt, avoiding eye contact with either Rachel or Charity. "It seems he announced that 'if they're going to allow that woman, that Jezebel, to organize women and be allowed to seduce men—' John Pike stopped himself. "Not sure thou want to hear this Rachel."

Rachel sighed, her voice sluggish. "He was on his way out back when there were the sessions over Charity's assault and disownment."

"'Tis true," John Pike nodded. "He's using the stance of those supporting thee as a reason not to participate." He knocked his pipe against the seat of his chair and then filled the bowl. "But there's a rumor that he and his cronies aren't done completely, that they're trying to organize a separate meeting at Holly Springs." John Pike looked up at the clouds and then chanced making eye contact with Rachel again. "'Twas a visitor to Cane Creek a couple of weeks back. A visiting Friend, John Griffith. He'd been to Holly Springs."

"Oh, the antislavery champion?" Charity asked enthusiastically. "I'd heard he's traveling in Virginia and here in the Carolinas."

John Pike nodded. "Though our division over Hermon Husband and his group leaving Cane Creek seemed more on the man's mind than that yearly meeting asks us to treat our enslaved people 'kindly.' He found all of us 'void of a solid sense of unity' when it comes to freeing Negroes. And," John caught Rachel's gaze, "he agrees that the argument causing the delay of thy transfer certificate should've been put to rest a long time ago."

Rachel raised an eyebrow at the mention of the transfer certificate. She gave John Pike a fragile smile.

"John Griffith told Abigail and me that he'd found a few sensible members at Holly Springs but that many in the meeting seemed indifferent or loose in their faith. He said Hermon Husband was bent on the separate Holly Springs Meeting, although John Griffith didn't see how that could happen with most of them, and these are *his* words: 'very unfit for the spiritual building and only taking counsel of their own will in their depraved hearts.'"

"Women, too, I suspect?" asked Charity.

"Those from the Deep River area are as vocal as their menfolk in their open complaint of all good order of discipline and denying any obedience to the hierarchy of the quarterly or yearly meetings," agreed John Pike. He gave his pipe a few puffs. "They say the structures have no basis in either scripture or the writings of the first Friends."

"And so they're calling themselves Friends but not practicing our ways?" asked Isaac, his lips thin. "The lot of them will bring discredit to the Society."

"John Griffith called Herman a 'wrong spirit,'" John Pike went on. "He's found him bent on challenging not only the ways of Friends but the colonial government as well. Seems he's going around to the farmers and pledging to eliminate excessive taxes and graft in the backcountry."

"Pretty grand promises," mused Majer, taking his turn, "but people of all manner of faiths are turning to him, is what I've been hearing. He has grand oratory skills, and he's using them to fuel the fire against 'taxation without representation'—that's the slogan for what's going on."

"Have no delegations gone to reason with Friends there, there in Holly Springs?" Rachel asked.

Charity looked over to her. Since they'd moved to Bush River, her mother no longer visited the women in Eno, Mill Creek, Holly, Rocky River, or Cane Creek meetings. *Because of my disownment?* Charity considered. *Or the rigors of frontier living?* Something had kept Rachel from the quarterly and yearly women's meetings as well, and so she hadn't seen Abigail Pike for a year or more. *Is it that Abigail doesn't want to associate with Mama or that Mama doesn't want to see her?*

"Oh, there's been delegation after delegation of Friends trying to talk with Hermon Husband and his gang," John Pike was saying, waving his pipe in the air. "They're constantly beefing over thy transfer certificate, Rachel, and the structure of our meetings. They've caused all manner of distraction and disorder at all levels of meetings and enjoy doing so!" John puffed on his pipe. "Just recently, it was decided that Hermon Husband and his followers be prohibited from the quarterly or yearly meetings. They're too disruptive, him going on and on in his arguments and keeping us at it for hours." John Pike moved his pipe to the corner of his mouth. "He seems to think that every member of the Society is entitled to *complete* satisfaction with whatever is being decided and won't ever step aside if he's in disagreement, let alone accept any guidance from the elders."

"But 'tis our way," complained Rachel quietly. "We are to move carefully, to discern the Holy Spirit, in the decisions that we make."

The Holy Spirit. Charity had never doubted the divine vastness that was in her, with her. It could pull her along when she was acting like a mule and show her a way through when she felt lost. "Hermon Husband never agreed with committee decisions," Charity said aloud, watching the sun flicker on her mother's worn face. "Or the restraint suggested in the Book of Discipline sent from London." She rose to take her turn with Sarah so that Danise could participate more fully in the discussion.

"But Herman has found a following, has he?" asked John Wright.

"Seems to have the support of Joseph Maddock and Jonathan Sell from Eno Meeting," replied John Pike, "and some of the others are willing to publicly admit that they are with him. Won over by his disparaging remarks about the actions and transactions of quarterly meeting."

"I heard something about a meeting at Maddock's Mill?" Majer asked tentatively.

"Yes," John Pike replied, leaning toward him. "But only because it's a meeting place for the community to grab a cup of coffee and be entertained by gossip. Mail carriers have made it a stop now, and Joseph Maddock hired on a blacksmith to keep business at his mill store steady. He's got a stock of Hermon Husband's pamphlets available for the few who haven't read them. It's a logical place to hold a meeting."

"Who's this Joseph Maddock?" asked Danise.

"A miller," replied John Pike, "him and his apprentice, Jonathan Sell, from New Jersey. Came a couple years back about the time . . ." he hesitated, and looked over Charity and baby Sarah. "When there were the sessions about the disownment and such. Joseph Maddock settled his family on a huge farm along the Eno River, near his Irish and English relatives. He operates a gristmill there with the little store and is well-respected among those who frequent it."

"And not worried that he'll be publicly linked to Hermon Husband?" asked Isaac.

"We are *all* going to be associated with Hermon Husband and his rebels," fussed Rachel, her head in her hands.

"His influence is spreading," admitted John Pike. "At least one member of the Spring Meeting is involved in the protesting of taxes, the group of them demonstrating peacefully at first, circulating petitions. But now it's an oath-bound group who are threatening to use force against anyone agitating for the raising or collecting of assessments. They call themselves 'Regulators' because they want the local taxes to be regulated. Their protests have become familiar sights on the road past Spring Meetinghouse to Hillsborough."

"And does William Tryon not control them?" asked Isaac.

"Oh, no one listens to Governor Tryon," scoffed Majer, giving Isaac a little jab with his elbow. "He's always making proclamations that have no meat to them."

"Perhaps distracted by issues of slavery and the French-Indian conflict," John Pike allowed, "but Majer's right. There's certainly plenty of opportunity for Hermon Husband's leadership in the spreading unrest. Why, Governor Tryon has already demanded that Friends take an oath of allegiance to the British government."

"They haven't done it, have they?" asked Charity.

John Pike gave a twisted smile. "Not all of them, but many are forced to provide drivers and teams of horses for his majesty's troops. Several wagon loads of flour were requisitioned from Lindley's Mill, here in Cane Creek. It's supposed to be a loan."

"They should be refusing," Rachel complained. She pushed at the loose strands of her hair to get them out of her eyes. "The epistle from London is clear that we are to offer only peaceful prayer over such disputes. Nothing more." She rubbed at her temples.

Charity fixed on her mother, worried for her condition.

"'Tis impossible," explained John Pike. His eyes circled the group of them. "The troops are insistent in what they take and leave little for the families. Word is that Joseph Maddock can't take the heat and is talking of going elsewhere."

"Who? Who's talking of moving?" asked Rachel, frowning.

"The Friends who were with Joseph Maddock at the meeting at his mill and then some," replied John Pike. "John Pyle's involved. It's that Joseph Maddock claims he's not in with Hermon Husband and the rest of them. Wants no part in any fighting with the authorities, but apparently, the government officials think otherwise. They've started harassing him, the sheriff, too, and anyone that comes to the store. He's talking of selling his farm and mill to move with some seventy families to Georgia."

"Georgia? Seventy families?" repeated Rachel weakly. She made eye contact with her husband, frowning.

"I've heard some about that," offered Majer. "The Assembly there has passed legislation that allocates land for a new town, Wrightsboro, named for the governor of the colony."

"I've heard that, too," agreed John Pike. "Maddock and his followers have had it with the Cane Creek leadership and want to be under the oversight of a new meeting altogether. At least ten Eno Meeting families showed up in force at Cane Creek women's meeting not long ago. All requested certificates to Wrightsboro for themselves and their children."

"I wonder how long it'll take the quarterly meeting to approve their transfers," mumbled Rachel.

Chapter 11

Charity, Danise, and Chelsea sat together, passing around Rachel's long overdue transfer of membership certificate. *"'Tis finally been awarded,"* signed Charity, tracing her mother's name with her finger.

Chelsea tapped Danise, searching for eye contact. *"Hermon Husband,"* she signed, shaking the handshape *"H"* twice as she arched it across her chest where the sign for *angry* was made. *"Why he, HH, never like Mama?"*

"Long story. Complicated," Danise replied, speaking, too, so that Charity could more easily follow the conversation. *"Hermon Husband and his men tried to stop Mama's transfer certificate at monthly and quarterly meetings."*

"Why?" Chelsea asked, exaggerating an expression of confusion.

Charity took a turn at explaining, pairing signs with her speech. *"When the meetings were discussing whether I'd be allowed at business discussions, Mama made a loud fuss of complaint. Thou know how she was, constantly questioning the unfairness of my disownment.*" She fingerspelled the word, not knowing a sign for it. "*After it was all said and done, quarterly meeting called Mama to apologize for her behavior. They held up her travel certificate for months and months as retaliation, I guess. So we moved without it.*" She held up the paperwork and laid it down again. "*Good to finally have the official permission.*"

"*But I thought she* did *apologize?*" Chelsea puzzled. "*I remember that, no?*"

"*Yes, but not sincerely enough for Herman Husband and his gang,*" explained Danise. "*I think the sour man saw a chance to cause difficulty for Mama, afraid of her, her bold ways.*" Danise stilled her hands, pausing, before she went on. "*He tried to do whatever he could to stop her in her organizing of women.*"

"*Women brave, strong like Mama threat to men, men like HH,*" Chelsea agreed, her signs made firmly to indicate her conviction.

"*Maybe HH was secretly attracted to her for the very reasons he feared her.*" Danise suggested thoughtfully. "*For her intelligent and abilities.*"

"*And she never backed down from him,*" agreed Danise.

#

"She's worn out," Anarcha, the midwife, surmised one afternoon. "Rachel's not getting out of this,

162

Charity. She's fifty-one, after all, and wracked from the hardships of frontier life, the birthing and raising of her fourteen children, and the challenges of repeatedly riding through the wilderness and camping out. And thou know that Danise and I have tried all combinations of bleeding, cupping, blistering, and leeching to halt her fevers."

As Anarcha and the Wright women tended to her, they failed to engage Rachel in much conversation. When she mumbled something, it was about her days at Cane Creek, raising her family, and working for her meeting. A couple of times, she confided in Charity that it nagged at her that she'd fallen out of favor with the women of the meeting to whom she'd dedicated her life. Rachel said something about losing her dear friendship with Abigail Pike, Charity not knowing how to console her. She'd never understood what had happened between Abigail and Rachel. Was it that her mother had been too bold and abrasive in the meetings and dealings around her disownment? Or had the two women had a disagreement and parted for different reasons? Maybe their leadership styles clashed when they went visiting together; maybe they were jealous over the attention that each was afforded. When Charity asked her older sisters, Mary and Margaret, they had no thoughts on the matter.

"I don't recall ever seeing Abigail even a single time after we moved here," said Mary. "Though she was nice enough to us if we saw her at quarterly or yearly meetings."

One afternoon, when mother and daughter were nested in bed like spoons, Rachel whispered hoarsely to Charity, "You're a chrysalis. Don't be the girl who was raped . . . wield your power and reinvent yourself . . . pray God will ask thee to take up the travel."

When she'd come to accept that the end was inevitable, Charity saw how her mother transitioned from an earthly reality to a spiritual one, working to establish the humility in her suffering that had been a challenge in her life. She wouldn't speculate on an afterlife, only saying, "I have tried to be a pattern of a Christ-like life . . . obey his commands . . . I go into the arms of uncertainty, embracing in death what cannot be controlled . . . my faith to guide me through."

Rachel Rebecca Ann Wells Wright died on day twenty-three, Twelve Month, 1771. Charity was sure she would have been pleased that her brother, Joseph Jr., had made her coffin. The pine had come from one of the trees they'd planted some twenty years ago in Cane Creek for this exact purpose. John Pike had chopped it and gotten it to Joseph Jr. and Majer, who honed the flat-topped box with all their craft, sealed the joints with pitch, and filled the bottom with sawdust. It gave Charity comfort to think that, in some manner, Rachel was with John Woolman, who they'd heard had died from smallpox in England. She prayed that he, too, was buried in the manner of Friends, the body lovingly washed and dressed at home by women. It had been Mary, the oldest of Rachel's daughters, who'd picked a dress for Rachel, choosing the familiar pieces that she wore to worship on First Days.

Six of the Wright children, both the men and the women, served as pallbearers, glovelessly carrying the coffin from the Wright cabin to the meetinghouse for the memorial. Once inside, Rachel's coffin was gently set at the front of the room. The family sat on the benches closest to it.

At the memorial meeting itself, Charity had listened with appreciation to those who rose to speak out of the quiet. Everyone was wearing their nicest clothes, their black hats and bonnets held to their hearts. The offered words had taken Charity out of her gloom and into an appreciation of Rachel's personality and contributions. She was grateful when Abigail Pike, now sixty-two years old and walking with a cane, stood to speak. She described Rachel as "a strong and pious mother of their faith, with endless energy and determination," and she was sure that her companion was in heaven, surrounded by the warmth of holy love.

Each of Rachel's siblings spoke as well, she and her father so choked with emotion that they were unable. And Charity's own Joseph, only seven years old, stood up to tell of his love for his gramma's blueberry pie with its lattice-top crust.

After a period of silence, the group of them filed out and made their way to the little burying ground near the back of the meetinghouse property. They watched Charity's oldest brothers, William, Joseph, Johnny, and James, lower the coffin in the gaping hole they'd managed to dig earlier, despite the hard winter ground. Even now, Charity could hear the noisy crows that watched the gathered group from the top branches of the evergreens.

John Wright, the patriarch of the family, found his voice at the grave site. Charity could only remember bits of what he'd said, how Rachel's soul was with God, no matter that the Anglicans believed it was scandalous for Friends to bury their members in unconsecrated ground. "All ground is God's," John reminded them, "and my dear wife is not deposited like a dog, as the outliers say. No, no." Charity had nudged Mary to interrupt whatever their father was going to say next and invite people to the cabin for refreshments.

'Twas my mother, the only mama I'll ever have, Charity moaned that day and many times after. She felt dizzy, as if she'd been hit on the head. Often her heart ached so fiercely that she held a hand over it as if to keep it from leaping out of her chest. *How can it be that I knew her, that she was right here, and now she is gone?*

When everyone had trudged back from the burial grounds, Charity turned to see her father still in place at the fresh mound of dirt. *If having all us children isn't proof of his love for her,* she decided, *it's confirmed by the way he's sorry to have to leave her alone now.*

There was no formal period of mourning. Life went on. Mary, Margaret, Charity, and Rachel packed up their mother's things, and each chose one of Rachel's scarves or shawls as a remembrance.

There'd be no headstone, but come spring, the women planned to plant some Carolina lupine, the flower that was dearest to Rachel for its brazen yellow heads. Still, there were many times in those first weeks after the death that Charity would crumble into the nearest chair and grope for the peace of the internal quiet. *Are thou there, Mama, with the women of your past? For I hope you are together and watching over the rest of us.* In her mind's eye, Charity would turn imagined black earth over and over, letting the dirt sift repetitively through her fingers. She waited expectantly like a farmer able to smell the rain for what the Spirit might offer to bring comfort. Often, she envisioned the many times in her childhood when she and her sisters had gone to bed, and her mother would come with a candle to the doorway, her shadow flickering on the wall. Charity would peek from under her covers to see her mother, the most loving expression on her face as she bent over each of them to kiss their sleepy faces.

And the Spirit does the same, Charity would think when she joined in meeting for worship after Rachel's death. *With us always. Kissing and cradling us.* She'd internally examined her undesired thoughts, taking up each one and letting it drop like a pebble into a great pool of water. She'd think about leaving Isaac and the children for her travel, her need for praise, her pride in her ministry, and how much she enjoyed the attention of weighty Friends. She imagined the ripples of water washing over each weakness until it disappeared in the ocean of Light. Trembling,

Charity would allow the Spirit to halt any excuse for her faults and, instead, give her new insights to see how she might improve herself. Almost always, at the rise of the worship, she felt wrapped in a peaceful bliss. *Mama wouldn't want my tears and sadness. She'd expect me to deepen my worship, tend to our family, and get about the work God has given me.*

#

"Was Hermon Husband a leader in the Battle of Alamance?" John Wright asked John Pike. Their old neighbor was visiting again and trying to distract them from their grief.

"He was," John Pike nodded, making eye contact at turns with John Wight, Charity, Isaac, and Majer as they sat in the front room at the Cook cabin, having coffee together. As usual, he had information about the world beyond the Quaker settlement and thought the Wrights and Cooks might be interested in the doings of Hermon Husband, the man who had been so against Rachel. "There's an excellent summary here in the *Gazette* of what happened leading up to the battle, new to you, perhaps, since Rachel was so in decline when these things were happening."

"The battle was last year in May, wasn't it?" asked Isaac. He scratched at his beard. "Only twenty miles away from Cane Creek, yes?"

"That's right," said John Pike. "Seems it all started with a bunch of ruffians complaining about the constant increases in taxes. Hermon Husband was a

168

representative to the state assembly in Hillsborough at the time, the newspaper—" John brought a page up to read from the article, "describes him as 'forcible and fluent in argument against the taxes and graft,'" John grimaced, "and well-suited to organize the men to take their complaint to court.'"

"Is this the same dissident group that had been meeting at Maddock's Mill?" asked Isaac. "The ones that had been giving Friends such trouble, with Joseph Maddock's fearing Governor Tryon would have the authorities confiscate his mill and store?"

"It was," John Pike looked over to John Wright. "The Regulators, three of them, the ones who'd questioned Rachel's sincerity over her apology back in '63, and another two, the ones who signed the dissenting minute in contesting Hermon Husband's disownment in '64."

"And so what'd they do?" Majer asked impatiently. He knew about the Battle of Alamance but not the details of what had led up to it.

"The mob of them came into the courthouse with clubs and whips, angry that the judge wouldn't hear their case," John Pike obliged Majer.

"Oh, Lord," whispered Charity. "Friends? Friends with clubs and whips?"

"Former Friends," John Pike corrected. "They don't claim us now, any more than we claim them." He took a sip of coffee and then looked mournfully to Majer. "In the aftermath at the courthouse, human waste was found on the judge's seat and the body of a dead enslaved man laid out on the lawyers' bar."

Majer put his hands to his head as if to squeeze away the image of it.

"Why? Why did they do it?" Charity whispered, as if there was possibly a reason. "How is that related?"

"It doesn't say," said John Pike, putting the newspaper down.

There was a long moment of silence before any of them thought it right to speak.

"There was a second skirmish," John Pike finally continued. He tapped the folded paper. "Within days, those who were sympathetic to the Regulators came storming from all areas of the colony to join their ranks. They burned the judge's house and outbuildings to the ground. Then, hundreds of them marched on Colonel Fanning's house and—"

"Who's he, Colonel Fanning?" interrupted Isaac.

"A protégé of Governor Tryon," replied Majer.

"And an enemy of the Regulators," John Pike agreed. The hooligans destroyed every piece of furniture in David Fanning's place, angry that he'd been extorting money from them and hadn't been punished for it. They threw his china and glassware into the streets, scattered his papers and books to the winds, stole money, and got drunk on the liquor they found in his cellar." John Pike sat back and took a few deep breaths. "Then they paraded through town in triumph, wearing bits of his clothing, wigs, and hats. They smashed windows along the way and terrorized the townspeople, beat some up—women, too!"

"Oh, that's awful," John Wright and Charity moaned in unison.

"They went on from David Fanning's to attack Governor Tryon's castle of a home in New Bern. The place was brand new, just finished two years ago."

"And no doubt paid for with our hard-earned tax assessments," Majer retorted.

John Pike gave him a nod of agreement. "This at William Tryon's mansion was all-out war."

"And Hermon Husband was a leader in it all?" Charity shook her head.

"According to the paper," John Pike tapped it, "he thinks he should be acquitted of any wrongdoings, but it's only a matter of time before he'll be expelled from the Assembly. Other representatives are quoted as calling him 'a promoter of the late riots and treason.'"

"So, what happened?" asked Majer. "Did the Quakers fight the governor's troops?"

"The *former* Quakers," John Pike insisted for a second time. "Yes. Those Hermon Husband led were largely untrained frontiersmen, without a plan or officers or adequate weapons. And certainly not a cannon."

"How many of these Regulators does the paper say were there at the Battle of Alamance?" asked Majer.

"Two thousand. Thinking they'd intimidate the governor with their numbers."

"Two thousand," Majer whistled incredulously.

"The Regulators taunted the governor's troops, the rag-tag lot of them surprised as anyone when the governor's cannon was rolled out onto the field."

"A cannon?" moaned Charity. "Oh, Spirit, guide us, guide us," she prayed aloud. She rose up and began to pace in a circle behind the chairs for the bloodshed, six months past.

John Pike directed his comments to the distraught Charity. "He tried to negotiate, tried to warn the Regulators that he was fed up. It says in the paper that the rebels were all arrogance and that their last message back to him was: 'Fire and be damned!'" John Pike turned back to John Wright, Isaac, and Majer. "And so, for at least the next two hours, the militia gave the country boys all they had until the Regulators broke and ran, leaving behind dead bodies, shoes, caps, powder horns, and seventy horses in their rush! Tryon's side counted nine dead and sixty-one wounded."

"And how many Regulators?" asked Majer.

"No one knows," admitted John Pike. "One of their leaders was hanged the day after without any hearing—and six more swung within the week."

"But the hanged man wasn't Hermon Husband?" asked John Wright.

"No, no. 'Tis said that, when the fighting started, he stayed about as long as thou can hold a hot horseshoe," scoffed John Pike, "and now he can't be found." He closed his eyes for a moment. "There's a quote from someone sympathetic to the Regulators, calling him a cowardly deserter who fled his followers in their hour of need."

"Could it have been that his Quakerism caught up with him?" Charity asked hopefully. She stared up at the rafters.

"Doubtful," said John Pike, wagging his head. "'Tis guessed that he scurried away to Pennsylvania. Those who lived through it, the ordinary fellows, were pardoned if they were willing to swear allegiance to the Crown. Most had their homes and barns burned, many of them now planning to leave North Carolina if they haven't left already."

"Was that the end of it, then?" asked Majer.

"Pretty much," John Pike replied. "The article ends with the prediction that our taxes will be raised here soon to pay for the fighting. 'Taxation without representation' is how they sum it up."

#

"Are thou sad today, Mama?" young Joseph asked his mother, his head tilted to one side. He'd come from a back room, wanting a cool drink from the can in the kitchen. "I was imagining Grammy galloping through the wilderness on a holy errand," the boy smiled. I thought it'd make thee happy. He came to her, circled her waist, and squeezed tight.

"Oh, dear boy," Charity embraced him, the words slipping out on a breath. She'd been thinking of her mother, too. "It's that I think I'm to travel, travel in ministry, and I am worried to leave you and the others." She rested her chin on top of the perfect head. *But wasn't I happy in Papa's care when Mama went off?* Charity considered. *Us Wright children surrounded by aunts and uncles and siblings?* She took a moment to let the leading sink deeper in her consciousness. *They'll be happy and well cared for with Isaac, and my sisters will help.* Charity walked Joseph to the door and released him to rejoin his playmates.

Suddenly, Danise was beside her. "He's written, he's written," she sang, a letter in her hand. She'd been corresponding with a Friend, Anthony Benezet. The Frenchman had earned a good reputation, Majer had told them, in Philadelphia, where he'd helped to persuade the yearly meeting to disown members who continued to buy and sell other human beings. The man had also arranged segregated meetings for worship for Negroes from Nantucket to Charleston where they could demonstrate their leadership and ministry abilities in their services.

Danise began to read to Charity, stopping after almost every sentence to squeeze her eyes and give a little joyful shake. Indeed, Anthony Benezet seemed to be a saint. A European Friend, he'd first taught at a school for Quaker children—White Quaker children—and tutored enslaved and free Negroes in the evenings out of his home. About twenty years ago, in 1758, he'd set up the first school for Negroes in Philadelphia with the support of the Religious Society of Friends.

"He has thirty-six students at the school," Danise read aloud, "most of them the result of unions between White, working-class women and freed African men." She kept scanning the letter and silently reread parts. "He says here he doesn't subscribe, as many do, to any theory of Black inferiority or to the idea that Africa is a barbaric continent, that for twenty years he's been publishing newspaper articles and tracts saying that 'it's a vulgar prejudice, founded on the pride of ignorance of their lordly enslavers, that Black people are inferior in their capacities.'" Danise looked up. "He uses the word 'Black' instead of 'Negro,'" she mused and then continued with the letter, quoting Anthony Benezet. "As a teacher, I've had the opportunity of knowing the temper and genius of the African Blacks." She looked to Charity with a wide grin and then continued, "And could with truth and sincerity declare amongst them as great a variety of talents, equally capable of improvement, as amongst a like number of White people."

Unexpectantly, Danise threw her arms up, waving the letter in the air. "He's, he's offering us teaching jobs, Chelsea and me both," she exclaimed. "At the school." She wrapped her arms around her sister. "Think what this means, Charity. We'll earn a living in our own right!" She danced Charity around the room, her sister giving into the glee and laughing for the first time in weeks.

Chapter 12

Charity bounced baby Mary and longed for Danise. It'd been a month since she and Chelsea had left the safety of Bush River, one of her Uncle Joseph's White employees driving them in a furniture wagon so that they could hide in the back if need be.

Finally, a letter had been delivered. Charity broke the seal and quickly scanned the first paragraph. Danise and Chelsea had arrived safely, walking once they had crossed into the safety of Maryland rather than bouncing in the jarring wagon. "I'm guessing the rutted, difficult Great Wagon Road hasn't improved much at all since you were four years old, Charity, a thousand more pioneers traveling it in the last thirty years."

Charity held the letter to her heart for a moment. *Safe, they're safe.* She ran her finger over the first sentences. How fortunate it'd been that Isaac valued literacy enough to find the time in his busy day to teach Danise, Charity, and Chelsea to read and write. Once he and Charity had married, he'd called the three young women to the Cooks' table most evenings, a lantern to light one of the religious pamphlets he collected, and patiently instructed them using the tracts and the Bible. When it'd been Chelsea's turn, Isaac gently asked her to watch his lips and tongue and give a try to saying some of the simpler words she was reading.

"Ess," Chelsea would nod, eager to comply. Understandably, she learned Isaac's lessons more slowly than Danise and Charity, who competed to outshine each other as they rapidly progressed in their reading fluency and cursive.

Charity's smile faded as she read the next part of Danise's letter. The condition of the Great Wagon Trail hadn't been the worst of the trip. Danise reported that, even with a White driver to vouch for them, she and Chelsea were denied accommodations at every boardinghouse along the route. They'd had to make do, sleeping fitfully in the hard bed of the wagon.

"A smack in the face to be sure," the twenty-seven-year-old Danise had written, "and a harsh introduction to a different kind of life than we lived in Cane Creek and Bush River. For heaven sakes, it's 1772, and thou would think people could be more accepting. Still, once we arrived to Philadelphia, Quakers offered us astonishing hospitality and kindnesses."

It had been a White woman, a Quaker abolitionist, Dinah Nevill, who provided Danise and Chelsea a room in her handsome brick home. It stood in a neat row with others on Elfreth's Alley, so named for the blacksmith who owned most of the properties on the cobblestone street. The neighbors were mostly tradesmen—shipwrights, silver and pewter smiths, glassblowers, and a furniture builder who knew well the reputation of Joseph Wright Jr. and Majer.

According to Danise, Dinah Nevill was "spoiling them rotten." She'd asked only that they help to maintain the common areas of the house and look after her daughter, Maria, for a period of time in the evenings after the housekeeper had left for the day. Dinah invited their questions about which shops and eateries were safe to frequent as long as they had a man with them and enjoyed discussing larger topics, too, such as abolition and women's education. She was quick to learn the basics of manual language and was sometimes able to haltingly sign her answers and comments without help from Danise. Some of the women in the meeting found the way the young women communicated such an intriguing curiosity that they had started a small sign class. They had asked Chelsea to be their teacher, and to no one's surprise, she was proving herself to be extremely capable. Her students loved her and were fascinated with what she explained of the Deaf culture she represented.

Danise also confessed that, while, for the most part, she and Chelsea dressed in their black bonnets, plain, long-sleeved dresses, and leather tie-up shoes, they sometimes wore the lace aprons that

Dinah Nevill had gifted them when they went downtown or to the Episcopal church they'd discovered. Apparently, Dinah was of the opinion that Quaker plainness wasn't in the style but in the color. She had a coat, reported Danise, that had been fashionably tailored, although it was dyed the expected dark brown. She'd gifted Danise and Chelsea each a new straw hat for everyday and a costly embroidered bonnet for services at Christ Church.

Are Danise and Chelsea lapsed in their attendance at the great Quaker meetinghouse of Philadelphia? Charity wondered. It seemed so. *At least they can't be disowned. They've never been members.*

In a long letter written at Christmas, 1772, Danise informed Charity that, although Philadelphia Friends had banned enslaving and had created societies to promote the emancipation of those who were enslaved, she and Chelsea were more comfortable at Christ Church. "'Tis where the students at the Negro school and their parents attend," Danise explained. "The pews are filled with Negroes and assorted people who have come to the colonies from many different countries. We can sit any place we please. During social times, we talk both with those in the congregation who support the ever-increasing taxes that the British impose and those who resent having to pay them. According to the paper, even the Natives are divided in their allegiance, some of them fighting for the king and some for the colonists."

Charity reached in her pocket for the intertwining rings of belonging that Danise had left with her. She turned them thoughtfully, missing her sisters.

#

Over the next three years, the letters between Danise and Charity were delivered sporadically. In 1774, Charity wrote to tell Danise that Catherine Payton had died and then their good friend John Pike, "Pneumonia." Most all of the Wrights and Cooks who lived in Bush River had ridden back to Cane Creek for the memorial, the first time they'd seen Abigail Pike in years.

"Abigail wept openly when we rode into her yard. After many a tender embrace and soft words of condolence, the whole group of us women sat just behind her during John's memorial meeting for worship. Papa, Isaac, and myself each moved to speak, to tell of our thankfulness for John Pike's consistent friendship."

Shortly after April 1775, when news of Lexington and Concord hit the *Philadelphia Evening Post*, Danise summarized relevant articles from the four-page paper when she wrote to Charity. She paid close attention to the growing discord between colonists and British forces and sarcastically commented about a White columnist who flippantly described himself as being "enslaved" by a corrupt English government.

"On a positive note, let me tell thee about Anthony Benezet," Danise wrote. "He is genuinely concerned to do the best for all his pupils at our school. And in an age that has ignored the education of children who cannot hear, he has compassionately devised a special program for a Deaf and mute girl whose mother came to him, begging that her girl be enrolled. True to his nature, he enrolled her in our school when no other school would. He immediately assigned Chelsea to the task of improving the girl's language and social skills so that she could share in the fellowship of the other students. Meanwhile, did I tell thee? He's found a speech teacher for Chelsea, a woman named Edith Fitzgerald, and she's already enabled Chelsea to clearly enunciate her name and address should she get lost, as well as useful, frequent phrases like 'I want' and 'I have.'"

In another letter, Danise recounted what she'd learned from the abolitionist. "'Twas the Quakers, Anthony says, who initially brought most of the Guineas, as we are sometimes called in the city, to Pennsylvania. They cleared the trees and rocks and built the first crude cabins. It was backbreaking work, and the White people didn't want to do it. During the Seven Years War," Danise went on, "Black people were in high demand because the supply of indentured Germans and Scots-Irish laborers had dried up. Even now, the British commanders recruit indentured men to bolster their militias, increasing the demand for Guineas to work in the capacities the White people have left behind. 'Tis why it's hard to persuade those who still own Guineas, Friends among them, to release them, indentured labor being so unavailable, and therefore, in high demand and expensive. Why, John Woolman spoke against slavery at the London Yearly Meeting four years ago, but Philadelphia Yearly Meeting is still dealing with the sin of it. Word is that most Friends, as well as many merchants, professionals, and politicians, are finally agreeing to manumit those they own. The people are often turned out like old dogs, without a trade or housing."

"Manumission," wrote Charity in reply, "is a horrible practice, the various forms of it not always favoring enslaved people. Some men and women have arranged to purchase themselves by paying the master an agreed amount, but then the transaction has to be approved by the state legislature—which is an arduous process and rarely allowed. You two were smart—and brave—to get out of the South. Does thou think thou will marry?"

Danise laughed out loud when she read the abrupt question. "There are plenty of eligible men here," Danise obliged her nosy sister, "and Anthony Benezet's wife, comfortable in the social circles of Philadelphia, is good to introduce me to many. Still, it'll be a cold day, a very cold day, when I allow a man to have power over me, and anyway, there were so few Black people in Cane Creek and Bush River that there was no sense talking about marriage. But here, unless a man is interested in going with Anthony Benezet and me to the offices of newspaper editors as far away as Lancaster, and interested in urging them not to publicize ads for enslaved runaways or auctions for enslaved people, I won't be wasting my time."

Chelsea wrote to Charity, too. Her grammar was sometimes a little odd because she didn't hear spoken language, but Charity could always understand her meanings. Now twenty-eight years old and in an employment where she could continue to improve her literacy skills and world knowledge, Chelsea was working as an assistant teacher at Anthony Benezet's school most days, as a dorm monitor on both Seventh Day and First Day nights, and teaching her sign class to community women. Always observant, she took up more superficial topics in her letters than Danise did and was tedious in her descriptions of city dress. In her most recent letter, Chelsea had described the men who dressed "macaroni," a funny word that seemed to mean "fancy," although Charity thought maybe Chelsea had misunderstood it. When she asked Danise, she was told that, indeed, Chelsea had it right. The term referred to English men's fashion when it was androgynous. Danise herself was attracted to the style.

After that, Charity accepted that Chelsea knew what she was talking about. Even as a child, she'd been a keen observer, her memory for what someone had been doing or wearing compensating for what she missed in conversations. To young Sarah Cook's delight, Chelsea wrote of Dinah's loose-fitting "bed gowns," with three-quarter length sleeves that alarmed Charity for their impropriety but delighted her daughter for their possibility. On one "exciting" afternoon when Dinah had been out, the maid had even taken the liberty of showing Chelsea into their hostess's bed chamber to see her hooped petticoats and corsets and the dresses and skirts that she'd had shortened to show her ankles.

Chelsea's descriptions of Philadelphian dress motivated young Sarah, now nine years old, to read her letters over and over. She'd taken to dressing up and pretending she was outfitted in the luxurious, imported satins and silks that Chelsea wrote were currently the fashion in London. Strutting around the cabin, she'd tease her younger sisters, Rachel, who was six years old, and Mary, who was a pesky three, for their homespun cotton and country look. She'd sashay past the baby Charity in her cradle, talking to the Cook's sixth child as if she was as an imagined "city man," dressed in a high-collared shirt, vest with ornate buttons, and knee-length coat.

"And thy wig?" Charity would ask her daughter if she were in a playful mood. She was pregnant again but not ailing from it.

"'Tis too uncomfortable. Too hot," young Sarah would retort, her nose in the air.

Charity watched her children play, wondering if God was calling her to travel in ministry. She was sure her mother had an opinion about it. She heard Rachel's voice in the wind and in the songs of the chickadees, nudging her to visit the women of Bush River as she'd once done in the Cane Creek region. Still, Charity wasn't sure she could leave the little ones, even if God commanded it.

What is the Spirit asking? she wondered as she watched Isaac in his lessons with Joseph, Sarah, and Rachel. She was torn between wanting to follow God's command and wondering if she had misinterpreted it. Finally, she requested a clearness committee.

When four members came to call, it was Sarah who opened the door to greet the visitors. "Come in, Friends," Charity welcomed, coming up behind her oldest daughter with Isaac just behind her. The group settled into the straight-backed chairs that had been circled around the large braided rug in the living room, Isaac among them, cradling the baby. Joseph and Sarah took their younger siblings to the back rooms.

"I understand thou are seeking clearness as to whether thou are called to visit others, to strengthen families in our faith," James Hollingsworth began after but a brief time of silence.

"Yes," agreed Charity hesitantly. "I believe God is asking me, with the meeting's support, to travel and serve. Isaac is willing, and Joseph's twelve years old now. He understands his part in helping his father with his younger sisters and brother."

"We have heard thee preach regarding the testimony against war and how you are constant in your messages regarding slavery," said William Wright, who was no relation to the Wrights or Cooks. "If you are approved for itinerant work, the meeting will cover thy expenses and watch over thy family."

"I thank thee, William, for it would be a great joy to travel independent of my worries of husband and home. The assistance of the meeting will allow me to go out often to visit the families in our faith community so challenged during these uncertain times."

"Thy papa joined Colonel Thomson's Rangers to campaign against Tory interference, did he?" interjected Iggy Richardson, silent for a moment with the shock of it. "I can't imagine thou won't be asked about it as you visit."

Charity worked to keep calm. When the Cooks had first learned of John Wright's decision, she'd gone with her youngest brothers and sister—Nathan, Thomas, Keziah, and Isaac—to appear before the committee for discipline and discuss it. Charity noticed that Keziah, fifteen years old, and Isaac, thirteen, had held hands as they stood nervously before the Quaker committee and told of their lifetime devotion to the beliefs and ways of the Religious Society of Friends. Surely they weren't responsible for their father's decision, mystifying as it was.

"My father hasn't been quite right since our mama died," Charity informed the committee members, "but you know he taught each of us to read with the Bible, and we all come regularly to meeting on First Days and Fourth Day evenings. We've made most everything in our home, buying little from the peddler, and drink only the mild beer we make ourselves. We've never played cards, sung, or danced." She turned to Iggy Richardson, who was clerking the committee. "We've never dressed and spoken in any manner other than the Quaker way." When no one said anything, Charity went on. "Our father will have to make his own way with God," for why he joined up—loyalty to England and our relatives there or because he's been continually threatened with treason by the Loyalists—I don't know. We've gotten no letters from him, no explanation." She paused, looking at the committee members, and slowly lit the pipe she'd taken to smoking with Isaac. She thought about the last time she could recall having embraced John Wright, the last time she'd told her father that she loved him. Charity shifted to address James Hollingsworth and Eli Cook. "Our pedigree is well-known, and my sister, Margaret, stays at my father's cabin to cook, clean, and watch over Nathan, Thomas, Keziah, and Isaac."

"I suspect that many a family in our community is divided in discussions about the impending war," Isaac said quietly, defending the absent John Wright, "but, as my wife says, isn't that between each member and the Spirit, that they decide for themselves their part in the revolution? For it is a challenge that our pacifist vow brings, that we are distrusted by all sides, that officers threaten to kill our boys on the spot if they don't muster. No doubt, you've heard that, if our youth refuse, muskets are tied to them, and they are forced to march to camps far from their homes."

"There are many such tellings," agreed Iggy Richardson.

"Do thou know that Abigail Pike rides to both the Tory and the Rebel camps and preaches to the soldiers?" asked Isaac. "That Nathanael Greene, a former Friend, must have endorsed her ministry because she's the only clergy permitted within the Rebel lines—although she's not allowed to dismount and delivers her sermons on horseback."

"We're in the middle of endless changes," Charity said firmly, looking at each of the clearness committee members in turn. "People are doing desperate things and are in need of prayer and counsel with one of faith deep enough to give it. I'm moved to go, Friends, no matter how far, to encourage them to trust God, to press forward through the many difficulties that face our sect. I pray for your spiritual support."

Chapter 13

Kitchen table ministry. That's what Charity called her way of conducting visits. When no one objected to her travel, when permission for it had been brought before the Bush River women's meeting and granted, she was greatly relieved. Some of those who approved the papers had been in attendance at quarterly meeting when her disownment from Cane Creek was upheld, but they'd not stood in the way of her calling.

The night before Charity left on her first overnight trip, she called the children to her. "I am led to go," she explained. "A holy order and I must obey. I am to do my part to create heaven here on earth and be an example of our faith."

"Will I be called someday?" young Joseph earnestly wanted to know.

"You might," Charity replied. Had Joseph been of a different religion, he would, at his age, have been studying for confirmation, but Friends had no ceremony for membership. There were no classes with explanations of Friends' testimonies or special verses for Joseph to memorize and recite before the Men's Meeting. It was not the practice of Friends to form a committee to probe their youth for a statement of faith or to extend a formal invitation to establish them spiritually, physically, and financially in the Bush River Meeting. Instead, he'd have to decide for himself if he was all and everything it meant to be Quaker.

"Am I counted as a member at the quarterly and yearly meetings?" Joseph probed sheepishly.

"Joseph, thy great grandfather, James Wright, was an esteemed minister," Isaac replied. "Thy gramma Wright began to travel when your mother was a little girl. Thou was born into a strong Quaker family. You are a birthright Friend. Of course, thou are counted as a member."

"But no one's ever *asked* me," Joseph complained. "And I've never been to any other service, Baptist or Presbyterian, to compare."

"To witness how women and Africans are devalued and that war is justified?" queried Isaac.

"Just to see that our way is the certain one," said Joseph, meeting his father's gaze. "I am convicted, Papa, that all people are equals. Convinced, Papa, that there is 'that of God' within me, showing me where I have gone wrong, that I must make amends. And for a good long while now, I have been turning my mind, my consciousness, to God for the strength to reject material and worldly cravings, and to stand up for peace in the fighting."

Charity and Isaac exchanged the slightest of smiles. "Thou seem righteous in thy path," smiled Charity, a hand to her heart, "but convincement is a long process, and it is well you have begun it." She came to stand in front of him with outstretched hand. "I am proud that you are one of us," she whispered, her voice quivering.

The next morning, Charity twisted up her tangle of chestnut hair into a bun, donned a newly sewn dark blouse and top skirt, and packed her additional garments—a shift, two pairs of stockings, two of her best black skirts, a long gown for sleep, a triangular scarf, and an apron. Most of the clothing was made of linen, but she'd rolled up a few wool pieces, too, for the windy days, those spent alongside the water, and for the cooler months. Her plan was to travel the Bush River jurisdiction, but she had no idea if the Spirit would call her elsewhere. She pulled on her hooded cape and took her wide-brimmed hat from the antler horns by the doorway, readying herself emotionally to leave her husband and seven children. *Abandoned as I was*, she thought, accepting that her mother had had no choice in the matter either.

Mary Steddom Pearson was waiting for Charity in the yard. At the mandate of the women's meeting, she was to serve as Charity's companion.

"Ready?" Mary asked now. She was about the same age as Rachel would've been, and Charity accepted that it was Quaker practice that she not

193

conduct her visits alone. It was more that she'd hardly ever spoken to the older woman and worried that Mary wouldn't accept Charity as the lead, the one to decide where they went and how long they stayed.

"Thou know 'tis typical," Charity's sister, Margaret, had reminded her, "for an older woman to go on God's errand with a younger one, to pray for her as she does the work. Mary Pearson might offer thee valuable spiritual experience, be a partner in prayer, and an advisor in seeking spiritual counsel. She might check thy perceptions. And consider, dear sister, she is putting herself at great risk to aid thee in thy calling."

Out in the Cook's yard, Charity tied her beaver hat. "I love you so, dear ones," she cooed to the children, all of them gathered around her. She kissed baby Ruth and pulled the other children into her skirts. "Be good for thy papa and thy aunt, Margaret," she counseled and then turned to Isaac who was cradling the infant.

Isaac handed Ruth to Sarah and took Charity's outstretched hands. "My love for thee is in my deeds," Isaac reminded his wife as he kissed the top of her head. His face was ruddy from farming, his palms rough. He wore no mustache, not wanting to look as the military officers did, but he allowed himself sideburns and a short beard. "And I pray that by waiting on God, by going on his errand, thou are renewed in strength. Thou are precious, my Charity, and I will miss thee greatly." His words brought tears to

Charity's eyes as she went to the mounting block and straddled the mare Joseph had led out from the barn.

From high on the horse, Charity addressed the cluster of Cooks. "Watch over each other," she called. "Might you older ones consider what you'd say to describe your faith if I were to come to visit you?" She made sure young Joseph was looking at her when she asked it.

Charity rode out, Mary Pearson behind her, but she stopped at the property line for a last wave, one hand on the grip that was tied securely behind her sidesaddle. Isaac stood rigid, holding baby Ruth again and making her tiny hand wave goodbye. "May God keep thee," she called back. She felt the wife and mother in her transforming into the itinerant minister. *Papa, Mama, Catherine Payton, I feel thee with me. Protect us from trouble with traveling strangers, Natives coming down from the Palmetto Trail, and any troublemakers.*

The two women followed the trail out of Bush River. *I'm a chrysalis, awkward in my upside-down hanging, but I'll emerge. I'll fly,* sang Charity to herself. She and Mary rode down a hill, across a slough, over a field, and through a wood of birch and oak before they came to the edge of the settlement. *Here I am. Here I am, God,* thought Charity as they entered the dense forest.

A little later, Mary brought her mare up beside Charity to tell about herself as they rode along. She was a birthright Friend, coming originally from Hopewell Meeting in Virginia, same as the Wrights.

She had been widowed there, but a couple of years back, she'd remarried. She and her new husband had come to South Carolina to make a fresh start of things. Her seven children were grown, all of them married or soon to be. Deep in her faith, Mary was unsure what God was wanting of her, but she was pleased to have been asked to accompany Charity.

"A 'seeker,' are thou?" Charity asked. "And not called to preach thyself?" There'd been two other women recorded in itinerant ministry when Charity had been, both of them closer to Mary's age, with no children left at home and their husbands dead.

"I've not the ability for it," Mary said a little too quickly. "I don't feel able to discern what I'm to share, the courage to stand and deliver the messages, and the cadence and emphasis that thou are able to give thy phrasing. Thou, Charity, are like a songbird, alternating thy pitches and melody so the most important ideas are emphasized."

Just then, a cardinal flew in front of them. "Oh, perhaps a sign of truth?" laughed Charity. "'Tis kind of you, Mary, but what I preach is not planned. I open my mouth, and the words and the rhythms of them fly out like butterflies. If I deliver one sentence, I seldom know what the next is to be. The Spirit and not my efforts sometimes brings scriptures to my remembrance, but other times, I have to simply trust that, if I am patient, God will provide what I am to share. Once, when I'd been sitting in silence, I felt I was to stand to speak, but when I did so, I stood silent for an endless time. I could only sit down again.

Another time, I thought I was to preach on one matter, but then, another one rose altogether. And the rhythm of my preaching? That starts up on its own accord, as well, when I am lost to myself and serving as a holy vehicle." Charity looked from the path ahead over to Mary.

"Ah, well." Mary looked up into the trees. "Perhaps there will come a day when God will choose me to give a word." She shifted her thoughts quickly to add, "I enjoy the young people at our meetings, wanting them not to be tempted by the world but to keep our manner."

"I've always felt that my call was to abolitionism," Charity shared. "For as Southern women, we know more of the atrocities of slavery than they do in the North. From what my sister Danise reports in her letters from Philadelphia, most there have never visited the Carolinas or Georgia and are sheltered from the evils of the institution."

At the end of the first day of travel, Charity and Mary agreed that the trail had been easier to follow than they'd expected. "And no Natives, soldiers, or wild animals harassing us," Mary half-joked as she dismounted, her skirt sliding down behind her like a waterfall.

The two set about their tasks. Mary fixed the evening meal of fried garlic, onion, and celery, covered with a thick gravy and seasoned with salt and pepper. Charity found a flat clearing and kicked away pine cones and sticks before stretching out the two bedrolls. With the chatter of the cicadas to welcome her, she took out two flour sacks she'd brought for the purpose and stuffed clothing into them to make pillows.

When the women were finished eating, they washed up the dishes, pan, and utensils together, and then walked down to a nearby river to sit on the bank and watch the sun go down. The way was downhill, and they walked with their bodies slightly tilted back as if they were pushing against a heavy wind. As they approached the water, a beaver slid off the bank and swam into the shallows.

Mary and Charity took off their boots and stockings, rubbed their feet, and then dangled them in the cool water. They said little to each other, relaxing and listening to the crickets and frogs. Charity hoped bats would hurry to come around and eat the annoying swarms of mosquitoes. "Let's go back," she suggested after a while, bites all over her calves.

"Look, there. Fox," whispered Mary, pointing to where three kits had begun to chase each other round and round through the low foliage, pouncing and rolling, biting and escaping.

"They have so much energy!" Charity sighed. She was dog-tired.

"Who, who?" an owl called.

"The fox, that's who," replied Mary. Then, still chuckling, the women went back up the bank to bed down for the night.

#

Almost immediately, Charity found a pattern to her visits. When she or Mary spied a cabin, they'd halt their horses in the camouflage of the forest and listen for a time to the screaming jays in the trees and the squirrels scrambling up and down tree trunks. Then, centered and with holy purpose, Charity would brush her skirts, straighten her hat, and lead the way to the hitching post.

It was the women Charity and Mary sought out. Their horses taken to the barn and fed, the two would find ways to gain the trust of the wives and oldest girls, helping with the cooking and children until Charity was able to engage one or more of them in serious conversation. She and Mary would each tell a bit of their spiritual journeys in Quakerism and ask the women to do the same. As models of Friends' worship, they made time for devotions, the older children joining them and the younger ones playing at their skirts. Almost always, one of the pioneers would take advantage of the silence and speak out about trying to deal fairly with the local Natives, a challenge in the treatment of an enslaved worker, or a fine or arrest for a husband, son, or brother not enlisted in the military. Charity would gently touch a hand, saying, "Shhh, that's enough now," and close her eyes again, seeking the peace and counsel of the silence. "The answers will come." Afterward, she'd explain how the Light might be deepened in discernment if those who waited were steadfast and patient in the practice.

"You can find victory over thy loneliness, sadness, and discord," Charity would assure those who seemed to desire her encouragement. "Trust in the Holy Spirit for what is unknown to us." Sometimes, she and Mary ate a meal with the family, and sometimes, they were offered a bed in a back room or the hayloft in the barn for a nightly rest.

Before they left, Charity would talk about the monthly meeting closest to the cabin and the schedule of worship there. She'd explain how business was done and ask whether the women felt their voices were considered in the discussions. If there was a women's meeting, Charity would ask how it was faring. If there wasn't one established, she'd share the advantages of forming one.

With passion and stamina, Charity refused to leave a community until she'd been to each cabin, planning to sup with some five hundred Friends in the Bush River Meeting jurisdiction. She and Mary visited as many as thirty families in a month, the work wearing and potentially dangerous but done with good intention and purpose. Many places were sparsely populated, the roads to the shabby cabins hardly more than a broad swath through the forest, muddy or dusty, depending on the unpredictable weather—unpleasant at best, hazardous at worst.

When it was necessary to cross a river, there were few available bridges, and a ferry was rarely an option. Most often, Charity and Mary had to ride their horses into the rushing water, although, at least once, it was too deep for it. That time, they had found a handful of men working nearby who felled four trees so the women could swim beside the logs, their horses following them to the opposite bank. Their belongings were soaked through, of course, and to make matters worse, a heavy rain started up. Mary caught a dreadful cold and ran a high fever for a week.

Still, such misery fueled Charity. She was driven to worship with every meeting, large or small, some throbbing with life and others in danger of dying from spiritual atrophy. Frequently, she was asked to return. She regularly attended quarterly and yearly meetings, reporting on her service. When she was moved to speak before the larger and larger gatherings, her ministry invariably brought the embarrassment of praise.

And always—always in the work, Charity's absence from Isaac and the children plagued her. It was one thing to understand that travel was required, another to pretend to ignore the ache and yearning in her heart for family. Once during a long period of feeling low, she'd actually startled Mary by turning unexpectedly toward home, set on being done with the trip. Mary, unrattled, had called her back. "The time is drawing near, dear one, for us to start for Cane Creek, but are thou sure God is asking it of thee now?" Charity had sat for a moment, settled back against the hard saddle. She'd listened to the birds calling and watched a butterfly as it moved close and then flew off in the direction opposite of Bush River. "The will of God be done and not mine,"

Charity agreed, demonstrating the self-suppression that was expected of her.

#

Eventually, Charity's certificate to travel outside of the Bush River jurisdiction was approved at the monthly, quarterly, and yearly meeting levels. After much prayer on where she was to visit first, she asked the Bush River women's meeting, and Isaac, of course, to hold her in the Light for a visit to Wrightsboro, Georgia. It was where Joseph Maddock and his followers, once members of the Eno and Cane Creek Meetings, had gone when Hermon Husband and the Regulators had begun using violence to dispute increasing taxes.

Mary Pearson was again appointed to serve as Charity's companion, and two men were to go along as well, the trip long and difficult enough to warrant it. Charity was displeased, uncomfortable that she would be out in the woods alone with men, cooking and camping together. She didn't like the idea of it at all, but she had witnessed the practice when others asked to travel. She'd be safe enough around them, she figured, but there was no guarantee that the men would behave themselves, was there? Jehu Stuart had been Quaker, and he had raped her and several other girls. And why were the men needed anyway? Didn't everyone in Cane Creek know how capable and self-sufficient she was, how only a week ago she'd swum against the torrents of Rayburn's Creek to rescue Isaac?

"Thank goodness that it was just Isaac and I with no children with us," Charity usually began the telling when someone asked about it. "The river was so swift and terrible that day, I'm sure I hit about every branch and rock available to me as I bounced down it."

The couple had been returning from the Rayburn's Creek meetinghouse, searching the red sandy bank of the river for a place to cross. It was already late in the afternoon, and a detour through the giant sycamores would have been too time-consuming, getting them home long after dark. The safest way to get across, they'd decided, was to ride through the rush, together on Isaac's gelding.

Charity had disrobed to her shift, not wanting her skirts to get tangled in the bobbing branches that were visible from the shore. She fixed her shoes around her neck and tied her grip tightly to her mare, thinking the horse would follow Isaac's. But before Charity could stop her, the mare had galloped down the bank and into the river, the rapid water exciting her, Charity supposed. She'd barely been able to mount up behind Isaac, his horse eager to follow his mate, and brace herself before the two of them were caught in the cold, fierce current. They were soaked within seconds, and then Charity was swept completely off the gelding and carried under and up and under and up downsteam, forced away from Isaac.

It'd been her strength that had allowed Charity to push off the boulders as she was swept to them, her solid faith that caused her to survive. She'd lost her shoes, though she later thought it was God's favor that kept the laces, initially looped around her neck, from strangling her. When her mare had come thrashing along beside her, she'd been able to grab the saddle horn and pull herself up on it. She was able to keep her face above the rushing water as the horse thrashed her way to shore, although she took in mouthful after mouthful. Once there, Charity had dropped onto the sand, coughing and coughing to catch her breath, but as soon as she'd been able to stand, she'd rushed to the riverbank to search for Isaac. She finally caught sight of him floating on a thick tree branch in the violent water and not wanting to miss her chance at a rescue, she immediately swam back out into the current and pulled him to land.

"My horse drowned," was the first thing Isaac managed to say before he wrapped his wife in his arms and kissed her hard.

#

For Christmas 1775, Charity received a letter from Danise that told of the Philadelphia Quakers and how the most articulate of them, along with Ben Franklin and Thomas Jefferson, had been successful in convincing the Continental Congress to ban the importation of enslaved people into America. "The

Black people are so grateful that, according to the paper, about five thousand of the men have enlisted in the Continental Army."

"Well, slavery is alive and well in the South," Charity wrote back, "and plantation owners will only free enslaved workers if they are willing to fight for the Tories. Not only that, but Friends who have been serving in the state assemblies are now being excluded because of their stand against slavery and the pending revolution."

"In Pennsylvania," Danise replied, "Quakers are resigning or refusing to run for re-election, giving up direct control over the colony their ancestors established. They face a great deal of ridicule here. Still, Anthony Benezet sees a positive, new role for Friends in the taking up of Christ's cross to suffer as he suffered. He is encouraged by compensation being paid by some enslavers, as well as the idea of sending free Black people back to Africa."

"Africa?" Charity scratched out on a return stationary as soon as she found time. "Back to Africa? Thou were born here, sister. Please, please, don't go to Africa. I will never see thee again."

"You misunderstand me," Danise quickly replied. "My place is here, doing the good work my freed brethren have initiated. There are some here called 'Free Quakers,' and I admire their activities: a lady named Betsy Ross, who sewed the first flag for America; Thomas Paine, who authored a popular pamphlet, "Common Sense," giving colonists the language to quote in expressing their discontent over

Tory taxes; Lydia Darrah, a spy for the Continental Army; and a man named Timothy Matlack, clerk of the Second Continental Congress. All are a different kind of Friends who accept the fighting, as does Thomas Mifflin, a major general in the Army, and the notable General Nathanael Greene, who is encamped on the outskirts of Philadelphia. All of these and probably others have been disowned, of course, expelled from their meetings."

"We pray in our meeting for those who have left us," Charity wrote back. "As I travel in the Bush River jurisdiction, I am moved to preach on our testimonies of peace and equality, that there is 'that of God' in each person. 'Tis why it's impossible for us to kill another human being. I suspect there is overwhelming pressure from the majority of those in Pennsylvania to support independence, but my work here is to encourage Friends not to cave to the worldly events that encircle us. It's a relief that our brothers, William, Joseph, John, and James haven't been lured into the fighting, although the younger boys are much excited by the battles. Perhaps thou has heard that, just recently, in February, the Rebels defeated the Tories at the Battle of Moores Creek Bridge in North Carolina.

#

On the day Charity was to leave for Wrightsboro, Mary Pearson, William O'Neall, and Henry Milhouse met her at her cabin. She was late getting ready for the eighty-mile ride, puttering over her packing and already missing Isaac. How lucky she was to have married a good man so deeply committed to his faith and his family, never complaining about managing the children when she was called away. Since that day she'd almost lost him in Rayburn's Creek, Charity stopped daily to thank God that Isaac hadn't listened to rumors of her rape or been influenced by her initial disownment. He'd married her and fathered their crop of healthy children. She flushed now, thinking about how'd they'd made love the night of the Rayburn Creek fiasco. And in the next days afterward, Isaac had been much more attentive than usual, asking about her plans and kissing her often, no matter who was around to witness it.

Charity made her way outside with her grip and called the children to gather around her. She planted a kiss on each dear cheek and waited for Isaac to hand off Baby Ruth to Joseph. He did so and then pulled Charity to his chest. "I'll pray for thee each morning and each night," he whispered. "Look to the stars and know I am doing the same."

Charity fixed on the wrinkles at the corners of Isaac's eyes and reached a hand behind his head to pull him closer still. His kisses had improved since they'd risked the first one, Isaac skinny and clumsy. How muscular and handsome he was now.

"I show my love for thee by the things I do," Isaac reminded Charity, "and pray that, by waiting on God, thou are renewed in strength. For thou, my love, are so precious in my sight. Neither the Natives nor the soldiers care who gets in front of them, so please, Charity, be careful to stay out of their way." He bent for one last, parting kiss on the top of her head.

"There's no greater show of love, Isaac, than what thou are doing in my stead. I thank thee for it," Charity smiled weakly. She raised herself on her tiptoes and kissed his shoulder through his shirt. Then she took both his rough hands, as was their custom, and met his blue eyes, trying to memorize the look of love in his eyes.

#

The trip to Wrightsboro was to take four days. For Charity, the isolation of the journey, the miles stretching out over the long hours, gave a release to her internal tension. The ride was almost boring. The changing leaves were so familiar, the bird calls, too. Once the group of them surprised a rangale of deer, but after that, there was only the waving, wild grass lining the narrow trail, the heads of black-eyed Susans and other woodland flowers wobbling a lazy greeting. Mary rode ahead of her and the men behind so that Charity found herself lulled into the deep of her memories.

There was no denying that she had been angry over Jehu's attack on her but also of how her meeting had not believed that she'd tried to get away. As she often did when thoughts of the horrid night bubbled up, Charity tried to let go of the festering injustice of it. She reworked the awful night, imagining different ways things might have turned out—her friends deciding to spend the evening at the Wright cabin where Mama surely would have fed them something sweet, and Papa would have given them a round of his home-brewed beer; Charity not separating from the others at the lone cabin; her yelling loud, kicking hard, and finally able to successfully fight Jehu off before he'd ravished her.

"Let's route around the possibility of Natives," William O'Neall called, interrupting Charity's thinking. She jerked vigilantly from left to right with the warning, memories of Jehu lingering. Is there danger? A light breeze gently stirred the leaves, and Charity sat up straighter, stiffly moving her head about like an owl. "Have you seen something?" she called back. She listened to the sounds of the whippoor-wills, thrushes, and mockingbirds to find calm.

"William's a cautious one," Henry Milhous assured the women. "There's only the annoyance of wild turkeys, mosquitos, and horseflies, as far as I can tell." He took a wide easy swipe at a cloud of gnats.

"And bushes plump with wild berries," sang Mary, riding close to the bounty and reaching to pick a few.

Charity rubbed at her shoulders and then her backside. She flexed her fingers and bent her neck from side to side. They'd stopped several times throughout the day to eat or recover from the stiffness of hours in their saddles, but the end of the day's ride couldn't come too soon as far as Charity was concerned. They continued on their way. As the sun emerged from behind a cloud, Charity tried to let sorrow for Jehu and his parents float over her. The lad's inadequacies had driven him from Friends, his own bragging the evidence the Men's Meeting had needed to disown him, too. Charity had been forgiven and was recorded as a minister in Bush River Meeting—but Jehu? What had become of him?

When they came to a clearing, Charity decided it was time to end the day's travel. The four of them dismounted and tied their horses, then went off in different directions into the woods. When they regrouped, they pooled their resources for a supper of dried meats and bread with butter and jam, each drinking from their own canteen of weak beer or stale water. Mary cooked up some beans and potatoes and boiled water for coffee. It pleased Charity to see that, when they'd finished eating, the men washed up the frying pan, tin plates, and mugs while Charity and Mary searched out a barren and level spot to lay out their bedrolls. When Mary began to write in her journal, Charity turned from her, worn out but happy, to lay quietly, listen to the applause of crickets, and figure out how long ago it had been that Joseph Maddock and the others had left Cane Creek and founded Wrightsboro.

Less than a decade, she decided. She'd been almost thirty years old, quite settled into married life. Joseph had been a little boy of seven and the girls each a couple of years younger. Thomas was a brand new baby. Her grandfather and mother had just passed away, as had Isaac's mother, and Charity hadn't cared much about Hermon Husband and the Regulator movement. She remembered her mother had been upset about the group of them from Eno Meeting leaving for Georgia and a whole series of disownments—Friends marrying non-Quakers, some having intimate relations before marriage or engaged in adultery, others taking governmental oaths, and the Quakers in the Regulators taking up arms. *Former Quakers*, Charity heard John Pike remind her mother. *Former Quakers*. She fell asleep, flitting from one imagined conversation about taxes and bloodshed to another, and woke in the middle of the night to find that a shawl had been laid over her.

I hope it was Mary who took off my shoes, she worried as she fell back to sleep.

The next day, Charity, Mary, Henry, and William reached the Savannah River. There was a large, planked ferry to take them across the wide water, but they had to ride down an embankment to the muddy landing to reach it. As Charity made the descent, the violent swirl of Rayburn's Creek came back to her, and she pulled up short on the reins, cautiously willing herself down the slope.

Henry paid the crossing fee to the old man who ran the conveyance, and the four of them waited while a couple drove a wagonload of tobacco aboard. Once on the ferry herself, Charity attempted to talk with the woman who had climbed down beside the wagon, her husband remaining on the buckboard. The snorts and stomping of the horses, the splash of the water, and the river wind made conversation nearly impossible. She heard enough to learn that the two were siblings, the man headed for business at a tobacco warehouse and the woman excited to shop for yard goods to make a new dress.

A new dress, Charity mused. Her sisters had banded together to sew her the outfit she was wearing. She'd been touched by their thoughtfulness, thinking that either it was a show of their support for her work or that they were concerned that, if left to her own wardrobe, she'd be a drab representative of Bush River Meeting.

"God keep you," the woman called after Charity when they'd reach the far side of the Savannah. Their wagon rolled past a slough of cattails, the soft, brown clubs and sharp, green leaves forming a barrier between the river and the road.

"And thee as well," Charity waved back just as a group of Tory soldiers came surging at the Quakers like mad geese. For reasons Charity couldn't figure, the men ignored the couple in the wagon and instead circled around the Friends, preventing them from progressing forward. One of the soldiers came close to William and Henry and insisted that the men and "the nuns," as he referred to Charity and Mary, follow them to a nearby stockade.

Neither Charity nor Mary corrected him. Charity could see reason for their confusion. She and Mary were dressed entirely in black, their capes draped over them and most of the rear of their horse. Their hair was pulled up off their faces. Mary's bonnet captured her bun, and Charity's was covered by the hood of her cape, it being too windy for her wide-brimmed hat, which was tied on her saddle horn.

"Governor Wright was captured by Rebels recently, and there's been a series of seizures of Tory supply ships," the soldier announced by way of explanation as he circled around them.

"And thou think we're involved?" asked Charity incredulously. "Us being Quaker?" she added sternly.

"We can't take any chances, Madam," was the reply. "The bunch of you are strangers here."

Chapter 14

At the stockade, the Friends were ordered to dismount and led to the office of a Colonel Thomas White. Charity had, of course, never been inside the towering walls of a fort and didn't know a whit about the expected protocol. She was so nervous that, despite the cold, she could feel her blouse sticking to her back. *Spirit be with me. Spirit be with me*, she prayed as she shuffled closer to Mary.

"I'm more fetching in my parade uniform," Colonel White joked half-heartedly. He stood up from behind his desk, a short man, as barrel-shaped as a bear in the fall. His hair was slicked back, and his mustache and short beard were carefully trimmed. He wore a long scarlet coat, buttoned up high to his neck, dirty-white leggings, and high muddy boots. A knife was sheathed in a white belt at his waist. There was a three-cornered hat and an impressive sword hanging on twin pegs behind him. "You're Quakers, are you then?" he asked with a chuckle. "Not nuns."

Charity extended a hand as was the practice among Friends, but the Colonel didn't take it. "We are Friends, Quakers, out of Bush River Meeting in South Carolina," she explained, retracting her hand. She felt as if the four of them represented the entire Religious Society of Friends from Massachusetts Bay Colony to Georgia. "Our traveling certificates," she announced, handing them over.

"Sit, all of you. Please," the Colonel bid them as he took the papers from Charity. His eyes flicked from their group to a long wooden table with five chairs on each side and one at each end. He strolled over to the head of it.

Introductions made, whiskey was offered. The Quakers accepted coffee.

"Would you prefer tea, *Loyalist* tea?" snickered Hugh Rees, who had been introduced as a major. Charity tried not to stare at his discolored, bulbous nose.

"Coffee is just fine, thank you," Charity replied as evenly as possible. It's what they drank over the campfire, and she preferred it to tea.

"We Friends—we don't take sides," Mary added politely.

Most of the soldiers had seated themselves in a row, all on one side of the table. The Friends took the chairs that were across from them. As she settled herself, Charity's shoes brushed the boots of the soldier, William Few, who was leaning toward her and scrutinizing her top to waist. "Never been so close to a Quaker woman," he said, smiling oddly. The familiar sick feeling of vulnerability crept up Charity's spine like a determined long-legged spider.

"Tell us what you're doing here, all the way from South Carolina," suggested Colonel White. He looked to William and Henry for an answer.

"We're headed to Wrightsboro to find Joseph Maddock and others of our faith," Charity replied, turning to him.

"Such a coward," hissed Lieutenant Colonel Few. He took a gulp of whiskey from a private flask, then surveyed the group of them pugnaciously. "Neither Maddock nor his men will join our ranks to help keep the foes at bay." The soldier sat back, his jaw jutted out, ready for an argument.

"Angry at us, are thou? For our vow of peace?" asked Charity innocently. She looked at the hollow expressions on the faces opposite her. There was no stubble on the clean-shaven jaws. "We're not fence-sitters or cowards," she continued. "The war is difficult for us. We only ask to stay neutral."

"Does she always answer for you?" asked Major Rees, smirking. He cupped his chin in his hands, his elbows on the table, as if he had spied an odd bird. He addressed William and Henry. "Do you speak?"

Charity rubbed at her neck, slightly dipping her chin as she did so to indicate that the men were free to answer.

"Surely thou know of the law that exempts Quakers from serving," asserted William. "A fine heaped on it, as well, and a replacement to be found."

"And surely *thou* know," Major Rees replied, chewing his words, "that for more than a dozen years, every man in every county is to be drafted, no matter their faith, and sent to the frontier to fight. Either in the French and Indian War or when the backwoods farmers rise up." He took a swig of his whiskey. "But what do Quakers do when the court date has been set? Your authorities select men to come to the hearings who go on and on with Bible verses and such, taking up everyone's time, to explain why an eligible man can't attend military assemblies."

"We do," agreed William, his expression solemn. "And surely thou know that, two years ago, the law was amended to excuse us from military activities."

"Lieutenant Colonel Few frowned. "Watch us take your farms."

"And why?" Colonel White interrupted with a different logic. "I don't understand how you can't be with us in this. Why, most recently, a Quaker man named Matthew Osborne, a gunsmith, directly disobeyed the government's demand for weapons for the army by going around to his neighbors and buying back the arms he'd made and sold to them! In his defiance, he heated the barrels until they were useless. 'Taxation without representation,' humph. Why, every one of the colonies has an assembly to deal with these matters, legislatures that give people the right to make decisions about their lives,

218

including the levying of taxes." He drew in a long breath of air. "You could have a say in such matters if you'd take advantage of the courts here. But no, you adhere to your stand against war, and in doing so contribute to the fighting, arson, and theft that is going on all around this region. When it's all at your door, you'll be grateful for us then us, the troops you won't support."

Charity thought of Isaac, so steeped in his faith. She twisted her hands in her lap and then interlocked her fingers as if to pray. These hands, they could hold a gun, or they could praise God. *Thank God that Isaac only uses his gun to hunt.* Charity couldn't imagine her husband, a man who never locked the cabin door, fearing another man so deeply that he'd try to kill him. *Thank goodness, Joseph is too young to be expected to kill "that of God" in another.*

Colonel White threw back what remained of his drink and, done with them, ordered Major Rees to show them to the Maddock farm.

"The Lord keep thee, Thomas White, and all those thou serve," Charity prayed aloud as she readied to leave the room. This time, when she offered her hand, he shook it.

#

Majer had told Charity to watch for a good size gristmill as a landmark on the north fork of the river. "And, Charity," he'd added, touching her forearm, "there've been bloody clashes with the Creek Natives all around Wrightsboro. Please be watchful."

"Whoa, smell that livestock!" exclaimed Henry, arching back in his saddle. He was the first of them in line behind Major Rees.

Majer had told Charity of the pens that rimmed the town. Those who'd first come to Wrightsboro had brought a great number of cattle, sheep, goats, and pigs with them from Eno Creek. They'd planned to raise it cooperatively and sell the animals if their first plantings failed.

"Sitting targets for the Rebels, these animals," Major Rees called back over his shoulder.

Charity could hardly take in how many cattle and such there were. Thousands, she guessed as they galloped past.

After that, Major Rees and the Quakers rode by fields of corn, wheat, and tobacco, Charity taking note of the wooden ploughs, the hayforks and rakes, and the scythes and sickles that lay about. The tools were a comfort, a sign that hardworking farmers had been tending to the fields.

"We'll check the meetinghouse first," yelled Hugh Rees when they'd reached the neat town square of Wrightsboro. Charity could see that he was used to giving orders. "We'll see if anyone's around."

As it turned out, it was Joseph Maddock himself who greeted them. He was coming out the door of the large, square-logged building as they rode up. A middle-aged farmer, Joseph wore a white cotton shirt tucked into breeches that came to the top of his work boots. He didn't look at all like the young hothead Charity had imagined from the days when he'd ridden with Hermon Husband and the other Regulators.

"Hello, hello, Friends," Joseph hollered as they approached, tipped off by their plain dark garments, cut without lapels, Mary's bonnet, and the unadorned broad-brimmed hats that the others wore. "And Hugh Rees, thank thee for bringing them along," he called to the Major who was already turning his horse back toward the fort.

"We're visiting from Bush River Meeting," Charity announced, trotting her mare up to the mounting block in front of the meetinghouse.

"Might you come to our cabin?" Joseph asked, stopping them from dismounting. "It's just over there," he directed, pointing.

Rachel Maddock was out in her garden when the five of them rode up. Dressed in traditional plain dress, cap, and apron, she greeted them with the smile of a well-seasoned hostess. Once they'd dismounted, she shook hands all around as they introduced themselves and led the way inside her humble home. "You women can stay with us. Our neighbors will be pleased to accommodate you men."

Charity, her cheeks cherry red with the cold, chose a rocker under the pelt of a black bear near the fire and settled into it. The others found places, too.

Rachel Maddock was already at the brick hearth, maneuvering the metal arm over the flame to reheat a pot of delicious smelling soup.

Charity relaxed back in the chair, glad to be off her mare and ready for a real bed this night.

"A round of fruit brandy?" asked Joseph Maddock, coming into the room. He hung his hat on the antler rack by the front door and circled the ring of them to learn their names.

Charity took in the wood smoke and tobacco that radiated off the farmer and fixed on his worn hands. For a moment, she thought of her father, wondering where he was and if he was alive.

Rachel Maddock brought mugs of pattypan squash soup and sliced bread into the room. "Go ahead and fetch that brandy for the men," she directed Joseph. "We've nothing sweet," she apologized. "Supplies are hard to get these days with all what's going on—the Creek attacks are almost constant. They've caused more than one of the original families to up and move to the safety of Augusta and Savannah. And since the Boston Tea Party, it's become a political decision whether to serve tea or coffee." She finished her work as hostess and sat down in her rocker.

Charity surveyed the split-log furniture, similar to that made in Bush Creek, and inhaled the perfume of freshly baked bread while Rachel launched into a soliloquy about the difficulties she and the others had faced when they'd first come to Wrightsboro. "My Joseph here left us to the wild turkeys when we were barely settled, to make the long trip to Savannah," she was saying. "Our survival was so threatened that he'd decided to ride to Governor Wright and make a plea for assistance."

"I asked for two companies of militia and a fort to protect us," Joseph explained, shaking his head, his face lined with responsibility," but the governor refused them. "He did eventually fund what's called Quaker Road that goes the five miles to Savannah. It's made it easier to move tobacco out of this area to the trading centers."

Sighing, Rachel Maddock reached for her husband's hand. "Last year, the Rebels got so angry over the Stamp Act that they forced their way into the governor's mansion and took him prisoner for a time." She looked to Joseph to explain it.

"It's true," Joseph obliged her. "You probably suffer for it in Bush River, too?" he asked, "London assessing an unbearable burden for anyone in the colonies who has to deal with the government for contracts, deeds, bills of sale, wills, or any other legal documents—and extra for newspapers and pamphlets, too." He inhaled loudly.

Rachel rose to fetch a second round of soup and coffee for her visitors.

"Tell me," Charity asked, diverting the talk from Joseph's tirade, "how has it been for the Friends that moved from Cane Creek and Eno Meetings? For Bush River carries the concern."

"Oh, most people are happy here, I think," Joseph allowed. "They're good families, productive and cooperative." He looked into the space above her head as if he could see the men and women there.

223

"I don't think you'd recognize any of the names. We built about twenty cabins that first year so that every family had a place to call home. We were given tracts for it, a parcel assigned to each man. The whole group of us worked together to clear our fields, get crops going. The women started their gardens, preserving, and sewing. Did you see our livestock when you came into town?" He gave them a crooked grin.

"You mean the unbearable smell of dust, feces, and urine?" Henry obliged Joseph, his smile skewed as well.

"Cattle sales and horse trading kept us alive our first winter till we got our farms up and operating," Joseph said with all seriousness. "After that, in the next couple of years, we built a school and the meetinghouse."

"Joseph was the first clerk," Rachel interjected proudly.

"But we rotate the job now," said Joseph modestly, and then diverted the conversation. "I'll have to show you Thomas Ansley's place. It's called the Rock House, if anyone mentions that, built from local stone—"

"By people enslaved by an early settler," added Rachel softly.

"A Quaker?" asked Mary.

"No, no," replied Rachel quickly. "You'll see no one enslaved among Friends."

"There's those Friends on the coast who are British-born, educated, and wealthy," Joseph, explained. "They enslave people for their tobacco plantations and side with the ones who protect their property." He looked at the four visitors thoughtfully. "I've heard that the North Carolina Yearly Meeting now prohibits its members from enslaving people and that Bush River has purged its membership of anyone who's failed to free those owned. But here, slavery is a means to economic advancement. We Friends don't buy, sell, own, or use enslaved people, and we believe that our actions make our position clear on the matter. We've worked to hide and help those enslaved people that the military claims are the spoils of war."

"Are members disowned if they enlist?" asked William.

"There's a lot of pressure on us to take sides with the Loyalists, the Rebels, or the Native peoples," Joseph's eyes darted from Mary to Charity, "but as a meeting, we are firm in our opposition to all violence. Still," Joseph sighed, "some of our members have enlisted just the same, and even though we need their vitality, we've read them out for it." He let go with a long exhale. "When you visit our families, you'll find hard feelings. 'Tis not at all like thy isolation in Cane Creek or Bush River. Here there are plenty of threats to our pacifist views and our antislavery testimony. And there's a constant drip of new settlers who influence our young." Joseph shook his head. "We were once thriving, hundreds of us here. We had stores, mills, farms, the school." He shook his head a second time. "But, first it was the thieving of the Creek and the Cherokee who stayed when the majority of their people were pushed to the west. They pillage Friends for whatever they can steal."

Joseph fixed on William and Henry. "Have you heard of the battles we've had around here? A shocking series of Native attacks. Back three years, a mass of Natives went to war against soldiers and settlers, burning forts and cabins. Then, a year after that, the Coweta Creeks attacked one of the stockades west of Wrightsboro, surprising the soldiers who were repairing the gate. Three of the soldiers and twenty frontiersmen were killed immediately, five were very badly wounded. I tell you, there was outright panic after that." He rubbed at his chin. "Later that same year, a relief force of militia were ambushed by a Lower Creek party, and twenty-five families left for Augusta or Savannah."

"And the raids have continued," Rachel repeated. "Almost nonstop, despite our pacifist reputation."

"We've just sent a letter to Governor Wright," said Joseph, "to ask again for more protection and to confirm our peaceable disposition."

"Not like the days with Hermon Husband and the Regulator rebellion?" asked William solemnly.

"We were never part of that," Joseph asserted firmly. "And moved here to get a distance from it." He sucked in his lower lip. "But I have made mistakes, allowing men who aren't Friends, who don't hold to our principles of nonviolence and non-militarism, to settle in Wrightsboro."

"Now, Joseph," began Rachel. "They were coming anyway, a steady stream from the North."

"Well, yes, and it's probably more because of men of other faiths that we have that fort nearby, protecting us." Joseph rubbed at his beard.

"And are Friends here in jeopardy?" Charity asked, her eyes on Joseph.

"The control of the region," the old man lamented, "shifts from week to week like a wild weathervane. It's impossible to determine the fate of the town." He tapped on his knee with a fist. "Gossip is that I'm a prominent Loyalist and that I procure volunteers for the militia, but it's not true. I did go with a Friend to Augusta when it was occupied by the British to meet with the commanding officer. And I did publicly lament the Boston Tea Party, more because the Rebels dressed in mockery of the Mohawk and senselessly ruined all those chests of tea." Joseph turned to Charity. "Pray for us, Friend. That's all I can tell thee." His gaze circled the group of them. "Hold us in the Light. For the young as well as the old among us are questioning the elders and ministers of the Wrightsboro Meeting. Pray we are wrapped in love and survive here."

There was the pop of a hunter's rifle firing in the distance and the gentler crackling from the fire in the stove.

"Come now," said Rachel, standing. "Let's get you to your rest." While Joseph took the men to the neighbors, she guided Charity and Mary to a back room for the night.

"I have my worries over what I'm doing, Rachel," Charity confided. "What's happening here and in the colonies in general, it's beyond anything I know."

Rachel put a hand on Charity's arm. "Stay strong, Charity. Thy sect needs thee. We're a tight community here despite what Joseph says, and we are working daily to tend the Light. We depend on each other for emotional, economic, and now especially, our physical survival." She gave Charity a little hug. "Our faith, well, our patterns, go way back, now don't they? You two know that, yes?" she glanced at Mary to include her and took her hand. "God holds the truth and has sent the two of you here, coming to us in holy service at the very time when we are being tested, when everything is pulling us apart." She looked to Charity, tears in her eyes. "Heaven knows we need thee. Thy plain dress, thoughtful questions and responses, the visits thou'll be making, and the messages the Holy Spirit will give thee to share. Thou being among us will strengthen us, remind us of our testimonies, our core beliefs, and give us what we need to stay resilient." Rachel reached her arms to encircle Mary and Charity. "We need you two to remind us that, even in these troubled times, we are to uphold peace and equality."

#

A couple days later, on First Day, Charity was moved to preach in the Wrightsboro Meeting. She had been seated on the facing bench with the elders, but now she stood to deliver the given message, composed and elegant in her style. "'Tis good to be with Joseph and Rachel Maddock and those who share our faith," she began, all eyes closed and not staring at her as had the soldiers at the fort. "I have much gratitude for those of you who hold this meeting, for you are a refuge for many. Here the pure wait, praying in our silent manner, for guidance and strength in our example." Her voice began to sing with her conviction. "We, Friends, serve this troubled town, offering our peaceful, virtuous behavior as a model to all others. We do not need the military to protect us. God's will be done. We live apart from the soldiers and their waring and the rules, a self-governing community of God's people, untarnished by the world. Still, Friends, I call you to action, to find a part in assisting those who do not have freedom. Work to release them from their enslavers, and get them west. Aid them. If not now, when?"

PART 3

PART 3

Chapter 15

Thirty-six-year-old Charity, rosy-cheeked and fit, came galloping through the woods near the Cook farm, excited to see her family. But before she could dodge them, she ran right into the middle of a band of loudmouth and disrespectful Tory soldiers. As if they were the drawstrings of a powder bag, the men quickly encircled her, riding closer and closer until Charity's poor mare was unable to move in any direction.

Trust God, Trust God, Charity prayed, choking on the dust that engulfed her. She didn't look at the faces of the men as they flew past but kept her eyes averted, watching the sweaty chest of each horse, each filthy pant leg and worn leather boot of a soldier as it went by.

Not getting the response they'd expected, some of the soldiers began to poke their rifle barrels at Charity as they circled. They hit into the mare's neck instead, causing her to buck, and Charity worked to still both herself and her horse. For no other reason than that she was in God's favor, one of the men suddenly yelled to the others, and the soldiers unwound and went on as if they were birding and had spied pheasant in the meadow ahead. Shaken, Charity continued on her route, distraught and distracted. Feelings of helplessness like when Jehu had pinned her to the floor plagued her until, finally, like a homing pigeon, she rode into the Cook yard. Joseph was the first to spot her.

"Mama, Mama," the eighteen-year-old cried as he ran toward her mare. He grabbed the bridle to halt her. "They—they almost got me, Mama. I was almost lost to thee."

Charity stared at her son in confusion. She quickly slid down off her horse to face him. "What are thou saying, Joseph? Thou was *lost* to me?" She rubbed at her weary eyes and blinked.

"A group of soldiers, they came on me when I was plowing, and the captain, he, he ordered me to join them. Right then!"

"They threatened thee to go with them?" Charity didn't want to believe it, that the influence of the fighting between the Tories and the Rebels had invaded her family. She hugged Joseph to her, his wide-brimmed, floppy hat falling to the ground. Her son's inability to join a militia seemed obvious to her. He was Quaker, from a Quaker farm, a Quaker community. Joseph wore the clothes of every man in Bush River Meeting, a homespun cotton shirt and breeches and work boots that were covered in red clay. "Rebels?" asked Charity.

"I-I don't even know," Joseph stuttered. He shook his head. "Their uniforms were rags, and I guess I was too scared to notice which side they were on. These hills are crawling with both these days." He gripped Charity's shoulders and met her dark eyes. "They need men, to fill their ranks, Ma." His voice trembled. "And they were going to shoot me, Mama, if I didn't fall in line right then and there. But here I am! For just when they had me bound up for it, with my arms tight to my sides—"

"No, no," Charity gasped. She squeezed her eyes shut with the image of it. When she opened them, a young woman had come to Joseph's side. She was about young Sarah's age, her hair still worn down.

Joseph glanced over and found the girl's hand. "Yes, but then Mary, Mary Harbert here—" He gently moved the young woman forward, "Mary came upon us and saved me."

"It's such an honor to meet thee, Charity Cook," Mary Harbert offered formally. Blushing, she reached out for the handshake.

Charity took the offered hand and held on to it. "Thou *saved* him? Tell me. Tell me what happened?"

Joseph cut back in. "Mary walked right up to the leader, the captain, and spoke so boldly to him, didn't thee, Mary?" Joseph puffed out his chest and straightened to his full height, "And she said, 'Thou can't kill him, he belongs to me.'"

"And I picked him up like a bundle of cotton and started to waddle away from the men," Mary laughed.

"Thou did, did thee?" Charity put her hands to her cheeks. "Thou brave girl!" She pulled Mary to her breast.

"Yes, and Mama," Joseph went on, "the captain was not humored. I could hear the anger in his voice as he called after us. 'When you can carry him no farther,'" Joseph mimicked, his tone deep and serious, "'my men will shoot the both of you.'"

"Oh, my word!" exclaimed Charity.

"But, Mama," the boy continued, "Mary, strong farm girl that she is, mustered all her strength and carried me over a rise until we were out of their range!" He hugged Mary to his side. "And we were saved!"

There were no local authorities to receive a complaint about the soldiers who had tried to kidnap Joseph, even if Isaac and Charity had wanted to seek justice outside the structure of Friends. "Our men are to be exempt," Charity seethed as she paced before Isaac later that evening. She knew her rights, but she also knew that it was 1781, and the war and its aftermath were sweeping the central region of North Carolina like a raging grass fire.

I'm glad you are dead and gone and not around to see this, Charity thought, not only of her mother but of Abigail Pike as well. The two of them would have been as angry as she was about the war invading

Friends' lives, but they were gone, Abigail passing just recently.

"The county governments have lost control," Charity said aloud to Isaac. "No meeting has been left untouched, troops kidnapping Friends and forcing them to serve."

"The soldiers are few and hungry," offered Isaac, sitting to take his boots off. "There are all kinds of tales of them thieving from the once bountiful Quaker farms, killing livestock and hauling off anything they can carry. They go after the Negroes, too, them lured by the promise of freedom, if they survive." He patted the arm of the chair that was positioned beside his own. "Come, sit down. Let me tell thee about Big Isaac."

"What about Big Isaac?" Charity gasped, searching Isaac's face as she took the chair. She didn't think she could withstand any tragedy involving the six-foot husband of her younger sister, Susannah. "What happened?" she whispered.

"He got into it with a Tory officer," said Isaac. "But it ended well," he added quickly. "Seems the man's squad was in his corn crib, stealing. Big Isaac saw them at it and ran to stop them. One of the soldiers unsheathed his sword and stood firm for the challenge."

"But Isaac is solid in the way of Friends," Charity interrupted. "He'd not fight."

"And he did not. He gripped the soldier's weapon, saying, 'Tis as far as thou are going to go with this, no further.' And then he asked if the group of them would want to come up to the kitchen to be fed." Isaac gave Charity a wide smile.

Charity matched it. "Ah, Big Isaac," she sighed, sitting back. "And Susannah fed them, then?"

Isaac nodded. "There's been worrisome fighting though in these parts, a battle at Cane Creek."

Charity's smile faded.

"All we love was safe afterward, but Majer told me folks could hear the gunfire from their yards and, later, the cries of those who'd been hit."

"When was this?" Charity asked, stiffening as she prepared for more difficult news. She was in the early months of pregnancy and not feeling particularly well.

"Just this fall. Thou hadn't heard?"

"I've been calling on rural families south of here, preaching and helping with the making of apple cider and apple butter. I haven't kept up on the battles."

"Well," Isaac sighed, "John Pyle was in the thick of it—"

"John Pyle from Cane Creek Meeting?" Charity moaned. "John and Sarah Pyle of Baldwin's Mill?"

"The very same," said Isaac, nodding. "Although thou know they were disowned after his involvement with the Regulators, with the fighting over taxes."

"Yes, yes, but what happened in Cane Creek?"

"Well," began Isaac, "let me tell thee of the massacre near his plantation."

"The massacre?" repeated Charity weakly.

"Yes, dear heart, for it was that. Just last month. John Pyle persuaded three or four hundred men in the vicinity of his place near Hillsborough to form a militia. He needed help to defend his cotton and enslaved people from the Rebels who were gaining ground in the Carolinas, although the Loyalists had been successful in Savannah, Charleston, and Camden. John requested reinforcements from Charles Cornwallis to ensure a victory over the 'vagabonds,' as the Tories called them, and the general agreed to send Banastre Tarleton's infantry to him. Trouble was, before the reinforcements arrived, John and his men were ambushed by a Rebel cavalry.

"How was that?"

"He was apparently fooled by the Rebel uniforms, their green jackets and white doeskin pants. Same outfit as what the Tarleton's Dragoons were purported to wear. When their captain, Henry Lee, rode up to John at the front of his lines and extended his hand, John thought the officer was leading the reinforcements that Charles Cornwallis had sent. By the time he realized his mistake, it was too late. Some three hundred Tory men and about ninety horses were killed in minutes."

"Oh, Isaac," sighed Charity. "I can make no sense of all the warring—the murdering, destruction of property, mistreatment of prisoners, and vigilante justice. 'Tis all such an awful waste of humanity on all sides." She leaned back in her chair, deflated. "What's happening to us? 'Tis hell on Earth."

"I don't know, I don't know," said Isaac, conveying his mutual sadness for the grim state of affairs. "The men at the meeting say the massacre of John

Pyle's troops is a turning point in the Revolution; that the former Rhode Island Quaker, Nathanael Greene, and his army are recovering in the North and will soon be in North Carolina to put an end to any remaining Tory dreams."

"And John Pyle?"

"He was spared. Shot from his horse and badly injured by a saber cut. He was able to crawl to a nearby pond and hide in the reeds of the icy Haw River, with only his nostrils protruding until he revived. Made his way to the Tory camp." Isaac bit on his lip. "He lost three fingers and an eye."

The Cooks sat in silence for a moment. "And Cane Creek?" Charity finally asked. "What happened there?" She put her folded hands to her lips to hear of it.

"Patrick Ferguson organized Tory sympathizers from the Carolina backcountry, some Friends among them, and brought them up the Cane Creek to fight the Rebels. The battle was right near Lindley's Mill, not fifteen miles from your old cabin."

Unwillingly, Charity envisioned the soldiers splashing to their slaughter in the shallow riverbed that had given the settlement its name.

"The Rebel boys were stationed on a plateau," Isaac went on, "overlooking the river. They watched the Redcoats high-stepping their horses around the rocks in the river, and then they flew down from the cliffs to attack. The battle went on for four hours." Isaac sucked in a loud breath. "When the Tories finally retreated, they left about two hundred dead or wounded. The rest of them were forced to hide out in the woods until they could safely escape."

"'Tis a sorrow, the Friends who will be disowned. So many of them now."

"Young Joseph's friend, Gus Richardson, was read out," said Isaac. He quoted the minute from the Men's Meeting. "Declared to 'no longer be a Friend' for 'having deviated so far from the principles of truth in his own breast, as to be guilty of bearing arms in a warlike manner.'"

"How can a boy like Gus be raised by pious parents in a protected community of Friends like this one," lamented Charity, "anchored in pacifism and standing strong against slavery, no longer be a Friend?" In the silence that followed the query, Charity felt the pain of her own disownment, some twenty years earlier. "How is it possible, Isaac? Our faith is a way of life. I am not a Quaker, I am Quaker. I was born Quaker, I will die Quaker, no matter what any meeting committee decides."

"They'll be allowed to apologize," Isaac carefully reminded his wife. He began to quote from the Bible. "Thou shall be forgiven for whatever part thou play in thy sins, and thy soul shall be filled with joy and peace unspeakable."

Charity bent her head to her breast with the pain of the fighting. She tried to imagine what John Pyle could say that would permit him back into the Religious Society of Friends.

Isaac took Charity's hand and pulled her to her feet. "Thou are Quaker, dear heart. Through and through. And we are all the better for it," he assured her. He hugged her to his chest.

Charity put a hand to Isaac's cheek. "As are thou and so many that I meet in my travels who are standing strong in their love of our communities, our pledge of integrity and plainness and our aversion to all manner of fighting." She kept her brown eyes firm on Isaac's blue ones. "Here," she stepped back, "I have a printing of one of the minutes." She pulled the crumpled paper from her travel grip, and read it aloud.

"Dear Friends and Brethren. Under a humbling sense of the many calamities that now abound in our land, and the prevailing difficulties which we as a people are likely to sustain, may all be resigned to divine will and be favored with the calming influence of truth in deliberating the weighty and important decisions that are upon us. It is our solid advice and judgment that all Friends faithfully maintain our peace testimony and refuse to act or willingly comply with any regulations or demands made by men in supporting or carrying on wars or the shedding of blood." She waved the paper slowly in front of Isaac.

"Well, that's all good and fine," said Isaac, taking the record of the minute, "but there's as many who are tired of being looted, their barns and corn cribs burned. And the Baptists and Methodists are putting fierce pressure on Friends to pay the county levied taxes and fines so *all* homes are better protected."

Charity knew the sentiment. The monthly meetings in the Western Quarter had written minutes that all carried a similar sentiment: "Friends are to be exceedingly careful in the course of their conduct when militia persons come to their houses to collect taxes. We demean ourselves in all things if we pay the assessments for we are the followers of Christ, the peace testimony informing our conduct."

When Charity looked over to Isaac, he was twiddling his thumbs, his eyes on the floor.

"Are thou keeping something from me, Isaac?" Charity guessed.

"Only thinking how to tell you. We've had some word about Wrightsboro. It's sad news. Raids by bandits, including a rebel colonel named Josiah Dunn, a former Wrightsborough Quaker who had been disowned before the war for horse-stealing, murdered thirty-five people, eleven of them in their beds."

"No, oh no," Charity yelped. She threw her hands to her head.

"Soldiers on both sides had been looting there as they do around here, haggard and hungry, and shooting whoever gets in their way. They're after food, jewelry, quilts, silver. This time, Joseph Maddock's home was burnt to the ground."

"But he and Rachel survived?" Charity asked, her eyes wide.

"They did, but Tories and Rebels alike have grudges against him, him having served as a justice of the peace, a governor's deputy, the head of the land grant office in Wrightsboro, and, most recently a representative to the Colonial Assembly. He's been in the position of having to enforce regulations on men who disregard the laws, and in return, they burned his house and barn, destroying valuable records, and let his horses and cattle trample his crops. His son was burned out, too, and has been in such straits that Wrightsboro Friends provided him with a horse so he didn't have to always walk. Native attacks have never let up, killing settlers, cattle, and horses in violent raids. Like so many in Wrightsboro, the Maddocks have a mountain of debt that they can't pay, the Continental money not worth the paper it's printed on. Their land is being confiscated to defray state expenses." Isaac inhaled loudly.

"What will they do? What will all those poor Friends do?"

"Rumor is the whole community is planning to move—again."

"Oh, Isaac! I should go there." Charity put a hand to her pregnant belly, wondering if the ride would be possible.

"Oh, I don't think there's need for that," Isaac replied, disapproval in his tone. He began to fix a pipe for Charity. "Majer has reported that neighbors are helping neighbors pack up, the lot of them headed in search of peaceable homes in Indiana."

"Truly?" Charity searched Isaac's worn face. She took the offered pipe. "Thank thee for telling it all, husband, this hard news." She gave his rough fingers a little squeeze. "And thou? How have thou been? We haven't even shared news about our own lives."

"Oh, the children and I have been fine." Isaac shrugged, seemingly glad for a change in topic. He reached to cup the bowl of Charity's pipe, then light it. "We miss thee when thou travel, of course, but thy sister Margaret is often around. She is a tender aunt to our brood. Meeting women occasionally stop by with a fine dinner. Oh, and thy uncle has been looking after me." Isaac smiled mischievously. "Majer was up to Salem not long ago on business with the Moravian furniture makers there. He came back with excellent beer and brought over a keg, compliments of Joseph Jr., with a reminder that I was not to partake in excess. He brought thee a huge bowl." Isaac pointed.

"How kind," smiled Charity, rising to examine the gift. She heard of the potters in Salem, skilled tradesmen and women from Chester County, Pennsylvania. They were famous for lead-glazed earthenware cups, mugs, and tankards. She had a set of mugs made by William Dennis, an Irish Friend. Last Charity had heard, the land and home of William's son, Thomas, had been confiscated by the Rebels.

"And Majer and Anarcha? Are they well?" asked Charity, worried for their Cane Creek friends. Majer had worked for her Uncle Joseph for as long as she could remember, and Anarcha was the area midwife. She couldn't think of a time when the Negro couple hadn't been part of the Quaker community.

"There is worry for them, especially Majer," Isaac admitted. "No Negro is safe these days. The Tories are snatching them up, no matter if they're free or not, for service in the militias. And if they escape, the

Natives go after the poor souls, sometimes returning them and sometimes enslaving them themselves. Thy uncle has asked Majer to stay as close as possible to his business in Cane Creek."

"Because there are catchers of enslaved people out in the woods, ready to pounce," said Charity.

"That's mostly around the Charleston area," Isaac corrected, "but I am grateful that Majer and Anarcha are careful. Patrols of catchers all over the South are able to police wide swatches of the region. They're allowed to apprehend, punish, and return any enslaved person." He sat back, smoking.

"Majer has a pass, yes, signed by my uncle?"

"He does," agreed Isaac, nodding. "But that's hardly enough protection anymore."

"Can we not all be safe, Isaac, our lives as they were?"

Isaac gave a half-hearted smile. "'Tis in God's hands, but many seem to think the war will soon be over, Charity. The governor's been arrested for his Tory allegiance, and the Rebels are chasing the Loyalists out of the backcountry to the coast and back across the sea." He held Charity's walnut eyes. "It seems that every bird in the forest is chirping of things coming to an end, that Charles Cornwallis is going to surrender the Tory army at Yorktown."

Chapter 16

That night, in her sleep, Charity gulped for air as if she were tumbling down Rayburn's Creek and rapidly losing sight of Isaac. It was the war that caused the reoccurring nightmares, the worry for those of her faith drowning around her. Because of the fighting, the *Gazette* had stop publishing, and she hadn't seen Majer in weeks. Charity had no idea what was going on in the North or how Danise and Chelsea were faring. She prayed Philadelphia Friends were watching out for them and that they hadn't taken sides in the war. She'd witnessed the challenge of it. There wasn't a family she'd visited in the year who wasn't filled with upset as they tried to protect their crops and animals from hungry soldiers. And Friends worried continuously for men and lads who could be kidnapped for the militias.

One day soon after, Majer came riding into the yard. Charity ran to him as he dismounted, happy to see that he was safe. Their good friend came with news. The women of New Garden Meeting were requesting that Charity visit; many of their brothers, husbands, and sons were being lured by the fighting.

Isaac and Charity knew New Garden Friends well from their many visits to yearly meeting. The oldest ones had traveled with the Wright family on the caravan when they'd first come to North Carolina. And truth be told, Charity, recovered from the birth of her ninth baby, Isaac Jr., welcomed the adventure of the holy call and the purpose it afforded her. It took but a moment for Isaac to agree that she should go.

The following day, Charity prepared to set off alone on the hard day's ride to New Garden. Majer had other business that needed tending, and no man in the meeting community could be spared to accompany her. It mattered not to Charity. She knew the trail well and arrived, without incident, to the farm of William and Priscilla Coffin. They caught her up on the threat to the Friends. Charles Cornwallis, commander of the Loyalist army, had been chasing Nathanael Greene, the Rebel major general, throughout the Centre and Deep River farms. "Now troops dotted the hills and fields near New Garden like red and blue wild flowers," worried Priscilla. She looked solemnly at Charity. "Will thou come to the women's meeting tomorrow and speak to us?"

But early in the morning, before hardly anyone knew what was happening, the war came to William and Priscilla Coffin's doorstep. Charity wasn't even dressed as yet, hadn't even had her coffee and mush when there came a heavy, relentless knocking.

"Can thou come? They're fighting near the meetinghouse?" a woman was shouting on the other side of the door. "There are more wounded than we can manage . . ." her voice trailed off.

When Charity went outside and looked about, the woman was running off through the golden leaves to the next cabin, her hair in tangles down her back. "Rise up. We need you! The fighting has started near the meetinghouse."

Charity didn't wait for the Coffins. She threw on the clothes she'd draped over a nearby chair the previous night and grabbed her shawl. The sky was only beginning to brighten as she hurried toward New Garden Meeting, the songbirds twittering in the cold.

As Charity approached a wooden structure similar to the size of the Bush Creek meetinghouse, she saw both men and women crawling over wagons, unloading wounded soldiers. She passed a burly fellow who was using a wheelbarrow to carry an injured Redcoat toward the meetinghouse entrance. Barely able to squeeze through the doorway, Charity took note of the men being hauled into the building, the smell of urine, sweat, and vomit in the air, and how the benches had been pushed against the walls to make room for the casualties who were laid out on every inch of the planked floor. Charity had lived on farms all her life, was the mother of nine children, and had assisted in several childbirths, but she'd never seen so much chaos or heard so many grown men crying. For a moment, she stood like a statue in the middle of the mayhem.

A bullet pinged a nearby window glass. *There is a plan that thou cannot know*, Charity heard in her consciousness as she fell to her knees, hunching over and balancing on her fingertips. As she tried to get hold of herself, she heard William Coffin, her host, call to her. Somehow, he'd gotten to the meetinghouse before she had.

"Here, wash up this man," William ordered as Charity rose back up to standing. He handed her a cloth and a bowl of water, both already pink with blood, and pointed to a soldier who was curled into a fetal position a few feet away. Charity bent to him, a young lad no more than young Joseph's age, who uncurled his body at her touch.

"Did you hear of us, how we fared?" the shaggy-haired lad asked. He fixed on her face.

"I heard some men say that Banastre Tarleton— the British general—and his scouts came into town at sunrise," Charity offered. She began to clean the arm that was closest to her and inspect it for serious wounds.

The boy stared at her curiously. "Didn't know his first name, but the general, yes." His eyes watered as Charity worked.

Someone bumped into her backside, and Charity threw an arm across the boy to catch herself as she fell forward. "Sorry, son," she apologized, scooting in a bit. "And thy name?"

"Eli, Eli Lootkey. From near Charleston. And yours, Ma'am?"

"Charity Cook. Quaker. A Friend," she answered. The water in the bowl she'd been given was dark red now, her cloth completely stained, but she couldn't imagine a way to get to the pump for all the commotion inside and out.

"I heard tell that General Greene was Quaker," Eli swallowed hard in pain, despite Charity's tenderness, "before he joined up. They came at us Rebs from where they'd been camped with General Cornwallis at Deep River meetinghouse," the boy continued as Charity cleaned dirt embedded deep in the cuts she found in Eli's arm.

Charity stopped in her work. *Cornwallis at Deep River meetinghouse?*

"Those Redcoats have been a-chasing after us Yankee boys for about six weeks. Us part of General Greene's army. They were probably plenty happy when they found a couple of our pickets posted on either side of Salisbury Road to check all those who wanted to pass through. 'Twas a saber that got me in my neck, Ma'am."

Charity left Eli's arm to inspect his pale neck. She found a slash that didn't appear to be very deep, just bloody. She cleaned it as best she could. Then she swiveled slightly to rip cloth from her underskirt, awkwardly lifted Eli's head, and ran strips of cloth around his neck to cover the wound.

"Ow—ow, Ma'am!" Eli teared up, stiffening with determination to continue his telling. "Talk around camp was that General Greene was interested in politics from the time he was a boy; that, when he was older, he circulated petitions against taxes and in support of boycotts against Tory goods." Charity nodded. She couldn't think of anything to say about the former Quaker. "It was George Washington himself who appointed Greene general of the whole Southern Army," said Eli. He was breathing a little easier and rattled on. "I tell ya, Ma'am, General Greene was good to us men. When he found our militia, we hadn't had supplies for weeks and were starving. He immediately ordered a grand meal for us and then gave us two weeks to rest up before we set out to find Cornwallis. And now this has happened to me."

"Someday, Eli, when this is all behind us," Charity said softly, tucking a loose strand of hair behind her ear, "thou will remember this ocean of death." Her eyes climbed the wall to the ceiling, and she borrowed from George Fox's famous quote. "But thou will see above it an infinite ocean of light and love, too—a goodness and peace that is flowing over the water. Thou will recall how we talked together today, a Quaker woman and a soldier lad." The boy closed his eyes. "Thou will heal from thy scars, thou will, Eli, inside and out."

"I hope so, Ma'am," croaked Eli, his eyes still closed, "because it's all so vivid now. I see us in the muddy, unplanted field by the crossroads." He opened his eyes and stared blankly. "The General ordered us into three lines and I was in the first one with the other riflemen, with nothing but a split rail fence for cover. We'd been told not to fire but to hold our line as long as possible. Then we were to fall back to the second line. But they were coming at us with their bayonets and swords, swinging and flashing," Eli paused to swallow, "and a bunch of us, well, we took off for the woods, thick with trees. I ran from tree to tree to get to this place, a hand to my neck and my bad arm swinging useless at my side."

"Hey, I was part of that," a fellow soldier unabashedly yelled from just on the other side of Eli. "There were about six hundred Redcoats, yes? Part of a much bigger cavalry with German mercenaries in the infantry."

"Sure, I heard a Welsh accent or two," said a man whose feet almost touched Eli's head. "And us running up Salisbury Road toward the Tories before General Tarleton turned his cavalry through this here settlement, mud flying everywhere."

The three of them began to relive the battle, and Charity moved on. For the next hours, she cleaned and bandaged wounds, trying to comfort the men as she worked. Some were eager to talk to her; others ignored any attempt. After one trip outside for clean water, she turned her attention to a scruffy fellow, his gray hair matted and his cheeks glistening with the sweat of a fever. His mouth was hanging open, his breathing labored.

Charity knelt beside the older fellow and picked a lock of his hair out of the crude stitching on his forehead. "Pa? Papa?" she asked, staring at the ashen face. She hadn't seen her father since he'd enlisted. "Papa!" She bent to kiss a grimy cheek.

John Wright opened his blue eyes and mumbled something through his blood-smeared lips. Charity couldn't make it out. "Papa, 'tis Charity," she whispered, unsure he recognized her. She found his hand and tenderly rubbed the freckled skin and knuckles. Then, considering his wedding band, the only piece of jewelry that Friends wore, she began to remove it, to keep it safe for him. When she purposefully poked the ring deep into her pocket, she felt Danise's trinket of belonging there. "Thou are loved," she whispered, the sentiment Danise had always said was the significance of the charm. "Come back to us, Papa. We love thee so," she choked, her face wet with tears. "Mary, young Charity, and baby Ruthie will all be wanting a horsey ride."

"Is it thy Papa?" asked William Coffin, coming up behind Charity.

"'Tis." Charity turned to her host, his clothes bloodstained.

"Well, God be praised." William put a hand on her shoulder.

Charity straightened the blanket that covered her father. "Heal us," she began to pray as William moved on. "Each Rebel and Tory in this room and Papa who bore arms." Her father's fingers weakly made their way into her own. "I only made shoes, Charity, shoes for the soldiers," he affirmed, barely able to open his eyes. "I didn't carry a rifle. I didn't

254

kill anyone. Never." He weakly squeezed her hand. "God forgive me, I only made repairs."

#

"Papa was with General Tarleton," Charity later told William Coffin as they stood together in the shelter of the giant oak tree in the center of the meetinghouse burying ground. A sprinkle of rain was freckling the area that, only hours earlier, had been a battlefield.

"It's wonderful thee found him, Charity," William sighed, utter exhaustion written across his face. "There's God moving in that." He offered a light for her pipe. "I heard General Greene had been inside, too, relieved to be among Friends. Sustained a serious injury to his hand, but once his wound was wrapped, went right out the door and back into action. Said he wouldn't take up space that was better used by someone more injured."

"I need to sit down," Charity muttered, completely worn out. She reached a hand to the stray tangles of what had once been a bun and sank to the ground. "I've never seen anything so horrible, so many men ripped up, then dead and gone."

"I heard a man say that there were almost two thousand Tories with Cornwallis here today and about four thousand of Nathanael Greene's rebel troops," said William Coffin. He cupped a hand around the bowl of his pipe to light it in the shelter of the grand tree. "And us carrying so many of them inside and then back out again for burial." The two stared across the way at pairs of Friends rhythmically wielding their shovels to dig one of three mass burial pits. "And now them altogether in these graves, red and blue, the lowest of the ranks with the highest." He patted the trunk of the oak. "This good tree to mark the spot," he predicted, moving to rub his upper back against the broad trunk. He exhaled loudly. "Another day like today, and General Tarleton's finished. George Washington will take him in Virginia and force him to surrender." William puffed on his pipe. "Friends are taking in the soldiers, too, caring for the worst of them is going to run several weeks. I stopped back by our cabin an hour or so ago. Priscilla is there now, turning the place into a hospital ward. We've been so severely pillaged these last months, I don't know how we'll feed them all." He looked over to Charity, who stared at him soundlessly. "Ran into Frederick McClure, a pious Friend," William went on, "who said that, when he heard that his home was to be included in the sweep of the contending armies, he went into his potato hole under the floor of his cabin to worship. Stayed there all day amid the roar of cannon and fierce clash of soldiers, asking God to keep him from harm. Priscilla said that William Armfield, a member here, wasn't so prayerful. He got so incensed about his land being constantly swept clean of grain, cattle, and horses by the Tory foragers, that when he saw he had the chance, he took up his squirrel gun and joined in the battle for a day of retribution." William chuckled, trying to get a response out of Charity. "His wife just made him a lunch as usual, and when he returned home last night, she asked him why he didn't have any game. He told her there was 'nothing worth bringing home.' Ha!"

"And he was a member of the New Garden Meeting?" Charity asked dully, not at all amused by the telling.

"He was," confirmed William, "'Tis said that as many as three hundred men from a wide area around Guilford County volunteered their services to the Rebs."

Surely, not all of them Quaker, prayed Charity.

Chapter 17

Twenty years. More than twenty years! thought Charity, wishing to be in the refuge of Danise's loving arms. She'd had five children since Danise and Chelsea had left to teach at Anthony Benezet's school in Philadelphia. John Wright had gone to war and come back to the Bush River community to live with Margaret. Charity had resumed her visits, gone for weeks for visits in the Carolinas and Georgia with Mary Pearson. It'd been grueling. She'd heard a hundred disturbing stories of how the war had destroyed families and farms, and she couldn't let herself think for a moment about all the death and dismemberment she'd seen at the Battle of Guilford Courthouse.

"Thou are simply worn out," Mary told her. "Perhaps thou should go north for a visit."

Danise and Charity had been keeping close through their correspondence. They found the time to write long letters to each other, Charity's next ones sent from the Carolinas, Georgia, and Tennessee. She worried Danise sick, telling her of how she came across renegade Natives and desperate settlers on the trails. In one letter, Charity's newly acquired spectacles perched on the bridge of her nose, she wrote that she'd found her way to an almost inaccessible settlement along the creeks of Tennessee and, in the next, of her attendance at a string of yearly meetings. She'd made visits back to Cane Creek, too, spending a few days as often as possible before she was off again.

If someone had asked Danise, she would have only offered words of praise for her sister, but secretly, she thought Charity's worry over her leadings might have merit. Her listings of where she'd been didn't make for interesting reading, sounding more like a merchant's travel log than the result of a spiritual order. She took Charity to task, asking carefully in a letter if the hardships she was enduring, all the dangerous, dramatic miles in the frontier wilderness and the months away from Isaac and the children, were somehow a reaction to her childhood rape and subsequent disownment.

To Danise's surprise, Charity thought it possible. "I desire torment," she stated frankly, "for perhaps the pain of saddle sores and backache while riding for hours bring me closer to God. I have discovered through the years that physical and mental anguish humble and strengthen my bond with the Spirit and heal me from the rape and the disownment."

The situation reminded Danise of the math equations the two of them had once done with Isaac: *Is the level of suffering endured in the itinerant work equal or unequal to the feeling of being adequate in God's eyes?* When she received Charity's letter, asking if she could visit, Danise was overjoyed. She would find a way to talk to her sister about all of this.

Charity had discussed the trip with Isaac and then the women's meeting. Everyone agreed that the respite would do her good. And so, in the late fall of 1793, when it was still warm enough to make the trip without need of heavy coats and cloaks or fear of riding in freezing wind and snow flurries, Charity and her son-in-law, Zimri, rode on an offshoot of the Great Wagon Trail from Bush River to Philadelphia. Once arrived to the expansive city and with address in hand, the two asked the way until they arrived at Dinah Nevill's home. She was the Quaker abolitionist who had offered hospitality to Danise and Chelsea when they'd first come to the city, and the women still lived with her. With the excitement of a child on her birthday, Charity quickly tied her horse and rapidly took the steps to pelt the handsome door with her knocking.

It was Danise herself who opened it. "Charity, Charity, Charity," was all she could manage, the two of them both in tears as they embraced.

"And this is Zimri, Zimri Gaunt," Charity eventually managed, introducing the young man who'd been patiently waiting about halfway up the stairs. "Married to my Sarah, remember?" She was dressed as Danise expected her to be, as were the rural Quaker women of her memories, in a boxy, loose-fitting brown dress with long sleeves that hid her wrists. It was hemmed so that her stockings were only slightly visible over the tops of her scuffed, black boots. Her hair was twisted into a mockery of a bun, a sure indication that she had ridden rather than taken a coach. Handfuls of it hung to her neck.

Zimri came up the remaining steps, an awkward grin plastered on his face. "Pleased to meet thee finally, Danise." He offered his hand, "I have heard so much about thee."

"Welcome, welcome, welcome!" Danise sniffed. "Come, come inside. She wore a two-piece, patterned gown with laced sleeves only to the elbow and fancy buttons down her front. A handsome pendant hung from her neck, and when she moved her right wrist, silver bracelets gave a jangle. She led the visitors to upholstered armchairs in the drawing room. "I don't know where Chelsea has gotten to," murmured Danise as she seated herself near Charity. "She has a surprise for you."

Charity had just begun to tell of the Wright and Cook family members in the South when Dinah Nevill came into the room with a service of tea, china cups on saucers, and a plate of tiny biscuits sweetened with bits of chocolate. "Welcome to you," she addressed Charity and Zimri formally. "Happy you have arrived safely to Philadelphia." She joined them for only a few minutes before she asked Zimri if he'd like to see some of the sites. "The State House and

262

the huge bronze bell that commemorates the fiftieth anniversary of Penn's Charter?" she suggested.

Zimri had never been in the North, let alone the grand city of Philadelphia. "That would be much appreciated," he replied, as if the two of them had magically conspired to give Charity and Danise time alone. He went to change from his riding attire and reappeared not much later in matching vest and breeches, a white shirt, white stockings, and buckle-less black shoes.

"We were sorry to miss the wedding," said Danise, resuming their conversation after Zimri and Dinah left them. "Travel to the South is still worrisome for us." Free Black people in the North were able to own land, homes, and businesses. The men paid taxes and voted. In the Carolinas and Georgia, Negroes lived under the shadow of slavery, forever at the mercy of catchers no matter whether they were free.

"We understood thy situation," Charity smiled apologetically. "We missed thee, of course, but the ceremony was beautiful." She sat back and took in her sister, her best friend, for a long moment. "Ah, Danise. To be with thee again," she sighed. "A prayer answered."

"Yes, yes, praise God," Danise beamed. "You didn't have any trouble traveling, did you?"

"No, Zimri and I stayed safe, though we'd heard tellings of Shays Rebellion and thought we might run into like-minded hooligans on the trail."

"That was in Massachusetts, three hundred miles from here," Danise corrected firmly. "And the farmers, mostly former soldiers, were attacking courthouses, not travelers. The agitators were broken men who'd fought in the war and gotten little pay for it. They were upset about the foreclosures on their farms." She shook her head. "None of that here."

"'Tis the Regulator's War all over again," lamented Charity. "Men in debt to those who sold them goods on credit or barter." She spied Danise and Chelsea's story quilt displayed on a quilt rack in a far corner of the room.

"Very much the same," Danise agreed. "Taxes always on the rise and no paper money in circulation. No way to earn gold or silver. When the authorities began arresting the farmers for what they owed, they organized and fought back. But not here," Danise said again. "You're safe on the routes around Philadelphia." She nibbled at a biscuit for a moment. "Are the Gaunts from Bush River Meeting?"

"Yes, Zimri's parents and his uncle came from the North," Charity began, setting her tea down and stretching back into the comfortable chair. "They moved to New Garden, then Cane Creek, and now Little Pine Tree. That's in South Carolina, too. They're good people, solid in the way of Friends. They helped to found the Little Pine Tree Meeting." Charity raised her eyebrows. "Zimri is also a nephew to John Woolman," she added, knowing Danise would find prestige in the association with the famous minister.

Danise nodded but kept silent, content to let Charity take the lead in the conversation.

"But here's a part about his family that Zimri told me as we rode to keep me entertained," Charity went on. "It seems that during the war, a Tory soldier came upon his uncle's cabin to steal whatever he could find, ready to kill anyone who got in his way. When he burst through the door, he met up with Hannah, Zimri's aunt. She's a good-sized, strong woman and was able to wrestle the scoundrel to the floor. She held him down until her husband, hearing the commotion, ran in, grabbed a skillet, and hit the man over the head to knock him out."

"And these are Quaker people?" asked Danise, her eyes wide with surprise.

"They are," replied Charit. "Respected in their meeting for not shooting the soldier." She took another sip of tea. "Isaac and I are pleased to have Sarah married into their family." Her eyes twinkled. "Sarah's pregnant, probably missing Zimri in these first days of it."

"Oh, that's wonderful news! Another grandchild for you and Isaac."

Charity closed her eyes with the blessing. "He's a good man, that Zimri. Younger than Sarah but very much in love with her. Told me of it on our ride."

"Did you see any of those Conestoga wagons?" Danise asked to change the subject. "They're made here in Pennsylvania, you know."

"Only one," replied Charity. "It was huge. Made of hickory and white oak with iron wheels that were as high as my waist. I talked with the driver at one of our inn stops and he showed me its features—wagon ribs covered with a canvas poke bonnet and a huge tailgate that dropped down at the rear for easy loading." Charity bit into another biscuit, liking the chocolate.

"And you, Charity, how are *you*," asked Danise when it seemed Charity was finished sharing. She leaned closer to her sister.

"Well," Charity paused, considering how much of her personal life to tell. She had always trusted Danise; it should be no different now despite the time that had passed. "I've been wondering about my leading," she admitted, taking the risk to talk about it. "I've been looking forward to this chance to discuss it with thee face to face." She looked into Danise's eyes and was given an encouraging nod to continue. "I sometimes think that I've misinterpreted the purpose of my travels. Are they only impulses toward self-sacrifice and suffering? Leaving Isaac and the children and riding for hours in service. It's not a subtle matter for me, and I wonder if I've misunderstood what I have interpreted as God's plan. Am I too fixed on the expectations of my family and community?" Charity let her concerns hang in the air.

Danise stared at Charity's weather-beaten face, the deep lines about the eyes and mouth. She hadn't heard the admissions in person before and felt she couldn't avoid responding to them. "Inside you, Charity, somewhere deep and buried," she thought to say, "you can find what the Spirit is asking of you.

266

You can trust that you will." It was the faith of her childhood speaking.

Charity nodded. Like the charm they passed between them, they were soldered in their love and admiration for each other. "I know thou only wishes to give me the balm of hope," she replied. "Perhaps as I am asked to explain myself to Friends here, I will confirm that I am, indeed, called to my work, that it's not based on ego." She nibbled at a biscuit and stared at the large commissioned portraits on the papered walls of the grand room. "Divine requests are often difficult and take people in different directions," she decided, straightening a bit from the arms of the plush chair that held her. "Do we not move through many baptisms, thou and I and everyone? Tested almost daily?"

"We do," Danise agreed, "but the grace of God is more than sufficient to carry you through your weaknesses and fears, dear sister. After all, Bush River Friends issues you travel certificates, do they not? They believe you are led by God. I don't have to remind you that, if any of the ministers and elders in Bush River had questioned your calling, they wouldn't have done so."

"Yes, yes, of course," Charity acquiesced. "And the meeting arranged for Zimri to accompany me here."

Danise reached to take Charity's hand. "Will you go out into the streets to preach tomorrow? As a Southerner, you bring a unique perspective to those here."

"Yes, though I am nervous for it. This is the city and changed by the war. I pray, as always, that the words I'm given will be well-received." She bit on her lip. "Do thou find Friends here more sophisticated than we are in the South? For thou know I have little education outside of what Isaac has provided me." She turned her hands over and over in her lap. "Of late, the messages that have come to me have been to urge others forward through their difficulties, but after Charleston, I feel more strongly than ever that I am to continue to preach against the evils of slavery." She laid a hand to her heart. "We in the North and South must work together actively to end the abomination."

"We do what we can here," said Danise. "At least thirty years ago, Pennsylvania Yearly Meeting took an official stance against slavery. Chelsea and I have been involved with the many groups about the city that are working to end slavery and assist those who have managed to escape from it. Currently, we are committed to the Pennsylvania Society for Promoting the Abolition of Slavery. And we've found a church where we're completely accepted. Appreciated even. We're involved there with abolitionists."

Charity sadly shook her head. She knew that, even in the North, Negroes were not allowed membership in the Religious Society of Friends. Danise had written to her of the insult to Abigail Franks, a faithful Black attender at the Concord Monthly Meeting. Her request for membership had gone first to the quarterly meeting and then on to an appointed yearly meeting committee. If she'd been White, her membership application would only have been reviewed at the monthly meeting level, but Abigail endured a lengthy process. She was first visited by a committee of White Friends who reported back to the Concord Meeting that "her color appeared no darker than some among them who were taken for White, her character worthy of Friends." All during the months and months of the membership process, Abigail waited patiently, worshiping on a back bench. Finally, more than a year later, the yearly meeting decided that it was "the sense and judgment of the Meeting that the membership application of Abigail Franks may be safely considered on the same ground as with other applications."

"That is right order, but it is a loss that thee, Chelsea, and countless others are not recorded as members," admitted Charity. She found her sister's dark eyes. "That's the truth of it, and I apologize for our behavior."

"Well, we both know that Black stillness has always existed, despite the lack of official record-keeping. Since the seventeenth century, I expect, but if our names are in the minutes, it is usually only our first names, and it is usually to track our sufferings."

"How so?" asked Charity.

"Well, I know of one story to give as an example of the many that no doubt occurred. You know that, as far back as 1676, Quaker plantation owners in Barbados and other such islands routinely brought the people they enslaved to meeting for worship. A law was passed to stop the practice, and constables and soldiers came on First Day to see who was in attendance. When a man called Toney was discovered, he was arrested, abused, and put in irons. The White people weren't arrested or even fined."

The two women sat for a moment, mulling over the injustice of it. "Tell me of thy church, how it differs from our meetings," Charity finally asked. "Thou knows I can't go to see for myself while I'm in the city. Friends are opposed to both pastoral worship and paid ministry."

"We go to Christ Church," said Danise. "It's a magnificent building in the oldest part of the city, founded in 1695, just thirty years or so after George Fox and the Valiant Sixty began preaching in Great Britain. 'Tis what George Fox called a steeplehouse with a spire that towers to the sky. We are met at the massive doors by two very proper ushers and are escorted down the center aisle of the sanctuary to a well-crafted oak pew with a backrest. And there are often flowers at the front of the sanctuary." Danise waved a hand. "We can sit anywhere, Charity. It's not segregated."

Not like Friends meetings, Charity thought, neither of them saying so aloud. "A part of the Church of England?"

"An Anglian church, yes." She gave a smile. "George Washington and his Martha are there if they're not at their home in Mount Vernon, Virginia. He's just retired as commander-in-chief of the Continental Army."

"Really?" Charity couldn't help but be impressed.

"We use *The Book of Common Prayer*, copies supplied in a wooden pocket on the back of each pew," Danise went on. "It lists out what we are to say in response to the parts that the pastor recites. George Fox would find fault with him as well. He wears all white robes with a narrow stole of violet about his neck. Not at all plain. And he always makes a lengthy plea for offerings."

"Is there any spontaneity of the Spirit?" asked Charity, feeling judgmental.

"Not so much," Danise replied with honesty. "There is a chosen Bible passage that a deacon reads. Several hymns are sung. I sometimes feel God moving in the music. A woman plays a huge organ so loudly that the notes vibrate in my chest."

"And do thou stay and talk together after, as we do?"

"Oh yes," sighed Danise.

In her mind's eye, Charity saw herself at the rise of the service, following Danise's family to a large room for refreshments. She was leaning against a wall, watching Danise flit about the room to visit with the other parishioners, the ribbons on her bonnet dancing as she laughed and gestured with a confidence that she'd not seen of Danise in the Cane Creek or Bush River meetings. "Is there someone special, someone thou met at church?" Charity asked.

Danise allowed a soft giggle. "There is. Someone of such wit and kindness and always dressed so crisp and clean. Proud that I write for the newspaper. Says my articles are engaging."

"Oh?" Charity was surprised to hear it. "Of what do thou write?" she asked, not wanting to pry into any more than what Danise was willing to share.

"Of late I have challenged the notion that our race is intellectually inferior, that Africans might be returned to Liberia, and that there should be an all-Black church where we'd be given more opportunities for leadership." She went to fetch another round of tea and returned with another plate of biscuits. "And Charleston?" she urged.

"Oh, yes, Charleston," Charity frowned, conjuring up her memories of the place. "There was building after building nestled one up against the other on the main street, and all sorts and sizes of carts and wagons rolled past Mary Pearson and me. Oh, sister, it's a woeful city, so much horror there. 'Tis nothing like in Cane Creek or Bush River or even Wrightsboro, for that matter, where there are few Negroes. In Charleston. Oh Danise."

"Tell me," Danise demanded, stone-faced. "I'm sheltered from it here and only hear the horrid stories or read about them in the paper."

"Mary and I headed for the auction house, thinking we needed to witness it, to see for ourselves. We went in the direction we were told to go, walking the planked sidewalk of a busy cobblestone street. Women passed us who had rouge on their cheeks and lips, and the men thought nothing of making loud remarks about our plain dress or my hat. We got tangled in a great thicket of bodies—people in front of us, behind us—jostling us until we simply held hands and stumbled along in the flow. There were people singing for coins on the corners, and children selling peanuts or outright begging. And there were so many, so many Negro people. More than I've ever seen, every one of them in rags, never walking alone but always with an enslaver, herding them with big sticks or thick whips like they were livestock."

"We made our way until we came 'round a corner, and there it was, a string of people standing like statues up on blocks, the men dressed in clean white tops and pants, the women in white cotton shifts. Their skin had been oiled to make them appear as healthy as possible. White men in the front row gawked at the lot of them as if they were prized hogs; and the enslaved people moved only when instructed to turn from one side to the other at the word of the dealer. We watched as he pulled down the lips of an elderly man to show an interested buyer that he had all his teeth." Charity wiped her mouth. "Then the bidding started. Family members were split up, the highest prices going for the strongest and healthiest."

"And the Black people themselves?" asked Danise.

"Dutifully standing there, expressions of hopelessness, despair, anguish, and sometimes, indifference on their faces. It seemed their hopes and hearts were crushed, one woman collapsing when she was separated from her children, and another moaning when she was sold but not with her husband beside her. When she was forced off the block, she moved as if she were sleepwalking. Her new owner put a rope around her neck and led her off as if she were a cow."

"After a time, a short time, I confess, Mary put her hand in mine, a signal that we'd seen enough. We left for the meetinghouse, unable to say a word to each other about what we'd seen." Charity rubbed at her temples. "It was truly a nightmare, Danise. I'm grateful thou has never seen the likes of it."

"We're looking to the Constitutional Convention to rectify the plight of the enslaved," responded Danise quietly, "so that the importing and exporting of Africans is stopped once and for all."

"At the national level and not to be decided by each state?" asked Charity incredulously.

"Yes, a congressional restraint on trans-Atlantic slave trade, one that will be implemented in the South as well as the North," Danise emphasized. "The commerce is inconsistent with the reason for the Revolutionary War."

"They'll stop the ships that go back and forth to Africa for their 'cargo'?" Charity's mouth twisted with her disdain for the word.

"Ten states have already signed the restraint," Danise assured her.

"But," Charity argued, "when I was at Western Quarter in Deep River, the talk was that the Convention delegates from South Carolina would refuse to sign any document without a clause upholding the slave trade."

"Hasn't South Carolina's own legislative assembly voluntarily banned the importing?" asked Danise, perplexed.

"That might be so," Charity conceded. "I've been gone from Majer a good long while and haven't been privy to his good accounts of the outside world." She drew a breath. "But those at the Western Quarter Meeting seemed very sure that the Southern plantation owners will hold fast to their claim that it's their constitutional right to import Africans." She ran a finger around the rim of Dinah Nevill's little china cup, letting the painted flowers distract her. "Friends are gradualists. A number of them have freed their enslaved workers, but others resist it for their 'investments.'"

"Then you and I must pledge to continue our work. Certainly it is what God intends for us, unity as sisters in the name of equality," Danise asserted firmly.

"If God wills it, I will preach it," Charity agreed, her face set firm in the pledge, "but I carry little influence outside of Quaker circles. In general society, I'm treasured as a leader only as far as women ministers are valued. Which is to say, ignored—seen as out of place and inferior."

Danise jerked her head suddenly, "I have a couple of people I want you to meet, one who represents that issue well. I'll invite them here before you are to go on to yearly meeting."

Just then, Chelsea came into the room. Her appearance shocked Charity, although she tried to hide her reaction. Chelsea had grown up. No longer their little sister or a country farm girl. Her black hair was beaded to her shoulders and she wore a colorful silk blouse that showed her forearms and wrists. Her bodice was laced over a prominent white stomacher, and her ankle-length split skirt revealed a lace petticoat.

Charity rose quickly to give Chelsea a warm hug. "And who's this?" Charity asked, reaching her arms to the cherub in Chelsea's arms. The little boy allowed Charity to take him into her arms for a cuddle, reminding her of her own Keturah. She'd been about the same size when she'd last seen her.

"My baby," Chelsea explained. *"C-L-E-A-V-E-N W-R-I-G-H-T,"* she spelled manually and then gave his name sign, *"CW"* on her heart for "Cleaven Wright."

To Charity, the name sounded like Klee Vee. *"Marry?"* she asked, her face glowing with the unexpected gift of a nephew. Last she knew, Chelsea was employed by Anthony Benezet, teaching signs to students who, for one reason or another, couldn't speak. There were no formal schools for Deaf students in Philadelphia or anywhere else in the newly formed nation. Anthony had recognized and appreciated Chelsea's wit and natural teaching ability. He'd offered her a teaching job almost as soon as she and Danise had arrived.

"No," Chelsea wagged her head. *"No marry."* She paired the signs with the spoken words, the combination allowing Charity, who was rusty in the manual language and not used to hearing her once mute sister speak, to understand her.

Chelsea, with her innate optimism, began to explain. She hadn't written about Cleaven because she wanted to explain her situation to Charity in person, not in her "poor writing." She'd asked Danise to keep her secret, the situation complicated. She'd met the baby's father, Ammon, who was Deaf as well, among those in the Philadelphian Deaf community. He had suffered horrible cruelties as a boy, neither fed nor clothed adequately. Brutally beaten, he'd lost his hearing. As a young man, he'd been forced to marry and then painfully separated from his wife, not allowed to say goodbye to her, and marched to a new owner. He'd had to work long hours, been kept in chains at night, and fed only enough mush to keep him alive. His life had been spared because a White witness had come by one day and caught the owner severely whipping him. The man immediately offered to buy his freedom, no matter the cost.

Ammon and Chelsea had met in church. They weren't married because Ammon didn't know the whereabouts of his wife or if she were still alive. He worked as a day laborer in the city, the two of them living in a brownstone not far from the Nevill home. *"Later, meet Ammon,"* Chelsea assured Charity. She tapped the handshape of the manual letter "A" twice on her heart.

"Later, meet Ammon," Charity agreed, copying the sign name Chelsea had used.

#

A few days later, Danise fulfilled her desire to have Charity meet a couple of her friends. She invited a young adult, a former Friend, whom she referred to as "the Public Universal Friend," and Rebecca Jones, a noted Philadelphian Quaker minister for afternoon tea. "So glad you could come and meet my sister," Danise welcomed the two of them.

The four settled into chairs in the Nevill parlor; Zimri was off exploring the city. Danise asked Rebecca to tell some about herself.

"Well," the famed preacher started, "it was Catherine Peyton who visited when I was at an impressionable age. She influenced my mother to permit me to attend meeting."

"She was a friend of my mama, Rachel Wright, as well," interjected Charity, pleased to hear again of Catherine Peyton's influence.

"Rebecca was recorded as an esteemed minister at Philadelphia Monthly Meeting only two years after she became a member," interjected Danise. "She was hardly twenty years old!"

"Yes," Rebecca agreed modestly. "But before that, I was known as 'wild Becky' and was often reprimanded for sitting with 'Black Rose' on the back benches." She stifled a giggle. "I preach now, yes, but I also work at my mother's school as well." She paused, pursing her lips. "Few know these plans, but I'm feeling led to go 'on an errand,' as Friends say, to England."

"Oh?" asked Charity. "England?" It was so far, the voyage a dangerous undertaking.

"Many American Friends are making the trip," replied Rebecca casually. "I am grateful I am led to go, to worship in the land where our faith began."

Charity turned to the Universal Friend, "And thee? Will thou share thy story?" Charity was curious as to why Danise had wanted her to meet the visitor, dressed in a plain but rose-colored, feminine blouse and white shawl, not unlike what a Friend would wear. This was coupled with the breeches, stockings, and boots of a man. *A woman in men's clothing?* she wondered. *Or a man dressed as a woman?*

The Universal Friend smiled as Charity reached self-consciously to a cheek and then down past the high neckline of a homespun dress to the folds that the heavy skirts created.

The expression was one of friendly mockery. "We are free to choose our garments, are we not? No matter whether we are male or female, no? But should it matter? For 'there is neither male nor female in Christ,' and when I preach, and even as I wander about, I insist I'm not to be categorized by either gender."

"Being female has its disadvantages," said Charity. "In my experience, women ministers are a shock to most people outside of our sect, as is my preference to ride horseback and not be driven in a wagon."

"And thou enjoy causing the confusion?" The Universal Friend chuckled. "I was raised Quaker and believe the teachings are echoed in the messages I give now, but I was disowned, them judging me prideful. I founded the Society of Universal Friends, preaching on Sixth Day so as not to interfere with Friends meetings. I hope thou will come and hear me."

"Thou knows well I can't do that, not as a recorded Friends minister," said Charity softly. "Is thy message given by the Spirit?"

"'Tis truth," the Universal Friend replied. Then, as if to avoid trouble, "Tell us about thyself. Thou are from North Carolina, yes."

"Yes," Charity nodded and gave a truncated version of her life to date.

"I'll come Saturday to your service," Danise told the Universal Friend as the group said their goodbyes, "and tell Charity all about it."

She had attended the services many times in the past, joining a respectable audience gathered on a large swath of public lawn. This time, she hurried home to report to her sister. "I find no argument with the predominant message of the sermon," Danise informed Charity. "That anyone, regardless of gender or having no specific gender, can gain access to God's Light. And at the rise of the gathering, I mingled with those around me, all of them welcoming and glad to see me. Many of them were raised Quaker and enjoy hearing of my being raised in a Quaker community in the South."

The weeks of visiting Danise and Chelsea's family worked their magic. Charity was ready to return to her family and rural work, to leave the noisy, smelly metropolis. As she said her goodbyes, Cleaven, who was tucked in his mother's arms, gave a series of waves with his fat little hand. "Bye, bye, Mama," he grinned, signing to her as she prepared to ride off. Charity assumed he thought the tapping gesture at his chin for "mama" meant "anyone who loves me," but the sign cut into her heart. She was glad to be returning to her own children and Isaac.

"May God keep thee, sweet thing," she called, her eyes filling with tears. She had no idea when she might see them all again

Chapter 18

"Thou should see the benches in the Cane Creek meetinghouse," Charity wrote to Danise in her next letter, "with the deep gashes where hundreds of sheep and almost as many of their cattle were butchered by Tory knives and axes. After the slaughter, the soldiers used all of the fencing they could pull up for firewood to cook the poor creatures. And Simon Dixon is dead."

Charity had sat a long while with her old neighbor, the crumbled Elizabeth Dixon. "My Simon was fifty-three years old when the war met up with him," the elder told her. "When the Tories came to our door, General Cornwallis among them, he took to the thick woods so as not to be kidnapped for service, and I—I was forced out of our cabin at gunpoint and made to stay outside and worry for him." The woman's hands trembled with the memory of it.

Elizabeth had tried to tell the soldiers that she didn't know where Simon was, but with their repeated badgering, she shut down completely, refusing to answer their questions. Instead, she made a distractive ruckus over her clay pipe, left inside her home, hoping the distraction would aid Simon in some way. She'd argued so loudly with the burly soldier who blocked the cabin door that Charles Cornwallis himself finally came stomping outside to hear her complaint. He'd allowed her inside to fetch her pipe and tobacco pouch, after which she couldn't think of anything that would help Simon. She sat on her garden bench looking like a country bumpkin, the soldiers ignoring her, in prayer for Simon's safety.

"But Simon, my poor Simon," Elizabeth lamented. "It turns out he jammed the gristmill wheel so it was inoperable and dumped all the flour in the river before the soldiers found him. They broke the millstones he'd brought all those years ago from Pennsylvania, and then they tied him up to torture him, deciding that he had hidden a great stash of profits from the mill store. When he denied it, they put iron tongs over the fire until they were glowing red and pressed them to his . . . down there." She pointed.

Charity had tried and failed to squeeze the image of the torture out of her mind. For days after she knew of Simon's fate, she suffered horrible nightmares, seeing her old friend's distorted mouth stuffed with a rag, his testicles scorched, and his body twisting in agony.

"Simon died a week later," Charity wrote Danise. "Typhus. Got it from the soldiers." She wrote in detail of the torture as well and sent it to quarterly meeting, wanting the suffering to be recorded as had been the practice of Friends for a hundred and fifty years. "Our beloved Simon died while sitting in this same chair that Charles Cornwallis used when he'd made the Dixon cabin his office. In his last days, Simon refused any liquid, it paining him to pee, and he became extremely dehydrated. He's at rest now in the Cane Creek burying ground."

When Charity visited Zachariah Dicks, the noted itinerant minister seemed overly philosophical about Simon Dixon's torture and death. Charity let him be, his own farm repeatedly robbed by the Tories during the war. Zachariah had been a friend of her parents, after all, one of the original Quaker settlers to North Carolina. He had moved on to New Garden but later married and returned to Cane Creek, his farm a mile west of Lindley's Mill and two miles west of Spring Friends meetinghouse.

"I prophesied it would happen," Zachariah unabashedly told Charity. "That there'd be a war to prune away the Society's dead wood." He pridefully pushed his chest out.

"Simon Dixon was a brave and beloved man," Charity firmly told the esteemed preacher. "An adventurer, a visionary, and something of a hero to many of us who came with him on the caravan. Are thou implying that he was overwise?"

Zachariah closed his eyes for a moment before responding. "I am sorry for it," he said solemnly, "but I did tell Friends, I did. I foretold them that there'd be mayhem in their meetinghouses. And what's happened these last years? Why, consider New Garden! So much blood gushed there that it seeped into the floor planks, and no matter how much soap and sand has been used to scrub those boards, do the stains of my prophesy not still remain?"

Charity found no reason to debate the man. She'd been there on that terrible day. She'd seen the blood on the boards as the Reb and Tory soldiers suffered.

"And now I prophesize that the enslaved people will explode in revolt in the islands south of these colonies," Zachariah declared. "They'll set fire to the world's most profitable stretch of sugar plantations." He raised his arms up and shook them dramatically. "They'll slaughter their enslavers, thousands of White people dying. I warn thee, Charity, the Negroes here will hear of it and rise up, too. We Friends must leave, leave these communities, sell our farms, no matter their true value, and take our families west."

Charity couldn't imagine it. How could she and Isaac ever leave Bush River? Her mother's grave? *And me, will my ministry against slavery and for equality never matter? Will we not release those we hold to freedom before this colonial revolutionary war occurs?* Charity thought it best not to probe Zachariah. She sat silent in her faith that the Spirit had an unknown plan and would keep Friends safe.

Zachariah seemed to care that Charity didn't heed his warning. He went on the attack. "And thou, Charity Cook, traveling all around, going north to preach, and wearing the white beaver hat?"

Charity's face colored. The man irritated her for his prideful manner and for how the comment reinforced her insecurities. No, she'd hadn't seen Quaker women in Philadelphia dressed plain as she did, walking as if they'd been on a horse day after day, or smoking as was the habit of the Southern backcountry women. And it was true that, more often, she wore a black bonnet to shield her face from the sun and wind, and only occasionally wore the wide-brimmed hat of a man. Still, Charity didn't say so. She found comfort in her homespun garments, a security as solid as wearing something that had belonged to her mother. And her distinguished beaver hat was a present from Isaac on their wedding day. She was known to sometimes wear it. No, no. Charity's style of clothing symbolized her commitment to living a Christian life, that she had risen above the ribbons, laces, and other temptations of the world, and was, as the Public Universal Friend had preached, living as herself, as a unique child of God.

"Are our colors to be pleasing to the eye, our quiet customs questioned?" Charity asked the preacher, her palms open at her sides. "Would thou rather that Friends, who are teased for being 'separate and peculiar people,' embrace the new ways? To take a seat in one of the enormous tents that are erected for the Second Great Awakening," she pushed, "that my sister in Philadelphia writes is crashing like a wave through the Northern cities. All manner of people attending the nightly revival meetings?"

"Ah, yes, the Second Great Awakening," mused Zachariah, dodging her question. "Did thou know that George Whitefield, the great orator, the originator of the First Great Awakening, was an enslaver?"

It pleased Charity that the comment gave indication that Zachariah was apprised of her holy messages. "I wonder if my Negro sister, Danise, knows that?" Charity allowed. "She lives in Philadelphia with our sister, Chelsea, and her family, and writes that, with this second wave, Friends like Elias Hicks and Anthony Benezet are kept busy defending the cherished testimonies of our Society."

"I've heard that the women at those revivals outnumber the men," mused Zachariah. "Shouting with the best of them." He laughed unkindly. "Women screaming out, summoning the Holy Spirit with their tambourines and fervent singing."

"We have lost many to it," admitted Charity, dismissing the preacher's disparaging remarks against women. For a moment, she considered that those at the revivals were being afforded the opportunity to unleash their anger for having fewer societal rights than their eldest sons. "For that's the real crime," she said aloud. "So many lost to us who might have been Quaker." She was thinking more of Negroes than of Protestants. "I suppose you've heard that Philadelphia Yearly Meeting has made it their practice that neither nation nor color will prevent membership," she asked, changing the subject.

"And about time," agreed Zachariah.

"Yes, but it saddens me that the good hearts and intelligence of most of our Negro attenders have been lost to our faith. Danise and Chelsea have joined a church founded by two men who were formerly enslaved. One of them was the property of a Quaker lawyer. Do you know a Benjamin Chew?"

"I don't," allowed Zachariah. "But I'm glad thy sisters are free and that they have found a spiritual home."

"Danise says that every Black person in Philadelphia was pushed to because of an incident at St. George's Methodist Church. Apparently, a man named Absalom Jones thought he was a member of the congregation, going faithfully each First Day. One day, out of the blue, it was announced to the Negroes that they were no longer to sit in the pews among the White parishioners but were to instead stand along the back wall. Danise wrote that when Absalom Jones saw two of his Black brothers being pulled from the pews where they knelt and manhandled out of the sanctuary, he abruptly left to join them. He eventually founded the African Methodist Episcopal Church. Danise and Chelsea are members there."

"The Negroes need a way to survive in that divided city, their own churches and meetings being the way of it," nodded Zachariah. "They have to put up daily with the indignities of White people."

The truth of Zachariah's comment quieted Charity, and her heart softened for the man. "God hears the sincere, no matter what their denomination," she replied.

#

In some ways, Charity's mother's death prepared her for the loss of her father. John Wright died in Ninth Month 1789, having slowly declined since the war had ended. As he lost interest in life, Charity had time to get used to the idea of his dying. Still, she and her thirteen siblings were now orphaned. She put her mind on the memorial, the hosting of it in Bush River, when her siblings would be in attendance. Charity planned to share her plans for wider travel.

As it turned out, she didn't find an occasion to mention to anyone the possibility of her working in the North or maybe even in Europe. Charity was kept busy seeing that her kin were fed and comfortable, some of whom had traveled a considerable distance out of respect for the family. She found everyone talking about their own busy lives, their own joys and sorrows—their own hopes and dreams. When the time came for John Wright's coffin to be lowered in the grave that his seven sons had dug, Charity took stock of them. William was now fifty-one years old and a grandfather many times over. Her youngest sibling, Isaac Joel, was twenty-five and living with his family in Tennessee. Danise and Charity had not made the long trip, but they sent cards that William read aloud, singing the praises for the only father they'd ever known. Charity's own eleven offspring, the three oldest in their twenties and the youngest, Keturah, a noisy three-year-old, huddled around their parents, missing their grandfather. They'd lived on his property their whole lives.

Testimonies of John's abiding love for Rachel were given, the two of them meeting overseers when they were in their twenties, and then walking from Virginia to North Carolina together with their young family. John was applauded for being a quiet, founding member of the Cane Creek Meeting, steady in his support of Rachel's work, and for sitting on the back seat at the Bush River meeting out of love for his adopted Negro daughters. Whatever breaches in John Wright's faith had occurred during the war, for whatever mistakes he had made, he was remembered for the good father and farmer he'd been, the one who had kept the huge lot of them fed and feeling loved when his wife had been galloping through the wilderness with Abigail Pike to organize women's meetings.

Later, as Charity watched her slender young nieces running in the yard with their long hair dancing behind them, she was reminded of her younger self, of how she and Danise had once run so carefree to the stand of oaks to tell each other their secrets. It was the time before—before the great pain and sorrow of the rape and disownment and the feelings of shame and unworthiness that had stolen what had remained of her childhood. George Fox had said that

Friends were to live in the cross, in the power of God, for that was where injustice was destroyed. *Then and now,* Charity thought, *God has the power to wash my heart. God can, as the Bible says, assist me to "bear and bring forth the living seed, and wait in that seed, for the Lord's season."*

Sitting in silence during one of the meetings for worship during the week of mourning, it came to Charity that, as a well-known recorded minister, no one would think that her desire to expand her ministry was unusual or inappropriate. Most itinerant Friends widened their visiting circle as their experience grew. What was important was that God asked it of her. *Was this the season?* she wondered. Was God showering mercy and blessings on her at this tender time, shining Light into her bones and heart, and offering her a transformation? *Fall to winter, winter to spring,* she thought. Might she make a significant change? Could she acknowledge that of God in Jehu, forgive him, forgive the Cane Creek Meeting, and move on with her life?

Set it all free, Charity heard internally; *in this very burying ground, set it all free.* And there was more. She was to pray for Jehu Stuart, pray daily for him as she did for her family and friends, pray that he was held in God's loving arms and remorseful for what he'd done.

#

For a couple of years after John Wright's burial, Charity stayed home. She took up her household responsibilities, adjusted to less adventurous days, and showed her appreciation for Isaac in the ways that occurred to her. She asked about the crops he was planting and how they were faring, and if he missed any part of taking care of the children who were still at home—Marion, thirteen, young Isaac, eleven, Susannah, nine, and Keturah, five. That brought a chuckle! Together, the two did the evening chores, Isaac telling Charity stories about the silly things the kids had done and said while she'd been away.

Often, Charity joined Isaac for the evening lessons with Marion, young Isaac, and Susannah, reading from his copy of Robert Barclay's *Apology* and leading them in a simplified discussion of the theological principles of their faith. Charity usually took a turn reading to all of them, Keturah too, from books she had been given as gifts on her travels. It was Susannah who was most interested in hearing from the autobiography of Jane Hoskins, a public Quaker preacher, and the journal of the abolitionist, John Woolman. Young Isaac was interested in a book written by Sophia Hume, Mary Fisher's granddaughter, who'd been born in Charleston and raised in the Anglican faith of her father. He was especially fond of Sophia's descriptions of her conversion to Quakerism in her midlife and of her famous seventeenth-century grandmother. The boy thought that, someday, he might like to be an author, too.

"What will thou write about?" Charity had asked him.

"About thee, Mama, about how thy parents caused us to come to Bush River, about thy travels and our lives here."

#

On her fifty-first birthday in 1793, Charity received an unexpected gift—the birth of a child that Thomas, now twenty-three, had fathered with Kesiah Henderson. Charity had seen the young woman was pregnant in meeting, but she didn't realize it was her grandchild until the night that Anarcha, the midwife, delivered the child and Thomas came to tell his parents. He was bursting with the marvel of it and assured them that he and Kesiah planned to marry. They had named the baby after her on Charity's otherwise uncelebrated day.

"'Tis said that Keziah's parents are unsure about having our Thomas, a landless farm boy, marry their daughter," Isaac confided in Charity as they got ready for bed. They knew the family, of course. The Hendersons and their relatives were upstanding members of Quaker communities in both North and South Carolina, some of them among the earliest members of Cane Creek Meeting.

"'Tis not a situation that pleases me," said Charity. "I pray Thomas and Kesiah go as soon as possible to their respective men's and women's meetings and apologize for the 'early birth.' It would break my heart to have them read out of meeting and not remain in the fold of Friends."

"I'll talk with Thomas tomorrow," Isaac promised.

As she slid into bed, Charity wondered how things would've turned out if her parents had insisted Jehu marry her. It wasn't their way, so it didn't surprise her that the possibility had never been discussed with her. Still, there hadn't been a clearness committee formed to talk with her about what had happened or any visits by meeting overseers or members of the women's meeting. Instead, Charity had been left alone to deal with the nightmare of the rape. She found Isaac's hand and listened to his soft snores. Then she let herself relive what Jehu had done.

Charity had grown up with farm animals in heat and overheard the joking of her older male cousins, but she hadn't been prepared for the pain, the bleeding, the smell of Jehu's ravishing. For days after his attack, spots of blood appeared in her pantaloons, and her vagina burned as if an auger had been drilled into it. Thank goodness she'd had Danise, difficult as it'd been to talk even with her.

Charity turned away from Isaac and shifted to the edge of the bed. She brought her hands to her lips. *Thank thee God, thank Thee for Danise*, she prayed as she thought back to the whispered exchanges of the time after, when she struggled with the words to tell her sister of her embarrassment. *Oh, God, how grateful that thou gave me the gift of that woman.*

As it turned out, the Thomas Cook and Kesiah Henderson wedding was cause for more discomfort. Isaac and Charity's daughter, Rachel, was in attendance, no lack of darts on her waistless dress able to hide the fact that she and her beloved Thomas Lewis, were also going to have an early child. "You know our marriage is already set for Second Month," Rachel, now twenty-five, quietly assured her parents, "and our clearness committee is aware of our circumstance. It's that we asked them to let us tell our parents before they brought the matter to the business meetings."

"And, and," Thomas Lewis stuttered, avoiding eye contact with Isaac, "we consider our engagements a sacred agreement. We have pledged to the clearness committee members that we'll halt our love-making until we're wed."

After the couple had departed, Isaac took Charity's hands in both of his. He found her wounded brown eyes with his twinkling blue ones. "'Tis good to know that the Cook women are fertile," he whispered.

Chapter 19

I will season my travel to London Yearly Meeting, Charity decided. *See if that is truly what God intends for me and not my own ego in wanting to go.* She was concentrating on traveling in the South, serving as a representative to the Western Quarter and to the annual sessions of Friends in North and South Carolina, Georgia, and Tennessee. She'd shoved her dreams of traveling to Europe far back in her thoughts, writing to Danise that, in her duties, she'd been gone on a trip that took her from Bush River for five months. She had ridden over four hundred miles of inhospitable roads and slept in open fields rather than in a household made comfortable by slavery. She was worried about the influence of the influx of Baptist and Protestant settlers who were rapidly migrating near Quaker communities, so close that too many of the younger members were being disowned for drinking to excess, playing cards, singing, and marrying someone of a different faith.

Danise wrote back that the trial of the travel Charity did "would challenge any man. Take care of yourself. Keep your center."

Danise's counsel seemed to open a vein. "The spiritual state of those I visit truly rests heavy on my heart," Charity began in a letter that took weeks to reach Danise via pony express. "Still, the poor women I meet bear me up in my low times. I trust that what I endure to serve them is in the name of holy obedience to my calling."

What low times? Danise wondered as she rested a hand on a glass inkwell and thought about how to phrase what she wanted to write to encourage Charity. She maintained a self-confidence, an internal compass of satisfaction and certainty that Charity seemed to lack. "I always thought that those in the meetings you visit provide a satisfying distinction and fuss," Danise decided to write. "Is that no longer satisfactory? And, Charity, there is not a doubt in my mind that your holy errands are done for the most sacred of reasons."

"Oh, Danise," Charity wrote, "it's been my lot of late to fall into deep discouragement for the work I am called to do. I try not to despair but to believe in the Spirit's mercy, accepting the guidance that sustains my life. It seems that a leading, my leading, any leading, is like the Virginia creeper, yes? How it wraps so tightly around those who sustain it that they can be suffocated. My desire for God's love is choking me."

It didn't help matters that Mary Pearson, Charity's companion over the years, had been so sickly for the last several months that she hadn't been able to attend the Bush River Meeting for worship, let alone accompany Charity on her wider visits. "I am in hopes she will yet be spared to us," Charity wrote Danise, "for if she were to be removed, I couldn't replace what she's been to me in my travels—a true friend who has shared the highs and the lows of my given life. When Mary is at my side, joys multiplied and grieving diminished. Now in my travels, I have only the letters from you, Isaac, and the older children to sustain me."

It was true, the letters anchored Charity. She read and reread what was sent to her until the folds of the paper were stained brown and sometimes ripped in the fragile places where the paper had been originally laid on the drying rack. Recently, Charity had sewn a card from Isaac into a pocket that she'd fashioned in the underside of her top skirt. "It is my part, how I show my deep love for thee, the Spirit having taken thee away from us to do the work," he'd written. "And be at peace for how we are together, seeing the same stars at night. I am waiting patiently for thy return."

It was Danise's tellings of her life in Philadelphia, the largest and wealthiest free community of Black people in the country, that gave Charity the most distraction. Her sister lived in such a different world, gone over thirty years ago from the worrisome life in the South to all that the northern city had to offer. Danise had made satisfying friendships with other women, joined associations of Black professionals—teachers, clergymen, hairdressers, bakers, tailors, teamsters, musicians—and the like. "It's easy enough to enjoy the Universal Friend's directives regarding sexual abstinence and avoidance of marriage," Danise had written. She, Chelsea, and Ammon had purchased a brownstone. Danise often sent copies of the articles she wrote for the newspaper, and in her letters were masterful descriptions of the attire, personalities, and activities of the women that surrounded her. She remained unmarried, seeming to prefer the regular company of the women who were abolitionists, especially those who followed the Public Universal Friend. Cleaven was five, already a handsome lad with wit.

The rest of Danise's most recent letter was a summary of an article that had appeared on the back pages of the *Gazette* regarding Hermon Husband. The coward who had tormented their mother for years and fled to Maryland after abandoning his followers in the Regulators War had died. "Hermon Husband played a part in something called 'the Whiskey Rebellion of 1794,'" Danise wrote, a conflict over a federal excise tax. The fee on whiskey, championed by Treasury Secretary Alexander Hamilton, caused a good deal of backlash from western distillers, and Hermon got caught up in it, the conflict turning violent," Danise went on, "and Hermon unable to successfully control the resistors. Federal troops were marched over the Allegheny Mountains to put down the ensuing revolt. Hermon, seventy years old, was arrested and held in miserable conditions until he was returned here to Philadelphia for trial. He spent six months in prison, his health deteriorating, until he was finally acquitted by President Washington. He died in a tavern just after his release, leaving a wife and eight children."

The news left Charity cold. She had trouble thinking of any comment about the man. Had Hermon Husband not tried for years to interfere with her mother's work? Had he not, in part, caused her falling out with the Cane Creek women's meeting that she loved? Charity wrote instead about the state officials in South Carolina who had begun rearresting Negroes that Friends had freed. "Majer says the legislature just passed an act to make it a penal offense for anyone to liberate those they've enslaved. Frankly, I am finding it difficult to trust God in this seemingly unending matter of slavery."

"Encourage Friends to help Africans and their children get North," Danise wrote back, as if Quakers couldn't be arrest and fined for doing so. "We will assist them. We are well organized to feed and clothe the runaways, to help them navigate the city and find those who won't take advantage of them. We are the guides, led by the Spirit. 'For what does it profit, my brethren, if someone says he has faith but does not have works? Can faith save him?'"

Charity reread the letter several times. *What is she involved with? Was it the invisible pathways to Canada?*

But Charity knew enough not to ask, not to write anything in a letter that could be intercepted and used against her sister. "Thou might be interested," she penned instead, "to know that Abijah O'Neall and David Pugh of Bush River Meeting have been appointed to find a solution for Friends in the South, a way that their testimonies of peace and equality can be upheld without being challenged constantly by war and slavery. The O'Nealls, Pughs—and Mills family, too—want Friends to move elsewhere, to give up our farms and businesses and buy cheap, fertile land west of here. But land that the *Book of Discipline* counsels has only fairly and openly been first purchased from the Natives."

Danise hardly remembered the names of the Bush River committee members. *The O'Nealls, Pughs, and Mills*, she repeated. She asked Charity about them in her next letter. "Aren't the O'Neall, Pugh, and Mills families the relatives of people who befriended our parents at the Hopewell Meeting in Virginia? Isn't Abijah O'Neall short and stout and cuts his hair close to his scalp? I remember that he and his wife, Anne, enslaved at least one man, who they called Jack. He helped in the house with 'Miss Anne.'"

When Charity wrote back, she answered Danise's questions and included impressions of Henry O'Neall, the younger brother of Abijah. She wrote, too, of their younger sister, Susannah, and her preaching. She was now recorded as a minister and had been serving for several years. Henry O'Neall had noticed that Susannah was always sure to sit beside Charity on the facing bench if her older sister was home. This was how it'd been on the occasion of Henry's telling.

"Henry O'Neall told Majer that our 'immense white beaver hats' were laid out beside us," wrote Charity, "and complained that Susannah was 'not gifted in her ministry.' Apparently, he and his young lads had their fun whispering the stale messages and Bible verses they guessed their 'Aunt Susannah' was going to use before she did so, making an audible ruckus with their sniggering when they hit the mark. Big Isaac was sitting right by the young men but has gone deaf and didn't hear them to stop their rudeness."

To Charity's chagrin, Majer had also told her that Henry O'Neall had described her as having a "round face and form."

"It's that I have lost the slender figure of my youth," Charity admitted to Danise, "the result of too many luscious dinners in the homes of Friends and my age, I suppose. But Henry also told Majer that he'd been impressed with my preaching against slavery." Charity also informed her sister that the Bush Creek Men's Meeting approved a traveling certificate for Charity and Susannah for travel to the 1796 summer business meetings in North Carolina, Virginia, and Maryland. "In the next year, we'll attend the yearly meetings in Baltimore, New York, and New England, too. And maybe Europe. At the risk of being called proud, let me quote some of the minute here:

"Our esteemed friend, Charity Cook, brought a leading to the whole, a weighty and increasing concern that she travel with her sister, Susannah Hollingsworth, in the South and then pay a series of religious visits to our Friends in New England—and then in Europe, as way may open, and with which this meeting unites. A certificate of travel will be prepared for approval at our next monthly meeting.

"Susannah" concluded Charity, "has the support of Big Isaac who claims his 'corn never grows better than when she is out on a preaching tour.'"

"E-U-R-O-P-E!" Danise spelled to Chelsea, trying to keep the manual letters on her hands from bouncing inarticulately with her excitement over the news. *"Charity might go to Europe."* She spun the globe in their spacious parlor and put a finger on Pennsylvania and another on England. *"Long, dangerous trip."*

"They'll cross the Atlantic," chimed in Cleaven from where he was reading on the sofa. He wore a short jacket over a white cotton shirt and blue ankle-length trousers. "The French and the English are fighting there."

"I think we should have our silhouettes cut for her," Danise suggested.

"Quakers not like P-O-R-T-R-A-I-T-S," Chelsea reminded her, fingerspelling the word.

"True," replied Danise, "but a likeness drawn by tracing our shadows should be acceptable. And I will send her my charm so she is reminded of our love."

#

304

Charity and Susannah came to Philadelphia in the winter, wanting a good long visit with Danise and Chelsea before they set off to the meetings in New York and New England. "Oh, Susannah," Danise greeted them. "Has it really been so long?" She introduced her younger sister to Ammon and Cleaven and, in the next weeks, to as many of the city abolitionists as they could visit. The sisters, of course, attended meeting for worship in the grand city.

Charity especially enjoyed her time with Rebecca Jones, who she'd met on a previous visit, and William Savery, too, a well-regarded Friend who found the women something of a rarity, them coming from the South and driven to expose the evils of slavery.

"'Tis said that William Savery is influential with President Washington," Danise informed Charity and Susannah after the minister and others had spent the afternoon together. "He's been invited to the new capital in the city of Washington."

"Was it moved from Philadelphia to appease the pro-slavery states?" asked Charity.

"Indeed," replied Danise. "For the fear was that a capital here was too close to abolitionist states." She caught Charity's gaze. "Built by enslaved laborers who toiled through every stage of the construction, from the quarrying and transportation of the stone to the impressive craftsmanship of the building itself."

"I hope William Savery is aware of that, such facts often unmentioned, although he told me that, at present, he's more involved with Native issues than with those involving Negroes. Said he's trying to stop the wars on the frontier that are spreading westward, increasing in size and intensity."

"According to the papers," said Danise, "most settlers are taking land along the Ohio and Miami Rivers in west-central Ohio, in what Congress has named 'the Northwest Territory.' 'Tis a vast wilderness as large as the whole of the thirteen colonies and long populated by Delaware, Miami, Potawatomi, Shawnee, and others. The tract includes all the land west of Pennsylvania, northwest of the Ohio River, and east of the Mississippi River below the Great Lakes." She frowned. "The homesteaders are invading the areas where the Natives have roamed for hundreds of years and hunting the animals they depend on for food. Bloodshed dominates the region."

"And the Natives?" asked Susannah.

"They want their land back and are forming alliances to stop the sale of any more of it. According to the paper, negotiations are at an impasse."

"The land is being sold, no?" asked Susannah quietly, "not stolen."

"'Tis not voluntary," Danise replied stern-faced. "The newspaper says that representatives of all the many Natives—the Wyandotte, Shawnee, Lenape, Ottawa, Ojibwa, Potawatomi, Kickapoo, and others—will meet in Ohio where they'll be forced to sign a treaty, a 'treaty of *friendship*,'" she mocked, "and moved farther and farther west."

#

"I've now attended five yearly meetings," Charity wrote in her first letter back to Danise after she and Susannah left their Philadelphia family. "Baltimore, North Carolina, Philadelphia, New York, and New England."

Danise read *pride* in the words, a Quaker cardinal sin, but she wrote back of the value she saw in the meeting attendance. "You're gaining a deep understanding of the wider Society, their social and economic life in the North. It will serve you well should you go to Europe, for surely you are seeing differences between Northern and Southern Friends."

It was true. Charity and Susannah were visiting Friends who were investing in textile mills and canals and those who, unwilling to educate their children in the local schools, were organizing their own. Many meetings had taken up education as a part of their meeting business, hiring teachers who would stress an understanding of living in the Quaker faith over the values of the local education system.

"We have met Friends in these parts who are making appropriate financial settlements to those they manumitted," Charity informed Danise, "assisting freed people to find homes and proper employment, and to build their own schools and churches. I've talked with Paul Cuffe, the whaling captain, who is the son of a Wampanoag mother and a formerly enslaved father. On Martha's Vineyard and Nantucket Island in Massachusetts, there'd been no shortage of Paul Cuffe stories. He'd won island hearts by delivering much-needed goods during the war, slipping through the Tory blockade in a small sailboat. "Now the good man is involved with aiding fugitive runaways from bounty hunters and helping them to get assistance in Cold Trail, the town on Nantucket where about fifty Black people live. They work as laborers, sheep and livestock farmers, and even whalers and mariners. And he's promoting a British program to send Black people to Sierra Leone, Africa."

"Paul Cuffe is a man of great intelligence and wealth," Danise wrote back. "After the war, he founded the first integrated school in this country! But Black people here in Philadelphia don't favor the idea of sending freemen and their families, who have lived here for generations, back to Sierra Leone. We are no more African than you are European."

Charity wrote that she'd found members of the Coffin family, all hearing people. "I told them how Chelsea is using signs to teach English vocabulary and grammar in Philadelphia, and they seemed pleased to hear it. They were interested to know how Tristram Coffin had taught thee more formal signs back in thy Bush River days, thou then using them to expand Chelsea's vocabulary. How curious the Spirit is, yes?" Charity ended the letter, "that we White Wrights learned to sign with thee and Chelsea, and now the manual language bonds us in a fast welcome to those on Nantucket and Martha's Vineyard. Everyone here signs, Deaf and hearing alike, and are grateful of our knowledge of it. Still, there are no schools for children who are Deaf that I can locate, no more opportunity in the North for education than in the South."

Charity was sure to report to Danise that she'd met Elias Hicks, the acclaimed abolitionist, in New Hampshire, and delivered a letter Danise had written to him. "The young, weighty preacher thanks thee for thy letter and offered Susannah and I the most lively conversation."

"The hats," Elias had teased, when they'd met, "the beaver hats are perfect."

Charity couldn't tell if he was teasing them for their unique Southern habit or giving them a sincere compliment. "I find the bonnets disagreeable," Charity had replied, "obscuring my vision and too tight at the chin." She touched the rim of her wide-brimmed hat, closed her eyes for a moment, and envisioned Isaac. "My husband trapped the beaver himself."

Charity wrote, too, of Elias's stand as an abolitionist, having manumitted the family's enslaved people on Long Island twenty years earlier, and of his opinions about the "second" Great Awakening. "It's sweeping across the states and generally mending morals," the preacher had told her approvingly. "Although I detest the method of it."

Still, it seemed to Charity that Elias grudgingly admired the success of the Protestant ministers, their revivals, huge social events, whether they were hosted in the cities or on the prairie frontiers. In her letter to Danise, she immodestly included Elias's comment about her work, him declaring that she'd become "one of the most experienced traveling ministers of the day." Charity continued, "He says that I've sat among so many in individual and corporate worship, my finger on the pulse of God, that I should share my discernment of it in Europe. But that would take me so far from Isaac and the children."

Danise didn't encourage the travel to Europe in her next letter. It was an extremely dangerous time to sail there, many itinerant ministers having died at sea or in a foreign land. Wasn't there plenty of work for Charity to do in America? Instead, she wrote of "Black Harry" Hosier, a famed Methodist orator, who, according to the *Gazette*, held revivals separate from the White people. Some criticized him for being illiterate, although he was indisputably a success. "Like Friends, he hasn't trained in theological studies at a college but is a man whose natural talent for ministry is widely recognized."

When Charity and Susannah reached the Redstone Monthly Meeting, west of the Appalachian Mountains in Brownsville, Pennsylvania, Charity got off another letter to Danise. "We are truly in the frontier, the ride here was extremely difficult. Worst were the rough men we met on the trail or in the taverns who misinterpreted our travel. They returned our attempts at polite conversation with whistles and hoots, teasing us for the way we talk and loudly telling each other dirty stories, knowing we could overhear them. A couple of times they circled around Susannah, smelling extremely unclean, like deer found dead and deteriorated in the forest.

"Keep thy distance, please," Charity had warned the men, rising to relocate herself and Susannah to a table farther from them. Despite her diminutive height, she took wide bowlegged strides to a table in the corner to reseat herself, the men taking note and calling out insults.

"It's sometimes difficult to trust in God's plan," Charity admitted in her letter, "and have faith that we're protected. Neither of us have been sleeping well. We use a place in a back room, husks for a pad, our saddle for pillows, and cover ourselves with our wool cloaks. We spend the days talking with the pioneers who will be the first Friends to cross the wide Ohio River and establish meetings in the Northwest Territory. And I feel needed here. We both deliver ministry and listen to the hopes and worries of the migrating pioneers, though I am unsympathetic of those who have strayed from the discipline in the manner of dress, speech, and sobriety.

"Your clothing should only be what is practical and worn to ward off the cold," Charity chastised the women. "Wear no lace or bows, with sleeves to your wrists, and nothing invented to excite lust."

To Isaac, Charity confessed that she was "short on sleep but long on reprimands." She wanted to profess her demeanor to someone who had witnessed it and to remind her husband that the work was difficult. She didn't want him to think she was away from her family responsibilities having a time of it. Still, it wasn't the Cook children that Charity dreamed of. It was the imagined comforts that might await her should she be led to travel to Great Britain. She longed for the adventure of it.

Before a week had passed, Susannah had had enough of Redstone, of travel all together. She wanted to go home. She'd tolerated New England where a good meal and a soft mattress were possible, but she told Charity that she felt out of place in the rugged West. With regret, Charity agreed to make the long journey back with her, writing to Friends that she would be in attendance at the North Carolina Yearly Meeting.

Once Susannah was delivered to Big Isaac, Charity rode to her own cabin. Isaac and children flocked around her. "Home earlier than I expected, my love," Isaac said, folding her into his warm embrace. "Thou look worn and thinner, but we'll get thee fed and bathed. And there's a letter that's come for thee from Rebecca Jones." The children at her heels, Charity tried to give each of them her attention, overjoyed to see their faces, their sweet supple bodies, and happy to hear their news. But later, when she sat in bed with Isaac, she anxiously read Rebecca's letter.

"She agrees I should go to England," Charity shared, her eyes held to the coarse page. "'With solid satisfaction,' she says here, 'I may inform thee that there is a newly established women's meeting in the London Yearly Meeting. It increases our sex in weight and experience. Women from all parts of America and Great Britain are encouraged to attend, although some men don't welcome our presence.'"

"Ah, Charity, off again so soon," sighed Isaac. He reached for her, nestling into her neck. "If thou are called, then thou must go, but tonight, tonight, thou are my sweet wife."

Chapter 20

When Charity wrote to Danise of the invitation to go to Europe, she included part of what the meeting had said in regard to her transatlantic travel certificate. She was introduced to those in England as "a member in good stead in the American Religious Society of Friends" and one whose leading had the support of the yearly meeting. The certificate declared her to be "a Friend of esteem, whose ministry is sound and edifying." She was "a credit to Bush Creek Monthly Meeting," the ministers and elders readily directing the treasurer to supply her with whatever amount of travel money she felt she needed.

Is it their true perspective? That I am a Friend of esteem? That I give enlightening ministry? Charity mused. She'd always been one to be grateful for the acknowledgment of others, to have her abilities recognized, but she also found it hard to believe the praise. "Seems that whatever the Cane Creek Meeting thought of me all those years ago," she added, "I have now made up for it."

Oh heavens, thought Danise as she read Charity's letter. *Long ago, dear sister. Long ago.*

Isaac insisted on making a large contribution for her travel from their own resources. "We need to support your goodness, Charity, and that the Spirit has chosen thee for this most holy errand. Thou are a pattern, 'an example in all countries, places, islands, and nations as thou preached among all sorts of people.'" It was what George Fox had said when he'd deployed pairs of seventeenth-century Friends to the most populated cities in England.

"I'll try to 'walk cheerfully,'" Charity continued the familiar quote, "over as much of Europe as I am led to visit, 'answering that of God in everyone.'" She kissed Isaac tenderly in deep gratitude for how he continually supported her calling.

By fall 1797, Charity was in New York on board the *Severn*. As was typical, she and her companions for the trip, Mary Swett of Haddonfield, New Jersey, and Sarah Harrison of Philadelphia, had been invited to examine the small ship before its departure. She paused to think of her family as she surveyed the dark, cramped cabin where she would keep her things and sleep. The Cook cabin rooms were so much bigger. *The children are so much older now*, Charity tried to assure herself. *They are better prepared to care for themselves than at any other time since I began traveling.* Five of her older children were married: Joseph, Sarah, Rachel, Thomas, and her Charity. Six were still at home—Mary, who was twenty-five, Ruth, twenty-one, Marion, nineteen, young Isaac, sixteen, Susannah, fourteen, and Keturah, only eleven. All of them were disciplined to take direction from their father, now fifty-four but still fit and able for the work that the homestead required of him. That evening, Charity wrote a letter to Isaac and each child, as well as to each of her siblings, wanting to send off the posts before she sailed.

To Isaac, Charity sent her love and gratitude and tried to joke that "ol' grandpa" had their twenty grandchildren to distract him in her absence. She assured him that she was ready for whatever lay ahead. She'd made her circuits for at least twenty-five years. She'd visited Friends in all the states, even those isolated on the wild frontiers. She had a depth of understanding of the American Society of Friends to share, and she was excited to do so. She had broken from her chrysalis and was ready to fly!

To her older brothers and sisters, the ones who could remember their Cane Creek home, Charity described the little, efficient cabin she was to occupy as it compared to their rooms in the Cane Creek home of their childhood. It was smaller, for sure. The ceiling was much lower, too. There was a hard mattress on an even harder wooden frame that was attached to one wall, with storage above it, and a single net across a corner for her toiletries. She had to go down a narrow hallway to use the head, and meals were prepared in the galley.

In the letters to her children, Charity included a description of the *Severn*, a seaworthy sailing ship with three masts and fore and aft sails that harnessed the power of wind and propelled the vessel across the ocean. She drew a little picture and ended each short letter with her prayer that "the Lord bless thee and keep thee. I'll be back before thee can miss me."

On the seventeenth of Eighth Month 1797, Charity sailed for Liverpool. She was in her mid-fifties, younger than Mary Swett and Sarah Harrison. She thought all three of them courageous, steeped in the faith, and *old*. Although hips ached, knees creaked, and feet cramped, the companions were spiritually ready for whatever lay ahead.

Charity's letter to Danise was written after she'd landed in Liverpool and didn't arrive for a month after the docking. It began innocently enough, praising God that she was healthy and safe, not seasick, and sleeping as well as could be expected. There was a description of Mary and one of Sarah.

"Charity arrive nineteenth, eleventh month," Danise informed Chelsea and Cleaven, who sat with her in the parlor, eager to hear the news. "Two Quaker women with her." Suddenly she sat back and pulled in her chin.

"What is it?" Cleaven asked, staring at his aunt's shaking hands.

"French privateers attacked Aunt Charity's ship!" Danise responded, signing and speaking simultaneously. She'd read about the situation in the *Gazette*, that because the United States had suspended repayment of French loans from the Revolutionary War, French privateers were robbing American ships. "With no American Navy, the privateers are free to roam the sea unchecked and capture ships," Danise explained to Cleaven and Chelsea. "The men came aboard the *Severn* and accosted the travelers, stealing jewelry and money." She looked up. "I've read in the paper that more than three hundred ships have been seized this year alone. They—Oh, my Lord!" Danise bit on her lip. "The men were armed and lined up all the passengers on the deck to interrogate them. They took what they pleased from their trunks."

"Storms," Danise signed next. She enlarged the sign and swirled it forcefully in front of her bodice. *"Water on ship."* She bent to indicate a water level as high as her knees. "For the next several days," she read, "the wind blew so hard, and the sea rose so much that the main deck was knee-deep in water. The fierce storms were relentlessly battering the ship so constantly that it tipped like a toy boat." Danise took the three-finger classifier that indicated the ship and circled it wildly in front of her. "One of the yard arms at the front end broke off and fell into the sea."

"The rain didn't let up," Danise read rapidly. "Everyone was ordered to their cabins. The three of us crammed into Mary and Sarah's room, even though the space was designed for only two adults. Those two were extremely seasick and constantly alternating their runs to the head to vomit. I tended to them, the stench suffocating."

Suddenly, Danise stopped. "Not again," she finally exclaimed. "A second French warship approached them, a fri . . . gate." She sounded out the novel word and then fingerspelled it. "*F-R-I-G-A-T-E* chased the ship, *firing on it* several times." She looked up. "Oh my word!"

"What's a F-R-I-G-A-T-E?" asked Chelsea.

"I know," Cleaven tapped his mother. "It's a big, fast ship," he explained enthusiastically, moving his hands to outline the large vessel, "mounted with lots of guns." He aimed the sign for "shoot" at an imaginary sailing ship.

"Well," exhaled Danise, shaking her head in disbelief. "A frigate caught the *Severn*."

"Prayer?" guessed Chelsea. She held her eyebrows high.

"Yes," nodded Danise, continuing to read and explain in both speech and sign. "Charity says she and the other women nestled on the bed, huddled tightly together for the size of it, and sat in silence until they got word that the men had departed without coming aboard. 'We keep our trust in the Spirit, our Helper.'" Danise waved the letter. "Oh! Listen to this. Charity says that, as if in answer to their prayers, a heavy fog of protection descended around the *Severn* and remained in place for several days, concealing it from the view of any other vessels. They weren't bothered again." Danise looked up. "Charity and Mary sighted a water spout!"

"What's that?" asked Cleaven.

"It's an eerie column of rotating air, like a tornado on the water," explained Danise, "that forms during a severe thunderstorm. Charity says the squall went on for the next nine days, the *Severn* unable to dock in Liverpool until it quit."

"She's finally there," smiled Chelsea. "She made it."

#

Almost seven months passed before Danise received a second letter from Charity, the contents focused on a single topic. "I am disheartened to tell thee of the slave trade in Liverpool," it began, "but I describe the situation here to fuel the work that occupies us both."

Danise tried to relax her shoulders, to ready herself for Charity's report.

"We were able to talk with a cabin boy awaiting his assignment in Liverpool, a talkative lad who seemed eager to tell of his part in transporting thousands of enslaved Africans from the east and west coasts of the continent." Charity had underlined the word "eager" twice. "He claimed the shipbuilders here are masters in the construction of the custom-built ships that allow men, women, and children to be chained and crammed, shoulder to shoulder, in their hulls. Oblivious to our sect, let alone our stand on slavery, the lad went on and on about the despicable voyages that carry some seven hundred people a trip from their homeland in Africa to new owners in

America. Then the boat returns to Liverpool, a city that so dominates the trade that one in five African captives is carried by a Liverpool ship—almost half of the entire transatlantic slave market!"

Tears blurred Danise's vision as she read on.

"We see the evidence of the evil in the tidy town, the newly paved streets named after the greedy captains and the other men who have been responsible for the kidnapping of over a hundred thousand Africans. That's one fourth the population of North Carolina!"

Danise put the letter down for a moment, closed her eyes, and tried to slow her breathing. Then she read on. "A man at the inn where we first stayed told us that, in this last decade, Liverpool has had three times as many transatlantic slaving vessels as London or Bristol. The captains use the network of rivers and canals out of Liverpool to access textiles from the Lancashire and Yorkshire mills, brass cooking pots, copperware, clay pipes, beer and liquor from Staffordshire and Cheshire, and guns and knives from Birmingham. They trade them in Africa for Africans—men, women, and even children. Nearly all the principal merchants and citizens of Liverpool are involved to some degree in the business. Why there is even a slave ship called the *Quaker,* although most of the sixty Quaker families here claim they are not involved. They won't talk much to us about it."

Danise wasn't sure where to send her return letter. She decided to mail it to London Yearly Meeting and hope for the best. In it, she told Charity of how she had held the pages of her sister's last letter to her heart and vowed aloud to fight harder to end slavery. "I'm working with the Pennsylvania Abolition Society against the Fugitive Slave acts, them providing the seizure and return of runaways who escaped from one state into another. Your telling of Liverpool makes our work here seen inadequate at best. My dedication to doing more has become the whole of my life."

Of course, Charity had written to Isaac, too. Her letter told of her arrival to Liverpool, although her description of the slave trade she had found there was condensed, and of her travels to Cheshire, Lancaster, and Westmoreland to preach. She apologized that she had not written sooner, admitting the three women had been slowed by coughs and colds.

In each letter that she wrote to family and friends, Charity emphasized the importance of the mail she'd received, begging they keep writing to her. She gave a London address although the next letters she received were delivered to her by William Savery. The itinerant Philadelphian Friend was traveling in England as well. He'd ridden hard to find her, checking with the network of Quakers who were known to offer hospitality to visitors. "He knew from his own experiences how hungry I'd be for news from home," Charity wrote Isaac, "but also seemed to want to keep track of what we women are doing, where we are going, and how our preaching is being received. Is it competition?"

After that, Charity had filled pages with the thrill of being in Kendal, a quaint village in northern England. "We are in the heart of George Fox country! Mary, Sarah, and I have walked the ridges, woodlands, and meadows where our faith first took hold. We've visited the places important to our history—Pendle Hill near Burnley, where George Fox had a vision of 'the people gathered,' and Fox's Pulpit in Firbank Fell where he preached to thousands. Oh, Isaac, we even stayed at Swarthmoor Hall in Ulverston, once the home of Margaret Fell, one of the strongest—and certainly richest—of George Fox's converts. We read from his huge Bible there and were told how Margaret's money sponsored George Fox and many others, including Mary Fisher, so that they were able to travel as we are doing now. Please remind the children of the Valiant Sixty, and tell them that three of them were from Kendal—Elizabeth Fletcher, Elizabeth Leavens, and Thomas Holme. The girls were fifteen—our Susannah's age. Does thou think we would let her walk over two hundred miles to tell others of our faith in times that were more dangerous than they are now? For Elizabeth Fletcher was brutally ravished by young men studying to be ministers in Oxford."

When Charity next wrote Danise, she repeated much of what she'd written to Isaac, but confided that when she'd been told about the rape of Elizabeth Fletcher, dismal feelings of her own assault had reared inside her.

"There it is," sighed Danise as she stared at the lopsided way Charity had written the word rape. "'Tis like a splinter, festering just below the surface of whatever occupies her," she murmured aloud. She laid the letter aside for a moment and began to pray in the language of her childhood. "Ah, dear God, may thou give my tormented sister eyes to see Jehu Stuart with a forgiving heart, so she may move on with all thy gifts. Danise sat back. *Black women are raped by White men as a matter of course, the fox always coming to the chicken coop, and there's no escape from it, no penalty. Charity must find a way to carry on.*

#

After a month in Northwestern England, Charity, Mary, and Sarah finally went south to London. When she wrote Isaac and Danise of it, Charity described the city in detail. "Seems equal parts wealth and poverty. There are throngs of hackney coaches," she wrote of the four-wheeled, horse-drawn carriages that filled London streets, "but despite the stench and noise, we prefer to walk. The people pour past us like milk from a spilled churn—Jews, Roman Catholics, Protestant dissenters, foreigners like ourselves, and of course, the begging children of the poor. I cannot help but be impressed by the golden church steeples, the bright colors of the women's dresses, and the many peculiar stores. Not to worry, we avoid the taverns, gaming houses, brothels, and theaters!" Charity tried to joke. "We find the public gardens and promenades of remarkable beauty and wander through them almost daily.

"As for the Friends here," Charity wrote on, "the men wear collars and cuffs but not wigs and no buttons or lace. The yearly meeting women wear the same tones we do, but most wear opaque bonnets, the strings left to dangle at their chin. I've scandalized the British Friends with my man's hat and pipe smoking and with what I've been told is my 'theatrical' preaching. I pray that the Spirit assists me in rightly stepping along in my bowlegged manner, my boldness used when necessary. I have written to King George III, seeking audience with him to discuss his influence in ending slavery.

"Oh, and the worship. I feel holy when I enter the huge chamber for it, the partitions pulled back so that we are among hundreds of men and women in attendance. We sit separate, of course, but I have been told that this yearly meeting includes representatives from each region of Great Britain, as well as a significant number of Friends who have traveled to Europe, the Americas, and Africa to preach. Anyone in need of travel funds for itinerant work is encouraged to see the meeting treasurer!"

It was not until the very end of the letters that Charity described the London women's meeting. It was held apart from the Men's Meeting in a separate house. "Our women's sessions begin with introductions and announcements. Everything is managed in great calmness, love, and unity. The women shiver and tremble as we worship, carried beyond the usual manner in the holy power of love. I weep openly during our time together, filled with the glorious presence of the Spirit, the rays and majesty of truth stretched over our assembly. Many say they feel it, too."

Charity went on, "It does seem that the weighty Friends are from families involved in commerce and industry. Some are deeply influenced by the rise of the Evangelical revivals, but there is also a group that much attracts me—the Society for Abolition of the Slave Trade. They were established a decade ago to educate the public about the abuses of the trafficking and to influence Parliament in ceasing all related activities.

"I admire the young adult Friends, who don't hesitate to speak up in the business that is taken up. One of them delivered an eloquent message with zeal and courage. She was concerned for the tensions between the wealthy and the poor in our ranks. Later, Mary Swett introduced me to a young woman named Mary Birkett from Dublin. She wanted to meet me especially, saying that she admires my courage to wear my beaver hat and smoke when we are enjoying social times. Members of her family are strong abolitionists.

"Mary is educated in art, French, drawing, literature, and music!" Mary Swett had gushed, her gloves and education novel in comparison to the practice of Friends in America. "She writes poems, too."

"Oh," Charity had managed. She didn't think she'd ever known a Friend to write poetry.

"Some of my poems are about the issues women face as Dublin Friends," Mary Birkett explained. "The women are only allowed a certain level of equality around preaching. The Men's Meeting makes the majority of important decisions."

"'Tis how it is in America, too." Charity acquiesced. She eyed Mary Birkett's gay, fashionable dress and suspected the young aristocrat wore a bustle pad under her green, well-constructed gown. The top had long pleats of good quality cloth that hung from the low neckline.

"Mary is very vocal in Ireland, encouraging women to take responsibility for slavery by boycotting products made by the enslaved," said Mary Swett. She glanced to Mary Birkett. "Might thou tell Charity of the medallion thou wears."

The young woman fingered the heavy necklace that encircled her neck. She held it out for Charity to see. "It was given to me by my uncle. See how it features a kneeling African in chains and the words 'Am I Not A Man And A Brother?' My uncle sells these to the people who have stopped using sugar in their tea or rum as their drink in an effort to raise funds for the cause."

"What a bold idea," said Charity. "I'd love to buy them for my sisters, especially Danise and Chelsea."

"Come join us," Sarah encouraged Mary Birkett, "in our public preaching this afternoon."

"To warn London to repent. To let in the Light," Mary readily agreed, "and let all know of the possibility of a personal relationship. I've heard that a very great number of people have been attending the public preaching sessions, the chance or perhaps a curiosity to hear some of the greatest itinerant Quaker ministers."

"Many heavenly testimonies are borne," Charity wrote to Danise and Isaac, "if they can be heard above the carts that grumble over the cobblestone streets. The zeal and devotion of olden times is with us as we go, and much counsel and good advice is given in the openings of truth. I admit, sometimes we're mocked, and we were once stopped and told we needed to seek permission from the town council before any of us were to preach again. We dutifully went to the mayor where a man cried out from a back row that he'd had preaching and praying enough from Quakers in the past week to be carried to heaven. Still, we were issued a permit to continue."

Charity was most always moved to take a turn to preach as the group of them walked the London streets. She would be helped up to stand on a barrel or crate so she could be better seen. "I am enjoying the public recognition," she admitted in her letters, "that gives me a satisfying feeling of assurance that my messages about slavery are what God has charged me to deliver. At the close of our public preaching, there is a very solemn, weighty parting, the sweet, pure current of life flowing through all of us in attendance. Oh, and I must be sure to tell you all, Sarah, Mary, and I are going next to Germany!"

#

The women didn't leave for war-torn Germany immediately, the trip requiring the approval of the yearly meeting. While they waited for the necessary travel certificates, the three were invited to visit in Hitchin, a market town in Hertfordshire in Southeastern England. They all took a turn to preach there and were befriended by a group of local women who wanted a demonstration of how to make yeast as they did in America.

A week later, the cadre of Friends returned to London and were granted their paperwork. In it, after only eight months in England, Charity was recognized as "a confident traveling minister."

Her reaction to the accolade confused her. "It seems, Charity admitted to Mary and Sarah, that others see me as whole, self-confident, and an adequate model of a good Quaker woman, but somehow, I just can't believe it of myself."

"Thou will find the way," Sarah assured her friend. She respected Charity a great deal. "Sometimes, it's easier for others to see our gifts and talents than it is for us ourselves."

"For thou have a perspective, an experience, that we in the northern states haven't had," agreed Mary. "Thou are authentic, Charity, and thy articulate ministry is powerful."

The women arrived in Hamburg on a sailing ship that had taken them across the North Sea. The trip took fourteen dull days, made longer than usual by storms. Then they bought tickets for a rickety stagecoach headed toward Hanover in central Germany and found an interpreter, as they had been advised by Friends in London. Michael Wold was middle-aged, his hair graying, as was theirs, but very spry and accomplished. He was friendly and easily able to maneuver the seven hundred books and pamphlets the London Yearly Meeting had given the women to distribute in Germany.

The roads as rutted and unbearable as any in the American frontier, the group of them arrived to a place called Bad Pyrmont in Saxony, to the west of Hanover and north of Frankfurt, where they'd been told they'd be well cared for. The tract of land was called Friedensthal or Vale of Peace and had been given by Prince Friedrich von Waldeck to three Quaker brothers. Ludwig, Friedrich, and Dietrich Seebohm were kind to the women but expected them to fix the meals for the men, including the interpreter, and attend to their own housekeeping.

"I'm afraid we were spoiled in England," Charity wrote to Isaac, asking him to send the letter on to Danise after he'd shared it with the children. "We had others to cook and clean for us but not here. Still, the attitudes of those in Vale of Peace are offset by the spacious brick house they've given us, the very one where the American Friend, John Pemberton, breathed his last. Michael Wold, our interpreter, has separate accommodations, but we gather together in the afternoons to entertain the German Friends who come to visit, many of whom are retired American Revolutionary War soldiers. They learned English in the States and tell us that Quakers in the colonies were good to them when they were so far away from home and hired for 'the bloody business.'"

"We were the Hessian Highlanders," one of the former soldiers, Curt Nickel, told the women, "a part of the thirty thousand that Britain hired during the war." He was as tall as Isaac, a little shy but with an easy way about him. When he glanced over to Charity, preparing to smoke, he dug in a pocket for a thin strip of wood, held it to the lantern to ignite it, and politely offered it to her.

"You'll discover that this is a time of conflict with our new governmental authorities in Germany," another one, Hans, explained to the women. "I trust they'll allow you to preach, but while you wait for permission, you should visit the healing mineral waters of Friedensthal—and come with us to see the beginnings of the meetinghouse we're building. It's to be quite grand with a committee room for men and another for women, all financed by London Yearly Meeting."

"And might we see John Pemberton's grave?" asked Mary.

"You may," agreed Curt, "although it's a plot of ground like any other. No marker, no tombstone. But John was the first laid to rest in it, interred under a large oak tree."

"We went next to Miden, Micheal Wold continuing with us to interpret," Charity wrote home. "Unfortunately, we arrived at night. Michael thinks that the guards at the city gate thought our motivation undesirable and reported our visit to the authorities. Early the next morning, constables came pounding on the door of the woman who housed us, demanding we not hold any public meetings. But that, of course, was why we'd come. The men weren't halfway down the cobbled street before we began to spread the word about a public meeting for worship on First Day.

"A good number of townspeople attended, although they were as much at risk as the three of us. Just as we were ending, constables barged in and arrested our host. They let us be, but when we met in worship a second time, they hauled us off. Michael, too. Thou knows I have never been the coward, and I was joyful through it all, singing God's glory as Mary Fisher had done as she was whipped and hauled to jail. 'Repent your sins, allow the Holy Light to shine in you, to see your flaws,' she'd called. 'Change your lives. Change your lives.' And honestly, I was glad for the harassment that assists those who seek God's favor to suffer in Christ's example.

"We four were forced to the justice chamber, where Michael was the first to be reprimanded and carried off to jail. We couldn't say anything to him, and we were left, unable to understand what the judge was saying. *Trust God. Trust God,* I prayed. And, praise God, we were released, ordered to leave town immediately.

"We were put on a stagecoach that took us to Friedberg, about fifteen miles north of Frankfurt but without Michael. We managed to rent a room in an inn there, and then we busied ourselves with posting notices for a meeting for worship. I am sorry to tell you that we were detained and put under house arrest for several days before it was held. Finally, we were released but taken by stagecoach under military escort to the port, required this time to leave Germany altogether. We never saw Michael Wold again."

When Charity's long letter was forwarded to Danise, the account was read with a sister's anger for the pain and suffering Charity endured. "Are you not already a child of God?" Danise wrote in her subsequent post, "worthy of God's love without putting yourself in such jeopardy? Held in house arrest! And in Germany of all places. According to the *Gazette*, the country is full of warring princes who fight continually for control over the provinces. There is no central government to which you could have appealed had they not released you. Thank heavens, you are gone from there."

Really? Danise worried as she addressed the envelope in care of London Yearly Meeting. *Is it necessary to be three thousand miles from home and gone for years now? Little Keturah is already thirteen, her childhood lost to your travels. What must the girl think?*

Chapter 21

While Danise, Chelsea, Ammon, and Cleaven were caught up in the turn-of-the-century celebrations, Charity gave no indication in the letter she wrote after First Month, 1, 1800, that she had done anything special to welcome the turning of the century. She'd been to Wales with Mary and Sarah, riding the two hundred miles on horseback because they'd been unable to hire a coach from Bristol to Cardiff. The women found relatives of Joseph and Rachel Maddock of Wrightsboro, Georgia, and stayed with them. They visited with the Friends who remained in the Coalbrookdale Meeting, the vast majority having left in search of religious freedom. Like other places in Great Britain, thousands of the Welsh people, Quakers among them, had endured fines and imprisonment for their faith, their relatives telling Charity, Mary, and Sarah of how some had sailed for Barbados to work as indentured laborers and servants on the island's plantations. Others had paid the cheap transport to go directly to America. This had been the story of John Griffiths, the itinerant Friend who had visited Charity's parents in Cane Creek, back when Hermon Husband was causing trouble for Rachel.

John Griffiths had been thirteen when he arrived in America, part of a wave of about two thousand Welsh Friends who'd braved the terrifying, three-month Atlantic crossing. By invitation of William Penn, the Welsh who didn't die of dysentery at sea established a holy Christian community in the Welsh Tract west of Philadelphia. As skilled laborers, the men found work in the iron industry or as coal miners, slate quarrymen, and tin-platers. The women raised their flocks of children and waited for the better life their husbands had promised.

In talks with the Welsh Friends who'd been left behind, Charity learned of their determination to keep the remaining Quaker meetings from disappearing altogether. "They continued to brave the harsh treatment of the church and state authorities," she wrote home, "but remain steadfast in their regular attendance at meeting and their committee work at all levels. I was surprised to see that they sing and dance a little and don't seem repentant for it."

Listen to this," Isaac directed young Isaac, Susannah, and Keturah as he read Charity's letter. "Your mama has been to Scotland and says that, back in the seventeenth century, it was men in the

English army, Oliver Cromwell's soldiers, who circulated our faith there."

He scanned the letter further. "Hmm, she writes that the three of them—" he looked up for a moment. "That'd be Mama and the women who are accompanying her, Mary Swett and Sarah Harrison . . ." He held the page of the letter up to find his place. "They've incurred the sarcastic censure of churchmen in both Wales and Scotland, the men saying that 'the ministry of the peculiar faith has fallen into the hands of women, that when a woman is giving a message, it's entertainment for the curious.'" Isaac grinned at Keturah, who had just turned fourteen. He read silently for a bit. "Oh, hear this! At one meetinghouse, it was difficult to settle into worship because of the boisterous cockfighting on the adjacent property!"

"A leading isn't always comfortable," young Isaac reminded his father, his expression grave with concern. He was almost twenty years old and filled with years of Quaker wisdom.

Isaac gave his namesake an assuring smile and returned to the letter. "She thinks the lack of Scottish Friends is because of the popularity of the national Presbyterian Church and that Scots don't seem to have the personality for our faith. That those who become Friends have open minds and are able to let new thoughts sink into their consciousness. It is a pity," lamented Isaac, "that each only notices the oddity of the other's faith and fails to see that we are all brothers and sisters in Christ.'"

Unknown to those at home, after Wales and Scotland, Charity, Mary, and Sarah had traveled on to war-torn Ireland. Only two years before, in 1798, the British had crushed the Irish revolt. Charles Cornwallis, defeated by General Washington in the American Revolutionary War, had been victorious in Ireland as the Loyalist commander in chief. Not long after, the Irish parliament had rejected a British plan for union with Great Britain, determined to have their independence. Despite the danger, the women had been invited to the explosive country by Mary Birkett, the young, flamboyant Friend they had met at London Yearly Meeting. They wanted to go, as others before them had gone, in support of Irish Friends.

"Can we be a comfort to those who are upholding their faith despite penal laws against them?" Mary had asked.

"They are blocked from government offices and unable to join trade organizations where an oath of allegiance is required," added Sarah.

"'Twill be a risk," Charity considered. She had talked with William Savery, who they'd met up with in London, about his recent visit to Ireland.

"The Friends in poor Ireland," William had informed her, "are surviving mainly in the trading towns where members often travel back to England. Many are being disowned for marrying outside our faith, marrying before a priest, drinking to excess, or for paying church tithes. They struggle to adhere to plainness in dress and manner, and with acceptable forms of entertainment. And be advised," William had looked directly at Charity, "the Irish Catholics and English Protestants will not try to keep thee out of their fighting. Murder, arson, and robbery are commonplace and widespread. Government officials have lost all control." He had taken her hand, "Charity, the risk to thee is enormous."

No matter, Charity and the others had sailed to Dublin, met on their arrival by Mary Birkett. She acted anything but depressed about the rebellion, bouncing excitedly around them as they collected their bags and eagerly flagging a coach to take them to her parents' home.

William and Sarah Birkett were delighted to have the American women stay with them. Mary and her mother escorted Mary, Sarah, and Charity to the second floor of their home where they were to occupy a roomy bedchamber. It had a polished plank floor and was wallpapered, and there were three small beds awaiting them that were covered with gay quilts.

Charity listened for a moment to the muffled sounds heard through the one wall of the room that was shared with the rowhouse beside it. "I'd like to get to preaching yet today, Spirit willing," she informed her hosts. "Come with me?"

It was only Mary Birkett who went along. Her parents needed to stay back and attend to matters of the family business. Sarah and Mary, who were now in their early sixties, decided they needed "a lay down." It had taken more than a week to ride to Port

Patrick in Scotland and cross the Irish Sea to Dublin. Their ship had battled headwinds and been chased by both Spanish and French privateers. Sequestered for days in a tiny cabin, they hadn't gotten much sleep. Now the two wanted only to enjoy the safety of their warm and comforting bed chamber.

Charity and Mary Birkett readied to go out. "We'll need to walk," explained Mary. "British patrols took our horses—and much of our food and supplies as well."

"Please don't worry," Charity tried to assure her, firm in the desire to get about the work. "A good, long walk will do me good," she added with a smile.

As Mary guided Charity through the Georgian buildings of the city, the architecture known for its exacting symmetry and proportions, she allowed Charity to choose the corners on which she was led to preach. Then, while Charity delivered the divinely inspired messages, Mary stood tall at her side, her head bowed as she held Charity in the Light and prayed they wouldn't be molested or arrested.

As always, Charity told those flocked around of the availability of a personal relationship with God. "No priest is needed to intercede," she advised. "Repent thy sins and change thy lives." She stressed living in peace with all neighbors, "For there is that of God in each person," she counseled. "Put thy trust for protection in God, not weapons."

Mary discovered that Charity wasn't at all intimidated by the prosperous residences on the north side of Dublin or their gawking wealthy owners, although the preacher admitted later that she was more relaxed when they reached the southern squares along the River Liffey. It was a rough part of town, famous for its slums and street fights between heavily armed rival gangs of Protestants and Catholics, but Charity felt more at home among these working-class people. As she walked boldly down the cobblestone streets, making eye contact with those on the street, their dress reminded her of the simple folks back home.

The following day, all four women went out to meet individually with the Dublin Quaker families. They discovered much criticism of the "New Light," people who "behaved excessively" and were advocates of the Great Awakening theology.

"Former Friends are curious about the Protestant revivals," summarized Charity when she met up later with the others.

"'Tis the same in America, their fervent meetings causing division between New Lights and traditional Quakers," asserted Sarah Harrison.

"I have found those of the New Light persuasion to be critical of our silent worship and our dress," agreed Mary Birkett. Her outfit was noticeably plainer than it'd been when Charity had first met her at London Yearly Meeting. "They want only to talk of their emotional conversion experiences, singing and shouting, dancing in the aisles, and speaking in tongues—born again with a new confirmation of faith."

Charity took the observation into consideration when she spoke in meeting on First Day. "In these perilous times, I beseech you to remember the value of our quiet, to keep the manner of the first Friends, to uphold our pacifist ways. Do not contribute in even the smallest of actions to the military companies stationed in your villages." She called out against the keeping of guns, a sign of wealth that most Irish Friends were hesitant to relinquish. When, during the social time, she heard Quakers talking of gaming and frequenting taverns, she called them to account for their weaknesses. Despite her sternness, she was thanked repeatedly for caring enough about Irish Friends to make the difficult sea crossing, visiting in their homes and sharing her powerful ministry.

Mary Birkett suspected it was while walking the slums of Dublin that Charity caught smallpox. It struck her hard, a rash of red spots first visible on her face and then on what could be glimpsed on her forearms. She complained of a throbbing headache that bored into her temples like a gimlet. Then it was that her back hurt, until there was no part of her body that wasn't hot to the touch, confining her to bed. By the time she began vomiting, the pox sores were pus-filled blisters.

Miraculously, no one else in the Birkett household or its visitors fell ill, but Charity was so sick and the disease so contagious that Sarah's father, William Birkett, had her moved to a pestilence house. The reports from those who nursed her were that she was limp and unresponsive and not expected to recover. Mary Swett felt compelled to send a letter to London

Friends, asking for advice, but she couldn't bring herself to write to anyone in Charity's family.

Three weeks into Charity's bout with smallpox, Mary Swett and Sarah Harrison decided to return to England. They'd preach and be useful as they awaited Charity's fate.

"I'll take care of everything," Mary Birkett told the women. "I pray she will recover, but while she is sequestered, it's wise to go and be with Friends in London."

"Awful dreams," Charity muttered when the doctor finally agreed Mary Birkett could visit. He'd had her inhale a powder made from the crust of Charity's scabs as a defense.

"My dreams are so vivid, so mysterious," Charity said weakly. She cleared her throat, trying to project her voice so that Mary could hear her complaint. "Often in my fever I am back in my fifteen-year-old self . . . a young Jehu Stuart coming toward me. It's awful." She paused to catch her breath. "Jehu has that strange look in his eye . . . oh, the way he stares . . . locking me down . . . and I see in his expression that, that I am not behaving like he expects."

Mary nodded. Charity had told her in the early days of their friendship of the rape and disownment.

"He comes at me . . . over and over again," Charity continued. She wagged her head from side to side. "And I'm back in it again and again . . . not able to shout out or escape him." She kicked weakly at the mess of her top sheet. "I protest, I try to get away . . . I yell at him that he has ruined my ability to see myself as good and whole, but he mocks my compulsion to always be doing . . . to be constantly on the go . . . seeking approval . . . searching for it, searching in the wrong places." She stopped and looked at Mary. "Then, somehow, I am swimming in the rush of Rayburn Creek, a dangerously fast river back home in South Carolina. My headache recedes. I feel nothing but forgiveness . . . for Jehu and for Cane Creek Meeting members who didn't believe me . . . and for myself, that I did nothing wrong. That I was an innocent young girl. And I am washed over from head to toe, cleansed, both inside and out."

Mary nodded. "'Tis the fever breaking."

"At those times, I feel the cool of the river current tumbling over me," Charity agreed. "Sometimes, when I close my eyes, Jehu Stuart appears to me as an older man as he must be now—a father, sitting with his children in meeting for worship. I am eyeing him from across the way, wanting him to know that God asked me to pray for him, that I obeyed."

"It's good then that he is returned to our faith, is it not?" asked Mary softly. "He must have apologized for his behavior and been believed in it."

"'Tis, yes," whispered Charity. Her eyes fixed on something on the ceiling. "And that we see how we are to accept God's plan . . . unknown to us . . .sometimes for years, sometimes never. In my fits, I rehearse what it is that I want to say to Jehu at the rise of worship, but when we are dismissed, I can't go to him."

"I have a cold compress here," offered Mary, moving to apply it, "to cool your forehead and help the sorrowful thoughts to vanish."

"Sometimes, I see my sister, Danise," Charity went on. "She takes my hands and gazes deep into my eyes . . . to tell me I travel too incessantly . . . to win an unnecessary awe from others. Could it be that she agrees with Jehu? That I am looking in the wrong places for the validation of my worth?"

"For thou are good and deserving, Charity. A babe in Christ's arms," Mary affirmed. "And I would hug thee close if it didn't make me nervous to do so."

#

Eventually, Charity's doctor decreed his patient was no longer contagious. With his approval, it was the giant Patrick O'Brian who was her first visitor. Eight feet tall and weighing over five hundred pounds, Patrick had braved the mocking crowds to hear Charity give public ministry before she'd taken ill. He'd been moved by the strength of her convictions and wanted to thank her personally for her courage to speak out against the established church, to not change course from the faith because of the fighting factions. Most of all, Patrick wanted to pray with her.

"I need to find peace with my massive, lonely self," the huge man explained when the two met. He knelt beside Charity's bed; his upper body towered over her even though he was on his knees.

"Thou have always been acceptable to God, Patrick," Charity told the sickly looking fellow. "'Tis all that matters." She reached her small hand to take his enormous one, and together, the two of them entered the beauty of the quiet. They worshiped for a long while before Charity felt she had a message to deliver. "This is not the time to question the cause of why we are the way we are, blaming ourselves or thinking we could have prevented it. Be confident that thou are a good person as thou have walked this Earth, kind and helpful to others." She returned to the inward silence, pondering how the words spoke to her condition as well.

Only a few weeks after he saw Charity, Patrick died from the effects of an abnormal pituitary tumor near his brain. No hearse could be found to accommodate his heavy, eight-foot casket. It was carried by fourteen men in relays to the grave.

Death did not claim Charity. In the last days of her recuperation, she was strong enough to write both Danise and Isaac, telling them of her six weeks of illness and the good care she had received in her recovery. "Such seasons of trial are given us to prove our faith, and we can't know the strength of it," she wrote.

The following day, Charity rose early, excited to see the sun greet the day. As she watched the pale strip of sunlight on the horizon progress into a stronger yellow, thoughts began exploding in her conscience: *When many in the Cane Creek Meeting did not believe that I'd tried to escape Jehu Stuart, my family had never questioned it. They had stood with me through the subsequent months of anguish, and in the end, packed up and moved to the frontier of Bush River for a fresh start. There, in meeting for worship, God pushed me to deliver a message, and despite my fear of doing so, I'd trusted God and obeyed. Would I have met Isaac otherwise, my most wonderful husband and partner?* Oh, how thankful she was that she'd been able to open up to Isaac's love, eventually birthing eleven healthy children, their own families now carried by the strength of their faith.

The morning sky looked as it always did, pale and expansive as it began to give way to the day. *God is with us always,* thought Charity as she watched the spreading light. In an undefined, sacred space, in unity with the Spirit, she floated outside time and place, the distance between heaven and Earth collapsing. *With us always if we only but realize and acknowledge it,* she thought. Bush River Friends had seen her gift of ministry and helped her to clarify God's call. She'd begun to travel, preaching itinerantly because she truly believed with all her heart and soul that each visit she made was a holy errand for God, her great Friend. Then and now, God was a constant in her life, giving her the tools for whatever was asked. In a moment of opening, of divine clarity, Charity realized that her desire to heed God's commands had resulted in an almost inhuman power and fortitude.

Let's see what love can do, thought Charity. The beloved William Penn had said that. *What it's already done.* She'd preached to those who were wealthier, more educated, and more articulate than she was—and had been admired for it. She'd become well-respected in the South, and later, when the time was right, a renowned Friend in the North. A hand to her heart, she thought now of all the good and decent Friends with whom she had held honest conversations and those who had provided hospitality and funded her leading in five countries. She'd spoken boldly against slavery, been arrested in Germany, and almost died in Ireland. Still, whatever challenge God had given her, she'd always prevailed—surviving, rising. For here was the rich treasure of a God-given life. She bowed her head and then lifted it skyward with overwhelming gratitude. She felt the warmth of the day on her forehead and supposed God was touching her there, reminding her of "that of God" moving in the cathedral of her heart.

Suddenly, the sun flashed brightly, Charity comprehending that there was no need to define herself by events, by what others had to say about her, or with an endless list of evidence that she'd done as commanded. She stretched her arms upward, her fingers splaying so that the sun peaked brightly between them. The words, *Live on! Keep going. You will see!* came into her as she was filled with God's grace in the miracle of her life. *Go forward as you have always done. Try to make a difference, touch a heart, encourage a mind, inspire a soul.*

Yes, oh yes. "I will. I will," Charity whispered. *Thank you. Thank you. Thank you.*

"My heart is clear," Charity wrote as she closed her next letter to Isaac and the one to Danise. "My work in Great Britain is done. Mary Swett has returned from her sojourn in London to fetch me, Sarah Harrison having already left for her home in New Jersey. Mary and I will attend the first days of Dublin Yearly Meeting in Meath Place and request our travel certificates to the States. I'm coming home, home to you, with all my riches and flaws." A month after she posted the letter, she and Mary sailed out of Liverpool aboard the *Allegheny*.

Charity spent much of the long voyage standing at the railings and watching the ocean—the ocean of darkness over which she felt sure there was an infinite ocean of light. She held fast to Danise's charm, rubbing over the edges of it with her thumb and going inward and beyond the expansive, blue sky and down below the solid deck of the ship and the sparkling water to a place that had no color or structure. She heard the still, small voice: You are loved. You are loved. Continue thy devotion, thy prayers of acclamation and thanksgiving. Come to me. Come to me."

Whenever the sun would come out from behind a cloud, Charity saw it as a sign—that she was in the beam of God's love, acceptable as she was and, she realized now, that she always had been. "I want everyone to know the truth of it," Charity said aloud. She found grace in how the sunlight danced on the waves. *Light. Love. For me, for everyone,* she thought happily, bursting with thanksgiving for her family, her Friends, and the opportunities she'd been given to share ministry with hundreds of people. *For we are all complicated combinations, and everyone has challenging difficulties.* She felt healed, finally healed.

#

The *Allegheny* docked in New York in December 1801, Mary taking a stagecoach to New Jersey and Charity another to Philadelphia. When Danise opened the door and saw her sister standing on the stoop, she let out a scream. She threw her arms around Charity with the passion of a youth gone by, despite being fifty-eight years old, same as Charity. "You're home! You're home! Praise God, you've come back to us!" she shouted.

It was a short visit, Danise hosting a luscious dinner for her revered sister. Chelsea, Ammon, and Cleaven, now a handsome lad of eleven, filling Charity in on the major events of their lives during the last five years. The most exciting was that a Philadelphian named Thomas Gallaudet had met a wealthy man with a Deaf daughter and had been sent to France to learn how to educate Deaf children. The men planned to open a school for the Deaf when Thomas returned.

Charity arrived in Bush River on First Day, when the whole community was in meeting. She slid out of the carriage at the women's side of the Bush River meetinghouse and quietly opened the door to the dim room. She slowly made her way to the front, where the ministers and elders sat on the facing bench, the divider pulled back, searching for family members. She couldn't see to the men's side, couldn't identify Isaac's head as she padded down the aisle to her place, but she knew he was there, sitting in corporate worship with the other men in their family.

Once seated, Charity struggled to relax into the peace of the familiar room. She scanned the bowed, uncovered heads to find her sisters, Margaret and Susannah, and then her girls, young Susannah and Keturah. All had their eyes closed, unaware of her arrival. She sat back, breathing in the oak of the fire and lifting her chin in thanksgiving to the sturdy ceiling beams. *Ah, home*, she sighed. *Thank thee for delivering me safely.* Then she entered her beloved internal space, imagining she was turning over rich soil and sifting it through her hands again and again as she sank down. In time, she was moved to offer ministry, expressing her gratitude for those who had held up the meeting while she'd been on an errand. When she finished, she heard footsteps coming across the room, from the men's side to the women's, and opened her eyes to see Isaac drawing near, his blue eyes sparkling as he caught her own. His hair was completely gray, his beard longer than she remembered, but, oh, he was handsome! A pleasant shudder went through her as she stood and reached her hands to him.

Isaac took Charity wordlessly in his arms and held her for a long while before they sat, and he took a place beside her, continuing to hold her close. At the rise of the meeting, there were shouts from Keturah and the other Cooks as they came forward to hug Charity.

"Mama, Mama," Susannah and Keturah cried in unison. Tears ran down their cheeks.

"God is so good," Charity heard Susannah murmur as her mama was engulfed in hugs and kisses.

An elder came from the men's side to sternly reprimand Isaac. Isaac laughed unapologetically, "If thou hadn't seen thy wife for five years, I think thou would go to her as soon as possible!" Then he moved out of the way so that others could have their turn with Charity. In the days that followed, he hosted large gatherings at the cabin so that his wife could get reacquainted with the forty-five members of her family, twenty-four grandchildren among them.

At the next women's meeting, a minute was written to celebrate the return of the distinguished minister: "First Month, thirtieth day, 1802. Our Friend, Charity Wright Cook, has returned to Bush River Meeting and provided her certificate of religious visits to parts of this continent and in Europe. She has traveled in the north of the country and then to England, Wales, Scotland, Germany, and Ireland. She attended many meetings in these places. All signators have expressed united consensus and admiration for the gospel labor of Charity Cook while she was among them, her contact and conversations appropriate with her actions."

By Second Month, with nineteen-year-old Susannah and sixteen-year-old Keturah riding beside her, Charity set off to visit the families in the quarterly meeting, geographically and numerically the largest she'd ever witnessed. They met with women in Rayburn's Creek, Tiger River, Padger's Creek, Mud Lick, Allwoods, White Lick, Edisto, and Rock Springs, everyone ecstatic to see her and wanting to hear about Friends in New England and Great Britain. She and her daughters were especially overwhelmed by the hospitality of anyone named Wright, Cook, or Hollingsworth.

In her visits, Charity expressed her continued concern for the almost nine hundred thousand enslaved people in America, approximately a hundred thousand of whom were trapped in South Carolina. Methodists and Baptists had joined Friends in urging enslavers to free their "property," but there was no victory over the White men with political power. They continued to legislate laws that kept most Negroes enslaved and separated from their families, the women and girls raped at will by their enslavers.

The situation was even worse than Charity remembered. One day, she and her daughters came upon an old Black man, quite crooked with years and labor, who told them he was forced to work every day but Sunday, even though he was far slower at it than the others. He wore the remains of an old, tattered shirt, and his pants, hanging from a rope belt at his waist, were in such disrepair that they barely covered him.

The women also came across a plantation owner whom they could not dissuade from only giving shoes to those who could work a full day—fixing the roads, doing carpentry, cooking or butchering, weaving or washing. It was wintertime and heavy, sharp frost covered the ground, but many of the children and old people were barefoot. Keturah was brought to tears by their plight and insisted she be allowed to give her own shoes to a little girl who stood crying by her grandma.

"These people have no say in their treatment, in the tasks they are forced to do or the length of their workday," Charity reminded the area meeting on First Day. "They are treated no better than dogs, even if they are shaking with fever. There is none of this in Europe. Can we not work harder to end it?"

In New Garden, Charity made a point of seeing Levi and Prudence Coffin. "I understand you've befriended my sister, Danise Wright, of Philadelphia, and I have met your relatives in New England, too," Charity began and then introduced Susannah and Keturah. After niceties, the group of them, Levi Sr. with his four-year-old son Levi Jr. in his arms, led them away from Prudence and the others clustered about to a private part of the old-growth forest on the edge of the homestead.

"I understand thee are aware of Danise and Chelsea's commitment to the fugitives who find their way to the city?" asked Charity when the five of them were alone. They'd reached a champion poplar tree that Charity surmised was at least a couple of hundred years old.

"I am," the tall and beardless Levi admitted, "and am sorry to hear that they are not members of a Philadelphia meeting. Has thou heard that Negroes are taken in membership now?"

"I have," nodded Charity, "but Danise and Chelsea waited years and grew impatient for it."

"'Tis understandable," Levi nodded sheepishly, then changed the subject. "There's talk of North Carolina Yearly Meeting becoming legal owners of those that the members in the Carolinas are trying to set free. Those on the run don't usually head toward Philadelphia, but Friends are willing to help them find safe houses to get to Ohio and Indiana where Congress has prohibited slavery."

Charity hugged her daughters to her sides, confident they knew to keep the secret. "'Tis odd, is it not," she said, looking up to Levi, "that by a strange necessity, the very Society that most objected to slavery might itself become one of the largest enslavers." She bit her lip. "And now creating this 'overground railroad' of sorts—'tis dangerous."

Levi checked left, then right. "My family is committed to the effort," he said resolutely, "to save lives and a great deal of torment." He made eye contact with Susannah and Keturah. "We predict that in the next twenty years or so, by the time you two are married with families of your own, a thousand formerly enslaved Carolinians will be transferred out of here, the way made safe by freemen and Friends."

"But thou aid these people now?" asked Susannah, proud of the Coffins, proud of Friends in general.

"We do," nodded Levi. He clasped his hands in front of himself, his expression grave. "And if we are caught assisting them or interfering with their recapture, we are arrested or worse. I am trusting you to keep this work quiet." He reached a hand to the giant oak. "Negroes on the run are told of this grand tree, that aid is not far from it."

"So, your family isn't planning to move to Ohio or Indiana?" asked Charity. "With so much challenge to our testimonies of equality and peace in the South, we've heard others talk of it."

"Oh, I suspect we'll migrate eventually," said Levi, "but not yet. We're needed here. There are enormous obstacles in operating the yearly meeting slaveholding system."

"Yes?" prompted Charity.

Levi raised a hand to enumerate the challenges on his fingers as those who knew sign often did. "Well, for one," he obliged her, tapping his index finger, "we're constantly harassed by lawsuits brought by disappointed heirs." He touched his middle finger. "And secondly, some who have already left for the Northwest Territory simply leave behind those they've had enslaved with no provision for them. We find them living in the forests or swamps, starving and freezing from the cold and damp. Levi indicated his ring finger. "Laws prevent Negroes from living unsupervised, and so they find abandoned sheds and try to make do, but they're in constant danger of being seized, beaten, and sold to other enslavers." He touched his little finger. "And, finally, it is best if the fugitives are accompanied to the Northwest Territories or Canada by those who can vouch for them and defend them against catchers."

"And so Friends are needed to stay here in the South," Susannah confirmed, "although so many have already left."

"Ah, yes. 'Tis been years since Zachariah Dicks predicted it and more since Abijah O'Neall and two other Bush River Meeting families, those of William Kelly and James Mills, left with their families. Charity," Levi asked, "I have used thy sister, Danise, but worry for it. Have thee advice as to how I can safely get messages to her?"

Charity thought for a moment. "My uncle's furniture business?" she suggested. "His workers go often to Philadelphia and can be trusted." She took Keturah's hand. "We best be on our way. Many visits to make."

Epilogue

Everywhere that Charity traveled in 1802, there was talk of migration to the rich, cheap farmland of Ohio and Indiana. The invention of the cotton gin had been perfected on the plantation of Nathanael Greene, the former "Quaker General" of the Revolutionary War, and its use was spreading. The machine increased cotton production and the need for enslaved workers, and Friends wanted desperately to live away from the greedy planters and their insistence on slavery.

It wasn't but the following year, during the time of Thomas Jefferson's presidency in the newly created District of Columbia, that members of Charity and Isaac's family joined the great Quaker migration to the Northwest Territories. The first to extricate were Isaac's cousins, their families becoming chartered members of Miami Monthly Meeting in Waynesville, Ohio. Friends there gathered into a log cabin built for the purpose, just as Ohio was becoming a state. The little meetinghouse had no stove, primarily because member Charity Lynch felt it was "too worldly" to have an internal heat source.

Also in 1803, Isaac and Charity met up with Zachariah Dicks, the notorious, itinerant Friend who believed that he prophesied events of influence to Friends. He was traveling to meetings in Georgia and South Carolina, giving Friends dire warnings of impending disaster if they did not move to the Northwest Territory and escape the curse of slavery. When Charity and Isaac heard him preach, he was expounding on the uprising of enslaved people in Haiti, advising that there would soon be similar riots in the South.

Rebellions of enslaved people weren't new to Charity and Isaac. They were well aware of the Stono Rebellion near Charleston in 1739, during which armed, enslaved men, many of them former soldiers, had gone on a killing spree. Twenty-five settlers had been murdered before White people set out in armed pursuit, eventually intercepting and defeating the enslaved men. Fifty of those captured were executed, and the rest were sold far from home to markets in the West Indies. Afterward, legislation was passed that outlawed Negroes from growing their own food, assembling in groups, earning their own money, or learning to read.

In Bush River, Friends had been so taken by what Zachariah Dicks was saying that the entire body of them soon moved to the Little Miami Meeting, leaving their well-established farms for unexplored land tracts in the frontier wilderness. Between 1802 and 1807, more than a hundred travel certificates were issued, most of them for whole families. The migration so depleted the membership of Bush River that the monthly meeting was all but abandoned by 1808. Those who remained were joined to New Garden Meeting by order of the New Garden Quarterly Meeting. The South Carolina Yearly Meeting sold the properties of Bush River, Rocky Springs, and Camden, and formally laid down Bush River Monthly Meeting in 1822. Two hundred years later, all that remains is a historic marker.

Between 1804 and 1807, five of Isaac and Charity's children moved from Bush River to Miami Monthly Meeting. Their daughter, Ruth, and her husband and children were the first to leave. Six months later, Isaac Jr., along with his wife and two children, followed. Then came the families of Rachel, Sarah, and Thomas. Life must have been lonely for Charity and Isaac with the absence of so many of their children and grandchildren.

In April 1804, Isaac accompanied Charity to both the Baltimore and Philadelphia Yearly Meetings. The Philadelphia gathering stunned the sixty-one-year-old with the number of Friends on the benches. At its rise, he shook hands with a Negro woman, the first he ever encountered who was a member of the Society.

In 1805, Charity's sister, Susannah Hollingsworth, and her husband, Big Isaac, relocated to Ohio, preceding Isaac and Charity by two months. The nine

Hollingsworth children traveled with their parents, as did Mary Pearson Jackson, the companion who had ridden hundreds of miles with Charity, serving as her companion. Mary, who was now sixty-eight years old, migrated with her husband, Joseph, and the families of two of their children.

In October of that same year, Isaac and Charity requested a certificate to leave their home of forty-three years. They packed up their belongings, bought a covered wagon, and started out on the five-hundred-mile, month-long trip to Ohio. The trail was so bumpy that they walked most of the way—and they weren't the only ones. Families they came upon were walking beside covered wagons and uncovered carts pulled by a single horse, all of them filled with precious few belongings. At night, a group of Friends camped together, sharing what they had around the campfire and telling each other what they knew of Ohio and the Miami Meeting.

The traveling certificates for Isaac and Charity were received in January 1806 by Miami Meeting. They were among one of 550 sets of papers, representing over two thousand Friends who migrated to Ohio between 1803 and 1808. Of these, 680 Friends were from South Carolina, such that Charity and Isaac were able to maintain close associations with almost all of their relatives and former neighbors. Within two years of their move, four more of their children arrived, but their son, Joseph, and his family didn't migrate until 1808, and the two remaining children, Mary and Keturah, moved elsewhere first before settling in Ohio.

By 1807, it had occurred to the sixty-two-year-old Charity that, while the pioneers of Ohio were busy building their cabins and clearing pasture land, they might be neglecting their faith. She requested a traveling certificate to visit the families in the Miami jurisdiction—Clear Creek, Lees Creek, Fairfield, and Fall Creek—and made her visits with her daughter, Rachel, then thirty-eight years old and the mother of four young children. While the women traveled mostly within the southwestern part of Ohio, six of their recorded visits involved extensive travel beyond the state's borders.

In September 1808, Charity left home for visits to meetings in the eastern part of Ohio and then traveled on to Virginia, Pennsylvania, and New Jersey. It was a time of vast western growth for the Society, with numerous subdivisions and rearrangements of meetings. Charity was among Friends at the Baltimore Yearly Meeting in 1812 and 1816 and kept busy with visits to those who remained in the Carolinas and Tennessee. A North Carolina Yearly Meeting minute noted the "esteemed attendance" of the sage itinerant minister.

The Southern Quaker meetings were seriously weakened by the western migration. By 1822, the Charleston Meeting, home in her aging years to the remarkable seventeenth-century itinerant minister, Mary Fisher, had so few members that, by the time the Civil War began, it ceased to exist. Except for some Northern Quaker women caring for newly freed people during the Reconstruction period, South Carolina was without the presence of Friends for more than a hundred years.

When Stephen Grellet, a prominent French-American Quaker missionary, visited Core Sound Meeting near Beaufort, North Carolina, in 1825, he recorded in his journal that he found the meeting-house preserved by an aged Negro man who resided nearby. His former Quaker enslaver had moved to Ohio. The loyal man had several times repaired the building, saying, "My old master or his sons may yet return here, and I wish them to find their place of worship in good order."

Not all Quakers went west, a few families remained. They wanted to provide some social protection (such as coping with crises, finding jobs, and aiding in the health and education of children) for free Black families that had worked and lived among Friends. In his report, Stephen Grellet asked if "Black families elected to stay behind or if they had simply been left."

Stephen Grellet wrote, too, of another forsaken meetinghouse in the area, the exact location of it unknown. An aged Black woman who used to attend meeting for worship there "with the family" continued to come regularly on "First and Fourth Days." She sat all alone in the silence, waiting upon and worshiping God, "who she was instructed to know and to love."

On July 30, 1819, Isaac and Charity moved to Silver Creek Meeting, fifteen miles south of Richmond, Indiana. It was home to four of their sons and their daughter Rachel. Quite possibly, the move was due to Isaac's failing health, the seventy-seven year old diagnosed with cancer by then. Charity spent most hours of Isaac's last days—her fingers intertwined in one of his brittle, bony, birdlike hands—telling her beloved husband of fifty-eight years what a remarkable partner and father he had been. Four months later, on January 15, 1820, Isaac died.

Charity returned to Caesar's Creek a few months after Isaac's death, the meeting of Friends from South Carolina set apart from the Miami one as a monthly meeting. All indications are that Charity continued to be given certificates of travel. Her name appeared in a Friend's journal regarding the 1820 Baltimore Yearly Meeting: "She is seventy-eight years of age, a fine specimen, and of a strong American constitution." Her hair was completely white, her face deeply wrinkled, and her skin translucent.

Charity died on her birthday, November 13, 1822. She was eighty years old.

Danise and Chelsea likely received the news of Charity's passing too late to attend Charity's memorial, but Danise might have spent twenty-five cents to send a lovely notecard to the Cook children. She might have enclosed the charm that she and Charity shared throughout their lives and asked that it be tucked in the fresh dirt of her sister's gravesite at

Caeser's Creek Friends burial ground, sixty miles from where Isaac was buried.

Charity died before the infamous "Quaker Split" that birthed the various branches of Friends meetings, some of which still exist today. One of these is credited to Elias Hicks, who preached traditional Quaker values, opposing the wealth and power of Friends, reminding followers, called Hicksites, of the core beliefs of the faith of the original Quakers. His messages drew support from many, his position leading to a schism in Philadelphia Yearly Meeting in 1827. Others were called Gurneyites, a term assigned to members who adopted the views of Joseph John Gurney, an English Quaker minister who espoused evangelical Christian doctrines. The remaining third of the Philadelphia Quakers became known as Orthodox Friends. They preached a more Protestant emphasis on Biblical authority and penance. Similar schisms rapidly followed in New York, Baltimore, Ohio, and Indiana Yearly Meetings, the situation soon complicated by strong personalities causing additional divisions.

Friends eventually sought reconciliation and partial reunification, although the process took half a century. New England Friends led the way by reuniting in 1945. Baltimore, New York, and Philadelphia Yearly Meetings reunified in the '50s and '60s. The twentieth century also brought collaboration between the three broad confederations of yearly meetings—now known as Friends United Meeting,

Friends General Conference, and Evangelical Friends Church International.

Over time and increasingly, Quakers worked actively for the equality of all races and social classes, reconciliation with Indigenous peoples, the end of war, immigration rights, climate crises, prison reform, temperance, and many other important issues. Today, members of the Religious Society of Friends continue to speak out, as Charity Wright Cook did, for equality among all people. A common bumper sticker distributed by American Friends Service Committee displays the slogan, "Love Thy Neighbor; No Exceptions."

Today there are approximately 400,000 Quakers worldwide in eighty-seven countries, most affiliated with the Friends World Committee for Consultation. They differ in language, culture, and national allegiance, as well as the theological emphases that they place on different aspects of Quakerism, upholding the unifying testimonies of simplicity, peace, integrity, community, and equality.

Additional Information

Danise and Chelsea are invented characters (see biographies). I used the word Negro/Negroes in the novel because that is the term used in the North Carolina Yearly Meeting minutes. At the time of the sisters relocation to Philadelphia, the term "Black" was in use in Northern cities. "Colored" wasn't used until about 1820. Accordingly, I also capitalized Native, Deaf, etc. to indicate a culture.

It is true that two of Charity and Isaac's children had babies out of wedlock and apparently were not read out of meeting. Between 1680 and 1790, there were 114 men and 100 women disowned and recorded by North Carolina Yearly Meeting for "premarital fornication" (the first of these in 1706, involving William Bogue).

A Recap of Slavery Among Friends During the Period of the Novel

Paragraphs below are adapted from Lynwood C. Winslow III, "Friends in the Albemarle," pg. 37; *A House in the Albemarle: English Settlers, Quakers, and the 1730 Newbold-White House,* Philip S. McMullan Jr. and H. John Ernst, III, editors; Pamlico & Albemarle Publishing, Nags Head, North Carolina, 2020.

Stepping back to the eighteenth century, a look at the wills and estate inventories tucked into the fine walnut desks of prosperous Friends shows that, among the silver tankards and livestock, there were listed human chattels, enslaved people, as bequests to their children. Quaker Abraham Sanders named four enslaved people in his 1750 will—Old Blind Mingo, Lame Mingo, Sambo, and Bess. Sanders left these workers to his children. Though Friends were admonished by George Fox to treat their "servants and slaves" with tender care, Quakers initially found no conflict between saying that there is that of God in someone and then claiming ownership of that same person. However, as they approached the mid-eighteenth century, and enslaving became more and more prevalent in the colonies, this dichotomy became clearer.

The issue made its official appearance in the North Carolina Meeting records with a 1738 minute asking Perquimans Quakers not to make those they enslaved work on First Day (Sunday). By 1755, caution was expressed by the Philadelphia Yearly Meeting against buying and keeping enslaved people. Slowly and somewhat painfully, Friends in the Carolinas began to divest themselves of their human property. In 1757, as depicted in the novel, John Woolman, a Friend from New Jersey who dedicated his life to traveling among Friends, traveled to North Carolina to preach against the evil of slavery for both the enslaved and their enslavers alike.

Once Friends saw that their faith would no longer allow them to enslave people, they faced multiple challenges. For example, the year after Woolman's visit, 1758, both Wells and Piney Woods meetinghouses burned to the ground. While the minutes are unclear as to the causes, there has been some speculation that these were cases of arson brought on by the growing unpopularity of Friends' new testimony against the enslaving of workers.

In the face of threats such as these, there were also the practical problems of what to do with those they had enslaved once they were free people. If left on their own, they were often captured and resold into bondage. This was the case in 1777 when Thomas Newby of Belvidere Plantation, along with nine other Quakers in Perquimans County, freed some forty of those they had enslaved. Nearly all were recaptured and sold back into bondage by the county court. Friends were launched into a series of legal battles that lasted for almost a century. In an effort to safeguard the actual liberty of those they freed, Friends decided it best to turn over legal ownership to the yearly meeting, making Negroes free in practice but still legal property and thus safe from recapture and sale. The result was one of the most ironic situations in Friends history: one of the most active opponents to slavery became one of the largest enslavers in what by then was the state of North Carolina. Finally, by about 1785, Eastern Quarter was able to report to the yearly meeting that it was "clear" on the issue of slavery.

A Partial List of References

Books and articles by Margaret Hope Bacon including *Mothers of Feminism* (1986), "Quaker Women in Overseas Ministry" (1988; published in *Quaker History* Vol. 77, No. 2 (Fall 1988), pp. 93-109) and *Daughters of Light* (1999).

Ball, Charles (1781?). *Slavery in the United States: a narrative of the life and adventures of Charles Ball, a Black man, who lived forty years in Maryland, South Carolina and Georgia, as a slave.* Published by J. S. Taylor in New York in 1837.

Bjorkman, Gwen Boyer (2013). *Hannah (Baskel) Phelps Hill: A Quaker Woman and Her Offspring.* This article first appeared in the National Genealogical Society Quarterly, v 75 no 4 (Dec 1987).

Bowden, James (1811). *History of the Society of Friends in America (2 vols.).* London: Charles Gilpin.

Butler, Lindley; editor (2006). *Quakers*. In the Encyclopedia of North Carolina. Chapel Hill: University of North Carolina.

Cane Creek Monthly Meeting of Friends (1942). *From Whence We Came: Cane Creek Meeting Sesquicentennial Remembrance Book*. Alamance County, N.C.: Cane Creek Monthly Meeting.

Chilton, M. (2020). *Faith, Rape and Charity: The role of Feminism and Primitivism in the rise and fall of eighteenth-century Quaker Meetings in North Carolina, South Carolina and Georgia*. Unpublished paper that received the 2019 Herbert L Poole Award for Southern Quaker History from the North Carolina Friends Historical Society.

Comfort, William Wistar (1948). *The Quakers: A Brief Account of Their Influence in Pennsylvania*. Gettysburg, Pennsylvania: Pennsylvania Historical Association.

Cook, J. (2009). *Geography of a Massacre: Cherokee and Carolinian Visions of Land at Long Cane*. Bachelor of Arts in History, University of California. A thesis presented to the graduate faculty of the University of Virginia in candidacy for the degree of master of arts' Department of History; University of Virginia.

Crabtree, S. (1981) *Quakerism in the Atlantic World, 1690–1830*. In Michele Lise Tarter and Catie Gill (eds.) *New critical studies on early Quaker women, 1650–1800*. Oxford: Oxford University.

Descendants of the Phelfps and Eleanor Moutton. In HeirsandRoots, Genealogy Resources. https://heirsandroots.com/MyFamilies/Phelps.htm.

High, E. (2022). "Significant Silence; the Fellowship of Early American Black Quakers." Friends Journal, p. 10–13, 47.

Hinshaw, Seth B. and Mary Edith Hinshaw (1972). *Carolina Quakers: Our Heritage, Our Hope: Tercentenary, 1672–1972.* Greensboro, North Carolina: North Carolina Yearly Meeting.

Janney, Samuel M. (1861). *History of the Religious Society of Friends from its Rise to the Year 1828.* Philadelphia, Pennsylvania: T.E. Zell.

Kars, Marjoleine (2002). *Breaking Loose Together: The Regulator Rebellion in Pre-Revolutionary North;* University of North Carolina.

McCarthy, A.L. (2013). *The Quaker Communities of Albemarle;: Friends Early Meetings.* AnceStory Archives; Genealogy Research, Family Stories and Photographs, Archival Resources.

Nakita, K (2016). *A Collection of Memories.* http://kikinakita.blogspot.com/2016/11/the-wright-family-ly-pedigree-15.html.

Newlin, Algie (1981). *Charity Cook, A Liberated Woman.* Richmond, IN: Friends United Press.

Northwestern North Carolina Stories, Early Quakers in Northeast Carolina. http://northeasternncstories.blogspot.com/2012/07/.

O'Neall, J. B. and J. A. Chapman (1892). *The Annals of Newberry: In Two Parts.* Newberry, S.C.: Aull & Houseal.

Opper, Peter (1975). *North Carolina Quakers: Reluctant Slaveholders*. The North Carolina Historical Review; 52 (1); 37–58.

Penney, Norman (1930). *Life and Travels of a Southern Quaker Minister. Bulletin of Friends Historical Association;* 19 (2); 8–90. Philadelphia: Friends Historical Association.

Jean Schubert. *Of Hearth and Highways*. Available from jeanieshubert2022@gmail.com.

Stoneburner, John and Carol Stoneburner (1986). *The Influence of Quaker Women on American History.* Lewiston, NY: E. Mellen.

Tarter, Michele Lise Catie Gill (eds.) (1981). *New critical studies on early Quaker women, 1650–1800.* Oxford: Oxford University.

Tracey, Grace L. and John Philip Dern (1987). *Pioneers of Old Monocacy: The Early Settlement of Frederick County, Maryland, 1721–1743.* Baltimore: Genealogical Publishing.

Tyson, Rae (Spring 2011). *Our First Friends, The Early Quakers. The Early Quakers.* Pennsylvania Heritage Magazine; 27 (2.) http://www.phmc. state.pa.us/portal/communities/pa-heritage/our-first-friends-early-quakers.html.

Teague, Bobbie (1972; eBook, 1995). *Cane Creek: Mother of Meetings* (1995). Snow Camp, North Carolina: Cane Creek Monthly Meeting.

Tuller, Roberta (2020). *An American Family History: Cane Creek Dispute*. https://www.anamericanfamilyhistory.com/Quakers/Meeting%20Cane%20Creek%20Dispute.html.

Whitaker, Walter (June 1, 1972, 1974). *Centennial History of Alamance County Chatham News.* Burlington, N.C.: Alamance County Historical Association.

Weeks, Stephen B . (1896; 1968). *Southern Quakers and Slaver 4: A Study in Institutional History.* New York, Bergman.

White, Steven Jay (1981). *North Carolina Quakers in the Era of the American Revolution.* master's thesis, University of Tennessee, 1981.

Winslow III, Lynwood C. (2020). "Friends in the Albemarle" (eds. Philip S. McMullan Jr. and H. John Ernst III), *A House in the Albemarle: English Settlers, Quakers, and the 1730 Newbold-White House*, pg. 37; Pamlico & Albemarle Publishing, Nags Head, North Carolina, 2020.

Acknowledgments

I am indebted first and foremost to the Obadiah
Brown's Benevolent Fund, established in Providence
in 1823 by bequest of Obadiah Brown, of New
England Yearly Meeting, for partially funding my
work. Then to Peggy Moran, my editor, for her good
work and suggestions. Gratitude for hospitality provided by Betsy Costello, Maggie and Kurt Keskinen,
and Art Luetke for writing retreats. Deep thanks to
historians Thomas Hamm, Max Carter, and Mark
Chilton, the latter two who gave so generously of
their time to take me sightseeing to relevant areas of
North Carolina. Thanks for the friendship of Marcy
Maury, Kat Rice, and Carol Cothern who partially
funded my first stay in Greensboro, North Carolina,
and, on a second visit, traipsed around with me to
see Cane Creek pottery and furniture. To Bruce
Baker, Gunnel Clark, Meg Butterworth, Mike Wold,
and Erin Walsh for their countless walks with me to

discuss events in the novel. To Sarah Crabtree who gave me permission to quote from her chapter in *New Critical Studies on Early Quaker Women, 1650–1800*, and Lynwood Winslow III who allowed me to quote (with edits) from her book.

My heartfelt thanks to the following beta readers who offered encouragement and useful suggestions. My apologies to anyone I have omitted: Meg Butterworth, Max Carter (for accuracy of North Carolina Quakers), Mark Chilton, Susan Storer Clark, Karie Firoozmand, Anna Higgins, Thomas Hamm (for accuracy of Quaker history and language), Mary Pat Luetke-Stahlman (for Deaf sensitivity), Peggy Mayer, Cai Quirk (for transgender sensitivity), Erin Walsh, Carol Lathrop White, and Lynwood Winslow. To Jay Marshall (for spirituality accuracy), Dwight Wilson and Jerry Williams (for language regarding Black people and Black history), and Jean Schubert, a kindred spirit, who also wrote about Charity Wright Cook, including information about her relative, Susannah Wright (see biographies). Collectively, these people joined me in sharing the story of the remarkable Friends of the eighteenth century.

Timeline of Relevant Events

1652 George Fox, founder of the Society of Friends
roams Great Britain with others of the Valiant
Sixty to preach. Among them was William
Edmundson, the first to preach in Ireland, and
Mary Fisher, Elizabeth Fletcher, Elizabeth
Leavens, and Thomas Holme, all of whom are
mentioned in this novel.

1671 After a voyage of seven weeks, during which
dolphins were caught and eaten, George Fox
and William Edmundson arrived in Barbados,
and from there, Fox sent an epistle to Friends,
spelling out the role of women's meetings in the
Quaker marriage ceremony, a point of controversy when he returned home. Though women's
meetings had been held in London for the last
ten years, this was an innovation in Bristol and
the northwest of England, which many there felt,
went too far. Fox and Edmundson went on to the

colonies where they visited in North Carolina in 1672.

1675 William Edmundson wrote an epistle to Friends in Virginia, Maryland, and other parts of America in which he denounced the holding of enslaved people.

1677–1678 Culpeper's Rebellion took place in Albemarle County (now Pasquotank County). The rebellion was in response to a variety of complaints about the government but arose primarily as a reaction to the Navigation Acts imposed on the colonies by England.

1682 The colony of Pennsylvania was founded by William Penn. Some of the early settlers of Philadelphia and surrounding towns were wealthy and purchased African natives to work on their large farms. Although they themselves had immigrated to escape religious persecution, they saw no contradiction in enslaving workers and indentured servants (who had signed agreements to work for several years in exchange for ship passage). Slavery was widespread in the colonies, and William Penn is noted as declaring that, during the course of a single year, Philadelphia had received ten ships with enslaved people.

1682 Benjamin Lay was born in England.

1688 German Friends in Germantown, Pennsylvania, issued the first protest against enslavement made by a religious body in the thirteen colonies. It was sent to the Philadelphia Yearly Meeting, but "it was adjudged not to be so proper for this meeting to give a positive judgment in the case."

1696 Philadelphia Yearly Meeting advised "that Friends be careful not to encourage the bringing in of any more Negroes."

1700 The Pennsylvania Assembly passed the first law concerning the different treatment of Black and White indentured servants. The statute declared that the penalty of a White servant for embezzlement of his master's wares would be additional time in servitude equaling double the value of the material stolen; if the servant was Black, he was to be harshly whipped. Sexual relations between the races were forbidden by law but were widespread.

1709 Abigail Pike was born.

1720 Rachel Wells was born.

1717 Mary Peisley was born.

1724 Hermon Husband was born.

1727 The London Yearly Meeting epistle censured those Friends who engaged in the importation of enslaved people.

1745 Charity Wells Cook was born.

1749 John and Rachel (and others) walk to Cane Creek, North Carolina.

1753 Mary Jackson traveled with Rachel Wright to Richmond and, therefore, knew for a fact that she had conducted herself properly despite Hermon Husband's erroneous allegations against the minister. This same year, Catherine Payton came with Mary Peisley to the colonies.

April 1754 Rachel Wright went to Cedar Creek in company with Jeremiah Piggott, and Mary Miller Jackson to support the women of the meeting in petitioning for the establishment of a women's meeting there. Renowned traveling Quaker ministers, Mary Peasley and Catherine Payton, were also at this meeting.

1755 Hermon Husband officially joined Cane Creek in December.

From 1755–1776, the Religious Society of Friends became the first Western organization to ban enslaving.

1756 Hermon Husband accused Rachel Wright of having improper relationships with men when she was traveling to organize women's meeting. He presented these accusations to a committee at Cane Creek Meeting.

1757 John Woolman visited Virginia and the Carolinas and complained of the minimal care shown to enslaved people. "Are there any concerned in the importation of Negroes or buying them after imported?" he asked. The answer to this query was unsatisfactory because Friends admitted to the right to buy those they enslaved for their own use but not for general sale. John Woolman wrote an epistle to the new settlement of Friends at New Garden and to Cane Creek against slavery, which was not well received.

In 1758, North Carolina Yearly Meeting (first organized around 1680) appointed a committee to consider "making provision for Negro meetings" at New Begun Creek, Head of Little River, Simon's Creek, and Old Neck at specified times. A sufficient number of White Friends were to attend these meetings to see that good order was observed. Also, in 1758, the Yearly Meeting asked, "Are all who have Negroes careful to use them well and encourage them to come to meetings as much as they reasonably can?" Finally, in this year, Joseph Wells married Mary Cook. The couple would later be killed by Natives.

1758–72 For fourteen years, the leading question among Friends was about slavery.

1759 Thomas Wells, Rachel's grandfather, died July 15, 1759. He was eighty-three years old.

1760 In the common form of a query, the North Carolina Yearly Meeting asked its members, "Are all Friends clear of being concerned in the importation of slaves or purchasing them for sale; do they use those well they are possessed of; and do they endeavor to restrain from vice; and do they instruct them in the principles of the Christian religion?"

1761 Jehu Stuart is first mentioned in the Cane Creek Monthly Meeting minutes. The matter of him having premarital sex with Charity Wright was continued at the February meeting. He was disowned at the April 1761 meeting. Also, as described in the first chapter of the novel, in January 1761, the Cane Creek women's meeting took up the issue of Charity's part in the assault. After repeated labor, the meeting disowned her in April 1761. Thus, the sensitive issue was seriously debated over a three-month period of time. As is included in the novel, Mary Hiatt and Rebekah Marshall were made overseers of Cane Creek women's meeting, unseating Rachel Wright. In June, Charity appealed to the Western Quarterly Meeting. Upheld were both hers and Jehu's disownments.

1762 Rachel Wright requested a certificate for transfer, but after months of discussion, Cane Creek was unable to reach consensus as to whether it should be provided. According to Mark Chilton (2020), "Her request triggered vigorous debate as some Friends wanted it denied due to Rachel's perceived 'lack of sincerity' when she had earlier repented for her misconduct. Others felt that she deserved a certificate because her apology had at the time been accepted as satisfactory" (Clinton, 2020). Nevertheless, the Wrights had already moved sometime between May and December 1761 to Bush River. "In November 1762, Rachel complained to the Quarterly Meeting, wanting the certificate to be given as was right order. It was issued, Hermon Husband out of town at the time. He married Mary Pugh (the sister of Simon Dixon), who in contrast to Rachel Wright, was "deferential, not confrontational" (Chilton, 2020). Also in this same year, Charity Wright married Isaac Cook.

1763 to 1783 Isaac and Charity Cook's ten children were born within the district of Bush River,

South Carolina. They were Joseph (1763), Sarah (1766), Rachel (1768), Thomas (1770), Mary (1772), Charity (1774), Ruth (1776), Marion (1778), Isaac (1781), Susannah (1783), and Keturah (1786). The birth and death dates of Charity's relatives can be found on Wikitree.

1764 Based on reports from quarterly meetings that there is a general deficiency in most places in instructing Negroes in the principles of the Christian religion, the North Carolina Yearly Meeting "weightily recommended to Friends who possessed to have the unhappy people more immediately under their care and notice, to endeavor towards their education, but also make a diligent inspection into their clothing and feeding." The yearly meeting further asked its members to impress on the minds of those they represented "the necessity of shutting the door against the increase of slaves among them by purchase" and that the wound is so deep "it seems incurable in the present generation."

1764 According to Clinton (2020), Cane Creek proposed to establish a new meeting at Holly Spring as an alternative to the Mill Creek Meeting because not everyone agreed with Hermon Husband's manner of theology. It was the opinion of a delegation of New Garden men sent to visit Holly Spring that this move was divisive, and they recommended deferring the decision of creating another meeting "in hopes a time more union may appear in this Quarter."

About this time, a romance was blossoming between forty-one-year-old Hermon Husband and twenty-two-year-old Amy Allen of Cane Creek Meeting, Hermon Husband's first wife, Mary Pugh, having died. Allen's love for Husband was not dampened by his disownment in early 1764, even though by marrying "out of unity," she, as well as the wedding guests, were eventually disowned also.

1765 John Griffith, an antislavery champion, visited meetings in Virginia and North Carolina. After attending most of the monthly meetings, he remarked that most Friends were "keeping Negroes in perpetual slavery. . . . I am satisfied Truth will never prosper amongst them, nor any others, who are in the practice of keeping this race of mankind in bondage. It is too manifest to be denied, that the life of the religious is almost lost where slaves are very numerous; and it is impossible it should be otherwise, the practice being as contrary to the spirit of Christianity as light is to darkness."

In January 1766 Visiting Quaker John Griffith remarked in his diary that "most of the members [of Cane Creek] seemed void of a solid sense and solemnity; a spirit of self-righteousness and contention was painfully felt; . . . and the few living sensible members were borne down and discouraged." Of Hermon Husband and his followers, Griffith lamented that they acted "in their own will . . . having taken counsel of their own depraved hearts" (Clinton, 2020).

In 1766 Husband announced in an open court session in Hillsborough that Maddock's Mill had been selected as a gathering place for Regulators to discuss their grievances. This publicly linked Joseph Maddock with Herman Husband, and afterward, Joseph constantly feared confiscation of his mill and mill property by Governor William Tryon. The meeting at Maddock's Mill included much the same dissident Quaker crowd that had been troubling Cane Creek Meeting. Of the twelve men at the meeting at Maddock's Mill, we know the names of just four—disowned Quaker Hermon Husband, Eno member Joseph Maddock, Mill Creek members William Cox Sr. and William Moffitt. Three of these men had questioned Rachel Wright's sincerity in 1763; two of them had signed the dissenting minute about Husband's disownment in 1764; and three of them had been at Husband's wedding. These four men and their neighbors would soon form what Husband called "the Sandy Creek Association," a radical but nonviolent forerunner of the Regulators (Clinton, 2020).

1767 The North Carolina Yearly Meeting recorded that Friends were divided in their sentiments based on their responses to a previously recorded minute (in 1766) and epistle concerning the steps to be immediately "respecting putting a stop to the further purchase of Negroes, which being solidly considered, and several weighty remarks made thereon, it is left for further consideration at the next sitting of this Meeting," Friends were requested not to "encumber themselves" with further purchases. All were encouraged to treat and clothe the people they enslaved well; also to allow them to "hire their time to pay them wages as servants."

1768 The Regulators entered the Hillsborough courtroom and dragged those they saw as corrupt officials through the streets. In this same year, the issue of slavery, carried over from the previous year, was again discussed at the quarterly and yearly meeting levels. Friends were "for the most part clear of importing or buying Negroes." Some Friends were also willing to release their enslaved workers if way could be made for it. It was agreed that no Friends from this time forward should purchase an enslaved person.

1769 The quarterly meeting being "uneasy" with the query related to Negroes, appealed to the yearly meeting that a "more fuller restraint" be made regarding "the unrighteous and oppressive gain and practice of buying and selling Negroes in all its various branches among Friends." Also in January of this year, Charity Cook offered a paper of condemnation that was accepted as satisfaction. Herman Husband and his troublemaking supporters were not in attendance when the letter was accepted, so the people who were there were largely supporters of the Wright family. The acceptance suggested to Chilton that it was probably vaguely worded. She returned to good standing in the Society of Friends and the Bush Monthly Meeting in particular.

1770 Enslaving was made a disownable offense by the Philadelphia Yearly Meeting.

1771 The Battle of Alamance.

Two years after the Western Quarterly Meeting registered its dissatisfaction of the advice on slavery to the yearly meeting, a new query was substituted with copies sent to each monthly meeting: "Are all Friends careful to bear a faithful testimony against the Innequitious practice of importing Negroes and refusing to purchase them; do they use those they have inherited well, endeavoring to discourage them from evil, and encouraging them in that which is good?" It was recorded for the first time that a member, James Crew, was disowned for buying an enslaved person.

Rachel Wells Wright died in December.

1772 The Bush River Monthly Meeting recorded Charity as a minister. John Woolman died in England, having traveled in steerage to London Yearly Meeting. Fortified by John Woolman's death, an epistle was written that included an abolitionist statement. In advices from the yearly meeting, Friends were not to buy enslaved people "except from Friends" or cause the parting of husband and wife or parent and child. They were not to sell people to enslavers. They addressed the state legislature, "being fully convinced in our minds and judgements . . . [that the] abomination of the importation of Negroes from Africa; by which iniquitous practice great numbers of our fellow creatures with their posterity are doomed to perpetual and cruel bondage . . . [and cause] pride and idleness to our youth in such a manner that morality, and true piety is much wounded where slavery abounds." From this time on, there were individual cases of tender conscience among North Carolina Friends. Friends were assisted by other Quakers to write documents of freedom to those whom they enslaved if "the persons proposed to be set free is able to get their own livelihood."

1773 North Carolina Yearly Meeting declared that "it is our clear sense and judgment that we are loudly called upon in this time of calamity and close trial to minister justice and judgment to Black and White, rich and poor, and free our hands from any species of oppression. . . . We do therefore most earnestly recommend to all who continue to withhold from any [enslaved people] their just right to freedom, as they prize their own present peace and future happiness to clear their hands of this iniquity, by executing manumissions for all those held by them in slavery who are arrived at full age, and also for those who may yet be in their minority, to take place when the females attain the age of eighteen, and the males twenty-one years."

1775–1783 Another Friend in the yearly meeting, Shadrack Stanley, was disowned for buying an enslaved person. The yearly meeting ordered the distribution of twelve copies of a pamphlet authored by Anthony Benezet, a lifelong abolitionist, be sent to every monthly meeting.

1776 As told in the novel, Charity Cook made her first journey as an itinerant minister outside of the Bush River area. She went to Wrightsboro, Georgia, with Mary Pearson. Two men, William O'Neal and Henry Milhous, are minuted to accompany the women. In this same year, the North Carolina Yearly Meeting "earnestly and affectionately advise all who held slaves to cleanse their hands of them as soon as possible." No Friend was permitted to "buy or sell any slave, or hire any slave from persons in unity [other Friends];" and "any member of this meeting who may hereafter buy, sell or clandestinely assign for hire any slaves in such manner as may perpetuate or prolong their slavery" was to be testified against. A committee was appointed to assist Friends regarding those they hold in bondage. All over the North and South, many individual Friends were led to manumit those they had enslaved.

1777 The committee appointed at the previous North Carolina Yearly Meeting reported that "about forty" people had been set free. This seemed to put a stop to the present work, although there were "several Friends who have yet Negroes in their possession, and are uneasy in remaining in a practice they are convinced is not consistent with [state law]. In many states, owners could be arrested by any freeholder, turned over to the sheriff, and kept in jail until the next term of court that should order them to be punished. Friends paid lawyers in North Carolina to take cases involving complicated state laws to court, resulting in the emancipation of many formerly enslaved people in North Carolina and Virginia.

1779 Friends continued to "labor with those who still held slaves in bondage to convince them if possible of the evil of the practice." A committee met with anyone who was in jeopardy of being disowned and also worked to assist those who had been manumitted, "to instruct them in religion, in education, and in worldly affairs."

1779 The North Carolina Yearly Meeting appointed a "committee of visitation whose duty it was to visit and labor with those members who declined emancipation. The committee reported progress from year to year; many were persuaded, some held back."

1780 Friends agreed not to hire Black people except such as were manumitted and were yet minors or the property of orphans. Those who continued to enslave people were not to be employed in the services of the monthly meetings.

1781–1782 The Yearly Meeting provided for the disownment of those who persisted in holding enslaed people after a committee at the monthly and quarterly levels had met with them. Way opened when a new state law on the subject was passed. It gave all enslavers "the power to emancipate by will after death or by acknowledging the will while still alive, in open court, provided they agreed to support all the aged, infirm and young people thus set at liberty." The great body of Friends did not hesitate to free those they still held when the law allowed emancipation and for them to protect and assist those they had emancipated.

1783 The work of persuasion continued among Friends, and a number of enslaved people were released with the prospect that others would soon be freed. Cases also demanded the attention of Friends where people, after being freed, had been taken to Virginia and sold. On one occasion, a committee was sent there to investigate.

1784 Hugh Judge, an itinerant Quaker who was visited in central North Carolina, went home with a woman Friend after meeting for worship. He and others "had some friendly conversation" with the woman concerning a Black man held in bondage. They proposed he be set free, and the wife "was very willing. [The husband had an] unwillingness to let him go free, and we labored with him till late. In the morning a manumissions was written out and the man came in and signed it."

It was witnessed by several Friends. Hugh Judge referred to Charity as "a living minister," meaning that she was one in which a strong spiritual life was clearly present.

1784 Those who continued to enslave people were excluded from membership in the Society of Friends. It was also noted that the education of Black people was very neglected and was to be the responsibility of owners. These weighty matters were given to the monthly meetings who were requested to send up an account of their progress with them.

May 1784, Abigail Franks, a faithful Black attender, was accepted into membership in the Philadelphia area three years after her original application.

1786–87 Two post-revolutionary agrarian movements were the Shays Rebellion, centered in Massachusetts, and the Whiskey Rebellion in western Pennsylvania.

1787 Visitations continued, but if Friends "remained in the practice of holding their fellow men in a state of slavery, endeavoring to convince them of the iniquity of such practice," and if they still refused, they were to be disowned. "From the time of the Revolutionary War on, the burden of the journal of every Friend who visited the South is always the same—slavery."

1788 North Carolina Yearly Meeting inserted in the discipline "that none amongst us be concerned in importing, buying, selling, holding or overseeing slaves, and that all bear a faithful testimony against the practice." During the same year, Cedar Creek Monthly Meeting (near Richmond, Virginia) disowned thirteen persons for enslaving people, and in some cases where Friends had sold enslaved people, they were required to find them and restore their freedom. The North Carolina Yearly Meeting reported that some "Quakers were not yet clean of slaveholding and a new committee was formed to report to the next yearly meeting to be held at Centre Meeting in Guilford County" regarding the state of this concern.

November 21, 1789, the General Assembly, meeting in Fayetteville, ratified the United States Constitution, making North Carolina the twelfth state.

1790 A statement was incorporated into Philadelphia Yearly Meeting's Discipline that "meetings are at liberty to receive convinced people into membership, without respect of nation or color."

1797–1802 Charity traveled to Europe to attend London Yearly Meeting and visit other meetings.

1801 North Carolina Yearly Meeting decided to call the enslaved people in their concern "Black people."

1802 Friends complained formally to state officials that, due to defects in the law, free Black people were carried out of the North Carolina state and sold.

1802 Charity returned from Europe to the United States.

1809 Bush River and Wrightsboro were almost void of any Quaker element because so many of the towns' inhabitants had left for Ohio and Indiana, leaving behind their dreams of a peaceful life. For example, "Francis Jones (1725–84), his children and grandchildren moved from Wrightsboro in a caravan of some forty families. They crossed the Ohio River at Cincinnati June 12, 1805. This town then consisted of one brick store, one frame building, and some log cabins. Francis was an old man of eighty years, very ill, and was carried through the Cherokee nation on a litter by Natives who noticed his Quaker garb, and called him one of Penn's men."

1809 The work of the Underground Railroad and the abolitionist movement in North Carolina, as elsewhere, included many from the Religious Society of Friends. Also in this year, Quaker enslavers in Guilford County deeded all of those they owned to the North Carolina Yearly Meeting, which over the next few years spent about thirteen thousand dollars relocating Black people in northern states, Haiti, and Liberia. As early as 1819, Vestal Coffin established an Underground Railroad station in Guilford County, along with free Black people. His sons, Alfred and Addison, carried on his work, as did his cousin, Levi Coffin. These four but especially Levi were unquestionably the best-known of Guilford County's abolitionists.

1810 North Carolina Yearly Meeting appointed a committee of seven Friends to have under care all suffering cases of "people of color." This committee seems to have evolved a system under which certain parties were authorized to act as agents for enslaved people who were gifted by their owners to the yearly meeting.

1813 In a case where some Indigenous people had been made enslaved workers, Friends brought suits on their behalf and won.

1816 Friends opened a school for two days in the week to last three months for the Black people who came under Friends' care. It was reported two years later "that some of them can spell and some few read. It was agreed that their education was to be extended until the males could read, write and cypher as far as the rule of three, and those of the females to read and write."

1817 Levi Coffin published the first issue of *The Philanthropist*, the first journal in America to advocate unconditional emancipation. Also in this year, the first school for the Deaf in the United States, The American Asylum, At Hartford, For The Education And Instruction Of The Deaf And Dumb, was founded in Hartford, Connecticut. Black students were not admitted until 1952. In its earliest years, the school was a mix of signs, some students bringing the gestures they had invented in their homes, others sharing the signs used on Martha's Vineyard, and Laurent Clerc, the first teacher at the school, sharing the signs of French Sign Language. Eventually, these three strains of manual communication merged into what would become American Sign Language (ASL). When sign is interpreted into spoken English, as it is in this novel, it is not ASL, which is not spoken. It is a form of manually coded English, which has many variants.

1820 Isaac Cook died on January 15, 1820, in Liberty, Indiana (Union County).

1821 Levi Coffin's cousin, Vestal Coffin, opened a First Day (Sunday) School for the enslaved people in New Garden, North Carolina. "Some masters were induced to allow their slaves to attend, and these were learning to spell in words of two or three letters, when other masters became alarmed, for it made their own slaves discontented and uneasy. They threatened the terrors of the law, the slaves kept at home, and the school closed."

1822 There were 450 Black people in the hands of North Carolina Yearly Meeting. They came from all parts of North Carolina, and people other than Quakers began to give over their Black people as well. That same year, North Carolina Yearly Meeting found it necessary to forbid their agents to receive Black people from any except members of Society because they were responsible to send these people "thus put into the hands" to Friends living in free states. As early as 1814, forty people had been sent to Pennsylvania.

1822 On November 13, 1822, Charity Wright Cook died at Caesar's Creek in Clinton County, Ohio.

She was buried in Caesar Creek Cemetery in Wayne Township, Warren County, Ohio.

Biographies

These biographies are provided in alphabetical order after the information about Charity Wright Cook.

Charity Wright Cook
(November 13, 1742–November 13, 1822)

Charity was born on the frontier near what is today Frederick, Maryland. She was the seventh child of John Wright and Rachel Wells Wright, who maintained a devout Quaker home (see Rachel Wells Wright below). The extended family included six ministers.

As told in the novel, Charity walked with her family on the Great Wagon Trail to Cane Creek, North Carolina, in 1749, when she was four years old. Details of the imagined trip were taken from accounts of similar migrations. The Wright family members, including her uncle, Joseph Jr. (a skilled furniture maker), were founders of the Cane Creek Meeting (now called Snow Camp, an unincorporated community in southern Alamance County). A man referred to simply as Majer/Major in the will of his owner, Joel Brooks, is the only known Black person who lived in Cane Creek at the time. He was enslaved by Charity's brother-in-law (husband of Mary Wright) and was emancipated when Joel Brooks died.

According to Cane Creek Meeting minutes, Charity was raped by Jehu Stuart, who was also a Quaker, when she was fourteen years old. She was accused by the majority of members of the Cane Creek Meeting of not doing enough to stop the assault and disowned, a process that took several months. The minutes of the meeting state that Charity was found "guilty of keeping untimely and unseasonable company with Jehu Stuart and for want of resisting to the utmost of her power his wicked and lustful design was overcome and defiled by him" (Chilton, 2020). As was the practice at the time, Charity could remain a part of Cane Creek Meeting if she would sincerely sign a paper of condemnation taking responsibility for *her* transgression. Charity refused to sign anything that accused her of any wrongdoing and was disowned.

Shortly after Charity was disowned or "read out of meeting" and as the result of "the struggle between feminism and misogyny" (Chilton, 2020), the Wrights sold their land and house to Peter Stout (a fellow member of Cane Creek Meeting), and most of them moved to Bush River, Newberry County (near Fredericksburg, South Carolina). While the Wrights were not the first Quakers to move to Bush River, they did play an important role in organizing Bush River Monthly Meeting.

Charity appealed her disownment to the quarterly meeting. She met Isaac Cook, a Quaker, and in 1762, shortly before her disownment was completed, she married Isaac in the Bush River Meeting. The marriage meeting for worship in the novel is based on Friends' weddings then and now. Not long after, Charity Cook became Bush River's first recognized woman minister. According to the Cane Creek minutes, about eight years later, in January 1769, Charity's Paper of Condemnation was accepted, and she was officially returned to good standing in the Religious Society of Friends.

During the American Revolutionary War, Charity traveled in the South, preaching pacifism and taking a solid stand against slavery. Isaac supported the holy work, raising their eleven children and working their farm. The incident at Rayburn Creek, during which Isaac almost drowned and Charity rescued him, is true. Although Charity's father was a captain in the military (see John Wright, below), the scene at New Garden Meeting during the war is invented.

Charity made hundreds of religious journeys, engaging in kitchen ministry in the homes of Friends; it was intimate and direct. She was away from home for long periods of time, supported financially by her faith community and by her and Isaac's resources.

She crisscrossed the country, visiting every region where Quakers were established.

Through the 1770s, '80s, and '90s, this inspired, vibrant, outgoing woman from the backcountry of the American frontier made a name for herself among Quakers everywhere. As depicted in the novel, Charity smoked a pipe and was distinguished by her white, broad-brimmed beaver hat. Smoking was not uncommon for rural, colonial women, as long as it was done privately and moderately. However, Charity was known to smoke her pipe in public, which caused quite a stir, especially in London, England. She would never have attended a service in Christ Church as depicted in the novel. This scene was created to describe the differences between this service and the way of Friends. However, had Charity actually done this Quaker historian Thomas Hamm is quick to point out that it would have been perceived by other Friends as supporting a hireling ministry, which Friends were against.

Charity displayed an uncanny ability to relate to people in all walks of life when she traveled in the North. She hobnobbed with the Pennsylvania Quaker elite and rubbed shoulders with much less sophisticated folks on the frontier. Her normal travel pattern was to ride with a woman partner, as well as men appointed by a meeting to chaperone the women. On a few of her journeys, she traveled with her much younger sister, Quaker minister Susannah Wright Hollingsworth.

In October 1797, Charity traveled on the *USS Severn* from New York to Liverpool, England. There, she attended London Yearly Meeting and visited Quaker communities throughout England, Germany, and Ireland. She spent many hours in people's homes, providing pastoral care and spiritual guidance. Newlin (1981) wrote that Charity created a bond that lifted the spirits of those she met and nurtured her own soul as well. Chilton (2020) noted that, "in Europe and in America both, the men who met Charity were sometimes taken aback by her outspoken nature. When she visited London in 1797, she scandalized English Friends by strolling around town with her pipe in her mouth., the broad-brimmed beaver hat atop her head. Her advocacy in Europe for the equality of all human beings was forceful enough to garner some negative feedback from fellow Quakers. Charity also had the audacity to intervene in an otherwise all-male debate at London Yearly Meeting in 1797 (Chilton, 2020). It is true that, in 1798, in French occupied (now German) territory, Charity was arrested for conducting Quaker meetings in defiance of government orders that forbade her from doing so. In Dublin, Ireland, in November 1799, Charity did contract smallpox and almost died. She was bedridden for six weeks.

Charity returned to the United States in December 1801. It being First Day (Sunday), she went immediately to Bush River Meeting. When she entered worship, Isaac was on the preachers' and elders' bench on the men's side of the church.

According to Newlin (1981), Charity crept to the preachers' bench on the women's side and eventually gave ministry. When Isaac heard his wife praying, he recognized her voice, and shattering protocol, hurried to her. He kissed her passionately, not having seen her for five years. At the rise of meeting, one of the men sharply rebuked Isaac for breaking into the worship in such an unseemly manner. Isaac replied: "If thou had not seen thy wife for over four years, thee would have done the same thing" Newlin (1981).

After getting readjusted to life with her family, Charity spent another four years making religious visits but closer to home in South Carolina. Some authors report that she returned to England for a second visit, but I didn't include this in my novel.

In 1805, Charity and Isaac joined family and friends in the five-hundred mile exodus of Quakers from the South. The Cooks went to Miami Monthly Meeting in Ohio. The mass migration saw almost every Quaker leave North Carolina, South Carolina, and Georgia. It is true that Zachary Dicks (see below), a noted Friend, prophesied an impending uprising by enslaved workers, influencing many to migrate to Ohio and Indiana. In the rush to leave, Friends sold their lands and homes at a fraction of their true value and abandoned much personal property.

As depicted in the novel, two of Charity and Isaac's children had babies born out of wedlock or shortly after their parents married. I included this in the novel to remind the reader that Quakers, as is true of those who practiced other religions, did not always follow the rules of their faith.

By the time the eighteenth century drew to a close, Charity had logged twenty years of religious travel and had become one of the best-known itinerant preachers of her time. The hardships she encountered on her journeys are difficult to appreciate: rough roads and arduous travel on horseback, severe weather, sleeping on hard and cold ground, assisting in the Revolutionary War, enduring emotional struggles, and being separated from family and friends.

Charity spent her last years as a member of the Caesar's Creek Monthly Meeting in Warren County, Ohio, northeast of Cincinnati. She continued to travel to visit and support Quaker communities, making her last religious journey with her son, Joseph, in 1820, when she was seventy-five years old. After forty-four years in active ministry, Charity finally ended her remarkable career. She died on November 13, 1822, on her seventy-seventh birthday. She is buried in Caesar's Creek Burying Ground.

By 1827, when the great Quaker split occurred, many of Charity's relatives, particularly the Hollingsworth and Cook descendants, became Hicksites (after Elias Hicks, who is mentioned in the novel) and Wilburites. At the time, Hicksites comprised about two-thirds of the body of Friends and emphasized the role of the Inward Light in guiding individual faith and conscience. Wilburites (Conservative Friends) maintained traditional Quaker values and habits. It was the poet, Walt Whitman, who wrote:

"Always Elias Hicks points the way to the fountain of all naked theology, all religions, all worship, all the Truth to which the listener is eligible. Others talk of the Bible and its verses, saints, churches, exhortations, and the standards of the outside world, but Elias Hicks talks of the only inward religion, inside human consciousness. This he incessantly labors to kindle, nourish, and strengthen."

A biography by Quaker author Algie Newlin, *Charity Wright Cook: A Liberated Woman*, was published in 1981. The book is difficult to obtain but available in historical Quaker collections.

Robert Barclay
(December 23, 1648–October 3, 1690)

This novel was published by Eric Muhr at Barclay Press in Newberg, Oregon. Named for Robert Barclay, whose *Apology* is mentioned as being owned by the Wright family in the novel, the mission of Barclay Press is spiritual, socially responsible, Quaker, and Christian literature.

Robert Barclay was born to a wealthy Scottish family. In 1648, he became a convinced Friend at eighteen years of age, after visiting his father in prison and coming under the influence of a fellow prisoner, John Swinton, who was a Quaker. With the benefit of family wealth, Barclay spent a good deal of time in scholarship and in 1678, at twenty-seven years of age, published in Latin the work for which he is most famous, *An Apology for the True Christian Divinity, being an Explanation and Vindication of the Principles and Doctrines of the People Called Quakers*. However, "Barclay's Apology" failed to end the persecution of Quakers, and Barclay himself was thrown in prison several times. The book is still the best and most thorough defense of Friends' principles that has ever been written.

In addition to his scholarly work, Barclay made an extensive evangelistic trip to Europe with George Fox, William Penn, and George Keith and served for a time, in absentia, as governor of the American colony of East Jersey. His later years were spent at his estate of Ury House, now a large ruined mansion in Aberdeenshire, Scotland. He died and was buried there.

In 1670, Robert married another Quaker, Christian Mollison. They had seven children: three sons (Robert, David, and John) and four daughters (Patience, Catherine, Christian, and Jean). David Barclay of Cheapside (1682–1769) became a wealthy merchant in London. He was one of the founders of the present-day Barclays Bank and was also in the brewing industry. As told in the novel, David manumitted an estate of enslaved workers in Jamaica.

Thomas Beals
(1719–1801)

Thomas Beals was born in Chester County, Pennsylvania, in 1719, the son of John and Sarah Beals. His brother, Bowater Beals, married Ann Cook, sister of Isaac Cook, who was the husband of Charity Cook. Many of John's relatives migrated south from Pennsylvania to North Carolina and later to Ohio and Indiana. Many of them had the gift of ministry.

It is thought that Thomas Beals married Sarah Esther (Antrim) on November 12, 1741, in Hopewell, Virginia. They moved to North Carolina in 1748, living first at Cane Creek and later moving to the frontier of New Garden, North Carolina. In 1753, Thomas came forth in ministry. About that time, he moved his family to Westfield, Surry County, North Carolina. Here, Thomas was instrumental in the development of a large meeting. He lived at New Garden and Westfield for about thirty years, during which time he paid lengthy visits to the Delaware and Indigenous peoples. He was once arrested near a fort not far from the Clinch Mountain in Virginia, accused of being in league with hostile Natives. He asked to speak and gave a powerful message, convincing at least one young man from the fort and earning freedom for himself and his party. The group then crossed the Ohio River into what is now the state of Ohio, held many satisfactory meetings with the Indigenous people, and returned home safely. Discussing the trip, Thomas told his friends that he saw with his spiritual eye the seed of Friends scattered all over that good land, and that, one day, there would be a greater gathering of Friends north of the Ohio River than any other place in the world. Thomas continued his peacekeeping work with Indigenous people for the rest of his life.

In 1781, Thomas and Sarah moved to Virginia, and it is not really known if they were in Guilford during the Battle of the Guilford Courthouse (March 1781) as depicted in the novel.

Thomas died August 29, 1801, in Richmond Dale, Ross County, Ohio. He was buried September 1, 1801, at the Beal Cemetery on the farm of Presley Caldwell in Richmond Dale, Ross, Ohio.

Anthony Benezet, born Antoine Bénézet (January 31, 1713–May 3, 1784)

Anthony Benezet was a French-American Quaker abolitionist and educator who was active in Philadelphia, Pennsylvania. He never had any interaction with Danise Wright as is depicted in the novel because Danise and Chelsea are invented characters.

Anthony Benezet was the second of thirteen children born into a wealthy Huguenot family in St. Quentin, France. He was two years old when his family fled to Rotterdam in the Netherlands to escape religious persecution in France. Soon, they came to London, where they changed their French names to

English. Anthony was probably educated in London at the Friends School in Wandsworth.

The family emigrated to Pennsylvania in 1731 and were members of the Religious Society of Friends. In 1736, Anthony married a Philadelphia Quaker minister, Joyce Marriot.

Anthony started teaching in Germantown, Pennsylvania, and later taught at the Quaker school in Philadelphia. He wrote several primers and a book stressing the importance of a well-rounded education. Anthony's greatest achievement as an educator was with those who had no access to traditional schools. In 1750, he started to offer evening classes to Black people, mostly in his own home. In 1754, he started the first Philadelphia secondary school for girls. In 1770, he convinced Quakers to build the first free day school for Black Americans. He always wanted to do his best for his students and to make school as inclusive as possible. As told in the novel, he devised a special program for a Deaf and mute girl (name unknown) at his school so that she could participate fully in school life.

Anthony was also an abolitionist and challenged the assertion of Black inferiority. At this time, many people, including many Quakers, did not regard Black people as equals. Anthony testified to his experience of the innate equality of all people. He wrote an epistle seeking to eradicate the enslaving of people among Quakers, as he believed it to be inconsistent with Christianity and common justice.

Anthony also founded one of the world's first antislavery societies, the Society for the Relief of Free Negroes Unlawfully Held in Bondage. He wrote to London Yearly Meeting, asking them to denounce slavery. In 1783, he wrote to Queen Charlotte, wife of George III of England, asking her to consider the injustice of those who were enslaved. In his "Observations on the Inslaving, Importing and Purchasing of Negroes," the first publication to use stories of slave traders and other eyewitnesses, Anthony argued that, if buyers did not demand enslaved people, the supply would end. Anthony was well-known in abolitionist circles and counted among his contacts Benjamin Franklin. His "Account of that Part of Africa Inhabited by the Negroes," published in 1762, was translated into French and German. Other of his antislavery tracts circulated in America and Europe and were used by abolitionists to argue against slavery.

Anthony also undertook one of the earliest relief initiatives, when he set up arrangements for helping five hundred refugees from Nova Scotia, fleeing the British-French colonial war of 1713. He obtained government grants and had houses built for them in Philadelphia. He helped the refugees with education and employment, enduring much criticism from fellow Quakers for his efforts.

Anthony was interested in many other social problems and wrote about temperance, pacifism, and the treatment of Indigenous people. Upon his death, May 3, 1784, he willed his estate to support the education of Black and Indigenous people. People of many races and creeds, including a large number of Black people, were amongst the funeral mourners. Anthony is buried in the Friends' Burying Ground, in Philadelphia.

Mary Birkett
(December 28, 1774–1817)

Mary Birkett was born in Liverpool, England, to William and Sarah Birkett. Her uncle was the abolitionist George Harrison, one of the founders of the Society for Effecting the Abolition of the Slave Trade. In 1784, the Quaker family moved to Dublin, Ireland, where they attended meeting but were less strict and plain than American Friends. It is unknown whether Mary Birkett met Charity Cook, as depicted in the novel.

Mary was educated in music, art, French, drawing, and literature. She married the merchant, Nathaniel Card, in 1801. The couple had four children who survived infancy. Mary wrote numerous poems about the financial difficulties of the family business, antislavery issues, and the various problems faced by a Quaker woman in Dublin. While the Quakers allowed women a certain level of equality around preaching, the major decisions were taken by the Men's Meetings. In her search to become the ideal Quaker woman, Mary's work increasingly identified the need to conform and submit. Some of this limiting of herself came as a result of the loss of four infants, which she believed was due to her inattention to them.

Mary was involved in running the family business as well as the Quaker women's meetings. She raised funds for a variety of charitable causes and held responsible positions on committees for relief and education. These roles often involved travel away from home. Mary pursued her work as an abolitionist throughout her life, encouraging women to get involved and to boycott products made by enslaved workers. As a result, thousands of people protested slavery by giving up sugar in their tea.

Mary suffered ill health and died in 1817. Twenty years after her death, her son, Nathaniel Card, collected and published her writings. This included her journal, letters, and over 220 poems.

The Coffin Family

Mary Coffin Starbuck (February 20, 1645–late 1717) was the youngest daughter of Tristram Coffin (1605–1681) and Dionis Stevens (died after 1682). Her parents and her five older siblings emigrated from Briston, England, in 1642 to the Massachusetts Bay Colony. Her father, called the "patriarch of Nantucket," was one of the original English proprietors of the settlement. Mary and her husband, Nathaniel Starbuck, were the first couple to marry on Nantucket and the parents of the first child born there. Even as the mother of a young family, Mary helped to run a trading post, which grew into a large mercantile business with the advent of the whaling trade. Unusual for the time, Mary was a prominent leader in civic and religious matters. She had ten children, and her family members were leaders in the Quaker meeting. It is unknown whether Charity Cook ever met any of Mary's relatives on Nantucket.

The Tristram Coffin character in the novel is an invented character.

Levi Coffin (October 28, 1798–September 16, 1877) was a Quaker, abolitionist, farmer, businessman, and humanitarian. He was an active leader of the Underground Railroad in Indiana and Ohio. His home in Fountain City, Indiana, is a museum.

Levi's parents, Levi and Prudence, migrated from Massachusetts as devout Friends and became members of New Garden Friends Meeting, North Carolina. Levi was born on their farm in Guilford County, North Carolina, near what is now Greensboro. He was their only son but had six sisters. It is unknown whether the Coffins knew sign language (see Danise and Chelsea Wright, below).

As Levi explained in his autobiography, *Reminiscences of Levi Coffin* (1876), he inherited his antislavery views from his parents and grandparents who had never owned enslaved workers. Their stance on the issue was influenced by the Friend, John Woolman, who held meetings near their home in 1767. Levi's cousin, Vestal Coffin, probably attended those meetings, too, and around 1819, became one of the earliest Quakers in the state to help enslaved fugitives.

The tree described in the novel exists in the woods between the Coffin family farm near Greensboro, North Carolina, along a southern branch of Horse Pen Creek near the New Garden Meetinghouse. Earlier known as the New Garden Woods, the approximately two hundred acres of old growth forest are now part of the Guilford College campus. The champion tree stands as a silent witness to the many men and women who were told that, if they found the tree, they could get assistance nearby.

When Levi was seven years old, he saw enslaved people who were chained together and walking along the road. With them was a child who was about his same age. The child was being abused to force them along. Coffin asked an enslaved man in the group why he was bound. The man replied that it was to prevent him from escaping and returning to his wife and children. The event disturbed Levi. He'd later say that was his awakening. By the time Levi was fifteen years old, he was bringing food to those hiding on his family's farm. As the repressive Fugitive Slave Law of 1793 was more rigorously enforced, the Coffin family and others in the area increased their antislavery work. Local scrutiny worsened as North Carolina passed the 1804 Black Laws. This legislation caused Friends to be openly persecuted by those who suspected them of helping runaways. Nonetheless, in 1821, Levi and Vestal continued their work and also established a Sunday school to teach Black people to read.

As persecution worsened, thousands of Quakers left North Carolina for the Northwest Territory, where slavery was prohibited. After a visit to Indiana in 1822, Levi married his long-time friend, Catharine White, on October 28, 1824. They had a son and then moved to Newport (now Fountain City) in Wayne Country, Indiana, in 1826. Like her husband, Catherine actively assisted fugitive slaves, providing food, clothing, and a safe haven in the Coffin home. She was known as Aunt Katie to those on the run.

In Newport, Levi continued to farm, and within a year of his arrival, opened the first dry-goods store. His financial success allowed him to be heavily involved in the costly enterprise of the Underground Railroad. A large community of free Black people also lived near Newport and worked with Levi to assist fugitives. Some of the White neighbors were encouraged to make a more formal route, known at the time as the "mysterious road," to move people to freedom along one of three general routes: a western route, which typically began in the southwestern counties of Indiana near Evansville, continuing toward the Indiana-Michigan border; a central route that began after crossing the Ohio River from the Louisville, Kentycky, area and passed through Indiana before entering Michigan; and an eastern route from the southeastern Indiana counties that followed stations along the Indiana-Ohio border. Levi estimated that the organization helped about a hundred people escape annually. Slave hunters frequently threatened his life, but the family's Quaker faith sustained them. Levi is quoted as saying that his life was "in the hands of my Divine Master," and "I feel that I have his approval."

In 1836, Levi expanded his business to include a mill and a hog-butchering operation, opened a paint shop, and eventually acquired 250 acres of land. In 1838, he built a two-story, brick home known as the "Grand Central Station" of the Underground Railroad that is a museum today. It had ingenious hiding places for runaways, including a secret door installed in the maids' quarters on the second floor that provided access for more than a dozen people to hide in a narrow crawlspace. Because Levi demanded to see search warrants and slave-ownership papers before he allowed men to search his home, no one hiding there was ever captured.

In the 1840s, when some Quaker meetings advised their members to cease participation in abolitionist societies and stop assisting runaway slaves, Levi and Catherine continued their work. They were disowned and, along with others, formed the Anti-Slavery Friends, a separate group that did not reunite again with the Religious Society of Friends until 1857.

Levi moved his family southward to the Ohio River port city of Cincinnati, where he ran a warehouse that sold only free-labor goods. When the Civil War broke out in 1861, Levi and Catherine spent almost every day at a military hospital, caring for the wounded. The Coffins prepared large quantities of coffee, distributed it freely to the soldiers, and took many of them into their home.

In 1863, Levi became an agent for the Western Freedman's Aid Society, which offered assistance to those freed during the war, as well as those who were behind Union lines. He and Catherine continued to lodge runaways in their Ohio home. By then, Levi had traveled to Canada to visit a community of escaped people to offer his assistance. He also helped found a Cincinnati orphanage for Black children and assisted freed Black people to establish businesses and obtain education.

In his final decade, Levi traveled around the Midwest as well as overseas, helping to form aid societies to provide food, clothing, funds, and education to formerly enslaved people. He retired from public life in the late 1870s and wrote an autobiography. "The President of the Underground Railroad" died on September 16, 1877, at his home in Avondale, Ohio. His funeral was held at the Cincinnati Friends meetinghouse. Four of Coffin's eight pallbearers were free Black men. Levi was first buried in the Friends burying ground at Cumminsville, near Cincinnati. Later, his body was moved to Spring Grove, where there is an impressive monument. Catherine, who died four years later on May 22, 1881, is buried there as well.

Susannah Wright Hollingsworth
(Sept 27, 1755–July 31, 1830)

Little is known about Susannah Wright, younger sister of Charity Wright Cook. She was born in North Carolina and died in Ohio, a recorded minister who sometimes traveled with her older sister, although not as extensively. She married Isaac Miller Hollingsworth, one of the early settlers in Bush River Meeting, on December 12, 1772. The couple were the parents of at least sixteen children. The story in the novel about her ministry is true, according to Newlin (1981), who also describes her as "rotund in form and features" and shorter than Charity. Jean Shubert has written a self-published novel that includes stories about Charity and Susannah, entitled, *Of Hearth and Highways*. It can be obtained by emailing jeanieshubert2022@gmail.com.

Zacharias Dicks
(1728–late 1809)

Newlin (1986) described Zacharias Dicks as a pioneer, itinerant Quaker minister, and abolitionist. He was born in Chester County, Pennsylvania, the son of Nathan Dicks Sr., who had moved to Pennsylvania in 1686 and was the grandson of Peter and Esther Dicks of Chester, England. In 1755, Zacharias and his brothers, Peter and Nathan, were among the early settlers in the New Garden settlement (now Guilford College community) in North Carolina. They were also members of the Warrenton Friends (Quaker) Meeting in Pennsylvania. On December 7, 1756, at New Garden, Zacharias married Ruth Hiatt, daughter of George and Martha Wakefield Hiatt. They eventually had eight children.

As a Quaker minister, Zacharias spent much of his time on religious visits to most of the Friends' communities from Georgia to New Hampshire and to Great Britain. In 1761 and again in 1767, he traveled by horseback to make the rounds of the American meetings and also went to England and Ireland.

In 1775, Zacharias moved his family to a 770-acre tract of land located on both sides of Cane Creek in North Carolina, their cabin situated one mile west of Lindley's Mill and two miles west of Spring Friends meetinghouse. On September 13, 1781, the Battle of Lindley's Mill was fought between Tory and Patriot armies within a mile of the Dicks' home. Immediately after the battle, the British hurried toward Wilmington with the Patriot army in pursuit, leaving their dead and seriously wounded where they fell. Zacharias later said that he and his Quaker neighbors buried between fifty and a hundred dead and oversaw the care of between a hundred and a hundred and fifty wounded. The people of the community took these soldiers into their homes and assumed complete responsibility for them.

In his home community and on his extensive travels, Zacharias was recognized as a powerful minister, said to possess prophetic insight. As told in the novel, he exercised this power on at least two occasions. About the time of the Declaration of Independence, he told New Garden Friends that blood would flow in their meetinghouse. Five years later, on the morning before the Battle of Guilford Court House (March 15, 1781), the advance guards of the Tory and Patriot armies did, indeed, fight there. New Garden Friends cared for about seventy seriously wounded soldiers, using the meetinghouse as a hospital. From the wounded men, much blood did flow, just as Zacharias predicted. As depicted in the novel, it seeped into the floor boards and couldn't be scrubbed away with soap and sand.

The most noted of Zacharias's prophecies was related to the migration of Friends to the Midwest. Zacharias was an abolitionist, and a major objective in his religious visits among Friends in America was to warn them about the dangers of slavery. In 1803, this concern led him to travel throughout Georgia and South Carolina. Deeply shaken by the massacres accompanying the recent uprising of enslaved workers in Santo Domingo in the Dominican Republic, Zacharias warned Friends that a similar fate awaited them if they did not leave their slavery-ridden communities and migrate to free territory north of the Ohio River. Though such a migration had already begun, the dire warnings of this able minister created something close to a panic. In the rush to leave, Friends sold their lands and homes at a fraction of their true value and abandoned much personal property.

In May 1808, Zacharias and his wife, caught up in the wave of migration, moved to West Branch Meeting, near Miami, Ohio. On September 23, 1809, they became members of Centre Friends Meeting. Perhaps exhausted after the journey, Zacharias passed away a few weeks after reaching his new home. The exact date is unknown. Ruth died a few years later, her grave marker in the Springfield Friends' Cemetery in Clinton County, Ohio, noting that she was the spouse of the prophet, Zacharias Dicks.

Simon Dixon
(1728–1781)

Simon Dixon was born in Lancaster County, Pennsylvania. He was the grandson of William Dixon, who moved to Pennsylvania from Ireland, circa 1688. His father, Thomas Dixon, a Pennsylvania Quaker, married Hannah Hadley on August 20, 1727, at New Garden Meeting, New Castle, Delaware. At a public sale, Thomas bought a cradle in which a baby had died of smallpox and rested it in front of himself on his horse as he rode home. A short time later, he developed smallpox and died in 1734 at age thirty. His widow was left with three small children: Simon, seven years; Rebecca, four years; and Ruth, about one year.

As told in the novel, twenty-year-old Simon led a small party of men from Maryland and Virginia to Cane Creek (today called Snow Camp), North Carolina. They arrived in the spring of 1748, Simon unloading his wagon on the north bank of the creek. He cleared some land, built a typical cabin of logs cut from the forest, and planted a crop of corn. As told in the novel, others in the group also obtained land and did the same. The men returned with their families the next year. Simon and his family constructed a house of stone, cutting and splitting logs by hand for flooring and doors. In 1752, Dixon married Elizabeth Allen, and the couple eventually had eight children. Dixon accumulated a good deal of property and built a store to serve the vast number of immigrants who were moving into the area. Each spring and fall, Simon traveled by wagon to Philadelphia to replenish his stock.

In 1753, Simon built a rock dam across Cane Creek, using a team of oxen to haul the rock. The creek provided waterpower for grinding grain in a mill that he soon built. Inside was a set of millstones brought from Pennsylvania. Known through the years as Dixon's Mill, the structure was repaired and partly rebuilt several times. The aged mill was torn down in 1946, but the millstones were saved. At a reunion of Simon Dixon's descendants in 1925 at Cane Creek Friends Meeting, one of the millstones was placed at his gravesite as a memorial to him and his family for their contribution to the community and to the meeting.

As told in the novel, about March 20, 1781, a week after the Battle of Guilford, British troops occupied the Dixon cabin as a headquarters. Dixon and his family were forced to take refuge elsewhere. Tradition emphasizes that Lord Cornwallis kept himself warm before an open fire in the Dixon home, sitting in a straight armchair. It is thought that the soldiers tried to run the gristmill but failed because Dixon had jammed the wheel. According to another legend (and as told in the novel), some of Cornwallis's men, believing that Dixon possessed a money box, tortured him with red hot iron tongs to make him reveal its location. A few days after the soldiers left, sixty-year-old Simon died from so-called camp fever contracted from the men. Death came while he sat in the same armchair that was much used by Cornwallis. He was buried in the Cane Creek Burying Ground.

"Big Isaac" Hollingsworth
(about 1737–November 24, 1809)

Isaac Hollingsworth was born in Virginia, the son of George Hollingsworth and Ann Robinson. He moved to South Carolina in 1767 to farm property on the Little River prior to his marriage to Susannah Wright (see above). According to Newlin (1981), Isaac was over six feet tall and of great physical strength and unbounded courage. He supported his wife's ministry, quoted as saying that his corn never grew better than when she was out on a preaching tour.

Stories retold in the novel are from O'Neall and Chapman (1892) in the *Annals of Newberry*. One is that Big Isaac disliked young Quaker lads wearing suspenders, a practice that he considered prideful. "Often at log-rollings, if the young men were not on the alert, he would slip his fore-finger under their suspenders, and snap them." Notwithstanding his rough exterior, he had a kind heart. Once a poor Irishman applied to him for much needed work, and he paid the man to move a pile of rock to one location and then back again.

Isaac was an overseer in the Bush River Meeting. As told in the novel, he stopped a British officer from entering his farm corn crib during the Revolutionary War. When the officer drew his sword, Isaac is quoted as saying, "Thus far shalt you go, but no further." The British officer succumbed.

According to a history of Miami County, Ohio, Isaac moved there with three of his brothers' families in 1805. There they built their "rude cabins" in what Isaac was purported to describe as a dark, mephitic tangled woods. He died just a couple years later and is buried in Miami, Ohio.

Hermon Husband
(October 3, 1724–June 19, 1795)

Hermon Husband was born in Cecil County in Maryland, near Philadelphia. His parents were William Husband and Mary Kinkey. In 1739, when Hermon was just fifteen years old, he heard the Rev. George Whitefield, the leading figure of the Great Awakening. After reading an old Quaker tract by Robert Barclay, *Apology for the True Christian Divinity* (1675), Hermon became a member of the East Nottingham Monthly Meeting in Cecil County, Maryland. He married Phebe Cox about 1745, and the couple had at least three children.

Chilton, author of *Faith, Rape, and Charity* (2020), described Hermon as "a bright, successful young man in his community" who turned his eyes toward the North Carolina frontier as a place that held better opportunities than the already settled areas around Philadelphia. In Cane Creek, North Carolina, Hermon became concerned that many of his contemporary Quakers had fallen by the wayside: "Thousands of those who bear the name of Quakers know nothing of this saving Power of God. They having as well as others trampled it under foot, setting up forms to shelter under" (Chilton, 2020). To Hermon, the meetings of elders and ministers, queries, and books of Quaker discipline were recent inventions that had no biblical authority. Hermon complained that "the Inward Light was an immediate and individual source of inspiration, not expressed in the work of a committee" (Chilton, 2020).

Hermon's first wife, Phebe, died between 1753 and 1762, before Hermon relocated in North Carolina and joined the Cane Creek Meeting. On June 16, 1762, he married Mary Pugh, who was the daughter of Thomas Pugh and Elizabeth Richardson.

Chilton (2020) advised that the issues of "Quaker hierarchy, the role of women in Quaker meetings, and misogynistic perceptions of female sexuality" are "as relevant today as they were in the 1760s." Further, Chilton (2020) noted that Hermon made his views on women's meetings clear: "I never had any evidence that Christ had any hand in setting them up." In fact, Hermon's two religious tracts lay bare his misogyny. In *Some Remarks on Religion* (1761), he related that once, while hurrying home to pray, a woman approached him from a distance. "Satan," he wrote, "suggested instantly in my mind, assisted by the lust of the flesh also, as ready to take hold of the woman as she passed me." After the woman passed, Hermon felt "ashamed, especially when I remembered how great a hurry I had been in, but how I had slacked my pace to consult with the Flesh and the Devil."

There is similar evidence of Hermon's misogynistic views in his other religious tract, *The Second Part of the Naked Truth* (1768), which Chilton (2020) advised might have been typical for men of his day. Still, "It is clear that the principles of equality propounded by the earliest Quakers were not a part of his worldview. . . . Husband could only see women as temptresses who could not be trusted to uphold the extremely high moral standards he believed in" Chilton (2020). Women made Hermon feel powerless and ashamed, the feelings exacerbated in the context of the powerful Rachel Wright.

"In *The Second Part of the Naked Truth*," reported Chilton (2020), "Husband recounted that Rachel Wright was a constant source of turmoil—'backbiting, frequenting young men's company all hours of the night, drinking, lying and abominable pretenses to revelations.'" As told in the novel, Hermon claimed that, while Rachel Wright and Jeremiah Piggott were en route to Cedar Creek Meeting, she laid down near him, complaining of the cold weather. "She opened her breasts, squeezing his head up to them. . . . It is notable that Hermon Husband's allegation here was that Rachel Wright's purported sexual impropriety was happening as a part of her effort to organize Cedar Creek women's meeting" Chilton (2020).

"Husband made a point of referring to both William Cox Jr. and Jeremiah Piggott as young men," noted Chilton (2020). While it is true that they were younger than he was, "six and ten years respectively," they were middle-aged at the time of the alleged incident with Rachel. It is interesting to note that Hermon was married twice in his life to women who were fifteen and nineteen years younger than he was, and although in eighteenth-century society, the man being older was normal, the woman being older was considered deviant (Chilton 2020). Men like Husband use women's sexuality both to discredit and to control them, which at the same time silences/ threatens other women and isolates the one being accused. Importantly, none of Hermon's accusations are corroborated in Cane Creek minutes, none of the people involved are documented as testifying to his allegations, and Rachel Wright was not disowned or required to submit a paper of condemnation about the situations described in Hermon's pamphlets.

Dissatisfied with the outcome at Cane Creek, Hermon Husband, Joseph Maddocks, and his assistant, Jonathan Sell, turned to their own meeting in Eno to "crack down on those who were so distant from humble living . . .[and be] more forthright about bad behavior that lurked below the surface within the larger Cane Creek Meeting" Chilton (2020). Hermon took out his revenge on Rachel by interfering with her travel certificate, claiming that her apology for her behavior during Charity's disownment was insincere. Hermon continued to complain within and outside of the Quaker community. He was so outspoken in his criticism of the monthly and quarterly meetings, that in January 1764, he was disowned by Cane Creek. He tried to appeal, but both the monthly and quarterly meetings refused to hear his argument. In the spring of 1764, when Hermon tried to read his appeal, the pacifist Quakers, unable to forcibly remove him, "made so much noise that he couldn't be heard" (Chilton 2020). His disownment was upheld by the yearly meeting, although his allies were reinstated.

About this time, according to Chilton (2020), "a romance was blossoming between forty-one-year-old Hermon and twenty-two-year-old Amy Allen of Cane Creek Meeting. Amy was born on February 18, 1743/44, in Chester County, Pennsylvania, the daughter of John Allen and Phebe Scarlett. Amy's love for Hermon was not dampened by his disownment, even though by marrying out of unity, she stood to be disowned herself. On May 10, 1765, the two married. They eventually had eight children.

Visiting itinerant Quaker John Griffith was at Cane Creek around the time of Hermon's marriage. He wrote in his diary that "most of the members [of Cane Creek] seemed void of a solid sense and solemnity; a spirit of self-righteousness and contention was painfully felt (Chilton, 2020). John Griffith wrote further that Hermon was trying to organize an independent church, although most of the congregation was unfit spiritually "[having] taken counsel of their own depraved hearts." The wedding guests and Amy were eventually disowned by Cane Creek Meeting.

In the summer of 1766, Hermon and his gang of dissenters attended a meeting at Maddock's Mill about the corruption in Orange County government. "For Husband, it was not a question of whether the people should pay their taxes, but rather whether those taxes were being fairly charged and justly handled. . . . In all, twelve men were to assemble at the mill in October 1766, to discuss their concerns and suspicions with the local officials" (Chilton, 2020). Three of the men were those who had questioned Rachel Wright's sincerity in 1763. The group formed the Sandy Creek Association, the radical but non-violent forerunners of the Regulators (Chilton, 2020). This is to say that, while the resulting Battle of Alamance shouldn't be blamed on North Carolina's Quakers, it is true that "Quaker dissidents were at the center of events that touched off the Regulator Uprising" (Chilton, 2020). Also during this time period, when no one from the Eno Meeting attended the relevant Cane Creek women's meeting, the participants took the opportunity to finally grant Rachel Wright a transfer certificate for Bush River (Chilton, 2020).

It is true that Hermon was elected to the North Carolina Assembly from Orange County but later expelled for being a "promotor of the late riots and seditions in the County of Orange and other parts" (Chilton, 2020). Some of the events around the Battle of Alamance are portrayed in Session 5, Episode 7, of the *Outlander* series (Netflix).

Hermon left North Carolina before the Battle of Alamance and hid in the Allegheny Mountains. His neighborhood of Sandy Creek was burned by Governor Tryon's militia in the aftermath of the battle, Quakers and others there forced to supply the British troops with grain (Chilton, 2020).

As told in the novel, in later years, Hermon was among the leaders of the Whiskey Rebellion in Western Pennsylvania. He was arrested in 1795 but pardoned by President George Washington. He died in a tavern outside Philadelphia, allegedly from pneumonia contracted in prison. His burial place is unknown.

Rebecca Jones
(1739–1818)

Rebecca was born in Philadelphia, the only daughter of William and Mary Jones, who were members of the Church of England. Her father died at sea when she was young, leaving her mother to raise two children. As a girl, Rebecca attended Quaker meeting with friends. Her mother disapproved when she began to refrain from music and dancing as a result. As is told in the novel, when Catherine Peyton visited in 1755, she assisted Rebecca in gaining her mother's permission to become a regular meeting attender. In 1758, after a long hesitation, Rebecca began to speak in meeting for worship, and two years later, her gift in ministry was formally acknowledged. She was recorded as a devoted Friend of great intellectual capacity, wit, and strength of character, with an easy and gracious manner. Rebecca was a friend of the great Quaker abolitionist and humanitarian, John Woolman, but it is unknown whether she knew the Public Universal Friend or Charity Cook as depicted in the novel.

After her mother's death in 1761, Rebecca combined ministry with teaching at her mother's school. In 1784, at the height of her power as a preacher, she visited Friends in England. On arrival, she went straight to London Yearly Meeting, where she was instrumental in petitioning for the establishment of a women's meeting. Over the next four years, Rebecca traveled in England, Scotland, Wales, and Ireland, preaching about simplicity, equality, and community. Her memorandum of her tour counted 1,578 meetings for worship, 1,120 meetings with servants, apprentices, and an unknown number of laborers (for whom she had a special concern).

Rebecca returned home in 1788, continuing to preach at yearly meetings in various parts of the Northeast. She fell ill of the yellow fever epidemic that took the lives of four thousand Philadelphians but survived. In the last years of her life, she contributed her knowledge of Friends' education from schools in England to the founding of Westtown (in 1799), a Quaker boarding school that remains open today. In 1813, Rebecca suffered an attack of typhus fever and was confined to her home. She remained there until she died in 1818, when she was seventy-nine years old. She was buried in the Friend's Burying Ground on Arch Street in Philadelphia.

Mary Jackson

According to Chilton (personal email, Dec. 29, 2021) there were at least two Mary Jacksons around the time of Charity's rape and disownment. One had a child born too soon after her marriage and was disowned for pre-marital sex. Chilton thought this to be Mary Miller Jackson, who was married to Isaac Jackson and is recorded in Eno Meeting (North Carolina) records.

The other Mary Miller Jackson was the one described in the novel, who clerked the women's meeting during the time of Charity's disownment. According to Alfred Cook Myers's *Immigration of the Irish Quakers into Pennsylvania*, p. 247, the Mary Miller who married Isaac Jackson at New Garden Monthly Meeting, Chester County, Pennsylvania, April 11, 1730, was a minister who moved with her family to North Carolina in 1751. She was the clerk/minister who accompanied Rachel Wright on some of her visits to organize various women's meetings, and knew her conduct to be appropriate (despite the accusations of Hermon Husband). It is unknown when she died or where she is buried.

Joseph Maddock
(1722–1796)

Joseph Maddock was one of many Quakers and other pioneers who migrated from Pennsylvania to North Carolina. He was a miller, horticulturalist, and carpenter who became an organizer and overseer of the sizable Eno Meeting settlement near Hillsborough, North Carolina. In 1755, he dammed the rocky Eno River a short distance below the mouth of McGowan's Creek and built a water-powered grist mill on the west bank. He cleared and built a road from the courthouse to his mill on the Eno River and then to the trading path such that Maddock's Mill and the road became historic landmarks of the area, the achievements important steps in the county's development by settlers. Maddock was promptly chosen as one of approximately thirty county road commissioners. He is also credited with building the first Orange County jail (1757).

In the autumn of 1767, Maddock led the first contingent of Quakers away from mounting Regulator disturbances in the Hillsborough area to a fourty-thousand-acre reserve in eastern Georgia. Altogether, 132 families eventually followed him to the new town of Wrightsboro, where he built a new mill, dwelling house, and cow pens and planted orchards. The settlement initially thrived, but attacks by the Seminole people eventually resulted in the destruction of Wrightsboro. Maddock did not participate in the great migration of Quakers to Indiana and Ohio but died in 1796 at the age of 74 in Georgia. The location of his grave is unknown.

Majer/Major/Mayer

The character of Majer in the novel is based on a man mentioned in the will of his owner, Joel Brooks (brother-in-law to Charity by marriage to Mary Wright). When I wrote this novel, he was the only Black person I knew to have lived in Cane Creek at the time of the Wrights. Since that time, Thomas Hamm, Quaker historian, has noted that, in the inventory of the estate of Henry Mayner, a Cane Creek Friend who died in 1760, there was listed "one old

441

negro man." It is possible, based on the similarities between Majer/Mayor/Mayer and the last name of Henry Mayner, that this man was the one mentioned as being owned, perhaps previously, by Joel Brooks. I fabricated the marriage to Anarcha, who I had read was a Black midwife in the area. I also invented the relationship between Joseph Jr. and Majer and Majer's ability to travel and spread news to the Wright and Cook families.

Dinah Nevill

The Dinah Nevill in the novel is based on the story about an enslaved woman by this name. She claimed her freedom in Philadelphia after she was sold alongside her three children to a Virginia slave-owner. Two Quakers, Israel Pemberton and Thomas Harrison, filed a court suit on Nevill's behalf and won her freedom (around 1775). Everything about her in the novel is fabricated.

Catherine Payton
(March 16, 1727–August 16, 1794)
and Mary Peisley

Catherine Payton was born in Dudley, Worcestershire, England, the daughter of Henry Payton (1671–1746), and his second wife, Ann (c.1673–1774), daughter of Henry and Elizabeth Fowler of Evesham. Catherine did not attend school until her late teens but studied and read widely at home until a time when she decided that poetry, philosophy, and history were distracting her from her faith practice.

Catherine was recognized as a minister at Dudley Meeting around 1748. She served in England, Wales, Scotland, Holland, and the American colonies. For her travel to Ireland in 1751, she was accompanied by Mary Peisley. They convinced Samuel Neale, who became an important Quaker minister and later married Mary.

Mary was born January 19, 1718, at Ballymore, County Kidare, Ireland. Her mother, Rachel (Burton), was from Mannin, County Tipperary, and her father John from Baltiboys, County Wicklow. Mary had little formal education and entered domestic service, a job she fulfilled until the age of twenty-six, when she began to offer ministry at Quaker meetings.

Catherine and Mary traveled to America in 1753–1756. Newlin (1981) reported that they rode eight thousand miles, often through thinly inhabited country, braving dangerous creeks, swamps, and wild animals, visiting North Carolina and South Carolina, Virginia, Pennsylvania, and New England. During their tour, Mary noted a "low state of discipline" among frontier Quakers in her journal (reported in Newlin, 1981), and saw a need for reformation. The relationship of Catherine and Mary to Rachel and Charity (and others) in the novel is based on information found in Newlin (1981). The part where Catherine talks to them about the power of love is taken from prepared sermon notes delivered by Margaret Webb, pastor of New Garden Friends Church. I was able to worship with these Friends on one of the visits I made to Greensboro to do research for this novel. The phrase "eyes to see" is a nod to Matthew 13:9–16, and the phrase "Love wins" is one that has become commonly part of progressive Christian theological language with roots in the book *Love Wins* by Rob Bell.

Mary Peisley died on March 20, 1757, three days after her marriage to Samuel Neale. She was buried in the Quaker cemetery at Mountrath, a small town in County Laois, Ireland. Her husband assembled and published a collection of her writings..

Catherine Payton married William Phillips, a copper agent and widower, in 1772, and moved to his home in Redruth, Cornwall, England. Always an advocate for a greater role for women within Quakerism, she attended London Yearly Meeting in 1784 to assist in the acceptance of a separate women's meeting.

Catherine died on August 16, 1794, and was buried at the Quaker burying ground, Come-to-Good, in the parish of Kea, near Truro (a hamlet in Cornwall, England). Her stepson, James Phillips, a Quaker printer, published her memoirs and some other writing after her death.

Mary Pearson
(1737–aft. 1824)

Mary was born in Chester County, Pennsylvania, the daughter of Jacob and Elizabeth Pearson. She married Isaac Jackson on May 5, 1762, in Province, North Carolina, and the couple had at least five sons and five daughters. As depicted in the novel, Mary did often accompany Charity Wright Cook on her travels and went with her to Wrightsboro, Georgia. She died in the summer of 1824, in Eno, Orange, North Carolina, and was buried at New Garden Meeting. Information about her in the novel is based on that found in Penney (1930) and Newlin (1981).

Abigail Overman Pike
(March 19, 1709–February 23, 1781)

Abigail Overman was the child of Ephraim Overman and Sarah Belman Overman. She grew up in Symons Creek Meeting on Little River in Pasquotank Precinct, North Carolina, where the women's meeting dates from at least 1715. On September 9, 1731, when Abigail was twenty-one years old, she married John Pike.

Abigail and John were living in the Pasquotank Precinct when they heard that a new meeting had been established in Frederick County, Virginia. They decided to move north about 1735 to assist there. They were granted a transfer certificate from Pasquotank to the new settlement of Hopewell Meeting (Virginia) on the Opequon River near Martinsburgy in what is today West Virginia. At the time, the couple had two small children, but they eventually had six more. They walked with their children to Cane Creek with the Wrights in 1749 and were founding members of the Cane Creek Meeting.

It is true that Abigail stood in meeting for worship in Cane Creek in the early part of the year 1751 to say, "If Rachael Wright will go with me, we will attend the Quarterly Meeting at Little River in Perquimans County and ask to be set up here" Newlin (1981). The Friends at Cane Creek prudently sent other persons with these two courageous women, although the exact number in the party is unknown (Newlin, 1981). When she set out for the quarterly meeting, Abigail Pike left behind a young son, Nathan, and Rachael Wright left a small child, Sarah. Both families were large, so the youngsters were not neglected, but the fact that they were left when so young reveals the depth of the women's concern for the spiritual life of the more than thirty families living in the Cane Creek settlement (Newlin, 1981).

Perquimans County lies about two hundred miles to the east of Cane Creek, a trip that would take approximately three hours by car these days but probably about ten using the same horses in the mid-eighteenth century. Abigail. Rachel, and the men that accompanied them rode on horseback through virtually uncharted wilderness. No doubt, there were few if any places along the route where a night's lodging and a simple meal could be obtained. Most likely, the group camped in the open. The establishment of Cane Creek Monthly Meeting of Friends was authorized at the quarterly meeting held at Little River, as recorded in their minutes, dated Sixth month 31st, 1751.

Shortly after the Cane Creek Meeting was established, Abigail was involved in the effort to secure a monthly meeting for Friends at New Garden, a trip of thirty-five miles. She also traveled extensively to promote the growth of numerous meetings and to represent Cane Creek at various assemblies.

As told in the novel, Abigail rode to military camps to preach to the soldiers during the Revolutionary War. It is not clear which armies allowed her to preach, and it is possible this occurred among both the Patriots and the Loyalists. General Nathanael Greene, himself a Quaker at one time, is said to have allowed her within his lines, although she was not permitted to dismount but had to preach from her saddle (Newlin, 1981).

There also is a story from Newlin (1981), retold in the novel, about Abigail and a group of Friends as they returned from a preaching mission. It is said that they came to where the road divided, one fork going straight home and the other leading up past a burying ground. When one of them said a ghost was to be seen every evening in the graveyard, Abigail whipped up her horse yelling, "We will go this way. I have long wanted to see a real ghost, shake hands with it, and ask it if all is well with thee?" Arriving at the cemetery, Abigail rode up to what seemed to be a creature with outstretched arms. She is said to have called back to the others, "Come on Friends, it is only a big cobweb on a bush" Newlin (1981).

Another story (Newlin 1981) is that Abigail had a set of "Queensware" porcelain china dishes. It was rare to find such finery in a backwoods cabin. One day, British soldiers came to her home, searching for food, and overturned her cupboard. She tried to catch some of the beloved dishes in her outstretched apron but was only able to save one small pitcher. That pitcher was passed down through the years from one daughter to another and is reported to be in a museum in Oklahoma.

After John's death in 1774, Abigail left Cane Creek for Muddy Creek, near Deep River, North Carolina, to live with her son. She died in February of 1781 and, at the age of seventy-one, was buried in a cemetery of this meeting that still exists on the outskirts of the town of Kernersville in Forsyth County, North Carolina. At the time of the novel, the town was called Dobson's Crossroads; the name changed in 1873. The grave which is thought to be Abigail's is outlined in handmade brick. A nearby marker tells of her remarkable life.

John Pike
(June 14, 1702–1774)

John was born in Pasquotank County, North Carolina, to Samuel Pike and Jean McGregory Pike.

(Samuel was born on October 29, 1678, in London, and Jean was born in 1695, in North Carolina). John farmed and served as overseer for the meeting.

John married Abigail Overman in North Carolina on September 4, 1731, or 1732. Friends met to inquire into the affair of John Pike and Abigail Overman and the couple was "left to their liberty to take each other in marriage when they please."

About 1738, the family moved to Westchester in Prince William County. John was granted a letter of transfer from Pasquotank to the new settlement on the Opequon River (Hopewell Meeting) in Virginia, where he and Abigail felt they could be of assistance in the forming of a new meeting. They remained there for eleven years and eventually had twelve children.

John and Abigail moved their family to the new Cane Creek settlement about 1749, where they were granted 280 acres of land along Cane Creek (*Cane Creek, Mother of Meetings*, published by the North Carolina Yearly Meeting in 1995). "One of the first acts of business of the newly formed Cane Creek Meeting was to record the births of four children in that year, one of which was Nathan, tenth child of John and Abigail Overman Pike." Those mentioned in the early minutes before 1751: John and Abigail Overman Pike, John and Rachel Wright, Joseph Jr. and Charity Wells.

Not much else is known about John Pike. His will was written March 30, 1771. He died January 15, 1774, when he was either seventy-one or seventy-two years old and was buried at Cane Creek. However, it is said the stone was moved several times (North Carolina Yearly Meeting, 1995). A memorial marker to John and Abigail is at Muddy Creek Friends Cemetery, Kernersville, Forsyth, North Carolina.

The Public Universal Friend
(November 29, 1752–July 1, 1819)

The Public Universal Friend was named Jemina Wilkinson at birth. Her Quaker parents, Amy (or Amey Whipple) and Jeremiah Wilkinson, lived in Cumberland, Rhode Island. As a child, Jemina was athletic and an avid reader. In 1776, after suffering a severe illness, Jemina claimed to have died and been reanimated as a genderless evangelist named The Public Universal Friend (TPUF). Shunning both their birth name and gendered pronouns, they began to wear androgynous clothes. TPUF preached throughout the northeastern colonies, attracting many followers to the Society of Universal Friends (which was never a part of the Religious Society of Friends). They were disowned from the Smithfield Meeting, their sister Patience dismissed at the same time for having an illegitimate child, and brothers Stephen and Jeptha "read out" in May 1776 for training for the Revolutionary War.

The Universal Friend usually wore long, black, loose clerical robes and a white or purple kerchief or cravat around the neck like men of the time.

Outdoors, they wore a broad-brimmed, low-crowned beaver hat of a style worn by Quaker men (and Charity Wright). They embodied Paul's statement in Galatians 3:28 that "there is neither Jew nor Gentile, neither slave nor free, nor is there male and female, for you are all one in Christ Jesus."

TPUF was accompanied by their siblings when they traveled. They used language similar to that of the Friends (e.g., thee and thou instead of the singular you), and their theology broadly echoed that of most Quakers, stressing free will and opposition to slavery. TPUF also advised sexual abstinence, did not bring a Bible to worship meetings, but preached long sections of the scriptures from memory. The meetings, which were held outdoors or in borrowed meetinghouses, attracted large audiences, making TPUF the first American to found a religious community. These followers included roughly equal numbers of women and men, some of whom were Black. They were predominantly under forty years of age. As described in the novel, most of those who attended the gatherings of TPUF were from Quaker backgrounds, though mainstream Quakers discouraged and disciplined members for attending. Roughly four dozen unmarried women, known as the Faithful Sisterhood, took on leading roles in the organization.

In the mid-1780s, TPUF began to plan a town for themselves in western New York. Amidst disputes about the land and multiple arrests for blasphemy, members purchased a site in 1789. The new town was called Jerusalem.

By 1799, TPUF's health began to decline, and they suffered from painful edema. Their final regular sermon was given in November 1818. The Public Universal Friend died at sixty-seven years of age on July 1, 1819. In accordance with the wishes of TPUF, only a regular meeting for worship was held, without a funeral service afterward. Obituaries appeared in papers throughout the eastern United States.

The Society of Universal Friends disappeared by the 1860s. An exhibit at the Yates County Genealogical and Historical Society's museums in New York includes TPUF's portrait, Bible, carriage, hat, saddle, and documents from the Society of Universal Friends. TPUF is credited as a pioneer of transgender history and is featured in a National Public Radio episode of *Throughline*.

William Savery Jr.
(July 14, 1750–June 19, 1804)

William Savery was a Quaker preacher and abolitionist as well as a defender of rights for Indigenous people. He was the son of Philadelphia cabinetmaker William Savery Sr. and Mary Petters, both devout Quakers. Following the completion of his apprenticeship as a tanner, his faith lapsed. Then, in 1778, he experienced a deep religious transformation. That same year, he married Sarah Evans, who was also Quaker. Their home was a dependable stop on the

Underground Railroad. The couple knew The Pubic Universal Friend, also from Philadelphia.

William was recorded as a minister in 1781, and in 1783, he was a signatory to the Quaker Anti-Slavery Petition. He also worked for equality, justice, and respect with Indigenous people. In 1792, he and the Quaker meetings in Philadelphia sent an urgent letter to President Washington, asking him to take prompt and just measures to terminate the Indian Wars.

In 1793, William was part of a Quaker group of White government men and Indigenous leaders who met in Ohio to negotiate territorial rights. A major obstacle was the demand of Indigenous people that settlers relinquish all their homes west of the Ohio River. The impasse forced Savery to return to Pennsylvania without a satisfactory solution, the long, hard journey weakening his health.

On May 18, 1796, William traveled to Europe with a small party of Quaker ministers. The group of Friends visited Bad Pyrmont, then and now the center of German Quakerism. While visiting Ireland, William was disheartened by the great poverty of the majority of the people and made a report to London Yearly Meeting on the sad state of affairs.

William returned home from Europe on October 18, 1799. Because of failing health, he traveled only to attend the 1801 yearly meetings in New York and Baltimore. Beginning in March 1804, he was confined to his home, suffering from fluid retention (dropsy). He died of a fever on June 19, 1804, and is buried in Philadelphia. William's diaries are kept at Haverford College, just outside Philadelphia.

Jehu Stuart
(October 10, 1740–1827)

Little is known of Jehu Stuart. He was born in Chester, Pennsylvania, to Robert Stewart and Martha Richardson. The family migrated to Cane Creek, North Carolina, and were early members of the meeting.

Sometime in 1760, Jehu raped Charity Wright and bragged about having assaulted other women as well. As told in the novel, Jehu and Charity were both disowned for their perceived parts in the rape. The Cane Creek minutes state, "At a monthly meeting held the 3d of 1st month. 1761: Complaints of Jehu Stuart for spreading of scandalous reports on several young women." Two men were appointed to labor with him and report to the next men's meeting. The minutes from a meeting held April 4, 1761, state that Friends were appointed to prepare a testimony against Jehu Stuart. As was typical of the times, Jehu Stuart apologized only a few years later and came back into the fold of Quakerism. At a monthly meeting held April 6, 1765, it is recorded in the minutes that "Jehu Stuart condemns his former misconduct."

John Woolman
(October 19, 1720–October 7, 1772)

John Woolman was an American merchant, tailor, journalist, itinerant Quaker preacher, and early abolitionist. He was based in Mount Holly, New Jersey, near Philadelphia, but traveled throughout the colonies, preaching against slavery, the slave trade, cruelty to animals, economic injustices, and conscription. Beginning in 1755, with the outbreak of the French and Indian War, Woolman urged tax resistance to deny support to the colonial military.

Woolman was born into a Quaker family. His father, Samuel Woolman, was a farmer. His maternal and paternal grandparents were early Quaker settlers in New Jersey. John married Sarah Ellis, a fellow Quaker, in a ceremony at the Chesterfield Friends Meeting in New Jersey. They had a daughter named Mary and a son who died in infancy.

As a young man, Woolman began work as a clerk for a merchant. When he was twenty-three years old, his employer asked him to write a bill of sale for an enslaved person. Though he told the man that he thought that slaveholding was inconsistent with Christianity, he wrote the bill of sale. Also, while Woolman was in his twenties, he felt called to preach "Truth and Light."

By the age of twenty-six, Woolman had become an independent and successful tradesman. On at least one occasion, he refused to write the part of a customer's will that would have bequeathed or transferred the ownership of an enslaved worker and instead convinced the owner to set the person free before he died. Woolman took up the trade of tailoring in order to have more time to travel in ministry and witness to fellow Quakers about his concerns. He viewed profit-making as distracting from his spiritual journey.

Woolman began refusing to use or wear dyed fabrics, almost always produced by slave labor. He avoided riding in stagecoaches, believing that the drivers were too often cruel and injurious to their horses. He published essays, many against slavery. In 1746, he went on his first ministry trip, preaching against the institution. He traveled about fifteen hundred miles and as far south as North Carolina, but never to Cane Creek. In 1757, Woolman addressed meetings in the Albemarle counties of Perquimans and Pasquotank. He wrote to New Garden Friends rather than visiting there.

The Coffins met John Woolman, and it is very possible that the Wrights did as well. The scene in the novel of him preaching at Cane Creek Meeting was fabricated.

In 1754, Woolman published *Some Considerations on the Keeping of Negroes*. He convinced many Quaker slaveholders to free their slaves. If, in his travels, he accepted hospitality from a slaveholder, he insisted on paying the owners for the labor of the enslaved workers who waited on him. He refused to use silver cups, plates, and utensils, as he believed that slaves in other regions were forced to dig such precious minerals and gems for the rich. He observed that some owners used the labor of their enslaved people to enjoy lives of ease, which he found to be the worst situation, not only for those who were enslaved but for the moral and spiritual condition of the owners as well.

Woolman's final journey was to England in 1772. During the voyage, he stayed in steerage but sometimes visited the cabins of others so as to escape the crowding and stench of his assigned berth. He attended London Yearly Meeting, helping Friends to include an abolitionist statement in their epistle (a type of letter sent to Quakers in other places) and later traveled to York, England, where he contracted smallpox and died. He is buried there.

Mary Swett
(1739–1821) of Haddonfield, New Jersey, and Sarah Harrison of Philadelphia

Little is known about Mary Swett and Sarah Harrison or how they came to know Charity Cook. As reported by Norman Penny (1930) in *Life And Travels of a Southern Quaker Minister*, Mary was the wife of Benjamin Swett, a minister in Haddonfield Meeting, New Jersey. The couple had two children, one of whom met Charity and Mary in England. Penny (1930) also included a pertinent entry from Samuel Dyer of Bristol, who wrote in his voluminous diary: "We have twice fallen in company with dear

Charity Cook and Mary Swett; I think them valued, choice (deeply religious) Friends. Charity's gift lies much amongst other societies; Mary's is confided to our own." Mary Swett's journal is available in the Haverford College Quaker & Special Collections in Haverford, Pennsylvania.

Historian Margaret Bacon (1988) noted that Sarah Harrison was twenty-two years old when she married Thomas Harrison, a devout foe of slavery and an early activist in freeing kidnapped Black people. They had ten children in short order, but six of them died in infancy or early childhood. In 1781, Sarah was recorded as a minister by her meeting.

In 1787, Sarah set out to travel among Friends in the South, preaching at meetings, holding prayer sessions with families, and persuading many to give up slaveholding. Some two hundred enslaved people were freed as a result of her efforts. After two of her adult children died, Sarah took up ministry abroad and traveled with Charity Cook and Mary Swett to Great Britain. In 1798, she was with them, as well, in Germany when they were arrested.

Joseph Wells Jr.

Born on July 30, 1729, in Anne Arundel County, Maryland, Joseph Wells Jr., Rachel's half-brother (same father, different mothers), was the son of Joseph Wells Sr. and Margaret Swanson Wells. He was christened at the All Hallows Church and lived with his parents on their farm (Boiling Springs) until his marriage to Charity Carrington (ca. 1730–1803) in 1750 at the Fairfax Meeting in Loudoun County, Virginia.

About the time that two of Joseph Wells Sr.'s daughters, Rachel and Charity, married into the Wright family of Chester County, Pennsylvania, Joseph Wells Jr. and his father had set up a sawmill and were making fine furniture in Chester County, Pennsylvania (Tracey and Dern, 2002). A 2016 analysis of Joseph Wells' Cane Creek Quaker furniture by June Lucas, a museum curator for the Museum of Early Southern Decorative Arts in Winston-Salem, North Carolina, concluded that the two Wells men learned their specific techniques of carpentry while in Pennsylvania, trained by a master there in the seventeenth-century style of Quaker cabinet-making. His work is on display at the Museum of Early Southern Decorative Arts, and some of his chests of drawers and dressers are also on display at the Moravian Museum, also located in Old Salem, North Carolina.

When Joseph and his father's families migrated to North Carolina, they continued to produce high-quality furniture. Joseph owned a sawmill approximately one mile west of the Cane Creek meetinghouse. Over his lifetime, Joseph Jr. and his wife, Charity, acquired hundreds of acres along Cane Creek and its tributaries. In 1804, his estate inventory listed various sorts of lumber, a glue pot, a horse shave, "one piece of brass," a workbench, a "case of drawers part made," and "joiner's tools" (https://

mesda.org/item/collections/chest-of-drawers/20629).
At his death, he had an atypical amount of furniture in his home: a desk, two chests of drawers, four chests, an oval table, a looking glass, a knife box, a "box and bottles," one armchair, seven side chairs, and an expensive, eight-day clock.

Joseph Jr. and Charity raised five daughters and six sons, two of whom, Jesse (1762–1794) and William (1766–1851), were also woodworkers. When Jesse died in 1794, his estate inventory included "joiner tools," a table frame, and a workbench, and quite a number of his father's tools. Joseph's sons, Isaac, John, and Nathan; and Joseph's son-in-law, James McDaniel, also purchased enough tools to suggest that they, too, were probably involved in the family woodworking business. Many of the members of Cane Creek Meeting bought from or traded with Joseph Jr. for furniture. More information about the furniture is available at http://www.chipstone.org/article.php/753/American-Furniture-2016/The-Early-Furniture-of-North-Carolina's-Cane-Creek-Settlement.

In 1764, Joseph Jr. was involved with the estate of Quaker Joel Brooks (who was married to Charity Wright's sister, Mary). Joel had requested aid in freeing his "Negro Major" (also spelled Majer). It is because of Joel's will that it is known that at least one Black person lived in Cane Creek.

Joseph Wells Jr. continued to operate his sawmill until his death on September 20, 1804, in Orange County, North Carolina. He didn't migrate to the

Midwest with the others in his meeting. In his will, he bequeathed each of his children seven dollars.

Danise and Chelsea Wright

Danise and Chelsea Wright are invented characters. They are named for my friends, Danise Ito Heisey, Chelsea Wright, and Ammon Wright. Living in rural North Carolina, the manual communication used by Danise and Chelsea would have been "home sign," invented by them and not known by other Deaf people. Later in the story their manual communication is influenced by the signs they learned from the invented character, Tristram Coffin, who was purported to be from Nantucket. His migration from Massachusetts to North Carolina would have been very possible. When the first school for the Deaf, the Connecticut Asylum for the Education and Instruction of Deaf and Dumb Persons (now the American School for the Deaf), was founded by Thomas Hopkins Gallaudet, Mason Cogswell, and Laurent Clerc in 1817, there were students from various New England states, and from the islands of Nantucket and Martha's Vineyard. On Martha's Vineyard, Massachusetts, and Henniker, New Hampshire, it is purported that Deaf and hearing residents alike used sign language. On Martha's Vineyard, the manual language originated with the Lambert family, who settled on the island in 1694 and brought the signing of Kent, England, with them as their language. Many of the colonial island whalers used it and taught it to their families. This story is told in *The Kendal Sparrow* by Barbara Schell Luetke. The signing from these various influences was used at the Connecticut Asylum and evolved into what is known today as American Sign Language.

John Wright
(January 4, 1716–September 17, 1789)

John C. Wright was Charity Wright Cook's father. He was born in Nottingham, Chester County, Pennsylvania, the son of James (then forty-eight years old) and Mary Bowater Wright, the two having already had five children at the time of John's birth.

John C. Wright married Rachel Wells about 1737 in Prince George's County, Maryland. The marriage records are unavailable and are assumed to have burned in a fire at the Hopewell Meeting. Their marriage is guessed to be a year before the birth of their first child. They eventually had at least sixteen children in the twenty-eight years before Rachel died. Both John and Rachel were appointed as overseers of their respective men's and women's business meetings in 1745. John was also a shoemaker and farmer.

In the late 1740s, Quakers in the Philadelphia area began to recognize that the cost of land in Pennsylvania was so high that it made sense to find fertile new lands on the colonial frontier. Western Pennsylvania was not an option because of conflicts there with Indigenous people. Many Quakers decided to move to the Southern colonies. John and Rachel Wright, along with seven young children, applied for a travel certificate, which was granted on May 5, 1749, for travel to Cane Creek, North Carolina. The three-hundred mile walk took about a month.

The Wrights were among the first members of Cane Creek Monthly Meeting in Alamance County, North Carolina, when it was established in October 1751. Six more children were born while they lived in the area. All thirteen children are listed in the Cane Creek records. Danise and Chelsea are invented characters in the novel and were not the adoptive children of John and Rachel Wright.

John and Rachel moved to the frontier near Camden, Kershaw County, South Carolina in 1761–1762, having sold their Cane Creek cabin to a member of the Meeting. They eventually resettled in Bush River, South Carolina.

When the Revolutionary War came, John was in his fifties. Although, in general, Friends upheld a testimony of peace, the Society allowed each man to make his own decision about joining the military. John became part of the celebrated American fighting group called Colonel Thompson's Rangers, a regiment recruited in the backcountry and on the frontiers. The regiment was established by the South Carolina Provincial Congress in June 1775 as mounted riflemen who used horses for transportation but dismounted to fight on foot. It consisted of a lieutenant colonel commandant, a major, nine captains, eighteen lieutenants, a surgeon, a paymaster, an adjutant, and a quartermaster, with each of its nine companies having two sergeants, a drummer, and fifty privates.

John was awarded the rank of captain while serving in the military and helped to defend Charleston Harbor in the Battle of Sullivan's Island on June 28, 1776. There, the regiment defended the eastern end of Sullivan's Island when the British attempted an amphibious assault during the naval attack on the fort, which was later named Fort Moultrie. John was also at the famous Battle of the Cowpens on January 17, 1781, where the Patriot army, made up of rough frontiersmen, defeated an army of elite Loyalist regulars under the command of Banastre Tarleton to win the first victory against Lord Cornwallis's army. It is unknown why John joined the military or if he used his shoemaking skills during the war as depicted in the novel.

At an advanced age, John lived with his daughter, Susannah (Wright Hollingsworth). According to Newlin (1981), he used to walk to and from the Quaker meetings. At a family reunion in 1908, someone recalled that his daughter prevailed on him to take her horse on one occasion. When the meeting was over, he walked home. When he got there, she asked him where the horse was, and he replied, "Dang, me Sue, I forgot her" Newlin (1981).

John wrote his will on September 17, 1789 (witnesses were Isaac Hollingsworth, John Coate, and

Charity Wright Cook). His executor was his son, Joseph Wright. Before he died, John supposedly gathered all of his descendants, which numbered 144 people, around him at Susannah and Isaac's home where he was living (Newlin 1981). He left his shoe-making tools to his son-in-law, "Big Isaac."

John died on September 17, 1789, and is buried in the Bush River Quaker Burying Ground in Newberry County, South Carolina.

Rachel Wells Wright
(March 27, 1720–Dec. 23, 1771)

Rachel was the first daughter of Joseph Wells, a farmer in Anne Arundel County, Maryland. (Joseph's father was Thomas Wells, who was born about 1653 in England). Rachel was named for her mother, who died in childbirth or soon after. Her mother's surname is unknown. Rachel's birth can be found in the registry of All Hallows Parish in Davidsonville, Anne Arundel County, Maryland. There, it is recorded that she was born on March 27, 1720, and christened in July 1721.

Rachel was raised by her stepmother, Margaret Swanson, who married her father, Joseph, on April 11, 1721. She had ten half-siblings, one of whom was Joseph Jr. (see above).

According to an article by Richard M. Kelly, published in 1994 by the North Carolina Friends Historical Society in *The Southern Friend*, Rachel came from "radical Puritan stock, as well as that of Catholic refugees who were seeking religious freedom in the tolerant colony of Maryland." All of her older male relatives were landowners and tobacco farmers. Most were enslavers. Joseph Wells paid taxes in 1733 on the family plantation in Prince George's County, Maryland, at a time when less than ten percent of slaveholders held forty-three percent of all Black enslaved workers in Charles and Prince George's counties.

Among Rachel's relatives were a lively group of settlers along the Chesapeake Bay. Her father, Joseph, was twice arrested for drinking and fighting. Yet he also was appointed as a constable and served as a member of the church vestry, an elected body in the Episcopal parish.

In 1742, Joseph and Margaret Wells moved their family west to a valley of the Monocacy River (now Frederick County, Maryland). Their land, a forty-acre tract, was known as Boyling/Boiling Spring. Quakers were early settlers there, and the Wells family eventually joined the sect.

Rachel Wells was just sixteen years old when, in 1737, she married John Wright, who was only twenty years old himself. He was born in Chester County of Pennsylvania Quaker stock,. When just a child, John's family relocated to northern Maryland and settled in the Quaker community of Fairfax Meeting near Frederick, Maryland. Rachel, presumably a nonpracticing Episcopal, met John in meeting. It is assumed she became Quaker herself before their marriage, the records unavailable due to a meeting-house fire. At the time, presumed to be about 1736, the Religious Society of Friends was the faith of choice for one third of all American colonialists.

In the spring of 1745, John was made overseer of the men's meeting and Rachel of the women's meeting. Even though there was this division of labor for the men and the women, the Quakers believed in the equality of the sexes and their ability to serve in leadership positions. As a young adult Friend, Rachel was recorded as a Quaker preacher and served with great energy, spirit, and determination. As told in the novel, she worked under the tutorage of Abigail Pike to establish women's meetings.

In 1749, when Rachel was twenty-four years old, she and John (along with some of their relatives and John and Abigail Pike) left the Fairfax Meeting to join the Great Quaker Migration that moved down the Shenandoah Valley to the frontier of Virginia, the Carolinas, and Georgia. The trip was a tremendous undertaking for this young family, evidence of the grit of John and Rachel, their faith in God, their strength of character, and their hope for the future.

As told in the novel, Rachel and Abigail Pike rode, unaccompanied by their husbands, over a hundred miles through the wilderness to Pasquotank County to obtain approval from the quarter to organize Cane Creek Monthly Meeting. Rachel and Abigail were active in the Cane Creek women's meeting, and Rachel, as a women's overseer, attended other meetings as a representative of Cane Creek.

It is unknown exactly why the friendship of Abigail and Rachel ended, but it had something to do with Rachel's behavior during the time of Charity's disownment. It may also have been influenced by the tales of Hermon Husband.

"It is evident that women's empowerment was a subject close to Rachel's heart," wrote Chilton (2020). "She was a founder of Fairfax women's meeting, Cane Creek women's meeting, and Cedar Creek women's meeting." It is true that, in the company of Jeremiah Piggott and Mary Miller Jackson, Rachel went to Cedar Creek in April 1754 to support the women of the meeting in petitioning for the establishment of a women's meeting there. The group were gone four months. If Rachel didn't conduct herself appropriately, Mary Jackson would have known—and she isn't recorded as agreeing with Hermon Husband and his tales.

Chilton (2020) continued: "The significance of women's meetings should not be underestimated. Prior to August 1754, all disownments at Cedar Creek were handled by the meeting. The dominant role of men in that process is clearly shown by the exclusively male signatures on the testimonies of disownment. After the women's meeting commenced, the disownment of women was judged by the women of Cedar Creek as the disownment signers are all women and these records are in the women's minutes. The creation of the women's meeting also resulted in the first ever women appointed as overseers, as well as its first female elders. All of this must have felt hugely empowering to the women of Cedar Creek, but the establishment of women's meetings was not welcomed by everyone."

In January 1761, when Jehu Stuart began to circulate scandalous reports about several young women in the Cane Creek community, the whole situation quickly came to the meeting's attention. None of the other women came forward, and it is true that Charity was found guilty of not doing enough to stop the assault. It is also true that neither Charity nor her mother accepted this result. They filed an appeal to the quarterly meeting, complaining that the disownment was "for a wrong cause." In June 1761, the Western Quarter appointed a panel of men to hear Charity's appeal.

According to Chilton (2020), appeals of this kind were a standard part of Quaker process, not only in matters of moral transgression but also in civil disputes. The Quakers did not believe in using the court system to resolve debts or other issues of civil liability between fellow Quakers. If someone was dissatisfied with a meeting decision, they could appeal to the quarterly meeting to get the judgment of more disinterested parties who lived farther away. If needed, they could then appeal to the yearly meeting.

Rachel Wright was the focus of a controversy in 1764, involving Hermon Husband (see his biography above) and known as the "Rachel Wright Affair" in some articles (e.g., *Southern Quakers and Slavery*, by Stephen B. Weeks). Hermon Husband accused Rachel of misconduct with men as she traveled in ministry. In addition, although Rachel was a weighty Friend, she also was considered loud. Hermon's concerns were taken up by her monthly meeting and seemed to be resolved, but when Rachel requested a travel certificate to move to Bush River, South Carolina, Hermon Husband and his followers stood in the way of it, not thinking her sincere in her apology for her behavior. The disagreement, detailed by Chilton (2020), resulted in the refusal of the paperwork and appeals to the Western Quarter. Meanwhile, Hermon was so vocal in his disapproval that, in January 1764, he was disowned for "speaking against the actions and transactions of this Meeting" (as is recorded in the meeting minutes). As the story goes, when Herman was informed of being read out of meeting, he sat down, took off his shoes, shook the "dirt of Quakerism" out of them, put them back on, and walked away from the faith for good (Chilton, 2020).

According to Chilton (2020), "By the end of 1761, Rachel Wright was disgraced to the point of no longer being able to be an effective leader within Cane Creek women's meeting. This coupled with the aftermath of Charity's rape caused the Wright family to move to a frontier Quaker settlement near the North Carolina-South Carolina border, the Bush River Meeting.

Little is written about the rest of Rachel's life. She died on December 23, 1771, at fifty-one years of age of unknown causes. She was buried in Bush River, South Carolina.

www.ingramcontent.com/pod-product-compliance
Lightning Source LLC
Chambersburg PA
CBHW011741010726
47498CB00012B/2890

* 9 7 8 1 5 9 4 9 8 1 7 6 0 *